D0028602

By Susan Sontag

Fiction

THE BENEFACTOR

DEATH KIT

I, ETCETERA

THE WAY WE LIVE NOW

THE VOLCANO LOVER

Essays

AGAINST INTERPRETATION

STYLES OF RADICAL WILL

ON PHOTOGRAPHY

ILLNESS AS METAPHOR

UNDER THE SIGN OF SATURN

AIDS AND ITS METAPHORS

Filmscripts

DUET FOR CANNIBALS

BROTHER CARL

A SUSAN SONTAG READER

THE VOLCANO LOVER

F
G
D
H
H

THE VOLCANO LOVER

A Romance

SUSAN SONTAG

Farrar Straus Giroux · New York

Copyright © 1992 by Susan Sontag
All rights reserved
Printed in the United States of America
*Published simultaneously in Canada by HarperCollins*CanadaLtd
Designed by Cynthia Krupat
Third printing, 1992

A signed first edition of this book has been privately printed by The Franklin Library.

Library of Congress Cataloging-in-Publication Data
Sontag, Susan.
The volcano lover / Susan Sontag.
p. cm.
1. Nelson, Horatio Nelson, Viscount, 1758–1805—Fiction.
2. Hamilton, William, Sir, 1730–1803—Fiction. 3. Hamilton, Emma, Lady, 1765–1815—Fiction. I. Title.
PS3569.O6547V6 1992 813'.54—dc20 92-71738 CIP

The images reproduced in this book are, with one exception, taken from plates in Sir William Hamilton's Campi Phlegraei, Observations on the Volcanos of the Two Sicilies. *2 Vols. Naples, 1776. Supplement, 1779. The artist was Pietro Fabris. The image on p. 359 is the dedication plate in the first volume of* Collection of Etruscan, Greek and Roman Antiquities from the Cabinet of the Hon. Wm. Hamilton *by D'Hancarville (Pierre François Hugues). 4 Vols. Naples, 1766–7.*

My Cavaliere is Sir William Hamilton's double, a fictional character on whose behalf I have taken what liberties suited his nature, as I have with the other historical persons given their proper names.
I wish to acknowledge the stimulation given by and information gleaned from the many modern historical studies and biographies as well as from memoirs and letters of the period.

I am grateful to the Deutscher Akademischer Austauschdienst (DAAD), which brought me to Berlin in 1989, when I began The Volcano Lover, *and again in 1990; to Robert Walsh and Peter Perrone; and, most of all, to Karla Eoff.*

FOR DAVID

beloved son, comrade

DORABELLA *(aside)*: *Nel petto un Vesuvio*
d'avere mi par.

Così fan tutte, Act II

PROLOGUE

It is the entrance to a flea market. No charge. Admittance free. Sloppy crowds. Vulpine, larking. Why enter? What do you expect to see? I'm seeing. I'm checking on what's in the world. What's left. What's discarded. What's no longer cherished. What had to be sacrificed. What someone thought might interest someone else. But it's rubbish. If there, here, it's already been sifted through. But there may be something valuable, there. Not valuable, exactly. But something *I* would want. Want to rescue. Something that speaks to me. To my longings. Speaks to, speaks of. Ah . . .

Why enter? Have you that much spare time? You'll look. You'll stray. You'll lose track of the time. You think you have enough time. It always takes more time than you think. Then you'll be late. You'll be annoyed with yourself. You'll want to stay. You'll be tempted. You'll be repelled. The things are grimy. Some are broken. Badly patched or not at all. They will tell me of passions, fancies I don't need to know about. Need. Ah, no. None of this do I need. Some I will caress with my eye. Some I must pick up, fondle. While being watched, expertly, by their seller. I am not a thief. Most likely, I am not a buyer.

Why enter? Only to play. A game of recognitions. To know what, and to know how much it was, how much it ought to be, how much it will be. But perhaps not to bid, haggle, not to acquire. Just to look. Just to wander. I'm feeling lighthearted. I don't have anything in mind.

Why enter? There are many places like this one. A field, a square, a hooded street, an armory, a parking lot, a pier. This could be anywhere, though it happens to be here. It will be full of everywhere. But I would be entering it here. In my jeans and silk blouse and tennis shoes: Manhattan, spring of 1992. A degraded experience of pure possibility. This one with his postcards of movie stars, that one with her tray of Navajo rings, this one with the rack of World War II bomber jackets, that one with the knives. His model cars, her cut-glass dishes, his rattan chairs, her top hats, his Roman coins, and there . . . a gem, a treasure. It could happen, I could see it, I might want it. I might buy it as a gift, yes, for someone else. At the least, I would have learned that it existed, and turned up here.

Why enter? Is there already enough? I could find out it's not here. Whatever it is, often I am not sure, I could put it back down on the table. Desire leads me. I tell myself what I want to hear. Yes, there's enough.

I go in.

•

It is the end of a picture auction. London, autumn of 1772. The picture in its bulging gold-leaf frame stands against the wall near the front of the huge room, a *Venus Disarming Cupid* thought to be by Correggio on which its owner had placed such high hopes—unsold. Thought wrongly to be by Correggio. The room gradually clears. A tall, sharp-faced man of forty-two (he was a tall man for that time) comes forward slowly, followed at a respectful distance by a man half his age bearing a marked family resemblance. Both are thin, with pale skin and cold patrician expressions.

My Venus, says the older man. I was confident it would sell. There was much interest.

But, alas, observed the younger man.

Hard to understand, mused the older man, when the distinction of the picture seems self-evident. He is genuinely puzzled. The younger man was listening with a becoming frown.

Because it grieved me to part with her, I suppose I should also be glad it failed to sell, continued the older man. But necessity obliged, and I don't consider the price I asked too high.

He gazed fixedly at his Venus. Most difficult, the older man went on, now referring not to the difficulty of understanding why the picture had not sold (nor to the hardship of keeping creditors at bay) but to the decision to sell; for I doted on this picture, he said. Then I knew I should sell it and so made myself apt to relinquish it; and now, since no one offered what I know it to be worth and it remains mine, should love it as before, but won't, I wager. Having stopped loving it in order to sell it, I can't enjoy it in the same way, but if I am unable to sell it I do want to love it again. It would be churlish of me to find its beauties spoiled by this misadventure.

What to do? How much to love it? he mused. How to love it now.

I should think, sir, said the younger man, that the only question is where to store it. Surely a buyer will be found. Have I your permission to try on your behalf among collectors of my acquaintance perhaps not known to you? I would be happy to make these discreet inquiries after your departure.

Yes, it's time to go, said the older man.

They went out.

•

It's the mouth of a volcano. Yes, mouth; and lava tongue. A body, a monstrous living body, both male and female. It emits, ejects. It is also an interior, an abyss. Something alive, that can die. Something inert that becomes agitated, now and then. Existing only intermittently. A constant menace. If predictable, usually not predicted. Capricious, untameable, malodorous. Is that what's meant by the primitive? Nevado del Ruiz, Mount Saint Helens, La Soufrière, Mount Pelée, Krakatoa, Tambora. The slumbering giant that wakes. The lumbering giant who turns his attentions to *you*. King Kong. Vomiting destruction, and then sinking back into somnolence.

Me? But I've done nothing. I just happened to be there, mired in my rustic routines. Where else should I live, I was born here, wails the dark-skinned villager. Everyone has to live somewhere.

Of course we can regard it as a grand pyrotechnical show. It's all a question of means. A long enough view. There are charms made only for distant admiration, says Dr. Johnson; no spectacle is nobler than a blaze. At a safe distance, it is the ultimate spectacle, instructive as well as thrilling. After a collation at Sir ***'s villa we go onto the terrace, fitted out with telescopes, to watch. The plume of white smoke, the rumbling often compared to a distant roll of timpani: overture. Then the colossal show begins, the plume reddens, bloats, soars, a tree of ash that climbs higher, higher, until it flattens out under the weight of the stratosphere (if we are lucky we'll see ski runs of orange and red start down the slope)—hours, days of this. Then, *calando*, it subsides. But up close, fear churns the guts. This noise, this gagging noise, it's something you could never imagine, cannot take in. A steady pour of grainy, titanically thunderous sound that seems always to be mounting in volume yet cannot possibly be any louder than it already is; a sky-wide ear-inundating vomitous roar that flushes the marrow out of your bones and topples your soul. Even those who designate themselves as spectators cannot escape an onrush of revulsion and terror, as you've never known them before. In a village at the foot of the mountain—we might venture there—what appeared from afar as a torrential flow is a creeping field of viscous black and red ooze, nudging walls that for a moment still stand, then devolve with a shuddering sucking plop into its heaving front; pushing into, inhaling, devouring, unfastening the atoms of houses, cars, wagons, trees, one by one. So this is the inexorable.

Watch out. Cover your mouth with a cloth. Duck! A night-time ascent of a moderately, punctually active volcano is one of the great excursions. After the trudge up the side of the cone, we stand on the crater's lip (yes, lip) and peer down, waiting for the burning innermost core to disport itself. As it does, every twelve minutes. Not too close! It's starting. We hear a basso-profundo gurgling, the crust of grey slag begins to glow. The giant is about to exhale. And the suffocating sulphur stench is unbearable, almost. Lava pools but does not overflow. Fiery rocks and cinders soar, not very high. The danger, when not too dangerous, fascinates.

Naples, March 19, 1944, afternoon, four o'clock. In the villa the hands of the big English pendulum clock stop at another fatal hour. Again? It had been quiet for so long.

Like passion, whose emblem it is, it can die. It's now known, more or less, when a remission should start counting as a cure, but experts hesitate to pronounce a long-inactive volcano dead. Haleakala, which last erupted in 1790, is still officially classified as dormant. Serene because somnolent? Or because dead? As good as dead—unless it's not. The river of fire, after consuming all in its path, will become a river of black stone. Trees will never again grow here, ever. The mountain becomes the graveyard of its own violence: the ruin the volcano causes includes its own. Each time Vesuvius erupts, a chunk of the summit is lopped off. It becomes less shapely, smaller, bleaker.

Pompeii was buried under a rain of ash, Herculaneum under a mud slide that raced downslope at thirty miles an hour. But lava eats a street slowly enough, a few yards an hour, for everyone to get out of its way. We also have time to save our things, some of them. The altar with the holy images? The uneaten piece of chicken? The children's toys? My new tunic? Whatever is hand-made? The computer? The pots? The manuscript? The cow? All we need to begin again is our lives.

I don't believe we're in danger. It's going that way. Look.

Are you going? I'm staying. Unless it reaches . . . there.

It has happened. It is over.

They fled. They mourned. Until grief had turned stony, too, and they came back. Awed by the completeness of the erasure, they gazed upon the fattened ground below which their world lay entombed. The ash under their feet, still warm, no longer seared their shoes. It cooled further. Hesitations vaporized. Not long after A.D. 79—when their fragrant mountain, matted with vines, crowned by the forests where Spartacus and thousands of slaves who joined him had sought to hide from the pursuing legions, first revealed itself to be a volcano—most of those who had survived set about rebuilding, reliving; there. Their mountain now had an ugly hole at the top. The forests had been incinerated. But they, too, would grow again.

One view of catastrophe. This had happened. Who would have expected such a thing. Never, never. No one. It is the worst. And if the worst, then unique. Which means unrepeatable. Let's put it behind us. Let's not be doomsayers.

The other view. Unique for now: what happens once can happen again. You'll see. Just wait. To be sure, you may have to wait a long time.

We come back. We come back.

PART ONE

I

His first leave home was over. The man to be known in polite Naples from now on as Il Cavaliere, the Chevalier, was starting the long journey back to his post, to "the kingdom of cinders." So one of his friends in London called it.

When he had arrived, he was thought to look much older. He was still as lean: a body swollen by macaroni and lemon pastries would have ill suited such a narrow clever face, with the aquiline nose and bushy eyebrows. But he had lost his caste's pallor. The darkening of his white skin since he'd left seven years ago was remarked with something approaching disapproval. Only the poor—that is, most people—were sunburned. Not the grandson of a duke, youngest son of a lord, the childhood companion of the king himself.

Nine months in England had restored his bony face to a pleasing wheyness, bleached the sun creases in his slender music-mastering hands.

The capacious trunks, the new Adam chimney-piece, the three cases of furniture, ten chests of books, eight cases of dishes, medicines, household provisions, two kegs of dark beer, the cello, and Catherine's Shudi harpsichord, refurbished, had left a fortnight ago on a storeship that would reach Naples within two months, while he would board a hired barque that would deposit him and his at Boulogne for an overland journey almost as long—with stops for visits and picture-viewing in Paris, Ferney, Vienna, Venice, Florence, and Rome.

Leaning on his walking stick in the courtyard of the hotel in King Street where his uncle and aunt had lodged these last busy weeks in London, the Cavaliere's nephew, Charles, contributed his sulky presence to the final readying of the two traveling coaches. Everyone is relieved when demanding older relatives who live abroad conclude their visit. But no one likes to be left.

Catherine has already settled with her maid in the large post chaise, fortifying herself for the strenuous journey with a potion of laudanum and chalybeate water. The broader, lower-hung coach behind had been laden with most of the luggage. The Cavaliere's footmen, reluctant to rumple their maroon traveling livery, hung back and fussed with their own compact belongings. It was left to the hotel porters and a lackey in Charles's employ to clamber over the coach, making sure that the dozen or so small trunks, boxes, portmanteaux, the chest of linen and bedding, the ebony escritoire, and finally the cloth satchels with the servants' gear were properly secured with ropes and iron chains to the top and rear. Only the long flat crate containing three paintings that the Cavaliere had bought just last week was strapped to the roof of the first carriage, to ensure the smoothest ride to the barque at Dover. One of the servants was checking on it from below with token thoroughness. The carriage with the Cavaliere's asthmatic wife was not to be jostled.

Meanwhile, another large leather case, almost forgotten, was brought at a run from the hotel and wedged into the load to be borne by the coach, which rocked and sagged a little more. The Cavaliere's favorite relative thought of the storeship, bearing far more cases of his uncle's possessions in its hold, which might already be as far as Cádiz.

Even for that time, when the higher the social station the greater the number and weight of things thought indispensable to the traveler, the Cavaliere traveled in exceptional bulk. But less, to the sum of forty-seven large chests, than when he had arrived. One of the purposes of the Cavaliere's trip, other than to see friends and relations and his beloved nephew, please his homesick wife, renew useful contacts at court, make sure the secretaries of state better appreciated the deftness with which he was representing British interests at that quite different court, attend meetings of the Royal Society and oversee the publication in book form of seven of his letters on volcanic matters, was to bring back most of the treasures he had collected—including seven hundred antique (miscalled Etruscan) vases—and sell them.

He had done the family rounds and had the pleasure of spending a great deal of time with Charles, much of it at Catherine's estate in Wales, which Charles now managed for him. He had impressed more than one minister, or so he thought. He had been received twice by, and once dined alone with, the king, who still called him "foster brother," and who in January had made him a Knight of the Bath, which this fourth son dared regard as but the first step up a ladder of titles to be won through his own accomplishments. Other Fellows of the Royal Society had congratulated him on his daring feats of close-up observation of the monster in full eruption. He had attended a few picture sales and purchased, judiciously. And the British Museum had bought his Etruscan vases, the whole lot, as well as several minor pictures, the gold necklaces and earrings from Herculaneum and Pompeii, some bronze javelins and helmets, amber and ivory dice, small statues and amulets, for the gratifying sum of eight thousand four hundred pounds (a little more than a year's income from the estate to which Catherine was heiress), although the painting on which he had placed his greatest hopes remained unsold. He was leaving the wanton naked Venus triumphantly holding Cupid's bow over her head, for which he had asked three thousand pounds, in Wales, with Charles.

He was going back lighter as well as whiter.

Furtively passing a bottle among them, the Cavaliere's footmen and cook chatted with the porters in a corner of the courtyard. The aureoled September sun was brightening. A northeast wind had carried a smoke cloud and the smell of coal into Whitehall, overriding the usual rank effluvia of early morning. The clatter of other carriages, carts, barrows, departing diligences could be heard from the street. One of the ponies of the first carriage moved restlessly, and the coachman pulled on the reins of the shaft horse and cracked his whip. Charles looked around for Valerio, his uncle's valet, to restore order among the servants. Frowning, he took out his watch.

A few minutes later the Cavaliere emerged from the hotel, in his train the obsequious proprietor and his wife as well as Valerio, who was carrying the Cavaliere's favorite violin in an ornate leather case. The servants fell silent. Charles stood waiting for a signal, his long face acquiring a more alert expression, which sharpened the resemblance between them. The deferential silence continued as the Cavaliere paused, looking up at the pale sky, sniffing the malodorous air, distractedly plucking a speck from his sleeve. Then he turned, offering a thin-lipped smile to his nephew, who moved quickly to his side, and the two men walked arm in arm toward the carriage.

Waving Valerio aside, Charles reached up and opened the door for his uncle to mount, stoop, enter, then followed to hand in the Stradivarius. While the Cavaliere settled onto the green velvet-covered seat, he leaned inside to ask, with unfeigned affection and concern, how his aunt was feeling and to say his last words of farewell.

Coachmen and postilions are in place. Valerio and the other servants mounted the larger carriage, which settled noisily a few inches nearer the ground. Charles, farewell. The window is closed against the coal-infested air, so dangerous to the asthmatic, against the shouts of starting and urging. The gates are opened, and things and animals, servants and masters surged into the street.

The Cavaliere removed his amber gloves, strummed his fingers. He was ready to return, he was in fact looking forward to the journey—he thrived on the strenuous—and to the new encounters and acquisitions it would bring. The anxiety of leaving had fallen away the instant he had stepped into the carriage, became the elation of departing. But being a man of considerate feelings, at least toward his wife, of whom he was as fond as he had ever been of anyone, he would not express the rising joy he felt as they passed slowly, sealed, through the erupting clamor of increasingly busy streets. He would wait for Catherine, who had her eyes closed and was breathing shallowly through her half-open mouth.

He coughed—a substitute for a sigh. She opened her eyes. The blue vein pulsing in her temple is not an utterance. In the corner on a low stool, licensed to speak only when spoken to, the maid bent her rosy, humid face into Alleine's *Alarm to the Unconverted*, which her mistress had given her. He reached with one hand for the case at his hip which contained the folded leather-bound traveling atlas, the writing box, the pistol, and a volume of Voltaire he had begun. There is no reason for the Cavaliere to sigh.

How odd, Catherine murmured, to be cold on such a temperate day. I fear—she had a penchant, born of the desire to please, for following a stoical utterance with a self-deprecating one—I fear I have got accustomed to our bestial summers.

You may be too warmly dressed for the journey, observed the Cavaliere in his high, somewhat nasal voice.

I pray I shall not be ill, Catherine said, drawing a camelhair shawl over her legs. I will not be ill if I can help it, she corrected herself, smiling as she daubed at her eyes.

I, too, feel the sadness of parting from our friends, and especially from our dear Charles, replied the Cavaliere gently.

No, said Catherine. I'm not unhappy to return. While I dread the crossing and then the hardships of—she shook her head, interrupting herself—I know that I shall soon breathe more easily. The air. . . . She closed her eyes for a moment. And, what is more important to me, you are happy to return, she added.

I shall miss my Venus, said the Cavaliere.

The dirt, the stink, the noise are without—like the shadow of the passing carriage darkening the mullioned glass of shop fronts. London appears a spectacle to the Cavaliere, time receding into space. The carriage sways, jostles, creaks, lurches; the vendors and barrow boys and other coachmen cry out, but in a different timbre from the cries he will hear; these are the same familiar streets he might be crossing to attend a meeting of the Royal Society, look in on an auction, or pay a visit to his brother-in-law's, but today he was not crossing to but crossing through—he had entered the kingdom of farewells, finalities, privileged last sightings that are instantly logged as memories; of anticipation. Each street, each rackety turning emits a message: the already, the soon-to-be. He drifted between the desire to look, as if to engrave on his brain, and the inclination to confine his senses to the cool carriage, to consider himself (as he is in truth) already gone.

The Cavaliere liked specimens and might have found a good many in the ceaselessly replenished throngs of beggars, maids, peddlers, apprentices, shoppers, pickpockets, touts, porters, errand boys who stream dangerously near and between moving barriers and wheels. Here, even the wretched scurry. They do not pool, cluster, squat, or dance, entertaining themselves: one of many differences between crowds here and those in the city to which he was returning that could be registered, pondered over—if there were a reason to note it at all. But it was not the Cavaliere's custom to reflect on London's din and shove; one is unlikely to see one's own city as picturesque. When his carriage was halted for a noisy quarter of an hour between fruit barrows and an irate knife grinder's wagon, he did not follow the sightless red-haired man who has ventured into the crossing a few yards ahead, extending his stave before him, heedless of the vehicles starting to bear down on him. This portable scented interior, layered with enough accoutrements of privilege to occupy the senses, says: Don't look. There is nothing outside worth looking at.

If he doesn't know what to do with his hungry eyes, he has that other, always adjacent interior: a book. Catherine has opened a volume on papal cruelties. The maid is with her alarming sermon. Without looking down, the Cavaliere slid his thumb against a sumptuous leather binding, the gold embossing of title and favorite author. The beggar, overtaken by one of the coaches, is knocked back and drops under the wheel of a plodding cooper's cart. The Cavaliere wasn't looking. He was looking away.

Inside the book: Candide, now in South America, has chivalrously, with his double-barreled Spanish gun, come to the accurate rescue of two naked girls whom he sees running gently on the edge of a plain, closely followed by two monkeys who are biting their buttocks. Whereupon the girls fling themselves on the corpses of the monkeys, kiss them tenderly, wet them with their tears, and fill the air with piteous cries, revealing to Candide that the pursuit, an amorous one, had been entirely welcome. Monkeys for lovers? Candide is not just astonished, he is scandalized. But the sage Cacambo, seasoned in the ways of the world, respectfully observes that it might have been better if his dear master had received a proper, cosmopolitan education so that he would not always be surprised by everything. Everything. For the world is wide, with room enough for customs, tastes, principles, observances of every sort, which, once you set them in the society where they have arisen, always make sense. Observe them. Compare them, do, for your own edification. But whatever your own tastes, which you needn't renounce, please, dear master, refrain from identifying them with universal commandments.

Catherine laughed softly. The smiling Cavaliere, thinking of naked buttocks—first women's, then a monkey's—looked up.

They were often in harmony, even if for different reasons. You're feeling better, he asked. The Cavaliere had not married a monkey. The carriage rolled on. It began to rain. London expired behind them. The Cavaliere's entourage was wending its way back to his passions—ruling passions. The Cavaliere went on with Candide and valet to El Dorado, Catherine stared down at her own book, the maid's chin dropped to her breast, the panting horses tried to pull ahead of the whip, the servants in the rear coach giggled and tippled, Catherine continued to labor for breath, and soon London was only a road.

2

They had been married, and childless, for sixteen years.

If the Cavaliere, who like so many obsessive collectors was a natural bachelor, married the only child of a wealthy Pembrokeshire squire to finance the political career he embarked on after ten time-serving years in military regalia, it was not a good reason. The House of Commons, four years representing a borough in Sussex in which he never set foot, turned out to offer no more scope for his distinctive talents than the army. A better reason: it had brought him money to buy pictures. He also had something richer than money. Yielding to the necessity of marrying—somewhat against my inclination, he was to tell another impecunious younger son, his nephew, many years later—he had found what he called lasting comfort. On the day of their marriage Catherine locked a bracelet on her wrist containing some of his hair. She loved him abjectly but without self-pity. He developed the improbable but just reputation for being an uxorious husband. Time evaporates, money is always needed, comforts found where they were not expected, and excitement dug up in barren ground.

He can't know what we know about him. For us he is a

piece of the past, austerely outlined in powdered wig and long elegant coat and buckled shoes, beaky profile cocked intelligently, looking, observing, firm in his detachment. Does he seem cold? He is simply managing, managing brilliantly. He is absorbed, entertained by what he sees—he has an important, if not front-rank, diplomatic posting abroad—and he keeps himself busy. His is the hyperactivity of the heroic depressive. He ferried himself past one vortex of melancholy after another by means of an astonishing spread of enthusiasms.

He is interested in everything. And he lives in a place that for sheer volume of curiosities—historical, natural, social—could hardly be surpassed. It was bigger than Rome, it was the wealthiest as well as the most populous city on the Italian peninsula and, after Paris, the second largest city on the European continent, it was the capital of natural disaster and it has the most indecorous, plebeian monarch, the best ices, the merriest loafers, the most vapid torpor, and, among the younger aristocrats, the largest number of future Jacobins. Its incomparable bay was home to freakish fish as well as the usual bounty. It had streets paved with blocks of lava and, some miles away, the gruesomely intact remains, recently rediscovered, of two dead cities. Its opera house, the biggest in Italy, provided a continual ravishment of castrati, another local product of international renown. Its handsome, highly sexed aristocracy gathered in one another's mansions at nightly card parties, misleadingly called *conversazioni*, which often did not break up until dawn. On the streets life piled up, extruded, overflowed. Certain court celebrations included the building in front of the royal palace of an artificial mountain festooned with meat, game, cakes, and fruit, whose dismantling by the ravenous mob, unleashed by a salvo of cannon, was applauded by the overfed from balconies. During the great famine of the spring of 1764, people went off to the baker's with long knives inside their shirts for the killing and maiming needed to get a small ration of bread.

The Cavaliere arrived to take up his post in November of

that year. The expiatory processions of women with crowns of thorns and crosses on their backs had passed and the pillaging mobs disbanded. The grandees and foreign diplomats had retrieved the silver that they had hidden in convents. The court, which had fled north sixteen miles to the colossal, grimly horizontal residence at Caserta, was back in the city's royal palace. The air intoxicated with smells of the sea and coffee and honeysuckle and excrement, animal and human, instead of corpses rotting by the hundreds on the streets. The thirty thousand dead in the plague that followed the famine were buried, too. In the Hospital of the Incurables, the thousands dying of epidemic illness no longer starved to death first, at the rate of sixty or seventy a day. Foreign supplies of corn had brought back the acceptable level of destitution. The poor were again cavorting with tambourines and full-throated songs, but many had kept the long knives inside their shirts which they'd worn to scout for bread and now murdered each other more often for the ordinary, civil reasons. And the emaciated peasants who had converged on the city in the spring were lingering, breeding. Once again the *cuccagna* would be built, savagely dismantled, devoured. The Cavaliere presented his credentials to the thirteen-year-old King and the regents, rented a spacious three-story mansion commanding a heart-stopping view of the bay and Capri and the quiescent volcano for, in local money, one hundred fifty pounds a year, and began organizing as much employment as possible for his quickened energies.

Living abroad facilitates treating life as a spectacle—it is one of the reasons that people of means move abroad. Where those stunned by the horror of the famine and the brutality and incompetence of the government's response saw unending inertia, lethargy, a hardened lava of ignorance, the Cavaliere saw a flow. The expatriate's dancing city is often the local reformer's or revolutionary's immobilized one, ill-governed, committed to injustice. Different distance, different cities. The Cavaliere had never been as active, as stimulated, as alive mentally. As pleasurably detached. In the churches, in the narrow, steep streets, at the court—so many performances here. Among the bay's eccentric marine life, he noted with delight (no rivalry between art and nature for this intrepid connoisseur) one fish with tiny feet, an evolutionary overachiever who nevertheless hadn't made it out of the water. The sun beat down relentlessly. He trod steaming, spongy ground that was hot beneath his shoes. And bony ground loaded with rifts of treasure.

The obligations of social life of which so many dutifully complain, the maintenance of a great household with some fifty servants, including several musicians, keep his expenses rising. His envoy's salary was hardly adequate for the lavish entertainments required to impose himself on the imagination of people who counted, a necessary part of his job; for the expectations of the painters on whom he bestows patronage; for the price of antiquities and pictures for which he must compete with a host of rival collectors. Of course he is eventually going to sell the best of what he buys—and he does. A gratifying symmetry, that collecting most things requires money but then the things collected themselves turn into more money. Though money was the faintly disreputable, necessary byproduct of his passion, collecting was still a virile occupation: not merely recognizing but bestowing value on things, by including them in one's collection. It stemmed from a lordly sense of himself that Catherine—indeed, all but a very few women—could not have.

His reputation as a connoisseur and man of learning, his affability, the favor he came to enjoy at court, unmatched by any other of the envoys, had made the Cavaliere the city's leading foreign resident. It was to Catherine's credit that she was no courtier, that she was revolted by the antics of the King, a youth of stupefying coarseness, and by his snobbish, fertile, intelligent wife, who wielded most of the power. As it did him credit that he was able to amuse the King. There was no reason for Catherine to accompany him to the food-slinging banquets at the royal palace to which he was convened three or four times a week. He was never bored when with her; but he was also happy to be alone, out for whole days on the bay in his boat harpooning fish, when his head went quiet in the sun, or gazing at, reviewing, itemizing his treasures in his cool study or the storeroom, or looking through the new books on ichthyology or electricity or ancient history that he had ordered from London. One never could know enough, see enough. Much longing there. A feeling he was spared in his marriage, a wholly successful marriage—one in which all needs were satisfied that had been given permission to arise. There was no frustration, at least on his part, therefore no longing, no desire to be together as much as possible.

High-minded where he was cynical, ailing while he was robust, tender when he forgot to be, correct as her table settings for sixty—the amiable, not too plain, harpsichord-playing heiress he had married seemed to him pure wife, as far as he could imagine such a being. He relished the fact that everyone thought her admirable. Conscientiously dependent rather than weak, she was not lacking in self-confidence. Religion animated her; her dismay at his impiety sometimes made her seem commanding. Besides his own person and career, music was the principal interest they had in common. When Leopold Mozart and his prodigy son had visited the city two years ago Catherine had becomingly trembled as she sat down to play for them, and then performed as superbly as ever. At the weekly concerts given in the British envoy's mansion, to which all of local society aspired to be invited, the very people who most loudly talked and ate through every opera during the season fell silent. Catherine tamed them. The Cavaliere was an accomplished cellist and violinist—he had taken lessons from the great Giardini in London when he was twenty—but she was the better musician, he freely allowed. He liked having reasons to admire her. Even more than wanting to be admired, he liked admiring.

Though his imagination was reasonably lascivious, his blood, so he thought, was temperate. In that time men with his privileges were usually corpulent by their third or fourth decade. But the Cavaliere had not lost a jot of his young man's appetite for physical exertion. He worried about Catherine's delicate, unexercised constitution, to the point of sometimes being made uneasy by the ardor with which she welcomed his punctual embraces. There was little sexual heat between them. He didn't regret not taking a mistress, though—whatever others might make of the oddity. Occasionally, opportunity plumped itself down beside him; the heat rose; and he found himself reaching from moist palm to layered clothes, unhooking, untying, fingering, pushing. But the venture would leave him with no desire to continue; he was drawn to other kinds of acquisition, of possession. That Catherine took no more than a benevolent interest in his collections was just as well, perhaps. It is natural for lovers of music to enjoy collaborating, playing together. Most unnatural to be a co-collector. One wants to possess (and be possessed) alone.

•

It is my nature to collect, he once told his wife.

"Picture-mad," a friend from his youth called him—one person's nature being another's idea of madness; of immoderate desire.

As a child he collected coins, then automata, then musical instruments. Collecting expresses a free-floating desire that attaches and re-attaches itself—it is a succession of desires. The true collector is in the grip not of what is collected but of collecting. By his early twenties the Cavaliere had already formed and been forced to sell, in order to pay debts, several small collections of paintings.

Upon arriving as envoy he started collecting anew. Within an hour on horseback, Pompeii and Herculaneum were being dug up, stripped, picked over; but everything the ignorant diggers unearthed was supposed to go straight to the storerooms in the nearby royal palace at Portici. He managed to purchase a large collection of Greek vases from a noble family in Rome to whom they had belonged for generations. To collect is to rescue things, valuable things, from neglect, from oblivion, or simply from the ignoble destiny of being in someone else's collection rather than one's own. But buying a whole collection instead of chasing down one's quarry piece by piece—it was not an elegant move. Collecting is also a sport, and its difficulty is part of what gives it honor and zest. A true collector prefers not to acquire in bulk (any more than hunters want the game simply driven past them), is not fulfilled by collecting another's collection: mere acquiring or accumulating is not collecting. But the Cavaliere was impatient. There are not only inner needs and exigencies. And he wanted to get on with what would be but the first of his Neapolitan collections.

No one in England had been surprised that he continued to collect paintings or went after antiquities once he arrived in Naples. But his interest in the volcano displayed a new side of his nature. Being volcano-mad was madder than being picture-mad. Perhaps the sun had gone to his head, or the fabled laxity of the south. Then the passion was quickly rationalized as a scientific interest, and also an aesthetic one, for the eruption of a volcano could be called, stretching the term, beautiful. There was nothing odd in his evenings with guests invited to view the spectacle from the terrace of his country villa near the mountain, like the moon-viewing parties of courtiers in Heian Japan. What was odd was that he wanted to be even closer.

The Cavaliere had discovered in himself a taste for the mildly plutonian. He started by riding with one groom out to the sulphurous ground west of the city, and bathing naked in the lake in the cone of a submerged extinct volcano. Walking onto his terrace those first months to see in the distance the well-behaved mountain sitting under the sun might provoke a reverie about the calm that follows catastrophe. Its plume of white smoke, the occasional rumblings and jets of steam seemed *that* perennial, unthreatening. Eighteen thousand villagers in Torre del Greco had died in 1631, an eruption even more lethal than the one in which Herculaneum and Pompeii were entombed and the scholarly admiral of the Roman fleet, the Elder Pliny, famously lost his life, but since then, nothing that could merit the name of disaster.

The mountain had to wake up and start spitting to get the full attention of this much-occupied, much-diverted man. And did so, the year after he arrived. The vapors that drifted up from the summit thickened and grew. Then black smoke mixed with the steam clouds and at night the cone's halo was tinted red. Hitherto absorbed by the hunt for vases and what minor finds from the excavations he could illicitly lay his hands on, he began to climb the mountain and take notes. On his fourth climb, reaching the upper slope, he passed a six-foot hillock of sulphur that hadn't been there the week before. On his next climb up the snow-covered mountain—it was November—the top of the hillock was emitting a blue flame. He drew closer, stood on tiptoe, then a noise like artillery fire above him—behind?—gripped his heart and he leapt backward. Some forty yards higher, at the opening of the crater, a column of black smoke had shot up, followed by an arc of stones, one of which sank near him. Yes.

He was seeing something he had always imagined, always wanted to know.

When an actual eruption began in March of the following year, when a cloud in the shape of a colossal umbrella pine—exactly as described in the letter of Pliny's nephew to Tacitus—poured upward from the mountain, he was at home practicing the cello. Watching from the roof that night, he saw the smoke go flame-red. A few days later there was a thunderous explosion and a gush of red-hot rocks, and that evening at seven o'clock lava began to boil over the top, coursing toward Portici. Taking with him only valet, groom, and local guide, he left the city on horseback and remained all night on the flank of the mountain. Hissing liquid metal on which fiery cinders floated like boats cascaded past him a mere twenty yards away. He experienced himself as fearless, always an agreeable illusion. Dawn rose and he started down. A mile below he caught up with the front of the lava stream, which had pooled in a deep hollow and been stopped.

From then on, the mountain was never free of its smoking wreath, the occasional toss of blazing scoriae, the spurt of fire, the dribble of lava. And now he knew what to do whenever he climbed the mountain. He gathered specimens of cooling lava in a leather pouch lined with lead, he bottled samples of the salts and sulphurs (deep yellow, red, orange) that he fetched from scorchingly hot crevices in the crater top. With the Cavaliere any passion sought the form of, was justified by becoming, a collection. (Soon other people were taking away pieces of the newly interesting volcano, on their one climb up; but accumulating souvenirs is not collecting.) This was pure collecting, shorn of the prospect of profit. Nothing to buy or sell here. Of the volcano he could only make a gift, to his glory and the glory of the volcano.

Fire again appeared at the top: a much more violent display of the mountain's energies was preparing. It grumbled, rattled, and hissed; its emissions of stones more than once obliged even this hardiest of observers to quit the summit. When a great eruption took place the following year, the first full-scale eruption since 1631, he had more booty, a collection of volcanic rocks large and varied enough to be worth presenting to the British Museum, which he shipped back at his own expense. Collecting the volcano was his disinterested passion.

Naples had been added to the Grand Tour, and everybody who came hoped to marvel at the dead cities under the guidance of the learned British envoy. Now that the mountain had shown itself capable of being dangerous again, they wanted to have the great, terrifying experience. It had become another attraction and creator of employment for the ever needy: guides, litter bearers, porters, furnishers of victuals, grooms, and lantern carriers if the ascent was made at night—the best time to see the worst. Anything but impregnable by the standards of real mountains like the Alps, or even of Mount Etna, almost three times as high,

Vesuvius offered at most an exertion, sport only for amateurs. The exterminator could be mounted by anyone. For the Cavaliere the volcano was a familiar. He did not find the ascent very strenuous nor the dangers too frightening, whereas most people, underestimating the effort, were appalled by its arduousness, frightened by its vision of injury. Upon their return he would hear the stories of the great risks they had run, of the girandoles of fire, the hail (or shower) of stones, the accompanying racket (cannon, thunder), the infernal, mephitic, sulphurous stench. The very mouth of hell, that's what it is! So people believe it to be here, he would say. Oh, I don't mean literally, the visitor (if English, therefore usually Protestant) would reply.

Yet even as he wished for the volcano not to be profaned by the wheezing, the overweight, and the self-congratulatory, he longed—like any collector—to exhibit it. And was obliged to do so, if the visitor was a friend or relation from England or a foreign dignitary, as long as Vesuvius continued to flaunt its expressiveness. It was expected that he would chaperone an ascent. His eccentric friend from school days at Westminster, Frederick Hervey, about to be made a bishop, came for a long month; he took him up on an Easter Sunday, and Hervey's arm was seared by a morsel of volcanic effluvia; the Cavaliere supposed that he would be boasting about it for the rest of his life.

Hard to imagine that one could feel proprietary about this legendary menace, double-humped, some five thousand feet tall and eight miles from the city, exposed to the view of everyone, indeed the signature feature of the local landscape. No object could be less ownable. Few natural wonders were more famous. Foreign painters were flocking to Naples: the volcano had many admirers. He set about, by the quality of his attentions, to make it his. He thought about it more than anyone else. My dear mountain. A mountain for a beloved? A monster? With the vases or the paintings or the coins or the statues, he could count on certain conventional recognitions. This passion was about what always surprised, alarmed; what exceeded all expectations; and what never evoked the response that the Cavaliere wanted. But then, to the obsessed collector, the appreciations of other people always seem off-key, withholding, never appreciative enough.

•

Collections unite. Collections isolate.

They unite those who love the same thing. (But no one loves the same as I do; enough.) They isolate from those who don't share the passion. (Alas, almost everyone.)

Then I'll try not to talk about what interests me most. I'll talk about what interests you.

But this will remind me, often, of what I can't share with you.

Oh, listen. Don't you see. Don't you see how beautiful it is.

•

It is not clear whether he was a natural teacher, an explainer (nobody did the tour of Pompeii and Herculaneum better), or learned to be one because so many people he was close to were younger than he and few were as cultivated. Indeed, it was the Cavaliere's destiny to have all the important relations of his life, counting or not counting Catherine, with people much younger than himself. (Catherine was the only predictably younger person, by eight years: a wife is expected to be her husband's junior.) The royal playmate of his childhood had been seven and a half years his junior; the King of Naples was younger by twenty-one years. Younger people were drawn to the Cavaliere. He always seemed so interested in them, in furthering their talents, whatever these might be; so self-sufficient. Avuncular rather than paternal—he had never wanted to have children—he could be concerned, even responsible, without expecting too much.

Charles, his sister Elizabeth's son, was twenty when he arrived for the southernmost stop on his Grand Tour. The pale self-assured little boy whom the Cavaliere had glimpsed a few times had become a highly intelligent, rather disablingly fastidious young man, with a modest, prudent trove of pictures and objects of virtu and an extravagant collection of precious stones and minerals. He wanted to impress his uncle and he did. The Cavaliere recognized the abstracted, wandering, tensely amiable look of the collector—mineralogy was to be the ruling passion of Charles's life—and took an immediate liking to him. Dutiful in the pursuit of entertainment, Charles procured the sexual services of a local courtesan named Madame Tschudi (distantly related to the harpsichord-making family), sat through a few evenings at the opera in his uncle's box, bought ices and watermelon from the vendors on the Toledo, and avowed that he found Naples neither charming nor picturesque but squalid, boring, and dirty. He listened devoutly to his aunt at the harpsichord (Kuhnau, Royer, Couperin). He inspected with envy his uncle's hoard of paintings, statues, and vases; but rough lumps of tufa with pieces of lava or marine shells embedded in them, the fragments of a volcanic bomb, or the bright yellow and orange salts he was shown only made him think with passion of his crystallized rubies, sapphires, emeralds, diamonds—these could be called beautiful. He washed his hands often. And he resolutely refused to climb the mountain.

A formidable though benevolent uncle would be too intimidating without some large eccentricity that made one feel a little protective. Declining the Cavaliere's second invitation to accompany him on a climb, Charles pleaded an intestinal weakness, the lack of a taste for danger. He hoped it would be taken as flattering rather than impertinent if he invoked the obvious classical allusion (many of the Cavaliere's friends in England made it): Remember, I shouldn't like to hear that you've suffered the fate of the Elder Pliny. And now the Cavaliere, having just acquired a favorite nephew, could return the compliment: Then you shall be the Younger Pliny and report my death to the world.

•

Then as now an ascent had several stages. The road, in our own century turned into a motorway, did not exist then. But there was already a trail on which one came about two-thirds of the way, as far as the natural trough between the central cone and Mount Somma. This valley, now carpeted with black lava from the 1944 eruption, had trees, bramble, and high grasses. There the horses were left to graze while the volcano pilgrims continued up to the crater on foot.

Having left his horse with a groom, grasping his walking stick, pouch slung over one shoulder, the Cavaliere marched firmly up the slope. The point is to get a good rhythm, to make it mindless, almost as in a daydream. To walk like breathing. To make it what the body wants, what the air wants, what time wants. And that is happening this morning, early morning on this occasion, except for the cold, except for the pain in his ears, from which his broad hat doesn't protect him. For the work of mindlessness there should not be any pain. He passed through the trees (a century earlier the slopes had been thick with forests and teeming with game), and beyond the tree line, where the wind cut more sharply. The trail darkened, steepened, past tracks of black lava and rises of volcanic boulders. It began to feel like climbing now, his stride slowed, the stretch of muscles became pleasantly perceptible. He didn't have to stop to catch his breath but he did halt several times to scan the reddish-brown ground, looking for the spiky rocks with seams of color.

The ground turned grey, loose, quaggy—hindering, by yielding to, every step. The wind pushed against his head. Nearing the top, his ears hurt so much he stuffed them with wax.

Reaching the boulder-rimmed summit, he paused and rubbed his soft, icy ears. He gazed out and down at the iridescent blue skin of the bay. Then he turned. He never approached the crater without apprehension—partly the fear of danger, partly the fear of disappointment. If the mountain spat fire, hurled itself into the air, turned to flame and a moving wall of ash, that was an invitation to look. The mountain was exhibiting itself. But when the mountain was relatively quiet as it has been for several months, when it invited a closer look, he was looking for something new as well as checking to see that everything is the same. The prying look wishes to be rewarded. Even in the most pacified souls the volcano inspires a lust to see destructiveness.

He scrambled to the top of the cone and looked down. The vast hole, hundreds of feet deep, was still abrim with early-morning fog. He took the hammer from his pouch and looked about for a layer of color in the edge of the chasm. The fog was lifting as the sun warmed the air. With each gust of clarifying wind the view dropped farther and farther, without disclosing any fire. Dirty white jets of steam drifted upward from fissures in the lengthening crater walls. The burning innermost core lay hidden below the crust of slag. Not a glimmer. Pure massiveness—grey, inert. The Cavaliere sighed, and put his hammer back in the pouch. Inorganic matter makes a very melancholy impression on us.

Maybe it is not the destructiveness of the volcano that pleases most, though everyone loves a conflagration, but its defiance of the law of gravity to which every inorganic mass is subject. What pleases first at the sight of the plant world is its vertical upward direction. That is why we love trees. Perhaps we attend to a volcano for its elevation, like ballet. How high the molten rocks soar, how far above the mushrooming cloud. The thrill is that the mountain blows itself up, even if it must then like the dancer return to earth; even if it does not simply descend—it falls, falls on us. But first it goes up, it flies. Whereas everything pulls, drags down. Down.

3

Summer. Indeed, by meaningless coincidence, August 24th—an anniversary of the great eruption of A.D. 79. The weather: clammily close, infested with flies. The stench of sulphur in the air. High windows opening out to the entire bay. Birds singing in the palace garden. A delicate column of smoke balancing on the mountain's tip.

The King is on the toilet. Breeches at his ankles, frowning as he strains, his fundament spluttering. Although only twenty-four, he is fat, fat. His belly, striated like his wife's (who has already gone through six of her eventual tally of seventeen pregnancies), rocks from side to side on the immense porcelain *chaise percée*. He had pawed his way through a copious meal, pork and macaroni and wild boar and zucchini flowers and sherbet, that had begun over two hours earlier. He had spewed wine at a favorite valet and tossed pellets of bread at his withered, disputatious prime minister. The Cavaliere, a spare eater even without these off-putting sights, had already been feeling stomach-heavy. And then the King announced that, having enjoyed an excellent meal, he hoped to have an excellent purge of his bowels, and wished to be escorted by one of the distinguished guests at his table, his friend and excellent companion of the hunt, the British minister plenipotentiary.

Oh, oh, my gut! (Groans, farts, sighs.)

The Cavaliere, in steadily dampening full court dress with his star and red riband, is standing against a wall, taking in the fetid air through his thin lips. It could be worse, thinks the Cavaliere, a thought with which he has consoled himself for much of his life. This time what he means is, the King could have had diarrhea.

I feel it coming!

The King's sottish boy's game of being disgusting, of trying to shock. The English knight's patrician game of not responding, of appearing not shocked. It would make a better picture, the Cavaliere thought, if I were not sweating almost as much as he is.

No, it's not. I didn't! I can't! Oh what shall I do?

Perhaps His Majesty could better concentrate on the call of nature if left alone.

I hate being alone!

The Cavaliere, blinking back the drops of sweat that had passed the escarpment of his eyebrows, wondered if this were not one of the King's nasty practical jokes.

Maybe it wasn't a good meal, said the King. I was sure it was a good meal. How could it not be a good meal if it was so tasty?

The Cavaliere said it was very tasty.

The King said, Tell me a story.

A story, said the Cavaliere.

(A courtier: someone who repeats back to you the last word or words that you've said.)

Yes, tell me about a chocolate mountain. A huge mountain all chocolate. That's what I'd like to climb.

Once upon a time there was a mountain dark as night.

As chocolate!

And inside it was all white, with caves and labyrinths and—

Was it cold inside, interrupted the King. If it's hot the chocolate will melt.

It's cold, said the Cavaliere, wiping his brow with a silk handkerchief soaked in essence of tuberose.

Is it like a city? A whole world?

Yes.

But a little world. Very cozy. I wouldn't need so many servants. I'd like a little world with people, maybe the people would be little too, who would do everything I wanted.

So they do already, observed the Cavaliere.

Not so, protested the King. You know how I'm ordered about by the Queen, by Tanucci, by everyone except you, my good dear friend. I need a chocolate world, yes! That's my world. Everything I want. All the women, whenever I wanted. And they could be chocolate too and I would eat them. Don't you ever imagine what it would be like to eat people?

He licked his fat white hand. Umm, mine is salty! Slipping the hand in his armpit, he continued: And it would have a big kitchen. And the Queen would help me cook, she would hate that. She would peel the garlic, millions of shiny cloves, and I would stick them inside her, and then we'd have garlic babies. And the people would run after me, begging me to feed them, I would throw food at them, I'd make them eat.

Frowning, he let his head loll. A roulade of spluttering noises climaxed in a deep cavernous exhalation of the bowels.

That was good, the King said. He reached out and thwacked the Cavaliere's lean rump. The Cavaliere nodded and felt his own bowels churn. But this is the life of a courtier, is it not. The Cavaliere was not one of the rulers of this world.

Help me, said the King to the Master of the Royal Bedchamber at the open door. He was having trouble getting to his feet, he is that fat.

The Cavaliere considered the span of human reactions to the disgusting. At one extreme, Catherine, who was appalled by the manic vulgarity of the King as by so much else at the court. At the other, the King, for whom the disgusting was a source of delight. And himself in the middle, where a courtier must be, neither indignant nor insensible. To be indignant would itself be vulgar, a sign of weakness, of lack of breeding. Eccentric habits in great ones must be borne. (Had not the Cavaliere been the childhood playmate, older by seven years, of another king who sometimes exhibited signs of outright lunacy?) There's no changing the way people are. No one changes, everyone knows that.

•

The ungainly King is easily impressed, almost as much by the thin English knight's imperturbability as by the cleverness of the Hapsburg wife imported for him from Vienna when he was seventeen, who since the birth of their first son sits on the Council of State and is the real ruler of the kingdom. How agreeable if, instead of that formidable, supercilious, gloomy man on the throne in Madrid, someone like the Cavaliere had been his father. The Cavaliere loves music, doesn't he? So does the King; it is, for him, like food. Is not the Cavaliere a sportsman, too? Besides always clambering up that beastly mountain, he loves to fish, ride, hunt. And hunting is the King's ruling passion, which he practices by excluding the exertion, difficulty, and occasional danger that limits and is thought to give zest and legitimacy to slaughtering animals. The beaters corraled endless columns of wild boar, deer, and hare, and then drove them past the King, who stood in a roofless sentry box of solid masonry in the park at his country palace or on a horse in the middle of a field. Out of a hundred shots, he never missed more than one. Then he descended and went to work, sleeves rolled to his elbows, carving up the steaming, bloody bodies.

The King relished the smell of the blood rising from the carcasses, of tripe or macaroni thickening in the cauldron, of his own excretory labors or those of his brood of young children, of pine trees and the intoxication of jasmine. The long bulbous organ that had earned him the nickname of King Big Nose was imperious as well as startlingly ugly. Hot smells drew him: peppery food, barely dead animals, a yielding moist woman. But also the smell of his terrifying father, the odor of melancholy. (He can just barely smell it on the Cavaliere, on whom it is much fainter, repressed.) The reassuringly animal-like odor of his wife would draw him into her body, but afterward, as he was falling asleep, another odor (or a dream of an odor) would wake him. The pungent molecules caressed the inside of his thick nostrils, flew to his brain. He liked everything that is formless, abundant. Odors focus, distract. Odors cling, follow. They extend, diffuse. A world of odors is ungovernable—one does not dominate an odor, it dominates you—and the King did not really like governing. Oh, for a tiny kingdom!

His sensuality was the only intelligence he possessed; deliberately left almost illiterate by his father, he had been designed as a weak ruler. Because of his taste for fraternizing with the city's immense tribe of layabouts, he was also nicknamed the Beggar King, but his superstitions were those shared by everyone here, not only the uneducated. His amusements were a bit more original. Besides nasty pranks and the killing sports, which he practiced at a uniquely wholesale rate, the occupations of servants diverted him from the constraints of royal mummery. Arriving at the grandiose palace at Caserta, the Cavaliere had once found the King busy taking down lamps from the walls and cleaning them. When a crack regiment was stationed on the grounds of the palace at Portici, the King set up a tavern in the encampment and sold wine to the soldiers.

The King doesn't act like a king (how disappointing!), he doesn't enact his pure difference from others: no wit, no grandeur, no distance. Only coarseness and appetite. But Naples often shocked, even as it bewitched. That good Catholic from provincial, relentlessly clerical Salzburg, Leopold Mozart, was appalled by the pagan superstitions of the nobility and by the rank idolatry of Church ceremony. English travelers became indignant over the indecent wall paintings and phallic objects at Pompeii. Everyone was scornful of the caprices of the juvenile King. And where everyone is shocked is a place where everyone tells stories.

•

Like every foreign diplomat, the Cavaliere had his much-polished store of tales of how outrageous the King could be with which to regale distinguished visitors. It is not the King's scatological humor that makes him unusual, the Cavaliere might start by saying. Jokes about defecation are common in most Italian courts, I am told. Really, his auditor would say.

If the Cavaliere began with a version of his accompanying the King to the privy, he might move on to another story in which chocolate plays a role.

This story, which he had told many visitors, concerned events that happened three years after his arrival as envoy. Charles III of Spain, who is the Neapolitan king's father, and Maria Theresa of Austria having concluded their negotiations for an alliance of the two dynasties, the empress having selected one of her many daughters, the acre's worth of trousseau having been assembled, and the tearful bride and her vast retinue having been readied for the departure—and in Naples, the ultra-pomp of a royal wedding having reached an advanced state of planning (the dressing of public spaces, the designing of allegorical fireworks and pastries, the composing of music for processions and balls), and the nobles and the diplomatic colony having girded themselves for the extra expenses of banquets and new finery . . . no one was prepared for the black-garbed emissary from the Hapsburg court who arrived with the deflating message that on the very eve of her departure the fifteen-year-old archduchess had succumbed to the smallpox then raging in Vienna, which had nearly carried off the empress as well.

Learning the news that same morning, the Cavaliere put on his court regalia and set out in his best carriage to perform the offering of condolences. Upon entering the palace, he asked to be escorted to the King and was brought not to the royal apartments but to an alcove inside the high archway opening onto a great gallery, some three hundred feet long and lined with pictures of the hunt, where the Prince of San ***, the King's tutor, stood musing. No, not musing. Fuming. Far down the gallery a noisy, aromatic, gilded procession, illuminated by torches and tapers, was advancing toward them.

I have come to express my sincere—

The prince's scornful eye.

As you see, His Majesty's grief knows no bounds, said the prince.

Advancing toward them, six young men carried a coffin draped in crimson velvet on their shoulders. A priest was keeping step, waving a censer. Two pretty servants bore gold vases filled with flowers. The sixteen-year-old King followed, swathed in black, with a black handkerchief to his face.

(You know what people here make of funerals, the Cavaliere would interject, ever eager to share information. No show of grief is too excessive.)

The procession neared the Cavaliere. Put her down, said the King.

He bounded over to the Cavaliere and seized his hand. Come, you can be one of the mourners.

Majesty!

Come! bellowed the King. I am not allowed to hunt, they won't let me take my boat out to fish—

For one day only, interrupted the old prince, furious.

All day—the King stamped his foot—I have to stay indoors. We were playing leapfrog for a while and then wrestling, but this is better. Much better.

He pulled the Cavaliere over to the coffin, in which lay a

young man in a lace-trimmed white gown, eyes with velvety lashes shut firmly, his rosy cheeks and his hands, folded over his chest, dotted with tiny lumps of creamy brown.

(The youngest of the chamberlains, often teased by the others because of his girlish good looks, who had been conscripted to play the dead archduchess, annotates the Cavaliere. Pause. And the drops of chocolate . . . you can divine what they signify. Actually not, says his auditor. These, explains the Cavaliere, were the pustules of smallpox.)

The boy's chest gently rose and fell.

Look, look, just like life!

The King seized a torch from one of the attendants and struck an operatic pose. Oh, my love. My bride is dead!

The pallbearers snickered.

No, you mustn't laugh. The light of my life! The joy of my heart! So young. Still a virgin, at least I hope so. And dead! With beautiful white hands I would have kissed, beautiful white hands she would have put here—he showed, on his anatomy, where.

(The Cavaliere does not add that he had already had more than one viewing of the royal groin—of the King's own very white skin, spotted with herpes, which his doctor considered a sign of good health.)

Don't you feel sorry for me, the King shouted to the Cavaliere.

(Neither does the Cavaliere relate how he finally extricated himself, but he does mention that throughout this farce a dwarf-like priest continued to recite the Mass for the Dead. Not a real priest, his auditor would say. Surely another chamberlain, got up in the garb of a priest. Considering the nonsense that priests lend themselves to here, the Cavaliere would reply, it could well have been a real priest.)

The youth in the coffin was perspiring and the chocolate drops beginning to melt. The King, trying not to laugh, put his fingers to his lips. I shall commission an opera on the subject, he exclaimed.

&c, &c, &c, concludes the Cavaliere.

And perhaps the word opera reminds the Cavaliere of a scene he witnessed recently at the San Carlo with Catherine, during the premiere of a new work by Paisiello. It was the last night of Carnival. Two boxes away was the King, who came regularly to watch and hum and shout and eat; rather than sit in the royal box he would often commandeer any of the upper boxes, whose regular subscribers considered it an honor to be so displaced. That night the King had ordered a dish of macaroni brought to him, first imposing the aromas of oil, cheese, garlic, and beef gravy upon those in his vicinity. Then the King leaned over the parapet and started throwing the scalding-hot food with both hands into the pit below.

(The Cavaliere pauses, waiting for a reaction. What did the wretched spectators do then, asks his auditor. You might think they would mind, says the Cavaliere, but everyone here seems to enjoy the King's waggery.)

While a few appeared discomfited by the blossoming of greasy stains on their best apparel—their efforts to clean themselves made the King roar with laughter—many treated the shower of pasta as a mark of royal favor and, rather than dodging it, pushed each other aside to retrieve some of it to eat.

(How astonishing, his auditor would say. It is like Carnival year round here. But quite harmless, I suppose.)

And let me tell you, the Cavaliere might continue, about another scramble for food incited by the King which is somewhat less comic. It took place the year after the mock burial I have described to you, when the younger sister of the dead fiancée designated as her replacement, who wept even more copiously than had her older sister upon learning to whom she had been affianced, had been dispatched from Vienna; happily, this archduchess arrived intact, and the days of wedding followed. Now what I must explain, explains the Cavaliere, is that all important court celebrations here include the building of an artificial mountain laden with food.

(A mountain? his auditor would ask.)

Yes, a mountain. A gigantic pyramidal scaffolding of beams and boards erected by teams of carpenters in the middle of the great square in front of the palace, which was then draped and sculpted into a very creditable small park with iron fencing and a pair of allegorical statues guarding the gate.

(May I inquire how high? I am not certain, says the Cavaliere. At least forty feet.)

As soon as the mountain was finished, tribes of purveyors and their assistants began ascending and descending. Bakers on the foothills were stacking huge logs of bread. Farmers were hauling up bins of watermelon and pears and oranges. Poulterers were nailing live chickens, geese, capons, ducks, and pigeons by their wings to wooden fences along the paths that led to the top. And thousands of people arrived to camp in the square while the mountain was heaped with its hierarchies of foods, festooned with garlands of flowers and pennons, and guarded round the clock by a ring of armed soldiers mounted on nervous horses. By the second day of banqueting inside the palace, the crowd had multiplied tenfold, and their knives, daggers, axes, and scissors were in plain view. Around noon a roar went up when the butchers entered the square, dragging the procession of oxen, sheep, goats, calves, and pigs. As they tied the animals by halters to the base of the mountain, a murmuring hush fell on the crowd.

(I see I must fortify myself for what comes next, says his auditor, after the Cavaliere paused for effect.)

Then the King, holding his bride's hand, stepped out on the balcony. Another roar went up, not so different from the one that greeted the procession of animals. As the King acknowledged the cheers and *vivas* of the crowd, the other balconies and the upper windows of the palace quickly filled with the leading members of the court, some of the more important nobles, members of the diplomatic corps most in favor—

(I have heard no one is more in favor with the King than you, interrupts the auditor. Yes, says the Cavaliere, I was there.)

Then the cannon sounded from the top of the fortress of Sant'Elmo, signaling that the assault could begin. The famished crowd gave an answering howl and broke through the ring of soldiers, who rode their rearing horses to the safety of the palace wall. Elbowing, kneeing, punching, shoving one another, the most able-bodied boys and young men pulled ahead and started to scale the mountain, which was soon aswarm with people, some clambering higher, some descending with their booty, others perched at mid-point carving up the fowl and eating it raw or throwing pieces to the outstretched arms of their womenfolk and children below. Meanwhile, others drove their knives into the animals tethered at the base of the mountain. It would be hard to say which of one's sensory organs were being more forcefully assaulted: one's nose, by the smell of blood and the excrement of the terrified animals; one's ears, by the cries of the animals being slaughtered and the screams of people falling or being pushed from some part of the mountain; or one's eyes, by the sight of the poor beasts thrashing about in their agony or of some wretch who, brought to frenzy by all these sensations, to which must be added the applause and shouts of encouragement from the windows and balconies, instead of plunging his knife into the belly of a pig or a goat, had plunged it into his neighbor's neck.

(I trust I am not making you think too ill of the lower orders here, interjects the Cavaliere. They are in most circumstances quite amiable. Indeed, exclaims his auditor—and, musing on human savagery rather than injustice, said no more.)

You would be surprised, the Cavaliere continues, how little time it took to pillage the mountain. It goes even more quickly now. For that was the last year in which the animals were dismembered live. Our young Austrian queen was revolted by the spectacle and entreated the King to put some limits on the bar-

barity of this custom. The King decreed that the oxen and calves and pigs would be killed first by the butchers and hung already quartered on the fence. And so it is done to this day. As you see, he would conclude, there is progress even here, in this city.

•

How can the Cavaliere communicate to an auditor *how* disgusting the King is. Impossible to describe. He cannot bottle the fetid odors the King emits and waft them under his auditors' noses, or post them to his friends in England whom he regales with his stories, as he does the sulphurs and salts from the volcano he sent back regularly to the Royal Society. He cannot call the servants to bring a bucket of blood and demonstrate, by dipping his own arms in it to the elbows, the spectacle of the King carving up hundreds of animals himself after a day's slaughter he calls hunting. He will not mime the King standing in the harbor marketplace at sunset selling his day's catch of swordfish. (He sells his catch? Yes, and haggles over the price. But it must be added, said the Cavaliere, that he throws his earnings to the suite of layabouts who always follow him.) Though a courtier, the Cavaliere is not an actor. He cannot become the King, even for a moment, to demonstrate or to show. That is not a virile activity. He only relates, and in the relating, the sheer odiousness of it dwindles into a tale, nothing to get wrought up over. In this kingdom of the immoderate, of excess, of overflow, the King is just one item. Since he has only words to tell, then he can explain (the dumbed-down education of the King, the benighted superstitions of the nobles), he can condescend, he can ironize. He can have an opinion (he cannot describe without taking a stand about what he is describing) and that opinion will already have shown itself superior to the facts of the senses, bleached them, muffled their din, deodorized them.

An odor. A taste. A touch. Impossible to describe.

•

This is a fable the Cavaliere had read in a book by one of those impious French writers he fancied, whose very names made Catherine sigh and grimace. Imagine a park with a beautiful statue of a woman, no, a statue of a beautiful woman, the statue, that is, the woman, clasping a bow and arrows, not naked but *as* naked (the way the marble tunic clings to her breasts and hips), not Venus but Diana (the arrows belong to her). Beautiful herself, with the headband on her ringlets, she is dead to all beauty. Now, runs the fable, let us imagine someone who is able to bring her to life. We are imagining a Pygmalion who is no artist, he did not create her but only found her in the garden, on her pedestal, a little larger than life-size, and decided to perform an experiment on her: a pedagogue, a scientist, then. Someone else made her, then abandoned her. Now she is his. And he is not infatuated with her. But he has a didactic streak and wants to see her bloom to the best of her ability. (Perhaps afterward he will fall in love with her, probably against his better judgment, and want to make love to her; but that is another fable.) So he proceeds slowly, thoughtfully, in the spirit of experiment. Desire does not urge him on, make him want everything at once.

What does he do? How does he bring her to life? Very cautiously. He wants her to become conscious, and, holding the rather simple theory that all knowledge comes from the senses, decides to open her sensorium. Slowly, slowly. He will give her, to begin with, just one of the senses. And which does he pick? Not sight, noblest of the senses, not hearing—well, no need to run through the whole list, short as it is. Let's hasten to relate that he first awards her, perhaps ungenerously, the most primitive sense, that of smell. (Perhaps he does not want to be seen, at least not yet.) And it should be added that, for the experiment to work, we must suppose this divine creature to have some inner existence or responsiveness beneath the impermeable surface; but this is just a hypothesis, albeit a necessary one. Nothing so far can be inferred about this inner aliveness. The goddess, beauty incarnate, does not move.

So now the goddess of the hunt can smell. Her ovoid, slightly protruding marble eyes under her heavy brows do not see, her slightly parted lips and delicate tongue do not taste, her satiny marble skin would not feel your skin or mine, her lovely shell-like ears do not hear, but her chiseled nostrils receive all odors, near and far. She smells the sycamores and poplar trees, resinous, acrid, she can smell the tiny shit of worms, she smells the polish on soldiers' boots, and roasted chestnuts, and bacon burning, she can smell the wisteria and heliotrope and lemon trees, she can smell the rank odor of deer and wild boar fleeing the royal hounds and the three thousand beaters in the King's employ, the effusions of a couple copulating in the nearby bushes, the sweet smell of the freshly cut lawn, the smoke from the chimneys of the palace, from far away the fat King on the privy, she can even smell the rain-lashed erosion of the marble of which she is made, the odor of death (though she knows nothing of death).

There are odors she does not smell, because she is in a garden—or because she is in the past. She is spared city smells, like those of the slops and swill thrown from windows onto the street during the night. And the little cars with two-stroke engines and the bricks of soft brown coal (the smell of Eastern Europe in the second half of our century), the chemical plants and oil refineries outside Newark, cigarette smoke . . . But why say spared? She would relish these odors, too. Indeed, it comes from a great distance, she smells the future.

And all these odors, which we think of as good or bad, putrid or enchanting, flood her, suffuse every marble particle of which she is made. She would tremble with pleasure if she could, but she has not been granted the power of movement, not even of breathing. This is a man teaching, emancipating—deciding what's best for—a woman, and therefore moving circumspectly, not inclined to go all the way, quite comfortable with the idea of creating a limited being—the better to be, to stay, beautiful. (Impossible to imagine the fable with a woman scientist and a beautiful statue of Hippolytus; that is, a statue of the beautiful

Hippolytus.) So the deity of the hunt has only the sense of smell, the world inside herself, no space; but time is born, because one smell succeeds, dominates another. And with time, eternity. To have smell, only smell, means she is a being-who-smells and therefore wants to go on smelling (desire wills its perpetuation ad infinitum). But odors do vanish sometimes (indeed, some were gone so quickly!), though some return. And when an odor fades, she feels—is—diminished. She begins to dream, this consciousness-that-smells, of how she could retain the odors, by storing them up inside herself, so she would never lose them. And this is how, later, space emerges, inner space only, as Diana began to wish that she could hold different odors in different parts of her marble body: the dog shit in her left leg, the heliotrope in an elbow, sweetness of the freshly cut grass in her groin. She cherished them, wanted them all. She experiences pain, not the pain (more precisely, displeasure) of a bad odor, for she knows nothing of good or bad, cannot afford to make this luxurious distinction (every odor is good, because any odor is better than no odor, oblivion), but the pain of loss. Every pleasure—and smelling, whatever she smells, is pure pleasure—becomes an experience of anticipated loss. She wants, if only she knew how, to become a collector.

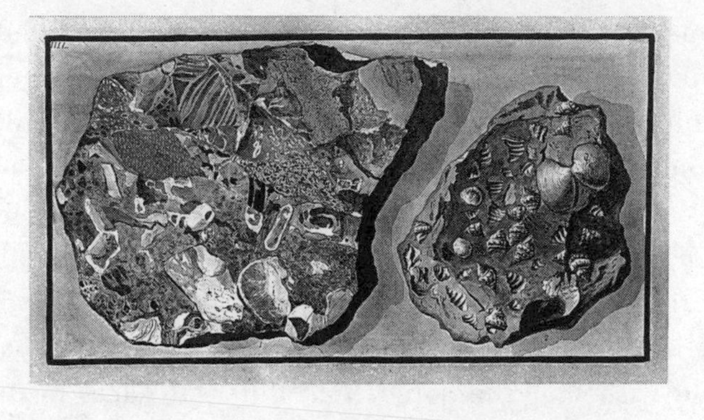

4

Another winter. A month of animal massacres with the King at the foot of the Apennines, Christmas balls, some eminent foreign visitors to entertain, his burgeoning correspondence with learned societies, an excursion with Catherine to Apulia to look at some new excavations, their weekly concerts (but Catherine is ailing). The mountain, draped in snow, fussed and fumed. The Cavaliere's collection of paintings, hitherto distinctly Old Masterish, now included several dozen gouaches and oils by local artists depicting the volcanic scenery and the natives in gaudy costume, frolicking. These are priced very cheaply (by the palm or yard of canvas painted) and hang in the gallery leading to his study. He attended the miracle staged in the cathedral twice a year, on which the city's well-being was believed to depend: the liquefying of a lump of the patron saint's blood. The city's best-known lump of superstition. Looking about for less familiar enactments of the local backwardness, the Cavaliere arranged for an audience with the famous sibyl Efrosina Pumo.

At first it was all atmosphere, the crooked street, the crumbling masonry, the battered door with the undecipherable writing on it, the woman's low dank room with whitewashed walls and soot-stained ceiling, the guttering votive candles, the cauldron on the fire, the straw matting on the tile floor, the black dog rushing to sniff his crotch. Leaving Valerio outside with a clutch of the sibyl's clients waiting for their ration of soothsaying and healing, the Cavaliere was feeling rather, well, Voltairean: in an ethnological mood. On his own. A tourist of other people's superstitions. Feeling superior, enjoying the feeling of being superior, disdainful of all superstitions, magic, zealotry, irrationality, yet not averse to the prospect of being surprised, confounded. Willing to hear a dead voice resound, watch a table prance, have this utter stranger divine the baby name he had called his mother, describe the raspberry mole on his groin . . . for then it would be after all, if not as vulgarly as is thought here, a miraculous world.

Instead, and one must be content with that, it was a world of wonders. Beauties. Marvels, chief among them the volcano. But no miracles, no.

It is said that some years earlier the woman predicted the month and year of both eruptions, the lesser and the greater, that had recently disturbed the volcano's long slumber. He intends to make her speak of that. But of course he cannot come to the point right away, as he knows from more than a decade among these indolent, sly people. He must listen to many servile expressions of gratitude at the honor of being visited by the most excellent and exalted Cavaliere, the dearest friend and counselor of the young King (may age bring him wisdom!), who had deigned to lower his head to enter her humble abode. He must sip a sweetish brew that she calls tea, served by a lanky boy of around fifteen whose left eye is like a quail egg, and allow his slim hand to lie open in her plushy palm.

She started by telling him he will have a long life, at which the Cavaliere raised his eyebrows, wrinkled his nose.

A long life here, she murmured. Not what the Cavaliere

enjoys imagining, and this was an exercise in imagination. He was still expecting Naples to be succeeded by a better post; say, Madrid. Or Vienna.

Then she told him that a great happiness lay before him.

Let us talk of other matters than my fate, said the Cavaliere, withdrawing his hand from her inspection. Actually, I am not seeking information about myself at all.

Really? Then His Excellency is indeed an unusual man, which I have every reason to believe. What man is not interested in himself?

Oh, said the Cavaliere. I pretend to no disinterestedness. I am as self-loving as the next man.

He guessed her to be about fifty, though one could never be sure with the inhabitants known as "the people" (that is, most people), since they, especially the women, usually looked older than they were. A shrewd, handsome face with amber, no, green eyes, with a strong chin, with greying hair braided and piled on her head; a squarish body whose outline was blurred by the volumes of pink and russet shawls that hung from her shoulders. She sat against an arched wall on a large oak chair. The Cavaliere had been ceremoniously installed in a chair piled with some ruptured cushions intended for his comfort.

Most of those who consult me want to know when they will fall in love, she was saying. Or come into an inheritance. Or die.

The Cavaliere replied that he was extremely fond of his wife, that he knew his prospects of inheritance to be nil. And that only a fool would want to learn the date of his death and poison the time still left to him.

His Excellency seems to think he is old.

I have never felt young, he said irritably. It feels like a new thought. This would-be sibyl had not surprised him yet but he had already surprised himself.

And such feelings keep you younger than your age now, she said with a rather theatrical wave of her arm. About youth and age Efrosina is . . . an expert! I've told His Excellency that he will live for many years more. Isn't that what everyone wants to hear?

He did not answer.

His Excellency is not curious?

On the contrary, he said sharply, I am exceptionally curious. Curiosity has brought me . . . here.

He made a gesture that said: this room, this country, this nonsense. I must be patient, he said to himself. I am among savages. Glancing away from the woman, he intercepted the one-eyed gaze of the boy—a servant? her acolyte?—squatting in the corner, who had the same penetrating look as she, more eloquent because halved.

I'm curious to learn how exactly you proceed. Do you read cards or consult the entrails of animals or chew on bitter leaves and fall into a trance—

You are impatient, my lord. A true son of the north.

How interesting, the Cavaliere thought. The woman is no fool. She wants to converse with me, not merely show me her tricks.

Efrosina lowered her head for a moment, sighed, then nodded to the boy, who took something wrapped in a malachite-green cloth from the corner cupboard and set it down on the trestle table between them. Under the cloth, which she removed slowly, was a lidless box of thick milky glass. Staring fixedly at the box, she laid the cloth over her bosom like a bib, muttered some inaudible words, made a few passes in the air, then crossed herself and bowed her head. The performance had started. Ah, said the Cavaliere, encouragingly.

I see too much, she whispered.

The Cavaliere, who always wants to see more, smiled to himself, relishing the contrast.

She lifted her face, eyes gone wide, her mouth twitching.

No, I do not want to see disasters! No!

The Cavaliere nodded in appreciation of the drama of the struggle against knowledge being concocted for his benefit. Sighing, she raised the cube with both hands before her face.

I see . . . I see water! Her voice had gone hoarse. Yes! And the bottom of a sea strewn with open chests, spilling out their treasure. I see a boat, a colossal boat—

Oh, water, he interrupted. Then earth. Then air, and I suppose we shall get to fire before nightfall.

She set the cube down. Her voice returned to its normal insinuating smoothness. But His Excellency likes water. All Naples enjoys seeing him out in his boat through the long day fishing in our splendid bay.

And I climb the mountain. This is known, too.

Yes, His Excellency is admired for his bravery.

He did not reply.

Perhaps His Excellency is interested in his death after all.

Death, death. He was closing the valves of his attention.

If I cannot reassure you, she was saying, can I frighten you, my lord?

I am not easily frightened.

But you have already, more than once, just missed being struck by a fiery missile. You could lean over and lose your balance. You could descend and not be able to climb out.

I am very surefooted.

You know how temperamental the mountain is. Anything can happen from one moment to the next.

I am very adaptable, he said. And to himself: I am observing, I am collecting evidence. He shifted his weight in the cane chair.

I am breathing, he said.

The closeness of the room was making him groggy. He heard her whispering, the boy leaving the room, a large clock ticking, a fly buzzing, a dog barking, church bells, a tambourine, a water seller's cry. A magma of sounds that fell away to reveal a silence, and behind that but more distinct, as if separately wrapped, the clock, the voices, the bells, the dog, the cry, the boy returning, the sound of his own heartbeat, and then silence. The Cavaliere was trying to hear a voice, a very faint, barely audible voice, while this large full-bodied voice droned on about the dangers of the mountain. He is still trying to hear the voice. Determined in his pursuit of experience, the Cavaliere is good at paying attention. You pivot your mind, train it on something fixedly: mental staring. Easy once you know you can do it. It needn't be dark. It's all inside.

Are you awake?

I am always awake, declared the Cavaliere. He had closed his eyes.

Now you are really listening, my lord.

From far inside his head he remembered to wonder why he was sitting here, and then recalled that it would be amusing to relate this exploit to his friends.

Shall we start with the past? Efrosina's voice asked.

What? he said querulously. The question was repeated. He shook his head. Not the past!

Even, she said, if I could raise the spirit of your mother?

Heaven forbid! exclaimed the Cavaliere, opening his eyes to meet her odd, penetrating stare. Since people here always claim to adore their mothers, perhaps they do, so she couldn't know how unwelcome would be even an imaginary visitation of that unaffectionate, august beauty from whom he learned as a small child to expect nothing. Nothing.

I should like to hear about the future, he muttered. He had forgotten to wonder why Efrosina would assume his mother was dead, until he remembered: he was old, so she would now be very old. Not beautiful.

The near future, he added prudently.

He closed his eyes again, without meaning to, then opened them at a farrago of convulsive sounds.

Efrosina had gone pale. She was staring into the cube, groaning and hissing.

I don't like what I see. My lord, why have you asked me to look into the future? No. No. No . . .

Trembling, sweating profusely, racked by violent coughs and hiccups, she was putting on a show of being extremely uncomfortable. No, surely that was not right, for someone who trembles, who sweats, who coughs and hiccups *is* uncomfortable. But it is still a show.

Let's go on with the game.

Are you seeing something? Something about the volcano?

She cannot fail to come to the point now.

I told the Cavaliere he was not old, she murmured huskily. *I* am old! My God, what a sight I am. Ah. I see, just when I get too old I will be saved. I will become young again. I will live for centuries! Next—she began to laugh—next I will be Emilia. Then Eusapia. Yes, then I will travel to many places, as Eusapia Paladina I will be famous everywhere and even the American professor will be interested in me. Then, where was I—she wiped her eyes with the edge of a shawl—yes, Eleanora. Eleanora is very bad—she laughs. But . . . then I leave Naples and move to London and I am Ellie and am head of a large—

The volcano! exclaimed the Cavaliere. Having directed Efrosina that the séance was not to be about his personal destiny, he hardly expected her to launch into this incomprehensible rant about herself.

Do you see when it will erupt again?

Efrosina looked at him impudently. My lord, I will see what you want me to look at.

She leaned forward, blew out the candle on the table, and peered into the cube. And now I see it. Oh—she shook her head in ostentatious wonderment—oh, how ugly.

What?

I see a blackened ruin. The cone is gone.

He asked when this would happen.

So changed, she continued. All the woods are gone. There are no more horses. There is a black road. Now I see something quite comical. Droves of people laboring up the mountain, pushing each other. Everyone seems so tall. Tall like you, my lord. But wearing such strange clothes, you can't tell the gentlefolk from the servants, they all look like servants. And near the top . . . someone in a little cabin selling pieces of lava and boxes of colored rocks, blue and red and yellow, and scarves and plates with pictures of the mountain. Oh, I fear I have gone too far forward.

Don't, said the Cavaliere.

The future is a hole, Efrosina murmured. When you fall in it, you cannot be sure how far you will go. You asked me to look and I do not control how far I see. But I see . . . Yes.

What?

Twenty-six.

And she looked up.

Twenty-six eruptions? You see that many?

Years, my lord.

Years?

How many you have. It is a good number. Do not be angry with me, my lord.

She busied herself relighting the candle, as if to avoid looking at him. The Cavaliere flushed with annoyance. Was there more? No. She was taking the cloth from her breast, she covered the cube.

I have disappointed you, I know. But come again. Each time I see something different. Forgive Efrosina that she does not tell you more about the volcano today.

A slow burn of noise outside the door.

People come to me with many fears, she said. I cannot relieve them all.

Someone was knocking. Perhaps it was Valerio.

I promise we will speak about it next time, she was saying. (The fear? The volcano?) She will talk with her son who has climbed the volcano since he was a child and knows its secrets.

The Cavaliere did not understand whom she was talking

about. But deciding he had wasted enough time on this evasive display of the clairvoyant's powers, he reached into his purse to put some money on the table. Efrosina stopped him with an imperious gesture, declaring that the honor of His Excellency's visit was payment enough and that it was she who wished to present him with a gift, and directed Tolo or was it Barto—what did she call the one-eyed boy?—to accompany the Cavaliere and his servant home.

•

The Cavaliere thought of himself as—no, was—an envoy of decorum and reason. (Isn't that what the study of ancient art teaches us?) Besides a most profitable investment and the exercise of his collecting lust, there was a moral in these stones, these shards, these dimmed objects of marble and silver and glass: models of perfection and harmony. The antiquity that was uncouth, alert to the demonic, was largely hidden from these early patrons of antiquity. What he overlooked in antiquity, what he was not prepared to see, he cherished in the volcano: the uncouth holes and hollows, dark grottoes, clefts and precipices and cataracts, pits within pits, rocks under rocks—the rubbish and the violence, the danger, the imperfection.

Few ever see what is not already inside their heads. The Cavaliere's great predecessor of a century earlier in the love of volcanoes, Athanasius Kircher, had watched Etna and Vesuvius in action and had himself lowered by a pulley into their craters. But these bold close-up observations, undertaken at such risk and with so much discomfort (how his eyes must have stung from the fumes, how his torso must have ached from the ropes), did not deter the wily Jesuit from proposing a wholly imagined account of the volcano's insides. The pictures illustrating his *Mundus Subterraneus* show Vesuvius, in cross section, as a hollow shell enclosing another world, furnished with sky, trees, mountains, valleys, caverns, rivers of water as well as of fire.

The Cavaliere wondered if he dared try a descent into the

volcano, while it still remained quiet. Of course, he no more envisaged that he would find Kircher's netherworld than he thought the volcano was the mouth of hell or that an eruption, like a famine, was a divine chastisement. He was a rational person, afloat in a sea of superstition. A connoisseur of ruins, like his friend Piranesi in Rome, for what was the mountain if not a great ruin? A ruin which could come alive and cause further ruin.

In the plates he commissioned to illustrate the two folio volumes he had made recently of his "volcanic letters" to the Royal Society, the Cavaliere appears in some of the pictures, on foot or on horseback. In one he is watching his groom bathe in Lake Avernus; in another—a memorable occasion—escorting the royal party to the brink of a chasm into which the lava was coursing. A snowy landscape, in which the mountain looks particularly serene, has no observer, but most pictures that show the odd shapes and mutations produced by volcanic activity have some human figures: a spectacle requires the depiction of a gaze. Erupting is its nature, the nature of a volcano, even if it does so only now and then. That would be the picture . . . if you choose to have only one.

As Vesuvius neared another eruption, the Cavaliere climbed more often, partly to taste how fearless he had become. Was it the sibyl's prediction of a long life? Sometimes he felt safer making his way up the seething mountain than anywhere else.

The mountain provided a different experience from anything else, a different measure. The land has spread, the sky has grown, the gulf has widened. You don't have to remember who you are.

He is standing at the summit in the late afternoon. Watching the steady decline of the sun, ever larger, ever redder, more succulent, toward the sea. Waiting for the most beautiful moment, the one he would like to prolong, when the sun falls to the horizon, for a second sits on a pedestal of itself—before dropping with sickening finality behind the sea line. Around him the atrocious din of the volcano, preparing for the next eruption.

Fantasies of omnipotence. To magnify this. To make that cease. To cut the sound. As in the rear of the orchestra, the timpanist, having drawn a roulade of booming sound from the two great drums before him, swiftly lays down his mallets and extinguishes the sound by putting his palms so lightly, so firmly, on the head of the drum, then lowers his ear to the drum to make sure it is still in tune (the delicacy of these gestures after the portentous motions of pounding and banging)—so one could silence a thought, a feeling, a fear.

•

The narrow street. A leper who lay in the sun. Whining dogs. Other visits to Efrosina Pumo in her lower room.

The Cavaliere continued to surprise himself. He whom everyone, including himself, thought so sceptical—impervious, to Catherine's despair, to any appeals of religion, an atheist by temperament as well as conviction—was the secret client of a vulgar soothsayer. It had to remain a secret because if he told anyone he would have to deride it. And then it *would* be nonsense. His words would slay the magic. But as long as his visits went unreported the experience could stay suspended in his mind. True as well as not true. Convincing as well as unconvincing.

The Cavaliere relished having a secret, a little weakness he could indulge in himself, an endearing frailty. No one should be entirely consistent. Like his century, the Cavaliere was less rational than has been reported.

The sleep of reason engenders mothers. This large-bosomed woman with cracked fingernails and a peculiar gaze teased him, amused him, challenged him. He enjoyed sparring with her.

She spoke oracularly of her powers, she proclaimed her dual citizenship in the past and in the future. The future exists in the present, she said. The future, as she described it, seemed to be the present gone awry. A terrifying prospect, he thought. Luckily,

I shall not see much of it. Then he recalled that she had prophesied for him another quarter of a century. May the future not arrive till after then!

•

On his third or fourth visit, she offered at last to read the cards for him.

The boy brought over a wooden box. Efrosina opened the lid and took out the Tarot deck, which she placed, still wrapped in a square of purple silk, at the center of the table. (Anything precious must be stored wrapped, and unwrapped slowly, slowly.) After freeing the cards from their wrapper she spread the silk cloth across the table. (Anything precious must be shielded from contact with a vulgar surface.) She shuffled the cards, then handed them to the Cavaliere to reshuffle.

They were greasy to his touch. And, unlike the beautiful hand-painted cards he had seen in the drawing rooms of noble families, these were printed from woodblocks, with crude, smudged colors.

When she took them back, she caressed them into a fan shape, stared at them for a moment, then shut her eyes.

I am making the colors bright in my mind, she murmured.

Indeed, the Cavaliere said, the colors are faded.

I'm imagining the characters, she said. I know them. They are starting to move. I am watching how they move, I see the breeze rustling their garments. I see the swish of the horse's tail.

Opening her eyes, she cocked her head. I smell the grass, I hear the forest birds, the sounds of water and moving feet.

They are only pictures, said the Cavaliere, surprising himself by his impatience: with Efrosina? or with pictures?

Closing the deck, she held it out for him to pick a card.

Is it not customary to lay out a spread?

This is Efrosina's way, my lord.

He pulled out one card and returned it. Ah, she exclaimed, His Excellency has picked himself.

The Cavaliere, smiling: And what do you learn about me from the card?

She looked down at the card, hesitated, then said in a sing-song tone: That you are . . . a patron of the arts and sciences . . . adept at diverting the tides of fortune into channels that suit your ends . . . ambitious for power . . . preferring to work behind the scenes . . . reluctant to take others into your confidence . . . I could go on—she looked up—but tell Efrosina, am I right, my lord?

You say this because you know who I am.

My lord, this is the meaning of the card. I invent nothing.

And I, I learn nothing. Let me see.

On the card she passed him between her second and third fingers was a crude drawing of a man dressed in elegant robes, holding a large cup or vase in his right hand, his left arm resting negligently on the side of his throne. No.

But it *is* His Excellency. The King of Cups. It could be no other.

She upturned the deck and spread the cards on the large silk square to show him that each was different, that he might have given her any card of the seventy-eight. But he had picked this one.

All right. The next card.

Efrosina shuffled the deck and held it out to him. This time, he looked at the card he selected before giving it to her. A woman holding a large cup or vase in her left hand, a woman in a long flowing dress, on a more modestly proportioned throne.

She nodded. His Excellency's wife.

Why? he said irritably.

The Queen of Cups is very artistically gifted, Efrosina said. Yes, and affectionate . . . and romantic . . . something otherworldly about her, you feel that . . . and unusually perceptive . . . with an inner beauty that does not depend on external aids . . . and without any—

Enough, said the Cavaliere.

Do I describe His Excellency's wife or do I not?

You describe the way all women wish to be described.

Perhaps. But not as all women are. Tell Efrosina if she has described truly or not.

There is a resemblance, said the Cavaliere grudgingly.

Is His Excellency prepared for another card?

Why not, thought the Cavaliere, with the next card we shall at least leave my family. He picked another card.

Ah . . .

What?

Enthusiastic . . . amiable . . . a bringer of ideas, offers, and opportunities . . . artistic and refined . . . often bored, in need of constant stimulation . . . with high principles, but easily led . . . That is the Knight of Cups!

Efrosina studied the cards a moment. A person capable of great duplicity, my lord.

She looked at him. His Excellency recognizes the man I describe, I can see it on his face. Someone to whom he is closely related. Not a son. Not a brother. Perhaps—

Let me see the card, said the Cavaliere.

The card showed Charles as a young man on horseback, bareheaded, with long hair falling around his shoulders, dressed in a simple tunic and short cloak, who holds a cup or vase before him as if offering it to someone ahead. The Cavaliere handed it back to Efrosina.

I cannot imagine who it could be, he said.

She looked at him quizzically. Shall we try one more? You do not believe Efrosina. But the cards do not lie. Watch while I shuffle them thoroughly.

Another card, another young man, it seemed.

But this is astounding, cried Efrosina. Never in a lifetime of reading the cards has someone drawn four consecutive cards in the same suit.

The card he had picked showed a young man who walks along a path, staring fixedly at the large vessel he grasps with his left hand and supports with the palm of his right. The top of the cup is covered by a fold of his cloak, as if to hide its contents. He wears a short tunic that shows his hips and the bulge of his genitals.

The Knave of Cups, she said solemnly, is a poetic youth much given to . . . reflection and study . . . with a great appreciation of beauty but perhaps not enough . . . application to become an artist . . . another young relative . . . I cannot see, but I think he is a friend of your wife . . . who will—

The Cavaliere waved his hand impatiently. Show me something else, some other skill, he said. I am interested in all your tricks.

One more card, my lord.

One more. Sighing pointedly, he reached out and took another, a last.

Ah, this is for me, Efrosina exclaimed. But also for you. What luck!

Not another member of the Vase family, I trust.

She shook her head, smiling, and held up the card.

His Excellency does not recognize the fair-haired youth carrying a satchel of indigo leather slung over his shoulder and a butterfly net?

The Cavaliere did not reply.

His Excellency does not see that the youth is stepping off a precipice?

Precipice?

But there is no danger, she went on, since he is immortal.

I don't see any of that! Who is it?

The Fool.

And who is the Fool? cried the Cavaliere, flushing. The one-eyed boy stepped from the shadows in the corner.

My son.

•

At Efrosina's another time.

She told him she could put him into a trance, though she was not sure he would like that. His Excellency wants to see what he already sees.

It took some urging to persuade her. All but the votive candle was extinguished. A drink was brought by young Pumo. The Cavaliere leaned back in his chair.

I see nothing, he said.

Close your eyes, my lord.

He drifted. He let the lethargy that was under the energy rise up and sweep over him. He let his temperament, like a retractile bridge, slide open to let the big ship of a vision pass through.

Open your eyes . . .

The room had disappeared. There must have been some opiate in the drink, which made him imagine himself inside a giant dungeon, a grotto, a cavern. It was shimmering with pictures. The walls were milky white like the glass box she had showed him on his first visit, like the King's fat hands. On one wall he saw a crowd of dancing figures.

Do you see your mother? Efrosina's voice asked. People always see their mothers.

Of course I don't see my mother, said the Cavaliere, rubbing his eyes.

But do you see the volcano?

He was starting to hear a low diffused hissing, rattling. An almost silent noise, like the nearly immobile movement of the dancers.

The noise and the movement of melancholy.

I see fire, said the Cavaliere.

He wanted to see fire. What he saw was the blackened, leveled summit she had spoken of. The mountain entombed, lying in its rubbish. He saw it for a moment, although he would forget it afterward: the terrible future. The bay without fish, without the swimming children; the mountain's plumeless top a desolate cinder heap. What has happened to the beautiful world, cried the Cavaliere, and flung his hand toward the candle on the table as if to will it lit again.

5

The Marquis de Sade described Italy—he was there in 1776, and met the Cavaliere, who was about to take another leave—as "the most beautiful country in the world, inhabited by the world's most backward people." Happy the much-traveled foreigner, who comes and leaves, sated with impressions, which are turned into judgments and, eventually, into nostalgia. But every country is lovable, and every people. Every variant, every piece of being has something lovable about it!

•

Four years after the Cavaliere's first leave he and Catherine had returned to England and again stayed nearly a year. While the insignificance of his post had become more obvious, with the secretaries of state preoccupied with the revolt in the American colonies and the rivalry with France, his contributions to learning and to the improvement of taste were more acclaimed than ever. He had become an emblem, like the star and red riband of the Order of the Bath he wore when he posed for Sir Joshua Reynolds; he could be identified by the signs of his passions. The portrait shows the Cavaliere seated by an open window, Vesuvius with a tiny white plume in the distance, and on his knee, above a shapely white-stockinged calf, an open copy of the book on his collection of vases.

Sometimes at an assembly, or at an auction with Charles, or at the theatre, he would think of the volcano. He would wonder what the state of its roiling insides was at this exact moment. He imagined the heat on his cheek, the ground trembling beneath his boots, the pulse in his neck beating after the exertion of the climb and the pulse of underlying lava. He recalled the boulder-framed view of the bay, the city's drawn-out curve. At the party the talk would flow on. It felt remarkable that he was here and that it was there. A Vesuvius could never be inferred from England, where there were disasters (an exceptionally cold winter, the Thames frozen over) but not a principle of disaster, monarchical, lording it over the scene.

Where was he? Yes. Here. In London. With friends to see, pictures to buy and vases he had brought back to sell, a paper on the recent eruptions to read to the Royal Society, attendance at Windsor, breakfast with his relations, visits to Catherine's estate in Wales. Little had changed. Nothing was changed by his return, though Catherine's asthma worsened. His friends seemed accustomed to his being away. No one found his tanned, lean, youthful appearance worthy of comment. They congratulated him on his enviable situation, in the sun, able to stay where everyone wanted to visit. And how beneficial for dear Catherine. He had become an expatriate. He was important because he was there. The Cavaliere's friends still chided him for what they construed as his recklessness. Skim off the treasures of that fabled land and bring them back to us, but don't take too many risks with your volcanic studies. Remember the fate of the Elder Pliny. It felt more like a visit than a leave home.

•

He had been back for a year. Charles wrote that Catherine's estate would yield a good income that year, and reported on his recent acquisition of a small collection of rare gems and scarabs. His friend Walpole wrote that he was unable to make the trip to visit him which he had been planning. It took one month for a letter to make the passage to or from London.

The Cavaliere's correspondence—in English, French, and Italian—claimed up to three or four morning hours of each day. There were dispatches to his superiors in London, with acerb portraits of the principal players on the local scene; the more candid were in cipher. A proper letter—to Charles, say, or to Walpole or to his friend Joseph Banks, the president of the Royal Society—was a long one and might touch on many subjects. What was happening of note at the court ("Politics is at a very low ebb here"), the state of the excavations at the dead cities, Catherine's tattered health, new sexual pairings among the nobles and foreign residents, the enchantments of a recent excursion to Capri or to a village on the Amalfi coast, "beautiful" or "truly elegant" or "curious" objects he has acquired, and the volcano ("a fund of entertainment and instruction"). Amorous entanglements were a full-time occupation in these parts, as he noted in a letter to Lord Palmerston. He keeps busy differently, considering how disagreeable such a use of his leisure would be to Catherine, and that he is sufficiently diverted by his study of natural history, antiquities, and the volcano. He reported on the mountain's antics, an experiment with electricity that verified one of Franklin's experiments, the discovery of a new species of sea urchin among the exotic fish he trapped in a rock pool at the little summer house he now rented at Posillipo, and the number of boar and deer he had slaughtered in the company of the young King, and of billiard games he had contrived to lose, prudently, to the King. Letters to encourage letters. That ask for gossip, that impart gossip. Letters that say: I am the same. With nothing to complain of. I am enjoying myself. This place has not changed me, I have the same homebred superiorities, I have not gone native.

Sometimes it felt like exile, sometimes it felt like home.

Everything here was so calm. Naples continued to be pretty as pictures. The main business of the rich was entertaining themselves. The King was the most extravagant of the self-amusers, the Cavaliere the most eclectic.

He wrote letters of recommendation . . . for a musician discharged from his post at the opera, for a cleric seeking ecclesiastical preferment, for the German and English painters flocking to the city, drawn by the abundance of subjects, for a picture agent, for a young Irish tenor with ginger hair, just fifteen years old, penniless and immensely talented (he would go on to have a notable international career): the Cavaliere was an assiduous benefactor. He arranged to have a pair of newly whelped Irish hounds shipped to the King. From the reluctant prime minister he wangled impossible-to-get tickets to a masked ball at the court for fifteen indignant English residents who had not been invited.

He wrote rapidly, in uneven lines and large letters, with little punctuation; even the fair copies he made had blots and crossed-out words—he was not compulsively neat. But like many who were melancholy as children, he had a great capacity for self-discipline. He never refused an exertion, nor a commission that he could include in his large sense of duty, of calculation, of benevolence.

Any week produced several dozen requests for aid or patronage or benefactions of some sort, including many from the other, even more exotic half of the kingdom over which the court of Naples ruled. A Sicilian count asked the Cavaliere's help in having him restored as the chief of archaeological studies in Syracuse, from which he claimed to have been ousted by a plot hatched in Palermo. This same count had been the Cavaliere's intermediary in prising several paintings, among them his beloved "Correggio" (still unsold!), out of the collections of newly straitened Sicilian noble families. Some petitioners sweetened their requests with gifts of information, or more tangible gifts. A monsignor in Catania, asking the Cavaliere's help in securing for him the archbishopric of Monreale, told him of a stratum of clay between two strata of lava on Mount Etna. A canon in Palermo, who had accompanied the Cavaliere on his one climb up Etna, sent with his request for help in securing ecclesiastical promotion a report on antiquarian researches in Sicily, some samples of his collection of marine fossils, a copy of an index on stones compiled over the last twelve years, two lumps of lava from Etna, and an agate.

As well as having a reputation for being an ideal enabler, the Cavaliere was known as someone with whom one might deposit the account of a passion, an interest, a picturesque event. A Frenchman living in Catania wrote giving him an account of the recent eruption of Etna. A monk in Monte Cassino announced that he was sending him a dictionary of Neapolitan dialects. Someone hardy enough, appetitive enough, to regard himself as interested in "everything" can expect a good many letters from strangers.

People sent him poems and samples of volcanic ash; offered to sell him paintings, bronze helmets, vases, cinerary urns. Directors of public libraries in Italy wrote to thank him for the gift of the four volumes he had brought out on his collection of vases, or the enlarged two-volume edition of his volcanic letters with the beautiful plates by a local artist-protégé he had trained—or to request copies of these works. A maker of papier-mâché boxes in Birmingham wrote to praise the Cavaliere for having made available to him and to Josiah Wedgwood the designs on the ancient vases he collected, which were now circulating everywhere on his boxes (he hoped for the favor of an order) and on Wedgwood's Etruria Ware, to the great improvement of contemporary taste. His admirations and his talent for benevolence connected him to many worlds. There were offers of honorary membership in the Accademia Italia of Siena and in Die Gesellschaft naturforschender Freunde zu Berlin (the letter was in French), whose president also asked that the Cavaliere send them some volcanic rocks for their collection. A young man from Lecce wrote asking the Cavaliere's help in obtaining justice for his sister who had been raped, and offering a charm that increases the flow of milk. One of his agents in Rome wrote giving an estimate of one hundred fifty scudi for restoring three pieces of sculpture—a Bacchic bas-relief, a small marble faun, and a head of a Cupid—which the Cavaliere had just purchased. From Verona came the prospectus for a publication on fossil fish by the Società dei Litologi Veronesi, with a request to the Cavaliere to subscribe. An envoy in Rome asked on behalf of the Prince of Anhalt-Dessau for help in securing the scarce volumes on the discoveries at Herculaneum published over the last two decades by the Royal Herculaneum Academy. Someone in Resina announced to the Cavaliere that he was sending him samples of volcanic ash. A wine merchant in Beaune wrote to inquire respectfully when he might hope to receive payment for the hundred cases of Chambertin shipped to the Cavaliere eighteen months ago. The silk manufacturer from Paterson, New Jersey, who had called on him last year, sent, as promised, a copy of his report on methods of fixing dyes with alumite used in Neapolitan silk factories. A local informant wrote to describe how the French, sailing in Neapolitan feluccas, were carrying on contraband in the region. Another informant gave an account of the career and death of the Calabrian bandit chief Tito Greco. Someone in Naples sent him an amulet to ward off the evil eye. And someone in Positano who has the evil eye, and whose neighbors were piling offal nightly before his door, asked for protection.

•

The Cavaliere had a prodigious memory. He wrote few things down. It was all in his head: the money, the sums, the objects . . . a prodigious profusion. He sent off lists of his library needs to book dealers in Paris and London. He corresponded with antiquarians and purveyors of art. He haggled with restorers, packers, shippers, insurers. Money was always a distraction, as it must be to a collector: both a measure and a falsifier of value.

the cup with both hands and drink like his master. Of what the Cavaliere ate, he particularly liked oranges, figs, fish, and anything sweet. In the evening he was sometimes given a glass of Maraschino or the local Vesuvian wine. The Cavaliere, who hardly drank at all, enjoyed watching his guests watching Jack dip and lick, dip and lick. He became tipsy as a child does, this wizened child with a beard, a little rambunctious, and then suddenly, awkwardly, he fell asleep.

In seashells, buttons, and flowers Jack found a rich hoard of objects to stare at and play with. He was astonishingly dexterous. He would meticulously peel a grape, put it down, look at it, and sigh, before popping it into his mouth. His sport was hunting insects. He probed in crevices of the masonry for spiders, and could catch flies with one hand. He watched the Cavaliere practicing the cello, his big, utterly round eyes fixed on the instrument, and the Cavaliere began seating him up front during the weekly musical assembly. But often when he listened to music—he clearly liked music—he bit his nails; perhaps music made him nervous too. He yawned, he masturbated, he searched for lice in his tail. Sometimes he just paced, or sat staring at the Cavaliere. Perhaps he was bored. The Cavaliere was never bored.

The monkey had a most extraordinarily sweet, trusting disposition. He would take hold of the Cavaliere's hand and walk with him, helping himself along at the same time with his other hand applied to the ground. The Cavaliere had to stoop slightly to accommodate the monkey's need. He did not like changing his posture, and he did not want a substitute child. He began adding a tiny bit of teasing to his treatment of the monkey, a little bit of cruelty, a touch of deprivation. Salt in his milk. A cuff on the head. Whoo-whoo-whoo-whoo, lamented the monkey, when the Cavaliere visited him in the early morning. Jack seized his hand. The Cavaliere pulled it away.

One morning, when the Cavaliere went to the cellar storeroom, the monkey's pallet was empty. He had chewed through his rope. He was hiding. The testy Cavaliere barricaded himself in his study. The servants, cursing, searched every room in the mansion. On the third evening they found him in the wine cellar with a leather-bound folio of Piranesi's work on chimney-pieces gnawed beyond salvaging. Alessandro stepped forward to put the rope on him; the monkey snarled and bit his hand. The Cavaliere was summoned. Jack cringed but let the Cavaliere pick him up. The monkey pulled at the Cavaliere's wig. The Cavaliere held him more firmly. It was as if Jack had gone on a retreat, to reconsider his own nature, and reemerged more monkey-like: sly, quarrelsome, prurient, mischievous. The Cavaliere did not want a mock child. He wanted a mock protégé, a jester . . . and poor Jack loved him abjectly enough to oblige. Now his training, his real use to the Cavaliere could begin.

He taught Jack to mime the connoisseur's hooded stare, putting him through his paces when visitors were poring over the Cavaliere's objects. They would look up and see the Cavaliere's pet monkey studying a vase through a magnifying glass, or leafing quizzically through a book, or turning a cameo over in his paw and holding it to the light. Very valuable. Yes. Decidedly. Yes, I see. Most interesting.

Glass to one eye, Jack would squint, look up, scratch his head, then return to his scrutiny.

Is this a fake?

Fake!

Fake!!

Then Jack would relent and put the object down. (If a monkey could smile, he might have smiled.) Just looking. You can't be too careful.

The Cavaliere's visitors laugh at the monkey. The Cavaliere laughs at himself.

He let the monkey torment the servants and even Catherine, who, loath to have too many tastes and inclinations that separated her from her husband, professed to be attached to the monkey, too. Jack always seemed to divine when Catherine was retiring from a room to go to the water closet, and would rush after her and clap his eye to the keyhole. Jack diligently masturbated in front of Catherine, kept grabbing the page Gaetano's cock when the Cavaliere took him fishing. His scabrous antics amused his master. Even when he once knocked over a vase, the Cavaliere was not really upset (to be sure, it was not one of the most valuable and, when repaired, no one would know the difference). Jack was a little footnote to his life that said: all is vanity, all is vanity.

•

The world seemed made of concentric circles of mockery. At the center the Cavaliere pivots with Jack. Everything in the social zoo could be predicted. He would not get another diplomatic appointment. He knew how his life would go on to the end: tranquil, interesting, unstirred by passion. Only the volcano held a surprise.

1766, 1767, 1777 . . . 1779. Each eruption bigger than the previous one, each further embellishing the prospect of catastrophe. This was bigger than ever. The doors and windows of his country villa near Portici were swinging on their hinges. Jack was jumping about nervously, hiding under tables, flinging himself in the Cavaliere's lap. Catherine, who disliked the monkey almost as much as the servants did, feigned concern for his little person, his little fears. He was given some laudanum. Catherine returned to the harpsichord. Admirable Catherine, thought the Cavaliere.

Watching from the terrace, the Cavaliere saw bursts of white vapor rising pile over pile to a height and bulk three times as great as the mountain itself, and gradually filling with streaks of black, exactly as the Younger Pliny had described his eruption: *candida interdum, interdum sordida et maculosa* (sometimes white, sometimes dirty and blotched) according to the amount of soil the cloud carried with it. A summer storm followed, the weather turned torrid, and a few days later a fountain of red fire ascended from the crater. One could read in bed at night by the gloomy blaze of the mountain a few miles away. In a communication to the Royal Society, the Cavaliere described these black stormy clouds and the bright column of fire with flashes of forked lightning as more beautiful than alarming.

•

You project onto the volcano the amount of rage, of complicity with destructiveness, of anxiety about your ability to feel already in your head. Sade took away from his five-month sojourn in Naples, near then-quiescent Vesuvius, the fantasies of evildoing that anything capable of violence inspired in him. Many years later in his *Juliette*, he was to write a volcano scene for this champion evildoer in which she climbs to the summit with two companions, a tiresome man whom she promptly casts into the fiery chasm and a desirable man with whom she then copulates at the brink of the crater.

Sade worried about satiety; he could not conceive of passion without provocation. The Cavaliere did not worry about running out of feeling. For him the volcano was a stimulus for contemplation. Noisy as Vesuvius could be, it offered something like what he experienced with his collections. Islands of silence.

•

May 1779. On the slope of Vesuvius, illuminated by the orange glow of molten rock. He stood motionless, his pale grey eyes wide open. The earth trembled under his feet. He could feel the hairs of his eyelashes, his eyebrows move with the uprush of burning air. They could climb no higher.

The danger was not in the ground but in the lethal, unbearable air. Surefooted, pushed down by the billowing smoke and falling rocks at their backs, they moved diagonally, away from the lava stream, keeping upwind to avoid being overcome by smoke. Suddenly the wind shifted, sending scalding jets of sulphur into their faces. The blinding, asphyxiating smoke swirled around them, cutting off their descent.

To the left, a chasm. To the right, the lava stream. Transfixed, he looked for Bartolomeo, who had vanished into the smoke. Where is the boy? There, going the wrong way, shouting and beckoning him to follow. This way!

But blocking the way was the enormous, terrifying spread of grainy orange lava, at least sixty feet wide.

This way, shouted Bartolomeo, pointing to the other side. The Cavaliere's clothes were starting to smoulder. The smoke was tearing his lungs, singeing his eyes. And before them lay a river of fire. I will not cry out, he said to himself. So this is death.

Come! shouted Bartolomeo.

I can't, groaned the Cavaliere, his mind receding as the boy sprinted toward the lava. The stifling smoke, the boy's shouts—he was already deep inside himself. Bartolomeo stepped up lightly on the lava ledge and started across. Christ walking on water could not have amazed his followers more. The boy did not sink into the molten surface. The Cavaliere followed. It was like walking on flesh. As long as one kept moving, the lava's crust would support one's weight. In moments they had crossed the gauntlet and on the far side were once again upwind, coughing off the fumes. Inspecting his scorched boots, the Cavaliere glanced over at Bartolomeo, who was rubbing his good eye with a dirty fist. It was almost like being invulnerable. The Cavaliere with his Cyclops, the King of Cups with his Fool—perhaps not invulnerable but safe. With him, safe.

•

August 1779. Saturday, at six o'clock. The great concussion must have rocked the foundations of the Cavaliere's villa at the foot of the mountain, if not worse. But he was at home in town, and from the safety of the observatory room watched the mountain flinging showers of red-hot stones into the air. An hour later a column of liquid fire began to rise and quickly reached an amazing height, twice that of the mountain, a fiery pillar ten thousand feet high, mottled with puffs of black smoke, scored by flashing zigzag lines of lightning. The sun went out. Black clouds descended over Naples. Theatres closed, churches opened, processions formed, people clustered at candlelit street shrines to Saint Januarius on their knees. In the cathedral the cardinal held aloft the vial of the saint's blood for all to see and began warming it with his hands. This is worth seeing up close, said the Cavaliere—meaning the mountain, not the miracle. He had Bartolomeo sent for, and set out on horseback along the glowing streets, into the country night, down black roads, past fields of blasted leafless trees and carbonized vines, toward the burning mountain.

Suddenly the eruption ceased and, except for the glowing cinder-heaps on Vesuvius and small lava rills on the upper slopes, all was dark.

An hour later, as the full moon was rising, the Cavaliere arrived in a village on a lower slope which lay half silted up under black scoriae and dust, shriveled with heat. The moon rose higher. The dark, dented, scaly village turned pale—lunarized.

After dismounting and turning his horse over to Bartolomeo, the Cavaliere was shown the moonlit lanes clogged with gleaming ashes and dingy rocks. The village had been pelted with stones weighing up to a hundred pounds; few of the houses had burned, but every window he saw was broken and some of the roofs had collapsed. Filthy-headed people holding flaming brands walked with him, eager to tell their stories. Yes, they had stayed in their houses, what choice did they have? Those who stirred out with pillows, tables, chairs, or the lids of wine casks on their heads were driven back, wounded by the stones or stifled with heat and dust and sulphur. He heard the horrors. Then he was taken to gaze at a family that had sought refuge prematurely, the day before, and had mysteriously perished. ("No one told them to go to the cellar, Excellency, or to stay there!") At the low entrance to the cellar, one of the villagers moved ahead with his brand to illuminate an artless tableau. Mother, father, nine children, several cousins, and a pair of grandparents: all sitting upright against the earth wall and staring straight ahead. Their clothes undisturbed. Their faces not contorted—so they could not have died from asphyxiation. Their appearance perfectly normal except for their hair, lifeless-looking hair thickened with white dust, which, since peasants don't wear wigs, gave them the appearance of statues.

It would be interesting to ascertain what killed them, the Cavaliere thought to himself. One sharp concussive strike of the volcano from deep under the earth? The swift suffusion of a lethal volcanic gas? From behind him the boy, his young Bartolomeo, answered his thought firmly. They died of fear, my lord.

6

The Knave of Cups arrived in late October. Of course, who else but he. The Cavaliere felt annoyed with himself for not having divined who it would be.

Indeed a relation, a second cousin of the Cavaliere, William Beckford was then twenty years old, stupendously rich, already the author of a slim ironic book of imaginary biographies, a militant collector and connoisseur, willful, self-pitying, greedy for sights, temptations, treasures. A restless, abbreviated version of the Grand Tour (he had left England only two months earlier) had brought him to its southernmost station with record speed, casting him on the shore of the Cavaliere's hospitality just in time for the hot wind, one of the great winds of southern Europe (mistral, Föhn, sirocco, tramontana) that are used, like the days leading up to menstruation, to explain restlessness, neurasthenia, emotional fragility: a collective PMS that comes on seasonally. The atmosphere was nervous. Whining dogs prowled the filthy steep streets. Women left newborn infants at church doors. Bright-eyed, exhausted, pulsing with dreams of the ever more exotic, William stretched out on a brocaded couch and said, Surely this is not all. Show me more. More. More.

The Cavaliere recognized in his young relation someone like himself, that rare species who would never, not for one moment in the course of a long life, be bored. He showed him his collections, his booty, his self-bestowed inheritance. (He could hardly forget that this boy was, or would soon be, the richest man in England.) The cabinets full of wonders. The paintings in three or four tiers on the walls, most of them seventeenth-century and Italian. My Etruscan vases, said the Cavaliere. Splendid, said William. A sampling of my collection of volcanic rocks. Objects to dream over, said William. And this is my Leonardo, said the Cavaliere. Really, said William. The youth's comments were wonderfully acute, appreciative. A genuine liking on both sides was astir. But the Cavaliere did not need a new (grander, more difficult) nephew. It was Catherine who was needy, Catherine who reached out humbly, passionately to acquire a soul mate and shadow son.

Each felt instantly appreciated by the other. He told her. She told him. They revelled in all the ways they were alike—the handsome, full-hipped young man with curly hair and chewed fingernails, the thin woman of forty-two with her wide, slightly staring eyes. They belong to different generations, have had such different lives. Yet they have so many of the same tastes, the same disappointments. From stories they passed to confidences, each unwrapping a package of grief and yearning. William, being younger and a man, thought it his right to go first.

He spoke of his inner life, filled with (so he tells her now) vague longings. He described his life at home, at Fonthill, moodily pacing in his rooms, reading books that made him weep, full of dissatisfaction with himself and foolish dreams (which he plans never to give up no matter how old he becomes), raging against the stupidity of his mother, his tutors, all those around him.

Have you read a book called *The Sorrows of Young Werther*? I think every line resplendent with genius.

This was a test that Catherine had to pass.

Yes, she said. I love it, too.

It happened quickly, as it so often happens. There is So-and-so, an acquaintance you meet from time to time at parties or at concerts and never think of. Then one day a door flies open and you tumble into a pit of infinity. Amazed as well as grateful, you ask: Can this deep soul be the person I thought merely . . . a mere . . . ? Yes.

I want to be alone with you. And I, my dear, with you.

From his study in the villa near Portici, the Cavaliere saw them lingering side by side on the terrace without speaking. From the terrace he saw them strolling slowly in the arbor surrounded by myrtle and vines. From the corridor he saw them at the piano together. Or Catherine played and William lounged on a settee beside a little tripod table and leafed through the Cavaliere's books. The Cavaliere was glad Catherine should have someone of her own, someone who preferred her to the Cavaliere himself.

They did not simply play together, as Catherine and the Cavaliere did. They improvised together, vying with each other to produce the most expressive sound, the most heart-rending decrescendo.

Catherine confessed that she composed, in secret. She had never played her "little movements" for anyone. William begged her to play them for him. The first was a minuet, with a darting gleeful melody. The others—his appreciation of the minuet gave her courage—had a freer form, a graver cast: slow, questioning, with long plaintive chords.

William avowed that he had always wanted to compose but knew he lacked the creative fire. She told him he was too young to know that.

No—he shook his head—I am good only for dreaming, but—he looked up—this is not flattery. You are a great musician, Catherine. I have never heard anyone feel music as you do.

When I played for Mozart, she said, I trembled as I sat down. His father noticed, I saw him noticing.

I tremble at everything, said William.

Each feels understood (at last!) by the other. William considered that it was the fate of a man like himself to be misunderstood by everyone. Now there was this angelic woman who understood him perfectly. Catherine may have thought, wrongly, that she was escaping male egotism.

He brought her flattering presents. A very cosmopolitan relation. He had found a wise, cultivated, stylish, encouraging older woman: every young man needs an authority. And she, at an age when she thought that no longer possible, has a new man in her life: every woman needs, or thinks she needs, an escort.

Catherine had taken a visceral dislike to the whole court from the beginning—this grande bourgeoise was more fastidious than the arrantly patrician Cavaliere. Her husband accommodated this by thinking of Catherine as reclusive, and respecting her the more for it. Catherine prefers the life of a hermit, was the Cavaliere's fond exaggeration in a letter to Charles, while he had often to be away with the King. Their union was designed to confirm their being different, in the way that most couples—two siblings, a wife and husband, a boss and secretary—divide up roles. You be retiring, I'll be gregarious; you be talkative, I'll be laconic; you be fleshy, I'll be thin; you read poetry, I'll tinker with my motorcycle. With William, Catherine was experiencing the rarer form of coupledom in which two people, different as they can be, claim to be as alike as possible.

She wants to do what pleases him and he wants to do what pleases her. They are moved by, admire the same music and poetry; are repelled by the same things (killing animals, vulgar conversation, the intrigues of aristocratic salons and an antic court).

The Cavaliere, whose life is unavoidably much taken up with killing animals, vulgar conversation, the intrigues of salons and the court, was glad that Catherine had someone to talk to, someone to be sensitive with. And it would have had to be a man—oddly, Catherine did not seem to enjoy much the company of her own sex—but one a good deal younger than she, so she could mother him; and, ideally, a lover of other men, so as to spare the Cavaliere concern there might be improper advances.

Without jealousy, no, with approval, the Cavaliere observed that Catherine looked almost youthful in the company of this stripling, and happier.

The two of them had been sitting on the terrace with a view of Naples and the gulf. Now it was six and they had gone indoors, to a room with windows facing Vesuvius. Catherine's favorite maid brought tea. Light softened, paled. The candles were lit. The bustle of servants and the screech of cicadas were sounds they would not hear. If the mountain made noise, they ignored it.

After a long silence, Catherine went to the piano. William listened with moistening eyes.

Please sing, she said. You have a beautiful voice.

Will you not sing a duet with me?

Oh, she laughed. I don't sing. I don't like to, I never could . . .

What, dear Catherine?

The Cavaliere came at night, booted, bloodstained, sweating, fresh from the King's animal slaughters, and saw them together at the piano, laughing softly, their eyes shining. But I am sensitive too, he thought. And now I am cast in the role of the one who does not understand.

•

William's light tenor voice held on to the last note, then let it go. The piano's sound decayed into inaudibility, the heart of this instrument's expressiveness.

Catherine, William murmured.

She turned to him and nodded.

No one has ever understood me as you have, he said. You angel. You precious woman. If only I could remain here, under your benevolent influence, I should be quite healed.

No, said Catherine. You must return to England, to your duties. I do not doubt that you will master these weaknesses, a product of your extreme sensitivity, which come from having too tender a heart. Such feelings are like a fever that passes.

I don't want to go home, he said, and wished he dared to take her hand. How beautiful she looked now. Catherine, I want to stay here with you.

William thinks he is suffering from a spiritual distress, which takes the form of a boundless appetite for vague, exotic things. How flattering to himself. What is happening is that he is not allowed to embrace what he wants to embrace. Most restlessness is sexual restlessness. The love of his life was eleven when they met, and William had been courting and fondling for four years before they were found one morning in the boy's bed. When Viscount Courtenay barred William from his house and threatened to bring suit if he ever dared approach his son again, William crossed the Channel and headed south.

He has sought the shelter of older skies. But no degree of otherness satisfies the restless sexual exile. No place is rude enough, foreign enough. (Until afterward—in the remembrance, in the telling.) In the north of south, he re-created the same scandal, from which he was again obliged to flee: a passion for the fifteen-year-old son of a Venetian noble family, the prompt discovery of which by another irate father had got him driven from the city and hurled him down the chute of the peninsula —into the Neapolitan fascination, the Neapolitan torpor, and into Catherine's lonely heart.

•

She feels stronger, has more energy, and (as the Cavaliere noticed) looks prettier. He was improving himself, under her benevolent influence. They had found a haven, the strongest variant of privacy: a voluntary social ostracism. Each was greedy for the other's exclusive company.

Of course, they were not literally alone. As befitted a man

richer than any lord, William was incapable of traveling without his tutor, his secretary, his personal physician, a major-domo, a cook, a baker, an artist to draw views that he wished to commit to memory, three valets, a page, etc., etc. And Catherine and the Cavaliere had a vast retinue for the mansion in the city, the villa near the royal palace at Portici, and the fifty-room hunting lodge at Caserta. Servants were everywhere, making everything possible, but, like the black figures in Noh plays who enter the stage to adjust a character's massive costume or furnish a prop, servants didn't count.

Yes, they were alone.

This relationship, which had the thrill of something illicit, was conducted in front of, with the blessing of, the Cavaliere. Though designed not to be consummated, it was still a romance. What released them to love each other was that each was unsatisfactorily in love with someone else. Indeed, it was Catherine's being abjectly in love with the Cavaliere after twenty-two years of marriage and William's convulsive passions for closely guarded pubescent boys in his own circles that allowed them to fall in love with each other, without having to worry about it or do anything about it.

Being in love and unable to acknowledge it, they were fond of generalizing about love. Is there anything crueler and sweeter, mused William. The heart so full it cannot speak, it can only dream and sing—you've known that feeling, Catherine, I know you have. Otherwise, you could not understand so well what I feel but must hide from everyone.

Love is always a sacrifice, said Catherine, who knew whereof she spoke. But the one who loves, she added, has the better part than one who lets himself be loved.

I hate being unhappy, said William.

Oh, Catherine sighed, and contemplated her long history of being unhappy without having any right to consider herself such, so grateful was she still to the Cavaliere for having married her. Thinking of herself as homely—and despising herself for the vanity this thought disclosed—she had an ugly duckling's reverence for her elegant husband, whom she found so attractive with his long beaky nose, his thin legs, his crisp sentences, his unwavering gaze. She still pined for him whenever he was absent for more than a day, still felt weak-kneed whenever he entered a room and came toward her. She loved his silhouette.

You don't judge me? murmured William.

You have already judged yourself, dear boy. You have only to continue on the better path to which you aspire. Your candor, your delicacy of feeling, the music we play, these tell me that your heart is pure.

Mutual avowals of each other's essential purity, innocence, however different their lives and impure his.

William, resist the lures of a soft, criminal passion! So she called the youth's love for his own sex, which could not fail to rouse Catherine's ever-ready talent for disapproval. It did not shock the Cavaliere, friend of Walpole and Gray, patron of that rogue scholar who had renamed himself the Baron d'Hancarville (he compiled the volumes on the Cavaliere's vases): even then the world of collectors and connoisseurs, particularly of the antique, featured a disproportionate number of men who loved their own sex. The Cavaliere prided himself on being free of vulgar sexual bigotry but thought the taste a handicap, exposing its adept to socially inconvenient situations and sometimes, alas, to danger. No one could forget the gruesome end of the great Winckelmann in a raffish hotel in Trieste twelve years ago, stabbed to death by a young hustler to whom he had shown some of the treasures he was taking back to Rome. William, beware! Stick to boys from your own class.

•

They are both misfits, loving what they can't have. And they are allies. She protects him; he makes her feel desirable. Each needs the other in such a congenial way. How flattering to them both if it is thought they *are* lovers. That means he is seen as capable of being a lover of women, she as still attractive. Both as brave souls capable of throwing all caution to the winds. This relationship, which only rarely ends in bed, is one of the classic forms of heterosexual romantic love. In place of consummation, there is elevation. A secret society of two, they were constantly high, exalted, flushed with complicity.

Their voices become deeper, shot through with pauses. Their hands coupled on the keyboard, her face tilted to his, leaning into his. Inner smiles, breathlessness, the piercing beauties of Scarlatti and Schobert and Haydn. Ignoring the volcano's spasms. Not to be distracted by any views.

When she played, he could see the music. It was an arc surging upward from her delicately tapping feet, streaming through her body, and exiting through her hands. She leaned forward, a strand of unpowdered hair falling across her forehead, her slightly flabby arms bowed as if to embrace the keyboard, her radiant face molded by feeling, her lips parted for soundless moaning and singing.

A lover would have recognized Catherine's expressions at the piano, and anyone else would have felt privy to an involuntary revelation of how she behaved with a lover. Grimacing, wincing, sighing, nodding, smiling beatifically—she spanned several octaves of abandonment to pleasure. It was then, when William saw her most clearly as a sexual being, that he was most drawn to her, most intimidated, and most touched. She was so innocent, he supposed, about what the music meant to her and did to her.

Sometimes, Catherine said, I feel that music invades me to the point of total oblivion, when my will and my intention do not exist any more. The music has penetrated so deeply into me that it alone directs my movements.

Yes, said William, I feel that too.

They had reached that state of perfect vibratory accord where everything they observed seemed a metaphor for their relationship. On an excursion to Herculaneum, they marveled together at the imaginary buildings—They must be imaginary,

Catherine!—depicted in frescoes in the Villa degli Misteri, whose slim columns are not asked to support anything but only to frame delicate space: freestanding elements of buildings that exist only for themselves, for light and for grace.

So I would build, said William.

At the entrance to the cave of the Cumaean Sibyl, they felt at one with the whole ancient world.

At Avernus they stood by the dank waters of the submerged crater, in ancient times thought to be the entrance to hell, where Virgil has Aeneas descend into the underworld.

Remember the Sibyl's warning to Aeneas? *Facilis descensus Averno*, William proclaimed in his high nervous voice, casting a fond glance at Catherine. *Sed revocare . . . hoc opus, hic labor est.*

Yes, dear boy, yes. You must not be idle.

With Virgil I can testify that it is easy to descend to hell. But to come back . . . Oh Catherine, with you, with your understanding . . . it is not work, not labor.

To be happy together they no longer need to feel superior to the local pleasures. During the premiere at the San Carlo of yet another opera about a fiancée rescued from a Moorish harem, the castrato Caffarelli makes them weep. Some of the worst music and most beautiful singing I have ever heard, murmured William. Did you mark how he sustained the legato in their duet? I did, I did, she said. It is not possible for any sound to be more beautiful.

Catherine came alive to the sensuality as well as the beauty of the city, seeing it refracted through William's responses. She had blocked it out until now, so put off was she by the riotous court, the indolent nobility, the heathenish religion, the appalling violence and poverty. With William, she allowed herself to notice the erotic energy coursing through the streets. Parented by William's lustful stare, she let her own glance linger on the ripe mouth and long dark lashes of a bare-chested young blacksmith. For the first time in her life, when too worn, too old to seduce, she was overwhelmed by the beauty of young men.

And the golden light. And the views. The pomegranate trees. And, my God, the hibiscus!

Beneath the layering of history, everything speaks of love. According to the local folklore, the origin of many Neapolitan sites is an unhappy love story. Once these places were men and women, who, because of unhappy or frustrated love, underwent a metamorphosis into what one sees today. Even the volcano. Vesuvius was once a young man, who saw a nymph lovely as a diamond. She scratched his heart and his soul, he could think of nothing else. Breathing more and more heatedly, he lunged at her. The nymph, scorched by his attentions, jumped into the sea and became the island today called Capri. Seeing this, Vesuvius went mad. He loomed, his sighs of fire spread, little by little he became a mountain. And now, as immobilized as his beloved, forever beyond his reach, he continues to throw fire and makes the city of Naples tremble. How the helpless city regrets that the youth did not get what he desired! Capri lies in the water, in full view of Vesuvius, and the mountain burns and burns and burns . . .

•

How devoted we are to each other, they might have said. (How much self-love comes in the guise of selfless devotion!)

Each got to exercise her, his forbearance: that she has her ways, that he has dangerous notions. But she is more cautious than he, because he will leave (he's young and he's a man) and she can't. For it must end. It is the woman, of course, who loses: the young man goes away and will love again, physically as well as romantically. He is her last love.

When he left in January, he was grief-stricken. He wept. She, no doubt sadder than he, was dry-eyed. They embraced.

I shall live for your letters, he said.

•

When I left you I was lost in dreams, he said in his first letter. He told her how much he missed her, he described the eloquent landscapes which reminded him of . . . himself. Each site pitched him into reverie, became a depiction of his own mind (and its powers), his own associations. His hand was wantonly difficult—Catherine found it hard to decipher—and he was a voluble describer.

Wherever William was, he was also somewhere else. At Misenum he was with Pliny the Elder. At the entrance to the Sibyl's cave he was with Virgil. Or just with his indescribable feelings. The dauntless churn of bookish references, the eager transformation of every reality into a dream or a vision, seemed less of an enchantment in his letters. No doubt this was because she was no longer the co-author of his fantasies but only the recipient of them.

She expected everything of herself: index of a strong character. (She had never thought it remarkable that she played the harpsichord as superbly as she did.) But she tried not to expect much from others, so as not to be corrupted by disappointment. She did not expect anything of William. She was William . . . or he was she. To love someone was to tolerate imperfections one would never excuse in oneself. And had she thought the egocentricity of his reactions needed defending, she would probably have invoked his youth, or simply his sex.

It was like a dream, he would say of something he had just seen. I dreamed, I cast myself back in the time of. I walked on, musing at every step. I lay for an hour gazing on the smooth level waters. I was vexed to be aroused from my visions.

He described every stop on his journey as a pilgrimage. And each place could be an occasion of inspired seclusion, of voluptuous disorientation. Wherever he went, there would be a moment when he would be able to ask: Where am I?

And, Catherine, Catherine, I have not forgotten. Where are you?

Their intimacy, this seemed like a dream, too.

I used to listen to her like one entranced, William said of Catherine's music-making, many years later. Transported, as I have been by no other performer. You cannot imagine how beautifully she played—referring, as he did whenever he evoked her at her instruments, only to how she played the music of others. It seemed, he said, as if she had thrown her own essence into the music, whose effects were the emanations of a pure, uncontaminated mind. The art and the person were one. She lived, uncorrupted, an angel of purity in the midst of the Neapolitan court, William remembered. Since to praise a woman then was invariably to call her an angel or a saint, William was anxious that his words be heard as more than the usual homage. You must have known what that court was, he wrote, to comprehend this in its full meaning. I never saw so heavenly-minded a creature.

Throughout his rapid journey up the peninsula, which included a futile stop in Venice (to sigh once more over the Cornaro boy), William continued to write Catherine, evoking the wild fantastic imaginings he could share only with her, and declaring that had he but sufficient strength of mind—I care not a farthing whether the world thought me whimsical or no!—he should change his resolution to proceed to England and instead would retrace his steps immediately to Naples. Nothing would make him happier than to spend a few more months in Catherine's company, and greet the spring with her, read to her under their favorite cliff at Posillipo, and listen to her music.

From Switzerland, he spoke of the music *he* has been composing.

Did you ever read of certain gnomes who lurk in the chasms of tremendous mountains? The strange exotic tunes I have just now been playing on the harpsichord were exactly what I imagine elves and pygmies dance to—brisk and humming—moody and subterranean. Few mortals except ourselves, dear Catherine, have ears to catch the low whisperings which issue in dark hours from the rocks.

And once again: How sorry I am, dear Catherine, to give up hopes of passing the spring in Portici and visiting the wild thickets of Calabria at your side. All my prayers will be to return and listen to you whole hours without interruption, my greatest anxiety that we shall not see each other again for some time. Never can I expect to meet another human being who so perfectly comprehends me. Let me hear constantly from you if you have any pity upon your most obliged and affectionate—

Crossing the Alps, he told her, he felt the air to be purer and more transparent than any he had ever breathed. He described long walks in which he traversed an infinity of vales, skirted with rocks and blooming with aromatic vegetation, and voyages in his head in which he shot from rock to rock and built castles in the style of Piranesi upon their pinnacles. And he told her that he never stopped thinking of her. Only you can conceive of the solemn thoughts I have on a clear frosty night, he wrote, when every star is visible. And: I wish you could hear what the winds are whispering to me. I hear the strangest things in the Universe and my ear is filled with aerial conversations. What a multitude of Voices are borne to me by the chill winds that blow on these vast fantastic mountains. I think of you, where it is always summer.

In Naples the winter turned unseasonably cold. Catherine began to decline. Her physician, an elderly Scot with leathery skin (she thought of William's smooth cheeks) who had settled in Naples years ago, drove out most days to see her. Am I that ill, she said. A mere ten miles, I am fond of the exercise, he replied, smiling. The softness in his glance made her uncomfortable.

Now I am in Paris, William wrote. My delicious seclusion is over. England awaits me. But oh, Catherine, I fear I shall never be good for anything in this world but composing exotic tunes, building towers, designing gardens, collecting Old Japan, and imagining trips to China or the moon.

In Naples it snowed for the first time in thirty years.

Far as Naples was from England, it was even farther from India, Jack's homeland. The Cavaliere observed with a tightening of his heart that the monkey was ailing. Jack no longer pranced about but dragged himself from table to chair, bust to vase. He lifted his head slowly when the Cavaliere called. From his tiny chest came a crinkly wheeze. The Cavaliere wondered if it was too cold in the storeroom. He meant to tell Valerio to have Jack's quarters moved to an upper story, but it slipped his mind. He would miss his little co-mocker. He had started to cut him out of his heart. And there were more than the usual distractions.

It was time for the King's campaign of boar hunting. The Cavaliere transferred the core of his household—Catherine, the indispensable musical instruments and choice books, and a reduced staff of thirty-four servants—to the lodge at Caserta, where the wind blew colder still. To spare him the further rigors of the upland climate, Jack was left in town in the care of young Gaetano, who was instructed not to let the animal out of his sight. The King summoned the Cavaliere for a week's shooting in the Apennine foothills. Oh I am accustomed to his absences, Catherine said to Doctor Drummond, who came every other day to visit her. And: I don't wish my husband to worry about me.

She wanted him not to worry about poor Jack, either. How to prepare him for the inevitable? For she thought with concern of that, even that, too. News was brought on a Sunday that Jack had not awakened that morning. The Cavaliere turned away and was silent for a long moment. He rebuttoned his hunting jacket and turned back. Was the ground still frozen, he inquired. No, came the answer. The Cavaliere sighed and ordered him buried in the garden.

She was relieved that he didn't seem too distressed, but found herself saddened by the fate of the little alien creature who had served the Cavaliere so ardently. She remembered how he sat in the shape of a treble clef, his hairy tail coiled neatly under his rump.

From England, William wrote that he had started and nearly

finished a new book. It was an account of his travels and all his fantasies and imaginary encounters with the spirits of place. But he hastened to assure her, lest she worry, that although it will be entirely suffused with her visionary accents, she will not be mentioned. He will assume full responsibility for all the ideas they have engendered together, shielding her from the world's malice and envy. No one will be able to criticize or implicate her. Her role in his life will forever remain a secret, a sacred mystery. He will represent them both to the world.

Indeed.

She feels annihilated. But at least something that represents both of them will exist.

He has had five hundred copies printed, he announced. Then he wrote that he has reconsidered and has ordered the edition destroyed, all but fifty copies. She was protected, he was not. In the wrong hands, the book could be misunderstood. He did not want to expose himself to ridicule.

But it will always belong to you, Catherine, he wrote.

She did not want to feel abandoned, but she did.

He wrote her that he was rereading his—no, their—favorite book.

Catherine, Catherine, do you remember the passage at the beginning of *Werther*, after the hero says, "It is the fate of a man like myself to be misunderstood," where he recalls the friend of his youth. Of course you remember. But I cannot resist copying it out, so perfectly does it express what I feel. "I say to myself: You are a fool to search for something that cannot be found on this earth. But she was mine, I felt her heart, her great soul, in whose presence I seemed to be more than I really was because I was all that I could be. Good God, was there a single force in my soul then unused? Could I not unfold in her presence all the wonderful emotions with which my heart embraces Nature? Was not our relationship a perpetual interweaving of the most subtle feeling with the keenest wit, whose modifications, however extravagant, all bore the mark of genius? And now?—Alas, the years she had lived in advance of my own brought her to the grave before me. I shall never forget her—neither her unwavering mind nor her divine fortitude."

Oh, thought Catherine, he is killing me off. The thought did not shock her as much as it should.

The Cavaliere returned, ruddy, nervous, from the hunt. The next morning at breakfast, looking at Catherine's pale lined face—how used she looked, while he still felt as vigorous as ever, his flesh tingled with exertion and the memory of keen sensations, with wind and shouts and acrid smells and the hard spread of his horse between his legs—and he hated her for becoming old, for always remaining indoors, for looking as vulnerable as she was. For being sad—why, he assumed he knew. And, jealous, he could not resist being cruel.

May I remind you, my dear, that we are both in mourning.

She didn't answer.

You have lost my young cousin. But I have lost Jack.

Another letter from William, in which he complained that Catherine did not answer his last and next-to-last. Do not abandon me, angel! Truth was, she was starting the end of mourning. William had begun to seem remote. Did I feel all that? So much? As sound decays into inaudibility, euphoria decays into indifference, and that is always unexpected, the way exalted feelings are weakened, undone by time. It was becoming harder to imagine what she had felt when William was there. That intensity seemed like, like a. . . . Even she might use the word dream now.

7

SYMPTOMS. A difficulty in breathing, a hurt around the heart. Loss of appetite. Complaint in the bowels, pain in her side and breast, chronic retching so that nothing stays on her stomach, feeling of weakness in her right arm—most of these symptoms subdued. Headaches. Want of sleep. Pale hair on the pillow each morning. A great difficulty in breathing. (Women's weaknesses: inform, generic. A man falls ill, a wellborn woman wanes.) Self-contempt. Anxiety at being a cause of concern to her husband. Revulsion at the futile chatter of other women. Thoughts of heaven. Impression of universal coldness.

DIAGNOSIS. Doctor Drummond suspects a paralysis. Or that the vital powers are quite worn out. She is only forty-four but she has been ailing for decades.

PRAYERS. Giving thanks to God for all his mercies, humbly asking pardon for her past sins, imploring indulgence for her impious husband. More thoughts of heaven, where all injury is repaired. Lord, pity and correct.

LETTERS. To friends and relations back home, of an exceptional dispiritedness. I fear I shall never see you again. And to her husband, in February, when the hunting orgy was still on and the Cavaliere was often away, a letter of excruciating abjection: How tedious are the hours I pass in the absence of the beloved of my heart, and how tiresome is every scene to me. There is the chair in which he sits, I find him not there, and my heart feels a pang and my foolish eyes overflow with tears. The number of years we have been married, instead of diminishing my love, have increased it to that degree and wound it up with my existence in such a manner that it cannot alter. How strong are the efforts I have made to conquer my feelings, but in vain. How I have reasoned with my self, but to no purpose. No one but those who have felt it can know the miserable anxiety of an undivided love. When he is present every object has a different appearance, when he is absent how lonely, how isolated I feel. I seek peace in company, and there I am still more uneasy. Alas, I have but one pleasure, but one satisfaction, and that is all centered in him.

MUSIC. It is not quite true that she has no interests, none, when he is absent. But the sounds at the harpsichord are more plaintive. Music elevates, but it does not erase.

PASSION. William's departure has left her more vulnerable than ever. But such passion in marriage is unnatural. And: it is always right to try to overcome this passion, to distract herself. She inspects some new sites at the dead cities, joins in a musical assembly at the mansion of the Austrian ambassador, and visits a Sicilian lady of high rank who, after dispatching ten, no, eleven people by dagger or poison, was finally denounced by her own family, and as punishment had been confined, luxuriously confined, in a convent near Naples. Her age was around twenty-three, Catherine related to her husband. She received me in bed, sitting up, satin pillows heaped behind her, offered me macaroons and other refreshments, and conversed politely and with great cheerfulness. It seemed unimaginable that someone with her gentle manners was capable of such atrocities. She had a shy, even kind face, Catherine reported in wonderment—a fact that would not have impressed even the most unreflective native of the country in which she was resident, since any peasant knows that rotten wares are often sold under a good signboard; but Catherine was a northerner, and gently reared, neither a peasant nor an aristocrat, and truly pious, a Protestant who assumed the match of inner and outer. She did not look like a murderer, Catherine said softly.

•

Catherine spoke in a very low voice, the Cavaliere was to remember. One had to lean forward sometimes to hear her. A plea for intimacy? Yes. And also a sign of her repressed rage.

•

Spring came, a warm fragrant April. She stayed in bed much of the time. William's letters spoke, jubilantly, gratingly, of a future. But Catherine knew that for her there was no future. She could only think of, only love the past.

The Cavaliere had been away on an archaeological expedition in Apulia for more than a week. Catherine, unable to leave her bed, felt herself growing weaker by the hour. On a hot April night, in the throes of a painful asthmatic seizure that she thought might be the beginning of the end, she sought relief in a letter.

Catherine had never been afraid, and now she was afraid. The long hard work of dying had given new urgency to the asthmatic's recurrent nightmare of being interred alive. What would help would be to write a note to the Cavaliere, requesting that he not seal up the coffin for three days after she died. But in order to say that, she must start by saying she fears that in a few days, nay, a few hours, she will be incapable of writing him; then declare that it is impossible for her to express the love and tenderness she feels for him, and that he, only he, has been the source of all her joys, he, the dearest of all her earthly blessings, which word, earthly, moves her from these extravagant and entirely unfeigned feelings for the Cavaliere to the thought of even greater heavenly blessings, and an expression of her hope that he might some day become a believer.

Catherine does not really think that he will ever become devout (and he did not). Her longing for him to yield to religious belief came from her own need for an exalted, rhapsodic language. She wanted him to acknowledge the reality of that dimension, therefore that language, so that they could share it—so that they could finally be truly intimate.

But, of course, he will never know the rhapsodic compensation. For all the dark constricting feelings that . . . and here she began to gasp for breath and recalled what she had wanted to put in this letter, a true letter of farewell, apart from declaring her love, asking him to forget and forgive her faults, exonerating him for leaving her alone so much, blessing him and asking him to remember her with kindness—yes, she wanted to request something. Let me not be shut up after I am dead till it is absolutely necessary. She finished by reminding him to give directions in his will to carry out the promise he has made to her that his bones will lie by hers, in Slebech Church, when God is pleased to call him, which she hopes will not be for many decades, during which interval—this is an exhausting, long-breathed sentence such as asthmatics take special pleasure in writing—during which interval she hopes that he will not remain alone. May every earthly and heavenly blessing attend you and may you be loved as I have loved you. I am, your faithful wife, &c.

She sealed the letter, felt the weight on her chest lighten, and slept more peacefully than she had in weeks.

Summer came, with its daunting, oppressive heat. The Cavaliere was angry with Catherine for dying—inconveniencing him, abandoning him. When in July they moved out to the Vesuvian villa, her favorite of their three residences, he found many reasons to linger for days at a time at the nearby royal palace. Doctor Drummond came out every morning to see her, with gossip to make her smile, little candies to stimulate her appetite, and, once a week, leeches to bleed her. One early August morning he did not arrive. She sent the dinner away uneaten at three o'clock and dispatched a footman to inquire, who returned with the news that the doctor had not taken his carriage but had decided to ride out on his new hunter and, a mile from the villa, had been thrown from the horse and hauled back on a litter to town. His injuries were serious, she was told. Then, very serious: a broken back and a punctured kidney. He died a week later. When this news was brought to her, Catherine wept for the last time.

The Cavaliere always maintained that her feeling somehow responsible for this frightful accident, incurred as the doctor was on his way to see her, hastened Catherine's death, which took place only twelve days later. Reading in a favorite chair facing the myrtle grove, she fainted and was carried into the house. As she was laid in bed, she opened her eyes and asked for a small oval portrait of the Cavaliere, which she set face down on her breast. She closed her eyes and died that evening without opening them again.

•

For those who hadn't known her well, he evoked her thus.

My wife, he said, was small, slender, of an elegant appearance and with distinguished manners. She had light blond hair, which age had not whitened, vivacious eyes, fine teeth, a witty smile. She was reserved in bearing, modest in gesture, and adept at contributing a few words to move a conversation forward without any thought of dominating it. Her constitution was delicate, and in the course of her life her poor health greatly influenced her frame of mind. Well-bred, cultivated, and a superb musician, she was much sought after in society, which she often avoided, however, for reasons of health and self-preservation. She was a blessing and a comfort to those who knew her, and will be sorely missed by all.

He reminisced about her virtues, her talents, her preferences. In fact, he mainly talked about himself.

Grief turns one into a queer being, the Cavaliere told Charles in a letter. I am much more bereft, much sadder than I expected to be.

Something terrible had happened to him, for the first time. The world is a treacherous place. You are going about, doing your life, and then it is over, or everything is worse. Just the other day at Portici, one of the royal pages opened the door of a disused chapel, walked into a *mofetta*, as pockets of cold poisonous gas secreted by the volcano are called, and died instantly. Since then the terrified King had talked of little else, and had added a few more amulets and charms to the large assortment normally pinned to his undergarments. And look what happened to old Drummond, while riding out to visit . . . no, the Cavaliere suddenly remembered, the one to whom something terrible has happened is himself. He had no magic charms; he had his intelligence, his character.

Something terrible. Something to meet with fortitude. I have had a happy life, he thought.

A wise man is prepared for all, knows how to yield, to resign himself, is grateful for the pleasures life has offered, and does not rage or whimper when felicity (as it must) ends.

And was he not a great collector? Therefore continually absorbed, distracted, diverted. He had not known how deep his feeling for Catherine was, or his need for her. He had not known he needed anyone that much.

Collectors and curators of collections often admit without too much prodding to misanthropic feelings. They confirm that, yes, they have cared more for inanimate things than for people. Let the others be shocked—they know better. You can trust the things. They never change their nature. Their attractions do not pall. Things, rare things, have intrinsic value, people the value your own need obliges you to assign to them. Collecting gives egotism the accents of passion, which is always attractive, while arming you against the passions that make you feel most vulnerable. It makes those who feel deprived, and hate feeling deprived, feel safer. He had not known how much Catherine's love also made him feel safe.

He expected more of his capacity for detachment, which he confused with his temperament. Detachment would not be enough to get him through this sorrow. Stoicism was needed, which implies that one really is in pain. He did not expect to be so slowed down by the press of grief, so darkened. Catherine's love seemed radiant now, now that it had been extinguished. No tears had bathed his eyes as he sat at Catherine's bedside and pulled his picture from her stiffening grasp, nor when he returned it to her, laying it in the casket before it was closed. Though he did not weep, his hair (suddenly greyer), his skin (drier, more lined) spoke for him, mourned for him. But there was no way he knew how to upbraid himself. He had loved as much as he could and had been more faithful than was the custom. The Cavaliere had always been good at self-forgiveness.

He sat beneath a trellis that looked out on the myrtle grove, exactly where Catherine was sitting when she fainted and was brought into the house. Where she had often sat with William. A thick complex web stretched across an ocular opening at the top of the trellis. He gazed absently at it for a while, before thinking to look for the spider, which he finally located hanging motionless from the outermost filament. Then he called for his climbing staff, reached up, and scythed through the web.

His letters speak of a settled, ungovernable melancholy. Heaviness, ennui, indolence—how tedious it was to write the words—is becoming my lot. The Cavaliere did not like to feel too much, but he was alarmed by the evident waning of feeling. He wanted to go on feeling not too much, not too little either (as he wanted to be neither young nor old). He wanted not to change. But he had changed. You would not recognize me now, he wrote to Charles. By nature lively, energetic, receptive, interested in everything, recently I have become indifferent to much of what once gave me pleasure. This is not indifference to you, dear Charles, or to another, but a general enveloping indifference. He lifted his pen, and considered what he had written.

I trust that apathy is not my inescapable condition, he went on, trying to strike the optimistic chord.

He had planned to bring out another edition, with more plates, of his book on volcanoes. The plan has been abandoned, he told Charles; he cannot surmount the feeling of weariness. Of a recent trip to Rome to look at pictures, he reported: Melancholy pursued me here also. My new acquisitions give me little pleasure. He described to Charles one of his acquisitions, a painting by a minor seventeenth-century Tuscan master evoking the transience of human life. Its message was voluptuously pertinent, its execution admirable. He gazed woodenly at the ingenious angle of the flowers and the mirror, at the soft flesh of the young woman gazing at herself. For the first time in his life, adding to one of his collections did not give him pleasure.

His lithe, reliable body allowed him to ride, to swim, to fish, to hunt, to climb the mountain as effortlessly as ever. But it was as if a veil lay between him and whatever he observed, draining everything of sense. Out for a spell of night fishing, attended only by Gaetano and Pietro, he watched the two servants jabbering in their incomprehensible dialect, butting the air as if words and phrases needed to be pushed forward with their jaws. The echoing voices from other boats crossing and recrossing the black bay, the black night, sounded like the cries of animals.

Yes, he still had the same physical robustness. It was an aging of the senses and of his capacity for enthusiasm that he noted. He felt his gaze becoming dull, his hearing and taste less sharp. He decided that it was because he was growing old. The reasons are innumerable for this general cooling, he explained —here the death of Catherine is being acknowledged—but perhaps it is mainly the passage of years. He struggled to resign himself to this reduced capacity.

He has never felt young, as he had told the sibyl. But when

Catherine died he felt, suddenly, old. He is fifty-two. How many years had Efrosina told him he had to live? He had dealt himself his hand and played it. He wondered how the devil he would occupy the eternity of twenty-one years to come.

•

To be unaccompanied. To be alone. To lower yourself into your own feelings.

There to find mists and vapors. Then little protuberances of old angers and longings. Then a large emptiness. You think of what you have done, done with brio—great slabs of actions, enterprises. All that energy has drained away. Everything becomes an effort.

Surfeited, his appetite for surfeit. Now it's enough.

•

A few months after Catherine's death, touring the devastation left by an earthquake in Calabria, gazing at the stiffened, dusty bodies dug out of the ruins, at their convulsed features and clawed hands—depressed people are often voyeuristic—then at a child brought up still alive, who for eight days had been lying under a collapsed house with her fist pressed against the right side of her face and had pushed a hole through her cheek.

Yes, show me more horrors. I will not flinch.

•

For a moment, just a moment, he saw himself as a madman, disguised as a rational being. How many times has he already climbed this mountain? Forty? Fifty? A hundred?

Panting, broad hat shielding his meager face against the sun, he paused and looked up at the cone. From the volcano's summit—far above the city, the gulf, its islands.

He was high up, looking down. A human dot. Far from all obligation of sympathy, of identification: the game of distance.

Before, everything affirmed him. I know, therefore I am. I

collect, therefore I am. I am interested in everything, therefore I am. Look at all that I know, all that I care about, all that I preserve and transmit. I construct my own inheritance.

The things had turned on him. They say, You do not exist.

The mountain says, You do not exist.

The priests say, The volcano is the mouth of hell.

No! These monstrosities, volcanoes or "ignivomous mountains," far from being emblems or presages of hell, are safety valves for the fires and vapors that would otherwise wreak havoc even more often than they do.

He knelt in the moat-like surround of the cone, placed his palms upon the dusty rubble, then stretched out, belly down, out of the wind, and lay his cheek to the ground. It was silent. The silence spoke of death. So did the thick, stagnant, yellowish light, as did the smell of the sulphur drifting up from the fissures, the rocks piled up, the tephra and dry grass, the slabs of clouds lying in the indigo-grey sky, the flattened sea. Everything speaks of death.

Let's take a positive view. The mountain is an emblem of all the forms of wholesale death: the deluge, the great conflagration (*sterminator Vesevo*, as the great poet was to say), but also of survival, of human persistence. In this instance, nature run amok also makes culture, makes artifacts, by murdering, petrifying history. In such disasters there is much to appreciate.

Under the ground were stretches of slag and clumps of bright minerals and fossil-studded rock and murky obsidian on its way to becoming transparent, beneath which lay more inert strata that enclosed the core of molten rock, as the mountain each time it exploded further deformed and layered and thickened the ground. And down the slope, under the tilted saliences of rock and the swatches of yellow broom, underneath, all the way to the villages below and riding out to the sea are ever more layers of human things, artifacts, treasures. Pompeii and Herculaneum were buried and now—a miracle of the age—have been exhumed. But offshore lies the Tyrrhenian Sea, which closed over the kingdom of Atlantis. There is always something more to be uncovered.

The ground holds treasures for collectors.

The ground is where the dead live, stacked in layers.

Cheek to the ground, the Cavaliere has descended to the mineral level of existence. Gone the court and the thuggish, jovial King, gone the beautiful treasures he has brought into his keeping. Is it possible he is not attached to them any more? Yes, at this moment he no longer cares.

•

The Cavaliere would have liked to have had a vision of redeeming plenitude and grace, such as one often has on mountain tops. But all he can think of is going higher still. He imagined taking to the air in that newfangled French marvel, the balloon, with a train of attendants; no, just young Pumo; and being able to look down on Vesuvius, from above watch the mountain becoming smaller and smaller. The cold bliss of effortless ascent, moving up, up, into the haven of pure sky.

Or, he would have liked to conjure up a lofty vision of the past, such as William had regaled Catherine with. But all that comes to mind is catastrophe. Say, a panoramic view of the great eruption of A.D. 79. The fearsome noise, the cloud in the shape of an umbrella pine, the death of the sun, the mountain burst open, disgorging fire and poisonous vapors. The rat-grey ash, the brown mud descending. And the terror of the denizens of Pompeii and Herculaneum.

Like a more recent double urbanicide, one murdered city is much more famous worldwide than the other. (As one wag put it, Nagasaki had a bad press agent.) So let him choose to be in Pompeii, watching death rain down, perhaps unwilling to flee while there is still time because he is, even then, some kind of doughty collector. And how can he leave without his things? So perhaps as his street, then his knees, vanish beneath the ashes, it would have been he who had recalled the line from the *Aeneid* the excavators found that someone had written on a wall of his house: *Conticuere omn* . . . ("All fell silent"). Gasping for breath, he had not lived to finish it.

As in a dream (just as one is about to die), he vaults out of the doomed city and tries to be someone watching. Why not be the most famous observer, and victim, of the eruption? For if, yielding to the obvious, he could imagine himself not like but really Pliny the Elder, if he could feel the slap of the wind on the prow of the admiral's boat rounding the cape of Misenum, if he could stay with Pliny right up to the end when, his lungs enfeebled by his asthma (O Catherine!), he succumbed to the lethal fumes . . . But unlike his young cousin, who is always imagining himself as someone else (and at the age of forty will congratulate himself for being forever young), the Cavaliere is hard put to imagine that he is anyone but himself.

That night, he slept on the flank of the volcano.

If he dreams, he dreams of the future—jumping over the future that remains to him (he knows it holds neither great interest nor happiness) to the future that amounts to his own death. Thinking about the future, the Cavaliere is peering into his own nonexistence. Even the mountain can die. And the bay, too—though the Cavaliere cannot imagine that. He cannot imagine the bay polluted, the marine life dead. He saw nature endangering, cannot imagine nature as endangered. He cannot imagine how much death lies in wait for this nature: what will happen to the caressing air, to the blue-green water in which swimmers frolic and boys hired by the Cavaliere dive for marine specimens. If children jumped into the bay now, the skin would slide from their bones.

People in the Cavaliere's time had higher standards of ruin. They thought it worth pointing out that the world is not as smooth as an egg. Fretted coastlines gave onto inchoate seas, and the dry land had broken, lumpy surfaces; and there were rude heaps: mountains. Blotched, stained, rutted—yes, compared to

Eden or to the primordial sphere, this world is a mighty ruin. People then did not know what ruin could be!

•

He waited for a clarifying wind. And torpor hardened over everything, like the lava stream.

He looked into the hole, and like any hole it said, Jump. The Cavaliere recalled taking Catherine after the death of her father to Etna, then in full eruption, and stopping on the lower slope at the cabin of a hermit (there is always a hermit), who insisted on retelling the legend of the ancient philosopher who jumped into the boiling crater to test whether he was immortal. Presumably, he was not.

•

He was waiting for catastrophe. This is the corruption of deep melancholy, that its sense of helplessness reaches out to include others, that it so easily imagines (and therefore wills) a more general calamity.

Ominous rumblings, which tourists as well as the Cavaliere welcomed. Every visitor wanted the volcano to explode, to "do something." They wanted their ration of apocalypse. A stay in Naples between outpourings of cataclysm, when the volcano seemed inert, was bound to be a little disappointing.

•

It was the time when all ethical obligations were first put up for scrutiny, the beginning of the time we call modern. If by merely pressing a button, one could, without any consequences to oneself, cause the death of a mandarin on the other side of the world (clever to have picked someone that far away), could one resist the temptation?

People can perform the weightiest actions if these are made to feel weightless.

How thin the line between the will to live and the will to die. How slight the membrane between energy and torpor. So many more could give way to the temptation to commit suicide if it were made easy. How about . . . a hole, a really deep hole, which you put in a public place, for general use. In Manhattan, say, at the corner of Seventieth and Fifth. Where the Frick Collection is. (Or a prole-ier address?) A sign beside the hole reads: 4 PM–8 PM / MON WED & FRI / SUICIDE PERMITTED. Just that. A sign. Why, surely people would jump who had hardly thought of it before. Any pit is an abyss, if properly labeled. Coming home from work, out buying a pack of wicked cigarettes, detouring to pick up the laundry, scanning the pavement for the red silk scarf the wind must have sucked off your shoulders, you remember the sign, you look down, you inhale quickly, exhale slowly, and you say—like Empedocles at Etna—why not.

PART TWO

1

Nothing can match the elation of the chronically melancholy when joy arrives. But before being allowed to arrive, it must lay siege to the weary heart. Let me in, it mews, it bellows. The heart must be forced.

That came four years later. First Catherine's death had to be absorbed by the Cavaliere's finely tuned metabolism. He requested another leave, to bring the body back for interment in Wales. There was no one here whose consolation consoled. Catherine's death brought him perilously close to a condition he did not enjoy, that of thinking about himself. He applied his usual remedy, which was thinking about the world. With what time he had to spare after the usual duties and distractions, he busied himself with a visit to some new excavations in stony Calabria (*Catherine is no more*). There he was taken to a festival in a nearby village honoring Saints Cosmas and Damian which culminated in a church service to bless a foot-long object, much revered by barren women, known as the Great Toe. *No more!* Dusty, exhilarated, the Cavaliere returned to Naples. To a learned society devoted to the study of antiquity (*Catherine is dead*), the Cavaliere sent a paper reporting on this savory discovery of traces of an ancient priapic cult still existing under the cover of Christianity, which furnished fresh proof of the similitude of the popish and pagan religions; recalling the prevalence of effigies of the female and male organs of generation uncovered in the digs; and speculating that the secret of all religions was worship of vital forces—the four elements, sexual energy—and that the cross itself was probably a stylized phallus. *Dead!* With Catherine gone, he had no reason to rein in the sceptic and blasphemer.

Everything has changed and nothing is changed. He did not acknowledge his need for company. But when his friend and protégé the painter Thomas Jones, about to return for good to England, gave up the house he rented, the Cavaliere offered him hospitality for a few months and came often in the morning to the room fitted out as a studio for Jones. He watched him filling small monochromatic canvases on his pretty olivewood easel with what seemed to him studies of emptiness: the corner of a roof or a row of top-floor windows of the building opposite.

How curious—but Jones must have his reasons. Everything rhymed with the Cavaliere's condition.

But what are you painting, said the Cavaliere politely. I do not understand the subject.

Moments of slippage, when anything seems possible and not everything makes sense.

Permission from the Foreign Office for his third leave home came in June, and he set sail. With Catherine's body in the hold of the ship and in his cabin a Roman cameo vase thought to have been made early in the reign of the Emperor Augustus, one of the rarest antiquities to come on the market for decades, which he had bought last year in Rome and was bringing back to England to sell. It was the most valuable item that would ever pass through his hands.

The Cavaliere had felt the bite of passion when he first saw it. Brought up two centuries earlier out of a newly excavated imperial burial mound just south of the boundary of ancient Rome, it was then and still is considered the finest piece of Roman cameo glass in existence. Nothing could be lovelier than the Thetis depicted on the frieze, reclining languidly on the nuptial couch. After he brought it back from Rome, the vase was often in his mind. He never tired of gazing at it, of holding it aloft so as to see the true color of the ground, a midnight blue indistinguishable from black except when pierced by light, and brushing the tips of his fingers over the low-relief figures incised in the creamy white glass. Alas, this was not an object he could afford to be in love with. Though Catherine's will had left everything, unencumbered, to him, he always needed more money. The vase was too famous for him to think of keeping it. Having got it for rather a good price, a thousand pounds, the Cavaliere had high hopes of making a substantial profit.

After depositing the vase in London, and receiving condolence visits from some friends and relations, he had brought the casket to the estate in Wales, now his in title as well as fact, set off in a light rain with Charles to see it slotted into the floor of the church, sent Charles away, and lingered in the house for several weeks. It was high summer. The rain pumped Catherine's native earth with green. He walked the estate and sometimes far out into the countryside every day, often with his pockets filled with small plums, and sat for a while staring at the sea. Mourning brought its distinctive languor. Mourning-thoughts, fond memories of Catherine, mingled with self-pity. Peace, peace for Catherine, poor Catherine. Peace for us all. The green leaves rustled over his head. This was the sun and temperate light that would prosper one day over his rotting body; and this—he'd entered the cool church for a moment—the tombstone that one day would bear his name as well.

Even before he had arrived, the London of collectors was astir about his Roman vase. News from Charles that the willful elderly Dowager Duchess of Portland coveted his prize brought him back to London. He asked for two thousand pounds. The duchess flinched. She said she would think it over. A month or two went by; the Cavaliere knew not to insist. Amusing himself as best he could, he toured her private museum of branches of coral, cases of iridescent butterflies and jewel-like seashells, insect fossils, mammoth bones (thought to be those of a Roman elephant), rare folio volumes on astronomy, antique medallions and buckles, and Etruscan vases. A grouping of objects no odder than many other collections of the period (its main oddity was that the collector was a woman), but decidedly too whimsical for the Cavaliere's taste. The duchess's son, already middle-aged and mindful of his inheritance, advised her against the purchase, for what was then a staggeringly high price. The duchess began seriously to want to buy the vase.

The Cavaliere spent less time at court and more with Charles, and allowed himself to be flattered and coddled by the exuberant, charming girl whom Charles had taken to live with him three years ago, and who, on Charles's instruction, called him Uncle Pliny and kissed him daintily on the cheek. She was tall and full-figured and her head, with its auburn hair, blue eyes, and ripe mouth, would rival the beauty of certain classical statues, thought the Cavaliere, if her chin were not so small. He already knew her story from his nephew: a village blacksmith's daughter, who had come to London at fourteen as an under-housemaid, was seduced by the son of the house, soon found more dubious employment, including posing semi-dressed as a "nymph of health" in the chambers of a doctor who claimed to cure impotence, was taken to the country estate of a baronet who cast her out when she became pregnant (her small daughter was being boarded in the country), and whose close friend, to whom the girl turned in despair, was . . . Charles. Sixteen years older than she, her rescuer did not marvel that so many eras had been crowded into a mere nineteen years. Women like her were supposed to climb as far as they could and be used up, quickly. There was, then, nothing special about her, apart from her physical charms. But there was. Charles wanted to be fair. He also wanted to boast. Just imagine, said Charles. She is actually quite gifted, Charles said. I've taught her to read and write and now she reads whole books of the self-improving sort, she's very fond of reading, and remembers everything she's read. The Cavaliere noticed that she remembered every word said in her presence. While her speech was vulgar and her laugh too hearty, when she was silent she seemed transformed. The Cavaliere saw her watching, observing, her eyes humid with attentiveness. And her judgment about pictures is rather fine, Charles went on, as well it might be, since she has lived with me for three years and since our friend Romney is obsessed with her. He has used her for dozens of paintings and drawings and will not hear of another model, except when I refuse to lend my girl to him. This reminded the Cavaliere that he must make time to sit again for Romney, for he wanted another portrait of himself.

The duchess counter-offered sixteen hundred pounds. The Cavaliere held firm.

He had not spent much time at court, thoughts of preferment or another appointment to Madrid or Vienna or Paris having long been abandoned. He felt older without Catherine at his side. He sat for his portrait. He told himself it was time to go back. He told others.

Eighteen hundred pounds, said the duchess angrily. Done. He made a few purchases, including Romney's painting of Charles's girl as a priestess of Bacchus, to take back with him to Naples.

He returned, he relapsed into his life, first addressing a backlog of duties, claims, and displays of well-being—he was still good at occupying himself. And he understood that one must combat apathy with new exertions. He undertook a vast project, one that would consume several years: designing fifty acres of English garden in the park of the palace at Caserta. He went on collecting and climbing and cataloguing. He got better at removing treasures from the excavations at Pompeii and Herculaneum under the very eyes of the King's archaeologists. Anything can be done in this country if you know whom to pay off.

Several agreeable, picture-loving English widows of his acquaintance seemed to be proposing to remedy his loneliness, one in London on the eve of his departure, another in Rome, where he stopped for a few weeks on his way back, principally to confer with Mr. Byres, his favorite picture agent there. The lady of Rome tempted him. She was rich, in excellent health, and she played the harp skillfully. With a certain glee he gave Charles an account of her charms, knowing how nervous this would make his beloved nephew, who was counting on being his childless uncle's heir. True, the age of the lady precluded children. However, being a decade younger than the Cavaliere, she still was likely to survive him. But the Cavaliere soon put aside the thought of a rational marriage. Even this lady, so dignified, so inhibited, portended a certain disruption of his habits, a readjustment. What the Cavaliere wanted above all else was calm. He had been meant to be a bachelor . . . and a widower he would end his days.

What he least wanted, consciously, was any change. He was as well-off as he could be. Yet the groin ached. Fantasy could not be denied. The inner fire was not entirely damped. And so, today, against his better judgment, he was allowing her to arrive. This naïve, innocent girl—she *was* innocent, the Cavaliere could see that, for all her experiences—arriving here, with her mother. Because Charles had his eye on a rich heiress (what was the second son of a lord to do?), Charles had to be serious. That is, he could no longer be guided by his affections. That is, he must be cruel to a woman. But having decided to get rid of the girl, he had not the heart to tell her and, further, had wondered if his newly widowed uncle might not enjoy her companionship. The uncle inherit the nephew's mistress? The Cavaliere knew that Charles was not simply relieving himself of an encumbrance and putting his uncle in his debt; he was also hoping to head off the possibility that his uncle might decide to console his late years with a new wife. He might soon find himself no longer his uncle's heir. But if his uncle liked the girl (whom clearly no one could marry) well enough, Charles was safe. Clever Charles.

She had left London with her mother in March, in the company of an elderly Scottish painter, a friend of the Cavaliere, who was returning to Rome and had agreed to take the two women under his protection. Valerio had been sent to Rome to bring them the rest of the journey. The Cavaliere was having breakfast and reading when he heard the great gateway swinging open. He went to the window and looked down at the traveling chaise pulling into the courtyard, being converged on by footmen and pages. Descending from the seat next to the driver, Valerio offered his hand to the young woman, who stepped lightly to the ground, then helped the stout older woman emerge from the carriage. As they crossed the courtyard toward the red marble staircase on the right, several maids reached out to fondle the girl's dusty yellow dress, and she dallied for a moment, smiling, touching the outstretched hands, responding with delight to the effect she was having. What the Cavaliere noted was a hat, a large blue hat, moving above the play of light on the cobblestones.

Suddenly he thought of Jack, and missed him. He returned to the breakfast table. It's all right to keep her waiting. A bookseller is waiting, too. He finished his cocoa, then went toward the Small Drawing Room, where he had directed that the girl and her mother be told to wait.

Passing through the door held open for him by Gasparo, he saw them sitting in the corner, whispering. The woman noticed him first and stood up hastily. The girl was holding the hat in her lap, and she turned and put it behind her on the seat as she rose. At that *contrapposto* of the body and then the turn back, he experienced a physical shock, as if his heart had plummeted into his belly. He hadn't remembered she was that beautiful. Stupendously beautiful. He must have seen how beautiful she was last year, since when he had possessed this beauty in the form of an image, as the Bacchante in Romney's picture hanging in the hall to his study, which he sees every day. But she is much more beautiful than the painting.

Heaving a deep and joyful sigh, he crossed the room and

acknowledged the girl's shy curtsy and the awkward lurch the mother intended as one. He directed Stefano to show Mrs. Cadogan the two rooms in the rear of the second floor that he was giving them. The girl leaned forward impulsively and brushed her lips against his cheek. He started back as if he had been scratched.

She must be exhausted from the long journey, he told her.

She was so happy, she told him. It was her birthday, she told him. She found the city so beautiful. She took his hand, she burned his hand, and drew him out on the terrace. And it was, indeed, beautiful—he could see that again—bathed in a sunlit haze, the red roofs tumbling down, the flower gardens and mulberry and lemon trees, the upthrust of cacti and slim, tall palms.

And that, uncle? she exclaimed, pointing to the mountain and its reddening plume of smoke. Will there be an eruption soon?

Are you afraid? he said.

Lordy, no, I want to see it! she cried. I want to see everything. It's so . . . fine, she said, smiling, pleased to have found such a genteel word.

She was young, still engulfed in the ecstasy of being alive, which touched him. And he knew of her virtues—her abject devotion to Charles, who had been campaigning for almost a year to make his uncle agree to receive her. Her passion is admiration, Charles wrote to the Cavaliere. She already admires you, said Charles. The Cavaliere thought he might enjoy behaving toward her more disinterestedly than other men had done. He will give her shelter—perhaps it would be better to put the two women in the four front rooms on the third floor—and show the girl the admirable sights.

You may make of her what you like, Charles had said. The material, I can guarantee, is good.

But he did not feel very pedagogic at first. For the moment he just wanted to look at her. He cannot yet master the emotion her beauty provokes in him. Is it a sign of old age that he so instantly doted on her? For he is old. His life is over. Add this beauty to his collection? No. He would polish a little. And then send her home. Charles really was a dastard.

So the Cavaliere temporized and delayed over the next weeks, unable to believe that he was being given another chance, that life erupts anew. What had such youth to do with him? Though he knew she was his for the possessing (or so he thought), he was afraid of making a fool of himself, and he was genuinely moved by her credulity. She really did believe that Charles was coming to fetch her in a few months. Still, he would be a fool not to take the gratification offered him, without fuss, without sentimentality. Surely the girl understood. She must be used to men and their wicked ways—being passed from one to the next. True, she did love Charles. But she must be expecting his advances. Poor Emma. Wicked Charles. And he put his bony hand on hers.

The sharpness of her rejection, her tears, her cries irked him—Charles had promised someone tractable—and impressed him, too. In the age-old way that men judge women, his esteem for her mounted because she refused him. Yet she seemed genuinely to enjoy his company, not only to look up to him. To be eager to learn. Surely then, happy. He gave her a carriage for her own use. He showed her—her placid, homely mother always in attendance—the marvels of the region. He took her to Capri, and together they visited the gloomy ruins of Tiberius' villa, stripped by predatory archaeologists of its ravishing floors of inlaid marble only a generation ago. To Solfatara, where they strolled on the scorching, sulphurous plain. To the dead cities, where they peered into a cluster of sunken houses. And to Vesuvius, setting out at four one morning beneath a full moon in a carriage that took them to Resina, where mules and Tolo were waiting to bring them as far as the lava sprawling three miles from the top. He watched her watching. She was enthralled by everything he showed her, he could tell; she besieged him with questions. She seemed only to want to please him; and if sometimes when he joined her on the terrace to admire a sunset her cheeks were wet with tears, that was understandable, she was far from home, that rogue his nephew really should have told her the truth, she was very young, what had Charles said? (He'd been vague about her age.) She must be twenty-three now. Which made the Cavaliere, at fifty-six, the age of the Elder Pliny when he succumbed to the noxious smoke, some thirty-three years older than this country Venus.

•

In fact, the difference between them was thirty-six years. She turned twenty-one the April day she arrived in Naples.

Oh Charles on that day you allways smiled on me & staid at home & wos kind to me & now I am so far away. From her first letter.

Charles was to follow in the autumn. He had told her. She wrote him every few days. The heat mounted, the fleas and lice multiplied. She tried to appear cheerful to the Cavaliere, who lavished gifts upon her, chief among them his own presence.

He breakfastes dines supes & is constantly bye me looking into my face, she reported to Charles. I cant stir a hand or a legg or foot but what he is marking it as gracefull & fine. Their is two painters in the house painting me but not as good as Romney. I wore the blue hat you gave me. He as given me a camels shawl & a beautiful goun cost 25 guinees & some little things of is wife. He tels me I am a grate work of art & I am sorry to see that he loves me.

Her letters to Charles became more abject, more pained. She tells her dear Charles, Charles, that she belongs to him, and to him only will she belong, and nobody shall be his heir apparent. She tells him of all the marvelous sights she has seen, which she would so much prefer to see in his company. She pleads with him to write her; to come to Naples as he has promised, now. Or to send for her to come back to him.

After two months there was a letter.

Dear Charles, she replied, oh my heart is intirely broke. And Charles Charles how with that cool indeference to advise me to go to bed with him. Your uncle! Oh that worst of all—but I will not no I will not rage. If I wos with you I wood murder you & myself boath. Nothing shall ever do but going home to you. If that is not to be I will go home to London & their go into every excess of vice tell I dye & leave my fate as a warning to young whomen never to be two good. For you have made me love you—you made me good—& now you have abbandoned me & some violent end shall finish our connexion if it is to finish. She ended: It is not to your intrest to disoblidge me for you dont know the power I have hear. Onely I never will be his mistress—if you afront me I will make him marry me. God bless you forever.

This was written on August 1st. She continued to write, to plead, to say goodbye, and held off the Cavaliere another five months. In December she informed Charles that she had resolved to make the best of things. I have decided to be resonable, she wrote. I am a pretty whoman & one cant be evrything at once.

•

Impossible to Describe . . .

It is impossible to describe her beauty, said the Cavaliere; impossible to describe how happy she makes me.

It is impossible to describe how much I miss you, Charles, wrote the girl. Impossible to describe how angry I am.

And of the volcano, erupting, in which the Cavaliere delighted anew: It is impossible to describe the beautiful appearance of the girandoles of red-hot stones, far surpassing the most astonishing fireworks, wrote the Cavaliere, who then went on to offer a batch of comparisons, none of which do justice to what he sees. For, like any object of grand passion, the volcano unites many contradictory attributes. Entertainment and apocalypse. A cycle of substance displaying all four elements: starting with smoke, then fire, then flowing lava, ending in lava rock, the most earth-solid of all.

Of the girl, the Cavaliere would often say to himself, to others: She resembles . . . she is like . . . she could play. . . . It is more than resemblance. Embodiment. Hers was the beauty he had adored on canvas, as a statue, on the side of a vase. She the Venus with the arrows, she the reclining Thetis awaiting her bridegroom. Nothing had ever seemed to him as beautiful as certain objects and images—the reflection, no, the memorial, of a beauty that never really existed, or existed no longer. Now he realized the images were not only the record of beauty but its harbinger, its forerunner. Reality splintered into innumerable images, and images burned in one's heart because they all spoke of one beauty.

The Cavaliere has beauty *and* the beast.

People were bound to say, because of the substantial loan he had made to Charles, that his nephew had sold the girl to him. Let them think what they will. If there was one advantage to living so far from home, in this capital of backwardness and sensual indulgence, it was that he could do what he wanted.

In the promenade of carriages at sunset on the Chiaia, he introduced her to the local society and, one Sunday, to the King and Queen. He could not take her to the palace, but outdoors, under the sky, she could be presented to everyone. All true lovers of beauty were captivated by her, he could see that. So were ordinary people, beggars and washerwomen in the streets, who took her for an angel. When he showed her Ischia, some peasants knelt before her, and a priest who came to the house made the sign of the cross and declared that she had been sent among them for a special purpose. The maids the Cavaliere had given her came to beg for intercession in her prayers, because, they said, she resembled the Virgin. She clapped her hands with glee at the sight of horses decorated with artificial flowers, crimson tassels, plumes on their heads. The driver gravely leaned forward, extracted a plume, and handed it to her. When people saw her, they brightened. She was so blithe, so full of joy. Anyone who didn't like her was a damned snob. How could one not admire her and be joyful in her presence?

Young as she was and without the advantages of birth and education, she had a kind of natural authority. Mrs. Cadogan seemed almost intimidated by her, treating her more like a mistress than a daughter. One could have taken this self-effacing, plain countrywoman who liked her drink for a more distant relative whom the girl had taken in as an unsalaried chaperone and companion. That her mother invariably accompanied them when they went out allowed him to cherish even more deeply inside himself the excitement he was feeling. Routine pleasures became suspenseful, acquired sweep and intensity. In the harsh sun of an early July morning, they rode along the piney hill road to his little day cottage in Posillipo, to wait out the heat of the day on the terrace under great curtains of orange cloth swelling and flapping in the sea breeze. With delight he watched her savoring the chilled fruit, the strong Vesuvian wine; remained in the shade of the terrace when she descended the stairs cut in the rock to bathe, and watched her standing breast-high in the water, first bravely splashing her arms, then cupping the nape of her neck with her wet hand and remaining in that adorable pose for a long moment, while some boys spied on her from behind the rocks and her mother and two maids waited nearby with robe and towels. It did not matter if she loved him, so much did he love her, love watching her.

He never tired of cataloguing the play of her moods, the flow of one appearance into another, the variety, the inclusiveness of her appearance. Sometimes she was provocative, sometimes chastely shy. Sometimes full, almost matronly; sometimes like a fidgety little girl, waiting to be plied with presents. How charming she was when she tried on a bonnet or a sash or a gown he had designed for her, laughing unaffectedly, admiring herself.

Shall I turn my head like this? she said to the young German painter the Cavaliere had installed in the house to paint her portrait.

Or like this?

Like an actress, she was used to having an effect on people when she came into a room. It was included in the way she walked, the exact slowness of the way she turned her head, put her hand to her cheek . . . just so. The authority of beauty.

What kind of beauty?

Not the beauty which is linear, and requires a purging of the flesh: beauty of contour, of bone, of profile, of silky hair and the flare of delicate nostrils. (The beauty that, after first youth, must diet, that wills itself to be thin.) This is the beauty that emerges from self-confidence, class confidence. That says, I am not born to please. I am born to be pleased.

Not that beauty, the beauty arising from privilege, from will, from artifice . . . but one almost as authoritative: the beauty of someone who has to fight for a place and can take nothing for granted. Beauty which is about volume, which is willing to be, cannot choose to be other than, flesh. (And eventually runs to fat.) Beauty which strokes itself with parted full lips, inviting the touch of others. Beauty which is generous and leans toward the admirer. I can change, yes, because I want to please you.

Her beauty, of the second kind, both naïve and sovereign, needed no completing or polishing. Yet she seemed to have become, if possible, even lovelier since she arrived, her beauty expanding as it chimed with something sensual, moist, sparkling in the air, under a sun so unlike the English sun. Perhaps she needed this new setting, these new modes of appreciation; needed to suffer, even (she wept for Charles, she really loved him); needed the luxury she had never enjoyed; needed to be—instead of some cautious, nervous dilettante's little jewel sequestered in a London suburb, obediently pouring his tea—the proud possession, publicly displayed, of a great collector.

•

What do you do with beauty? You admire it, you praise it, you embellish it (or try to), you display it; or you conceal it.

Could you have something supremely beautiful and not want to show it to others? Possibly, if you fear their envy, if you worry that someone will come and take it away. Someone who steals a painting from a museum or a mediaeval manuscript from a church must keep it hidden. But how deprived the thief must feel. It seems most natural to exhibit beauty, to frame it, to stage it—and hear others admire, echo your admiration.

You smile. Yes. She is quite marvelous.

Marvelous? She is much more than that.

What is beauty without a chorus, without the whispers, the sighs, the murmurs?

But who knows better than the Cavaliere what beauty is, beauty into which one falls. I am cut, I am felled. I fall, cover me with your mouth.

•

Beauty must be exhibited. And beauty can be taught how best to exhibit itself.

Her perfections and his happiness did not mean he did not want to improve her. The Cavaliere's mansion was stocked with tutors from morning to night. She had her singing teacher, her drawing teacher, her Italian teacher, her piano teacher. A natural student, she soon became fluent in Italian—speaking it better than the Cavaliere did, after more than twenty years of residence—so he added lessons in French, which he spoke well, with an English drawl. She quickly mastered French, and with less accent, which testified to the excellence of her ear. The Cavaliere himself gave the rain-in-Spain lessons to make her accent in her own language more acceptable, and ceaselessly reproved her for her childish spelling.

Her English remains incorrigible, a flurry of dropped aitches and puerile yelps, no matter how firmly he instructs her. She can add new skills, like French and Italian; learn arts, such as singing and drawing, that she has never practiced before. She can become accomplished on top of being vulgar, she cannot pull out the supporting layer of vulgarity. She cannot walk over her own feet.

She had thought herself abandoned. She had been passed on. She moves on, rapidly. All around her were women of her age, highborn women, each more languid than the next. She does not walk, she rushes. She was also naturally very intelligent, which compounded the energy at her disposal. She asked for more lessons: she wants everything, starting with days, to be filled. Eight o'clock . . . nine o'clock . . . ten o'clock . . . and so forth, as many as can be crammed into a day. The Cavaliere asked if she was tired.

She laughed boisterously, then covered her full mouth with her palm.

Tired!

The Cavaliere added botany and geology lessons. She has a dancing master now. She learns to play the piano, passably. But she sings like an angel. The castrato Aprile, engaged to give her advanced singing lessons, three a day, said that he had never heard so natural a voice, which the Cavaliere did not take as gross flattery but as the simple truth. He loved hearing her airy melismas as he worked on his morning correspondence. When she was not studying languages or music, she was feeding at his library. She hoped to please the Cavaliere, and did, by telling him she liked Sterne and Voltaire.

Flushed with pleasure, pitching her voice up and over the guests' heads to the torches and footmen at the rear of the room, she sang at the Cavaliere's assemblies. She longed to go to a ball at the palace. Although she accompanies the Cavaliere everywhere, she can't be received at the court. But she met the King often with his *al fresco* train of loafers and louts. He pulls at her hand and kisses her fingers. Even the Queen has smiled at her. Everyone pays her the most lavish compliments. She sits beside the Cavaliere in his silk-hung box at the San Carlo.

Mrs. Hart she calls herself.

She does not know who she is anymore, but she knows herself to be ascending. She sees how much the Cavaliere loves her. She feels her mastery. Skills fly in like birds and settle in her head. She drinks, she laughs loudly. She is hectic, full of blood. She warms the Cavaliere at night, he lays his angular head on her ripe soft bosom and slips his knees between hers.

•

Like many legendary beauties, she did not look for beauty in those with whom she fell in love. (A truly great beauty always has enough beauty for two.) She had not loved Charles more for his smug good looks, she did not love the Cavaliere less because he was a hollow-chested old man.

Insatiably eager for the Cavaliere's approval, she read him aloud passages from a manual of self-control for women which Charles had given her, *The Triumphs of Temper*. She knew its author, Mr. Hayley. He was one of Romney's friends. He had encouraged her. I am triumphing over my temper, she said to the Cavaliere. I have become reasonable. You will see. My adorable darling, said the Cavaliere.

Was it the way her eyes followed him? Not meek, like Catherine's; not pleading for attention, hoping to be met, drawn in, by an answering gaze—but playful, ardent, drawing him inside her gaze.

Her talent for enjoyment, her lack of fastidiousness, her superb health, delighted him. He was done forever with putting up with a woman's frailty, a woman's complaints.

In Mr. Hayley's poem, which she pointedly kept by her bed, Serena, the protagonist, is always calm, good-natured, obliging, unfazed by rebuke or difficulty. In a word, serene. That was the way the Cavaliere wanted her—not all the time of course, for then she would be bland and unseductive and without charm, but whenever he opposes her will or disappoints her. She was not to complain when he left her, because he must leave her now, even though he doesn't want to, must join the King to hunt or play billiards. In January, when the King's hunting lust was at its peak, the Cavaliere brought her out with him to the lodge at Caserta, where Catherine had spent so many lonely weeks. It was a test, which she passed splendidly. When he had to absent himself to be with the King, she wrote him little notes about how she studied to please him and how happy he made her. He dreamed of her full thighs.

Even her imperfections were dear to him: her small receding chin, the blush of eczema on her elbows that showed through the sleeves of a muslin dress, the stretchmarks of pregnancy on her belly, her laugh that sometimes became a guffaw. Which means he really loved her.

His passion defied what everyone knows about passion: that it is stimulated (indeed, kept alive) by doubt, separation, menace, withholding, frustration; and is incompatible with possession, security. But possession diminished nothing. The Cavaliere was bewitched sexually. He had not known he wanted so badly to be embraced.

Out of habit, out of affection, out of incapacity to hold a grudge, she continued to write to Charles—about her triumphs. I have a sweet of four rooms overlooking the bay & my own carridge & my own footmen & servents & cloathes are being made for me. All the ladys of the court admire my hair. I sang at a musical assembley 2 searous songs & 2 buffos & was told my voyce is as good as a castrato. Their was such claping. People wept when they herd me. And your uncle really loves me & I love him & my onely study is to make him happy. We walk in the public garden evry evening. We go to the oppera all the time, & have taken some foreyners to see the Greke temples at Pesto. . . . Besides the "we" of the couple (as in "We think the Dorick colums two heavy and not so ellegant"), there is the "we" of a place (as in "We may have some very large erruption soon, I wish we may"). She has adopted the mountain, seeing how much the Cavaliere's thoughts dwell on it, and speaks offhandedly of the eruption that took place soon after his arrival twenty-three years ago ("It was most memerable but not so terrable"), as if she had been there too. Your uncle laughs at me, she wrote to Charles, & says I shall rival him with the mountan now.

She is displacing the volcano.

She is becoming a local marvel with an international reputation, like the volcano. The Russian ambassador, Count Scavronsky, must have thought her beauty worth a description in a dispatch to his sovereign, for Catherine the Great has asked for a likeness of the girl to be sent to Saint Petersburg.

How could the Cavaliere not cherish her?

He began to trust her. Horrible to think of all she had suffered. An object is not sullied because it has been in the possession of less worthy owners. What counts is that it has reached its destination, been locked into the circle of possessions of the one who most deserved to own it.

•

Pity the uniquely valuable objects whose destiny is to be made available, in toy form, to everyone. Being safe in some great private collection or museum will not prevent this shadow despoliation.

Such was the fate of the celebrated object whose sale had been the Cavaliere's greatest coup as an art dealer. A year after yielding to the allure of his exquisite Roman cameo vase, the Dowager Duchess of Portland died and the vase passed to her son, the Third Duke, who leased it for a spell to the Cavaliere's alert accomplice in the great project of elevating public taste, Josiah Wedgwood. Some twenty replicas of the midnight-blue glass vase were made in smooth black stoneware—the industrial potter and professed lover of simplified forms was to consider it his masterpiece. Wedgwood did not even attempt to match the color or patina of the original and, by simplifying, vitiated its aristocratic contours. The vase's handles lean inward instead of following the curve of the body, the shoulders are more rounded, the neck is shortened. Perhaps the Cavaliere found the slightly dumpy rendering acceptable, having long ago overcome any patrician resistance to this new, mercantile way of spreading the influence of his collections. But he would surely have been startled by the progeny of the vase that the Wedgwood firm began turning out by the tens of thousands in the next century. Olive-green, yellow, pale pink, lilac, lavender-blue, grey, black, and brown Portland vases; Portland vases in many sizes, including small, medium, and large. Everyone could have, should have a Portland vase—and however desired: that was the company's plan. It grew, it shrank, it could be any color. The vase became a notion, a tribute to itself.

Who can really love the Portland Vase now?

The most valuable possession is always identical with itself. She is now his most valuable possession. And a valuable object confers value on its owner. A collector is happy to be known, mainly known, as the proprietor of what—through so much effort—has been collected.

•

So the old man collected the young woman; it could not have been the other way around. Collecting is both a sociable and a piratical activity. Women are reared not to feel competent at or gratified by the questing, the competing, the outbidding that collecting (as distinct from large-scale acquiring) demands. The great collectors are not women, any more than are the great joke-tellers. Collecting, like telling jokes, implies belonging to the world in which already-made objects circulate, are competed for, are transmitted. It presumes confident, full membership in such a world. Women are trained to be marginal or supporting players in that world, as in many others. To compete for approbation—not to compete as such.

•

You tell me a joke. I *love* your joke. It makes me laugh so much my sides ache, and my eyes moist over. And so witty and subtle. Rather deep, even. All this in a joke. I must pass it on.

Here comes somebody else. I'll tell your joke. I mean *the* joke. It isn't yours, of course. Someone told it to you. And now I'll tell it to someone else if I can remember it. Before I forget it I want to share it with someone, see that person have my reaction (roar with laughter, nod with appreciation, eyes moistening a little), but in order to be the pitcher, not the catcher, I have to not botch the telling. I have to tell it the way you told it, at least *as* well. I have to get behind the joke's wheel and drive it properly without jamming the gears or running into a ditch.

Being a woman, I'll worry more about my ability to get the joke out and into this new person's mind than if I were a man. (You, of course, are a man.) I may start by apologizing, and explaining that although I'm not good at remembering jokes and hardly ever tell jokes, I can't resist telling this one. And then I start, nervously, trying to recall exactly how you did it. I imitate your intonations. I make your emphases, your pauses.

I get through it, though it doesn't sound just right, not as good as the way you did it. The new person grins, laughs, sighs. But I doubt that I'm getting as much pleasure from telling this joke as you did. I'm doing something that doesn't come naturally to me, that's an imitation of a skill. I like to be witty, I'm good at turning phrases—my way with words. A joke is never mine. Stop me if you've heard this one, says the joke-teller, about to share his latest acquisition. He is right to assume that other people must be telling it too: a joke circulates.

The joke is this impersonal possession. It doesn't have anyone's signature. It was given to me—but you didn't make it up; it was in my custody, and I chose to pass it on, keep it going. It isn't about any of us. It doesn't describe you or me. It has a life of its own.

It goes off—like a pop, like a laugh, a sneeze; like an orgasm; like a little explosion, an overflow. Its telling says, I am here. I know enough to appreciate this joke. I'm convivial and expressive enough to pass it on. I enjoy entertaining. I enjoy showing off. I enjoy being appreciated. I enjoy feeling competent. I enjoy being behind my face and driving this little vehicle to its quick destination—and then getting off. I'm in the world, which has many things which are not me and which I appreciate.

Pass it on.

2

Tableau. Their backs are toward us, and we see what they are looking at, saluting, pointing out to each other, with one arm stretched out and up, the age's characteristic way of greeting some prospect of the marvelous in long-shot. A spread of ruins; a brilliant moon sailing behind a rim of clouds; the enlarging smoky plume of the mountain.

They have already marveled from afar—experience as promontory—before trudging up the side of the mountain, where they had to keep their eyes trained on the spiky rocks beneath each step so as not to stumble, and now, after the final clamber, they are at the top, they have reached the broad moat surrounding the cone, where once again, on level ground, they are looking up—and they can make the gesture, the gesture that says *there* —but it is *here*, dangerously near. They are being pelted with a shower of stones and ash. The cone is belching black smoke. A fiery rock falls only a few yards away—watch your arm! But they are bent on a view, at least the poet is. Another view. He hasn't climbed this far to continue to look up. He wants to look down, inside.

See, it's stopping. The poet took out his timepiece. You go

cower over there, behind that crag. I'm going to see just how long the monster can behave. This stricken monster, it's like the breathing of a stricken monster, with some twelve minutes between each breath, his watch tells him, during which the shower of stones subsides as well; and in one of the intervals, the poet suggested to his timorous friend, the painter, that they might get their guides to pull them swiftly to the top for a quick look into the crater.

It was done and they stood on the lip of the enormous mouth, as the poet was later to write. A light breeze blew the smoke away, the burbling and gurgling and spitting ceased, but the steam that rose from a thousand fissures veiled the interior of the crater, allowing no more than a shifting glimpse of the cracked rock walls. The sight, he wrote, was neither instructive nor agreeable.

Then the monster took another breath and from its entrails came a tremendous thundering roar—no, from the depths of the cauldron rose a cloud of searing steam and dust—no, from the mightiest of bombards hundreds of stones, large and small, were lobbed into the air—

Their guides tugged at their coats. One of them, the one-eyed boy whom the Cavaliere had recommended to the poet, rushed them to a boulder behind which they could shelter. It was too noisy to appreciate the great sweep of the gulf below and the city in the distance, whose contours, like an amphitheatre in oblique view or like a titanic chair, you have the impression you can take in as a whole, in one glance. The painter shouted, I shall descend now. After the poet crouched under the lee of the boulder a few moments more to demonstrate his courage and to turn over in his mind several other images, he too made a prudent retreat.

That was Goethe, with his friend the painter Tischbein, on the first of his three climbs up the mountain. The poet, no longer in his first youth but an exceptionally fit thirty-seven, has dutifully braved the fire-breathing dragon. If the old English knight can do it regularly, then he can too. It's what every able-bodied gentleman tourist does when he comes here. But the poet does not, like the Cavaliere, find it beautiful. He is both cold and hot, and tired, uncomfortable, a little frightened. It all seems a bit foolish. One does not see the feckless, pleasure-loving natives tramping up the awesome hill that rises some miles outside their paradise. Definitely a sport for foreigners. And among foreigners, rather English. Ah, these English. So refined and so coarse. If they did not exist, nobody would ever have invented them. So eccentric, so superficial, so reserved. But how they enjoy themselves.

One must try to enjoy oneself with them.

The poet arrived in the evening. Accompanied by another German painter resident in Naples, he and his friend had already been received by the Cavaliere and been shown the treasures in his public rooms. The walls covered with paintings, gouaches, and drawings, the tables piled high with cameos and vases, the cabinets crammed with geological curiosities. There seemed no method or organization in it, which is the first thing the German visitors noticed. And this created a certain unpleasing impression, not just of abundance but of disorder or chaos. But if you looked closely (the look every collector craves), you could recognize the sensitivity and sensuality of the person who had brought together these expressions of his taste, as Tischbein was to recall many years later. The walls, he said of the Cavaliere's walls, showed his inner life.

Then the poet, the poet alone, was invited to tour the Cavaliere's cellar storerooms. (The privilege of such a visit was reserved for only the most distinguished guests.) And the poet, who reported everything to his painter friend, was amazed at a different kind of profusion. There was an entire small chapel in the cellar. From where had he taken it? The painter shook his head, raised his eyes to heaven. The poet saw two ornate bronze candelabra which he knew had to have come from the excavations at Pompeii. And many objects of no distinction whatever. The collections upstairs were a map of the Cavaliere's fantasies, an ideal world. The cellar was the cavernous underbelly of the Cavaliere's collecting, for every collector soon reaches the point where he is collecting not only what he wants but what he doesn't really want but is afraid to pass up, for fear he might want it, value it, some day. He can't help showing these objects to me, the poet thought, even those he should not.

Of course to show off one's possessions may seem like boasting, but then the collector did not invent or fabricate these things, he is but their humble servant. He does not praise himself in exhibiting them, he offers them humbly for the admiration of others. If the objects a collector has were of his own making, or even if they were a legacy, then it would indeed seem like boasting. But building a collection, the anxious activity of inventing one's own inheritance, frees one from the obligation of reticence. For the collector to show off his collection is not bad manners. Indeed, the collector, like the impostor, has no existence unless he goes public, unless he shows what he is or has decided to be. Unless he puts his passions on display.

•

People told the poet that the Cavaliere had acquired, then fallen in love with, a young woman who was beautiful enough to be a Greek statue, had begun improving and educating her in the manner of any protector who is a man, older, rich, wellborn (all the things his beloved is not), and had become a kind of Pygmalion in reverse, turning his Fair One into a statue; more accurately, a Pygmalion with a round-trip ticket, for he could change her into a statue and then back into a woman at will.

In conformity with the Cavaliere's taste, she was dressed on these evenings in antique costume, a white tunic with a belt around her waist, her auburn, some say chestnut, hair falling free down her back or turned up by a comb. When she consented to begin a performance, according to one account, two or three cashmere shawls were brought to her by a stout elderly woman, some kind of housekeeper or perhaps a widowed aunt; certainly more than a servant, for she was allowed to sit at the side and watch. Maids would bring an urn, a scent box, a goblet, a lyre, a tambourine, and a dagger. With these few properties, she took her position in the middle of the darkened drawing room. When the Cavaliere came forward, holding a taper, the performance had begun.

Over her head she threw a shawl long enough to reach the ground and cover her entirely. Thus hidden, she wrapped herself with other shawls and started making the inner and outer adjustments (drapery, muscle tone, feelings) that will permit her to emerge as someone else, someone other than she is. To do this —it was not like donning a mask—one must have a very loose relation to one's body. To do this one must have a gift for euphoria. She floated up, she drifted down, she settled—her heart pounding, while she wiped the perspiration from her face. A flurry of grimaces, tightening of tendons, stiffening of hands, head rocketing back or to the side, sharp intake of breath—

And then she suddenly lifted the covering, either throwing it off entirely or half raising it, and making it form part of the garment of the harmonious living statue she had become.

She would hold the pose just long enough for it to be read, then cover herself again. Then she threw off the long shawl to reveal another figure, under a different disposition of shawls—she knew a hundred ways of arranging this drapery. One pose followed another, at least ten or twelve, almost without a break.

•

The Cavaliere had first asked her to pose inside a tall velvet-lined box open on one side, then within a huge gilt frame. But he soon saw that her artistry was frame enough for these simulations. Her whole life had prepared her to be the Cavaliere's gallery of living statues.

At fourteen, newly arrived in London, she had dreamed of becoming an actress, like the splendorous creatures she watched at night prancing out of the Drury Lane stage door. At fifteen, a scantily-veiled figure in the tableaux vivants staged by a fashionable sex therapist, she learned to stand without moving, breathing shallowly, the muscles in her face tightened to impassivity—expressing obliviousness to the sexual exertions taking place nearby, under Doctor Graham's supervision, in the Celestial Bed. At seventeen the favorite model of one of the great portrait painters of the era, she learned to think inventively about emotions and about how to express them, and then to hold these expressions for a long time. The painter said she often surprised him and inspired his conception of his subject; that she was a true collaborator, not a passive model. For the Cavaliere, she posed as herself posing—in a sequence of poses, a living slide show of the iconic moments of ancient myth and literature.

•

This was an extremely precise enterprise. First the subject had to be chosen. The Cavaliere would open his books and show the young woman the plates, or lead her to a painting or a statue in his collection. They would discuss the ancient stories. She always wanted to play them all. Then, once she was in possession of the subject, came the challenging part—finding the right moment, the moment that presents meaning, that sums up the essence of a character, a story, an emotion. It was the same hard choice painters were supposed to make. As Diderot wrote, "The painter has but one moment; he may no more record two different moments than two separate movements."

•

Illustrate the passion. But don't move. Don't . . . move. This is not dance. You are not a proto–Isadora Duncan in freeze-frame, for all your bare feet and Greek costume and loose limbs and unbound hair. Illustrate the passion. But as a statue.

You can lean—yes, like that. Or clasp something. No, a little higher. And turn your head to the left. Yes, you can seem to dance. Seem. Absolutely immobile. Like that. No. I don't think she would kneel. The left foot a little bit freer. Loll a little. Without the smile. Eyes half lidded. Yes. Like that.

•

Everyone said her expressions were altogether remarkable and convincing. But even more remarkable was the rapidity with which she moved from one pose to another. Change without transition. From sorrow to joy, from joy to terror. From suffering to bliss, from bliss to horror. It seems the ultimate feminine gift, to be able to pass effortlessly, instantly, from one emotion to another. How men wanted women to be, and what they scorned in women. One minute this. The next minute that. Of course. Thus do all women.

In principle, every kind of character and emotion was represented. But nymphs and muses, Juliets and Mirandas, were far outnumbered by the forlorn and the victimized. Mothers bereft of their children—her Niobe; or driven by an intolerable injury to kill them—her Medea. Maidens dragged by their fathers to the sacrificial altar—her Iphigenia. Women yearning for the lovers who have discarded them—her Ariadne. Or about to kill themselves in despair at being abandoned—her Dido; or to atone for the dishonor of a rape—her Lucrece. These were the poses that excited the greatest admiration.

When the poet saw her, only a year after she arrived in Naples, she had just begun performing at the Cavaliere's assemblies. Her lover had released an astonishing talent, which she would practice for many years and which would never cease to be admired, even by her fiercest detractors. Her gifts as a performer seemed at first identical with her beauty. But her beauty was more like genius, with its conviction of its own persistence, even in discouraging circumstances. For after her beauty went, she still felt like a beauty—available for display and appreciation. Even when she became heavy, she still felt light.

She did not want to be a victim. She was not a victim.

She doesn't miss Charles any more. She is resigned, she is triumphant. She knew she would never experience passionate love again, nor does she hope to. But she was genuinely fond of the Cavaliere, and easily faithful to him. She knows how to give pleasure, and does so as wanted. That Charles was rather chilly and strained in bed had not made her feel rejected. That the Cavaliere turned out to be more amorous than his nephew made her understand, for the first time, what it was to have sexual power over someone. Now she feels like a woman (which is safer than being a girl)—like many women, all of them irresistible. Her capacity for expressiveness, her unslakeable desire to make contact with others, had found its highest outlet in this theatre of simulated, ancient emotions.

•

What people made of antiquity then was a model for the present, a set of ideal examples. The past was a small world, made smaller by our great distance from it. It had only familiar names (the gods, the great sufferers, the heroes and heroines) representing familiar virtues (constancy, nobility, courage, grace), embodying an irrefutable idea of beauty, both feminine and masculine, and a potent, unthreatening sensuality—because enigmatic, broken, bleached of color.

People wanted to be edified. Knowledge was fashionable then—and philistinism unfashionable. Since each of the poses of the Cavaliere's protégé was a figure from ancient mythology or drama or history, to watch her run through her Attitudes, as they were called, was to be subjected to a kind of quiz.

She unbinds her hair, she rises from her haunches, she lifts her arms in supplication, she drops the goblet to the floor, she kneels and points the knife at her breast . . .

Gasps. A murmur from the audience. The beginning of applause, while somebody who doesn't recognize the figure is coached in a whisper by a fellow guest. The applause mounts. And the shouts. "Brava, Ariadne!"

Or "Brava, Iphigenia!"

And the Cavaliere standing nearby, both stage manager and privileged spectator, nodded gravely. He would have smiled had he thought it becoming to smile. Observing the old man's tense immobility, his age and thinness contrasting with her youth and opulent body, the poet smiled.

•

The significant moment! said the poet in his stilted French. That is what great art must render. The moment that is most humane, most typical, most affecting. My compliments, Madame Hart.

Thank you, she said.

Yours is a most unusual art, said the poet gravely. What interests me is how you move so quickly from one pose to another.

It just comes to me, she said.

But of course, he said, smiling. I understand. It is the function of art to conceal the difficulties of its execution.

It just comes, said the young woman, reddening. Surely he was not really asking her to explain how she did it.

How do you do it, said the poet. Do you see the personage you are incarnating in your mind's eye?

I think so, she said. Yes.

Her hair looked damp. The poet wondered what it would be like to embrace her. She was not his type. He was attracted to women who were more articulate, or who were humbler, less animated. Her talent had made her feverish. For there was no doubt that her performance was remarkable. She was not only, as was said knowingly by all, a work of art, but was herself an artist. The model as artist? Why not? But genius was something else. And so was happiness. He thought again how lucky the Cavaliere was. He was happy because he did not want more than he had.

There was a long, uncomfortable pause. The young woman did not flinch while this stiff German stared at her.

Would you like some wine?

Later, said the poet. I am not used to such heat.

Yes, the young woman exclaimed. It's hot. Very hot.

The great end of art is to strike the imagination, the poet told her. She agreed. And, in pursuing the true grandeur of design, it may sometimes be necessary for the artist to deviate from vulgar and strict historical truth. She was sweating. And then she told the poet that she had read, she had admired to distraction, his *Werther*, and was very sorry for poor Lotte, who must have felt so guilty for having inspired, innocently, the fatal passion in the too susceptible young man.

You don't feel sorry for the too susceptible young man?

Oh, she said, yes. But . . . but I feel more sorry for Lotte. She was trying to do what was right. She meant no harm.

I feel sorry for my hero, said the poet. At least I did. All that is very remote to me now. I was only twenty-four when I wrote it. I am not the person I was then.

The young woman, who is only twenty-two, cannot imagine the man standing before her ever to have been someone her own age. He must be about the same age as Charles. Strange what happens to men. They don't care for being young.

And was it a true story? she asked politely.

Everyone asks that, said the poet. Actually, everyone asks if it is my story. And, I confess, I did lend myself—but, as you see, I am still here.

I'm sure your friends are very glad, the young woman said.

I think Werther's death was my rebirth, the poet said solemnly.

Oh.

The poet was always—would always be—in the process of being reborn. Definition of a genius?

To her great relief she saw the Cavaliere approaching. I was just congratulating Madame Hart on the vivacity of her performance, said the poet.

Surely the brilliant Cavaliere would be a match for this ponderous visitor. The men would talk to each other, and she could watch.

But, as it turned out, the conversation between the Cavaliere and the poet was not much more successful than that between the Cavaliere's protégé and the poet. Neither greatly appreciated the other.

The Cavaliere had never read the notorious lachrymose novel about the lovelorn egotist who shoots himself; he suspected he would not like it. Luckily, his illustrious guest was not only one of the most famous writers on the continent and the principal minister of a small German duchy but had scientific interests, particularly in botany, geology, and ichthyology. So they talked about plants and stones and fish.

The poet began to unfurl his theory of the metamorphosis of plants. For some years I have been examining the leaves, pistils, and stamens of many species, and this study has led me to postulate a model from which it would be possible to construct an infinite number of plants, all of which could exist and many of which do. Walking along the seafront here, I had a new thought. You could say that I had an illumination. I am convinced that this Primal Plant does exist. When I leave Naples, I shall go to Sicily, which I am told is a botanist's paradise, and where I have hopes of finding a specimen. &c, &c, &c.

I am making an English garden on the grounds of the palace at Caserta, said the Cavaliere, ever eager to herborize, as soon as the poet had finished. Caserta may indeed rival Versailles, but I have persuaded Their Majesties that they need not yield to French fashion in the matter of gardens. At my suggestion they have engaged the most eminent landscape gardener in the English style, and this garden when completed will contain flora of the most enjoyable variety.

How disappointing the Cavaliere was. The poet changed the subject to Italy.

I have been completely transformed by Italy, he said. The man who left Weimar last year is not the same man who arrived in Naples, and whom you see before you now.

Yes, said the Cavaliere, not any more interested in self-transformation (the poet's favorite subject) than he was, for all his knowledge of gardens and the volcano, in botanical or geological theory. Yes, Italy is the most beautiful country in the world, I suppose. And truly there is no city more beautiful than Naples. Allow me the pleasure of showing you the view from my observatory.

Beauty, thought the poet scornfully. What a simple-minded epicurean this Englishman was. As if there were no more to the world than beauty! Here was a man incapable of delving deeply into what interested him. A mere dilettante, he would have called him, had dilettante not been then a term of praise.

Transformation, sighed the Cavaliere. Here was a man incapable of not taking himself seriously. He reflected that the poet undoubtedly exaggerated the extent to which he had been transformed by his Italian journey and that this concern with self-transformation was a rather overbearing piece of egotism.

And both were right. But the poet's convictions are more valuable to us; his vanity more pardonable; his sense of superiority more . . . superior. With genius, as with beauty—all, well almost all, is forgiven.

Thirty years later, in his *Italian Journey*, Goethe will write that he had a delightful time at the Cavaliere's assembly. He was not telling the truth. He was young enough then, restless enough, to have not enjoyed himself very much at all. To have minded that he learned nothing from any conversation that evening—for he felt himself undernourished mentally as well as underappreciated. I am bent on my own improvement, the poet was writing his friends. Pleasure, yes—that too. I have pleasures and these quicken and enlarge my ability to feel. How superior he had felt to these people. And how superior he was.

•

In most of the stories in which a statue comes to life, the statue is a woman—often a Venus, who steps off her pedestal to return the embrace of an ardent man. Or a mother, but then she is likely to remain in her niche. Statues of the Virgin and of female saints do not become ambulatory; there is movement only in compassionate eyes, a tender mouth, a delicate hand—speaking or gesturing to the kneeling supplicant, to console or to protect. Rarely does a female statue come to life in order to take revenge. But when the statue is a man, his purpose is almost always to do or to avenge a wrong. A male statue who wakens —in the modern version, a machine given human form and then animated—comes to kill. And his being-really-a-statue packs him full with the martial virtue of single-mindedness, makes him unswervable, implacable, immune to the temptations of mercy.

It's a dinner party. Sophisticated people who have dressed up in handsome and revealing clothes are enjoying themselves in the atmosphere in which such dedicated partygoers enjoy themselves best—something of both brothel and salon, minus the exertions or risks of either. The food, whether chewy or delicate, is bountiful; the wine and champagne are costly; the lighting is muted and flattering; the music, and the aromas of flowers on the table, enveloping and suffusing; some sexual tomfoolery is taking place, both of the wanted and of the other kind ("We're just having fun," says the would-be Don Juan, interfered with by the one who notices him relentlessly pressing his unwanted attentions on some woman); the servants are efficient and smile, hoping for a good tip. The chairs are yielding, and the guests profoundly enjoy the sensation of being seated. There are treats for all five senses. And mirth and glibness and flattery and genuine sexual interest. The music soothes and goads. For once, the gods of pleasure are getting their due.

And in comes this guest, this alien presence, who is not here to have fun at all. He comes to break up the party and haul the chief reveler down to hell. You saw him at the graveyard, atop a marble mausoleum. Being drunk with self-confidence, and also a little nervous about finding yourself in this cemetery, you made a joke to your sidekick. Then you halloed up to him. You invited him to the party. It was a morbid joke. And now he's here. He's grizzled, perhaps bearded, with a very deep voice and a lumbering, arthritic gait, not just because he is old but because he is made of stone; his joints don't bend when he walks. A huge, granite, forbidding father. He comes to execute judgment, a judgment that you thought outmoded or that didn't apply to you. No, you cannot live for pleasure. No. No.

He reaches out and dares you to shake his hand. The earth below rumbles, the floor of the partying room gapes open, flames start to rise—

Perhaps you are having a dream and you wake up. Or, perhaps, you are experiencing this in a more modern way.

He enters, the stony guest. But he is not going to kill you, and he's probably younger, even young. He is not coming to take revenge. He even thinks that he wanted to go to a party (he can't be a monument all the time) and he is not above wanting to enjoy himself. But he can't help being himself, which means bringing along his higher idea, his better standards. He, the stony guest, reminds the revelers of the existence of another, more serious way of experiencing. And this, of course, will interfere with their pleasures.

You did invite him, but now you wish you hadn't, and if you don't take the necessary precautions, he will break up the party.

After meeting a few of your guests, he starts giving up on the evening. Too quickly, perhaps. But he's used to scything through such matters. He doesn't think your party is all that much fun. He doesn't dissemble—mingle. He keeps to corners of the room. Perhaps he looks at the books, or fingers the art. He doesn't resonate with the party. It doesn't resonate with him. He has too much on his mind. Bored, he asks himself why he came. His answer now: he was curious. He enjoys experiencing his own superiority. His own difference. He looks at his watch. His every gesture is a reproach.

You, one of the guests—or, better, the host—make light of this scowling presence. You try to be charming. He refuses to be charmed. He excuses himself and goes for something to drink. (Is he moping or getting ready to denounce you?) He returns, sipping a glass of water. You turn away and make common cause with the others. You make fun of him—he's easy to make fun of. What a prig. What an egotist. How pompous. Doesn't he know how to have a good time.

Lighten up, stony guest!

He continues to contradict what is said to him, to make plain that he is not amused. And he can't really get your attention. You flit from guest to guest. For a party is not a tête-à-tête. A party is supposed to reconcile its participants, to conceal their differences. And he has the bad manners to want to expose them. Doesn't he know about the civilizing practice of hypocrisy?

You can't both be right. The fact is that if he is right, you are wrong. Your life is revealed as shallow, your standards as opportunistic.

He wants to kidnap your mind. You won't let him. You tell yourself that frivolity is a noble pursuit. That a party, too, is an ideal world.

Sooner or later he leaves. He shakes your hand. It's chilling. You settle back. The music is louder again. What a relief. You like your life. You're not going to change. He is pretentious, overbearing, humorless, aggressive, condescending. A monster of egotism. Alas, he's also the real thing.

•

On another visit, the poet asked the Cavaliere to recommend one of the lava dealers in Naples, so that he could take back with him a proper range of specimens.

To travel is to shop. To travel is to loot. No one who came here left without a collection of some sort. Naples made amateur collectors of everyone. It made a collector even of the Marquis de Sade, who, fleeing arrest in France, had arrived eleven years earlier under a pseudonym—though his false identity was unmasked by the French envoy, and he had to submit to being presented at the Neapolitan court under his true, already infamous name. When Sade left the city five months later to return to France, he sent ahead two huge chests filled with antiques and curiosities.

Before leaving for Sicily, the poet paid several more visits to the royal museum at Portici, which he proclaimed the alpha and omega of all collections of antiquities. He visited Paestum and avowed himself irritated by the stumpy Doric columns. (After his return from Sicily, on a second visit, he was able to appreciate them.) He did not, however, return to Pompeii and Herculaneum, which he had toured rapidly soon after arriving and had disliked. Better to observe the movements of crabs in the breakwater. What a delightfully splendid thing is something *living*, he wrote. Better to stroll in the garden at Caserta of which the Cavaliere was so proud, and look at the rose bushes and camphor trees. I am a friend to plants, he wrote. I love the rose. And he felt a wave of health and self-approval sweep over him. How pleased I am to keep up my little study of life in all its multifarious forms. Away with death—this hideous mountain, these cities whose cramped dwellings seem to foretell that they would become tombs.

He wrote letters back to his sovereign and to his friends in Weimar. I carry on looking. I am always studying. And, again: You will not recognize me. I scarcely recognize myself. This is why I came to Italy, why I had to abandon my duties. He had finished the final version of his *Iphigenia*, and added two scenes to the ever-unfinished *Faust* during his sexually revelatory stay in Rome. He had made many observations of plants and Palladio. To stave off the temptations of nostalgia for the lost classical past, he took notes on the picturesque behavior of common people in the streets. He had made progress with his drawing. He was not disappointed in himself. This productivity was yet another sign of his well-being.

It was important not to appreciate too much. Once one takes

it upon oneself to go out into the world and enters into close interaction with it, he wrote to one of his friends, one has to be very careful not to be swept away in a trance. Or even to go mad.

He was getting ready to go back. Naples is for those who only live, he wrote—thinking of the Cavaliere. Beautiful and splendid as it is, of course one couldn't settle here. But I look forward to remembering it, he wrote. The memory of such sights will give savor to a whole life.

People saved every scrap of paper on which the poet set down words. His fame had made him an instant antiquity—to be collected by his admirers. This great poet whose thirst for order and seriousness has led him to live as a public official, a courtier, is already one of the immortals. He was performing in public, being a work of art himself. He felt the echo of eternity in every one of his utterances. Every experience was part of his education, his self-perfecting. Nothing could go wrong in a life so happily, so ambitiously, conceived.

What we agree with leaves us inactive, but contradiction makes us productive. Words of the poet. Words of wisdom. A wisdom and a brand of felicity unavailable to the Cavaliere, and which he would never miss.

•

Everything should be understood, and anything can be transformed—that is the modern view. Even the alchemist's projects seem plausible now. The Cavaliere was not trying to understand more than he already did. The collector's impulse does not encourage the lust to understand or to transform. Collecting is a form of union. The collector is acknowledging. He is adding. He is learning. He is noting.

The Cavaliere commissioned a suite of drawings of twelve of the Attitudes from a local German artist. *Drawings Faithfully copied from Nature at Naples*, they were titled. But they conveyed nothing, the Cavaliere thought, of the seductiveness of these performances.

And he commissioned someone to take notes on and to draw the mountain's poses and performances.

Conscientious as the Cavaliere was, he could hardly be a full-time observer. For some years now, ever since the great eruption of 1779, he had been subsidizing a studious reclusive priest from Genoa, who lived alone and servantless near the foot of the mountain, to keep a diary of whatever he saw. This Father Piaggio never left his hermit's post—a mountain is a solicitation to hermits—rising at dawn and performing his observations, regular as devotions, at fixed intervals several times in the day. From the window of his tiny house he had a perfect view. He had already filled four manuscript volumes with his earnestly legible notations on the mountain's behavior and with fluent pencil drawings of the downward splaying and spreading of lava streams, the upward curling and soaring forms of the crater's effusions of smoke.

Much in these notes and drawings was repetitive. How could it be otherwise? Who could change the mountain? The Cavaliere particularly relished a story the priest told him about the natural philosopher from Prague who had arrived at the court forty years ago when Charles of Bourbon, the present King's father, was still on the throne, with a detailed plan for rescuing the villages surrounding Vesuvius from the danger that loomed above them. His various specialties, which he named as mining, metallurgy, and alchemy, had led him to study the volcano for many years in his laboratory in Prague. There he had devised his solution. It was to reduce the mountain to a mere thousand feet above sea level, and then open a narrow channel from its filled-in summit down to the shore, so that if the mountain explodes again, what remains of its fire will be concentrated and run directly into the sea.

Considering the magnitude of the task, the work force he would require was not large, the man from Prague pointed out. Give me twenty-nine thousand men, Majesty, he said, and in three years the monster will be decapitated.

Was the man from Prague just another charlatan? Possibly.

Should he be allowed to try anyway? The king, who liked bold projects, consulted with his ministers. They were appalled by the plan. To alter the mountain's shape, they declared, would be a sacrilege. An anathema was read out in the cathedral by the cardinal.

Since this was a new age, with new thoughts, new machines—people were discovering new forms of leveling, making shapely—it was not surprising that the project had been recently revived by a local engineer, armed with a more solid technology, who presented his drawings for the royal couple's inspection. The Queen, who fancied herself a patron of enlightenment, aware of the need for judicious reforms in politics and manufacture, put the proposal out to be studied by competent ministers and local savants. Exclude the thought of sacrilege, she instructed them; think only of feasibility.

The answer came back: Yes, it is feasible. Did not the people of ancient times, without any of our wonderful modern means at their disposal, build higher and with greater precision than one would have thought possible? And to dismantle is easier than to raise up. If a human machine of many tens of thousands of laborers could erect that marvel, the Great Pyramid at Giza, a similar mobilizing of energies and obedience by a visionary ruler could achieve another marvel, the lowering of Vesuvius. But changing the shape, scaling it down, would not alter the mountain's nature. It would not deter an eruption or make it easier to channel. The danger was not the mountain but what lay under the earth-pedestal on which the mountain was set, far below.

But it can be done, said the Queen irritably. Yes, it can be done. Then we shall do it, if we so decide. Remote as they were from the god-kings of the ancient Mediterranean, these enlightened despots still laid claim to rule with absolute power sanctioned by a divine mandate. In fact, their authority had been steadily undermined by mockery, by enlightenment. In fact, they no longer had anything resembling absolute power at all.

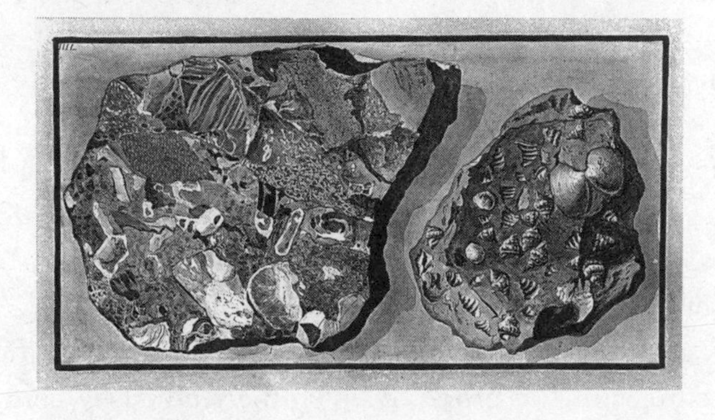

3

It had been freakishly cold that winter throughout the peninsula, from Venice, where the lagoon froze over and could be crossed on foot, even skated on as in a Dutch painting, down to Naples, whose winter was even harsher than the one seven years ago that had done in poor Jack. Snow stayed for weeks on the lava-paved streets and covered the mountain. The hail was as withering as a rain of hot ash. Orchards and gardens perished, along with the less hardy of the tens of thousands of the city's poorest, who lacked even a roof between them and the icy wind. Among the well-sheltered the unprecedented rigors of the season stirred up a mood of apprehension. Surely such anomalies were not mere facts of nature. These were emblems, equivalents, harbingers of a catastrophe that was on its way.

•

Like a wind, like a storm, like a fire, like an earthquake, like a mud slide, like a deluge, like a tree falling, a torrent roaring, an ice floe breaking, like a tidal wave, like a shipwreck, like an explosion, like a lid blown off, like a consuming fire, like spreading blight, like a sky darkening, a bridge collapsing, a hole opening. Like a volcano erupting.

Surely more than just the actions of people: choosing, yielding, braving, lying, understanding, being right, being deceived, being consistent, being visionary, being reckless, being cruel, being mistaken, being original, being afraid . . .

•

That spring, Vesuvius continued to be active, bringing more travelers to the city to marvel at it, sketch it, when possible climb it, and creating an ever greater demand for pictures of the volcano in all its moods, which skilled artists and local image-purveyors stepped up their production to supply. And by late July, as news of the fall of the Bastille spread, demand fell sharply for images of the volcano as the crowning element of a serene landscape. Now everyone craved an image of Vesuvius erupting. Indeed, for a while hardly anyone painted the volcano another way. Both to the revolution's partisans and to the horrified ruling class of every European country, no image for what was happening in France seemed as apt as that of a volcano in action—violent convulsion, upheaval from below, and waves of lethal force that harrow and permanently alter the landscape.

Like Vesuvius, the French Revolution was also a phenomenon. But a volcanic eruption is something perennial. While the French Revolution was perceived as unprecedented, Vesuvius has been erupting for a long time, is erupting now, and will erupt again: the continuity and repetitiveness of nature. To treat the force of history as a force of nature was reassuring as well as distracting. It suggests that though this may be only the beginning, the beginning of an age of revolutions, this too will pass.

The Cavaliere and those he knew did not seem directly threatened. Statistically speaking, most disasters happen elsewhere, and our capacity for imagining the plight of those disaster strikes, when they are numerous, is limited. For the time being we are safe and, as they say, life (usually meaning the life of the privileged) goes on. We are safe, though everything may be different afterward.

To love volcanoes was to put the revolution in its place. To live in proximity to the memory of a disaster, to live among ruins—Naples, or Berlin today—is to be reassured that one can survive any disaster, even the greatest.

•

The Cavaliere's beloved had never stopped writing to Charles. She had written to plead with him, reproach him, denounce him, threaten him, and attempt to rouse his pity. Three years later, she still wrote almost as often. If Charles was not her lover, then he had to be her friend. So large was her gift for fidelity that she rarely understood when people didn't like her or had had enough of her. She had such an aptitude for being pleased that she couldn't imagine Charles would not welcome her letters, be glad to know about her doings and those of his dear uncle, whom she was doing her best to make happy (wasn't that what Charles wanted?) and who was so kind, so generous to her.

She wrote of accompanying the Cavaliere on climbs up the mountain, and how she never saw so fine a spectacle, though she pitied the moon, whose light seemed pale and sickly alongside that of the erupting volcano (it took little to get the fountain of her compassion flowing); and of going with him to the excavations at Pompeii, where she mourned the people who had perished so many centuries ago. Unlike Catherine, who had never entertained the idea of climbing Vesuvius and had not enjoyed being taken in her husband's entourage to contemplate the dead cities (though she had visited them with William), she was ready to do everything, anything the Cavaliere proposed, and seemed to have unlimited energy. If she could, if he would have permitted it, she would have gladly gone, booted and bundled up in furs, on the boar hunt with the Cavaliere (she was an excellent rider, which he did not know). She would have watched the King standing waist-deep in bloody offal and found some way to enjoy the ghastly sight, though she was not in the least voyeuristic—reaching into a not very large personal experience of that kind of savagery (though her lover before Charles, the father of her daughter, who had taught her to ride, had been an animal-slaughtering country squire) or into what she was learning from books.

Amazing, yes. Once I saw . . . I mean, it's like, it's like, like . . . Homer, she might have exclaimed. And not have been entirely wrong.

The Cavaliere watched her fondly as she expanded to her role as his companion, as a lady in training. She had always been a very quick learner. That was how she had survived, and how she triumphed.

She was, he thought, taking his impress as clay does a sculptor's thumb. She was buoyantly, expertly accommodating. The ways in which he had to accommodate to her were slight. He had to restrain in her presence some of his natural tendency to ironical statement. Clever as she was, she could not follow him there. Both by temperament and by class, she was not sensitive to irony. Her temperament had virtually nothing in it of melancholy, which is the obverse of irony; and she was not born to that kind of snobbery which prides itself on an indirect expression. Irony is the staple response of the English gentleman expatriate to the weirdness, the uncouthness of the locals among whom he finds himself obliged (even if it be by his own choice) to live. Being ironical is a way of showing one's superiority without actually being so ill-bred as to be indignant. Or offended. The young woman saw no reason not to show herself offended when she was; or not to be indignant, which she often was—never at injuries done to her (of these she was very indulgent, or easily placated), but at an injury or slight done to others.

If she had a snobbish reaction, she could only express it directly. Oh lordy how vulgar they was, she would exclaim, returning from an evening out—the Cavaliere took her everywhere, and everyone welcomed her. Nobody is as good, as wise, as attractive as you, she said to the Cavaliere.

And no one, thought the Cavaliere, was as versatile as she.

As a woman she has become, like the Cavaliere, another champion intervener. Her sphere of activity is the one usually claimed by women: paying attention to feelings, to ailments. Another talent unfolded: a quickness to divine what others were thinking, feeling, needing; what others wanted, wanted for themselves, wanted her to be. Egocentric though she might be, her most predictable sentiments were admiration, loyalty, sympathy . . . not the passions of a narcissist. Anyone's emotional distress brought her to tears. She cried at the spectacle of a child's funeral in the street, at confidences she received during a party from a young American silk merchant sent abroad on a mission by the family firm to get over the woman who had jilted him. Anyone's physical distress made her think she could do something about it. She concocted a Welsh folk remedy for Valerio's headaches. Anyone's silence made her try to draw the taciturn person out. She tried to talk to the young man with one eye who is the Cavaliere's guide. Oh, his poor eye!

•

In 1790, after spending her first post-Bastille year in Rome, the itinerant Elisabeth Vigée-Lebrun arrived for a prolonged stay in Naples, inevitably furnished with an introduction to the city's leading patron of painters both local and foreign, whose companion happened to be a young woman who had been one of the most famous painter's models of the era. Vigée-Lebrun lost no time in asking the Cavaliere to commission from her a portrait of his much-depicted charmer and the Cavaliere gave his consent with alacrity, agreeing to a substantial fee. He already owned some dozen portraits of her. He could not have too many. Probably he gave no thought to the fact that this would be the first portrait of her by one of the few professional painters who was a woman.

Since the Cavaliere's companion was still a model, not yet a subject, the question was which figure from myth, literature, or ancient history she would represent. Vigée-Lebrun decided, not without a little malice, to paint her as Ariadne. The moment chosen is after Ariadne has been unceremoniously dropped off by Theseus, much against her will, at Naxos. Though it must be soon after, Ariadne looks anything but desperate. In the foreground, just inside a grotto, wearing a long loose white dress partly covered by the meandering fall of her luxuriant auburn hair from her shoulders, over her belly, to her plump knees, she is sitting on a leopard-skin rug, leaning against a rock, one hand held decoratively against her cheek while the other clasps a brass goblet. She has her back to the entrance, facing the grotto's interior, as if both the spectator, whose gaze she meets with wide-eyed inane candor, and the source of the brilliant light that irradiates her face, her bosom, her bare arms, were farther inside the grotto. Behind her lies the open sea and far in the distance, on the horizon line, a tiny ship. Presumably it is the one commanded by Theseus, the hero whose life she had saved and who had promised to take her back to his homeland and marry her, but who, instead, has cast her off in mid-passage and left her to die on this deserted island.

Yes, it must be her lover's ship—just picking up wind in its sails after the treacherous, cowardly deed. It cannot be the ship of Dionysus, the god of pleasure and wine, who will rescue her, and make her *his* consort, thereby supplying her with a destiny far more glorious than the one she had thought the best she could do. Not being a mere mortal, Dionysus does not need to arrive by ship. He can just fly in. But perhaps he has already flown in, and it is he in the rear of the cave, preparing to make love to Ariadne, and she has already forgotten Theseus, who is barely out of sight (and, though relieved to be rid of her, feeling a bit remorseful, as remorseful as a cad who also thinks of himself as a gentleman ever gets), and she has already drunk the wine the god had proffered to become more dry-eyed (Forget

Theseus! But I have . . .), more loose-limbed, in anticipation of their embraces.

Or is it just the spectator who is being seduced, here in the rear of the cave, as the real woman seduced everyone, shone her bright glorious emphatic smile on everyone. But not with the directly suggestive smile in the painting. She is more wholesome, more anxious to please, less self-confident than that. Never, in all the portraits made of her, was she depicted so patently as a courtesan. Unpleasant depiction by one independent woman surviving out in the great world by her wits and talents, of another woman at the same perilous game. But impudent as the portrait was, it was a success. The artist knew her patrons. She must have wagered that the Cavaliere (infatuated) and the young woman (innocently vain) would not see the portrait as others might see it, would see only one more tribute to her all-conquering beauty.

Among the large number of roles and personae that she deemed herself suited to play, there was a special pleasure in portraying women whose destiny was so unlike her own happy one, such as Ariadne and Medea, princesses who sacrificed all —past, family, social position—for a foreign lover and then were betrayed. She saw them not as victims but as persons who were inordinately expressive: persons affecting and heroic in the intensity of their feeling, in the recklessness and wholeheartedness with which they gave themselves to a single emotion.

She elaborated her Attitudes, improved the stagecraft and the dramaturgy. It was not necessary anymore for the Cavaliere to stand nearby, holding a taper. She was lit by two tall thick candles, placed on either side behind screens. Sometimes she used human as well as physical props. The Countess de ***, another refugee from the appalling events in Paris, who had settled in Naples, near the court ruled by the French queen's sister, to await the prompt punishment of the godless revolutionaries and the restoration to their full, divinely prescribed powers of their revered majesties Louis XVI and Marie Antoinette—this countess had a daughter, a sallow clever child of seven or eight, about the same age as the daughter whom the Cavaliere's companion had not seen for more than four years (and the small sum for whose yearly board Charles now paid, on the Cavaliere's instruction, from the revenues of the estate in Wales) and who, she fancied, resembled her daughter, or what her daughter (poor abandoned babe!) must look like now. She wept thinking of her daughter, and conscripted the countess's daughter into the Attitudes. Before the Cavaliere's guests one evening she constructed three tableaux vivants with the child. These materialized in strobe-like succession, for she no longer needed even the slight pause afforded by covering herself between one Attitude and the next.

The first subject was the rape of the Sabine women, the emotion was terror, and the moment was the mid-flight capture of a young Roman matron, vainly attempting to escape with her child clasped to her bosom. She had prepared the nervous, trusting child for this subject, showing her pictures from the Cavaliere's books. But the two subjects that followed were inspired improvisations. In a single movement, she pushed the child's body to the floor and pulled upward on the little arms, locking the hands in prayer, took one step back, seized her by the hair, and pressed a dagger against her throat. Applause and "Brava, Medea!" Then she fell to her knees, enveloping the petrified swooning girl with her whole body, her frame contorted by a silent frozen sob, and received the consecration of "Viva la Niobe!"

It was beyond acting, thought the Cavaliere, watching with his guests. And once again he was struck by how extraordinary were her powers of imagination, of sympathy, for emotions that she could not have known, and basked in the *bravas* as if they were praise for himself. What an amazing creature she was.

•

It was the beginning of the age of revolutions, it was the beginning of the age of exaggeration.

The young woman was becoming everything he wanted her to be. It occurred to the Cavaliere that he might consider the hitherto unthinkable, becoming the one thing she wanted him to be—though she had the grace never to mention it.

What more could he want to possess in the autumn of his life than this adorable, and adoring, creature?

Look how she won everyone over.

A small party, only fifty guests, in honor of the Duke del ***. The Cavaliere's consort presiding on her side of the long table. She was wearing a Greek robe, a chiton, which the Cavaliere had ordered made for her, after the robe worn by Helen of Troy on one of his vases. While she was dressing, Mrs. Cadogan had refused to let him enter. And when she appeared he was overcome. She looked as beautiful as ever—could one say more?

On her right was the rubicund, perfumed Prince ***, a notorious local seducer; on her left, Count ***, a notorious local bore. She had an amazing talent for pleasing, bending her lovely face now to one, now to the other. She counter-seduced the seducer, by talking to him of the charms of his wife, and with such ingenuity and fervor that even he began to think fondly of that much ignored woman, becoming more interested in his dinner partner's astuteness than in her snowy bosom. She enthralled the bore, too, with less difficulty, by listening to him go on about each one of his social triumphs on a recent trip to Paris, and how he had met a lawyer named Danton and the journalist Marat and, though it was not well thought of here to say so, found the revolutionaries not the ogres and would-be regicides he had expected but men of common sense, who wanted only to bring some much needed reforms, such as could be carried out under a constitutional monarchy. Yes, she said. Yes. I see. And then? And what did you say? Oh. What a clever reply.

She laughed loudly, and lifted her glass first to one, then the other. The Cavaliere listened to her voice, relished the sheen of her cheek. From time to time she looked at him, received the nod of his approval. No matter how busy she was with others—

and no one listened more ardently than she—he felt she never ceased to be aware of, passionately concentrated on, *his* existence, as if to say: I do all this for you, so you will be proud of me. What more could a Pygmalion ask than that?

Now the count was boring the woman on his left, the Princess ***, with his ideas about the turmoil in France: that the revolutionaries were anything but hotheads, and would pull back from the brink, you'll see, had no interest in plunging the country into chaos or disturbing the relations of France with the other powers of Europe, etc., etc.; and while the princess was still in the middle of her vaguely assenting reply, the man on *her* left, Sir ***, who had been listening to the count's words, and had just taken in what was meant by them, interrupted impetuously and, talking past the head of the princess, over her head actually, as if she did not exist, as a man will often do when his interest is piqued by what another man has just said, denounced the count as a damned republican and subversive, and spilled his wine, and caused the whole table to stop talking, and while the Cavaliere interposed his calming affability and the Cavaliere's consort added her earnest agreement with what Sir *** had said about the dangers of the situation in France (the opposite of what Count *** had said), but said it in such a warmhearted and innocent way that the boring count did not feel betrayed; indeed, each man felt that the Cavaliere's spirited and lovely young companion was in agreement with him on that vexatious subject. So winning were her social skills—in spite of, no, even because of, the indelible streak of commonness, thought the bewitched Cavaliere. She was warm, she was bounteous. He could not live outside the summer of her smile. And he tipped his fine dry smile toward her as the uproar about the damned events in France subsided, and she swung back to him, cheeks flushed, glorying in his approval, and raised her glass of red wine to him, blew him a kiss, and drank it in one endearing, admittedly less than elegant, draught.

When the right person does the wrong thing, it's the right

thing. And so she was, he had concluded (flushed with joy, he had no need of wine), eminently, surprisingly, inexhaustibly, right for him.

She had returned now to amuse Prince ***, who, lacking any opinions at all about the events in France, was sulking, and to whom she had apparently promised to tell the story of something that had happened when she came to Naples with her dear mother four years ago, a mere girl, as she said, unschooled in the ways of the world, before her dear friend and protector had taken her in hand, but knowing enough to have been immediately enamored of the city—the story of a horrendous drama that had taken place a few weeks after her arrival.

But you'll not believe it, she said.

What, dear Mrs. Hart, said a visiting English lady seated across from her.

Eighteen murderers what had taken up residence in the courtyard—

How many?

Eighteen!

And then she proceeded to tell how a bandit gang, pursued by the municipal soldiers, had broken into the courtyard and seized two of the servants, a young groom and a page who was one of the household musicians, and, threatening to cut the hostages' throats, had barricaded themselves in the eastern wing of the courtyard, and how the soldiers wanted to charge and take them but the Cavaliere had refused permission for them to enter, wishing to avert the inevitable carnage and particularly concerned to save the lives of the groom and the violinist, who lay trussed up in a corner, and how they had camped there for a whole week—

A week?

Yes! And built fires and sang and shouted and drank and committed indecencies with one another, which, alas, she had been obliged to witness from a window, because they, she and her dear mother and the Cavaliere and the entire household, were prisoners too, unable to leave the mansion, of course they had plenty to eat and to drink, and she had her lessons and the Cavaliere had his books and his studies, but still they were much at the windows looking down on the eighteen murderers, who had begun to quarrel among themselves, though they had to keep the windows closed because of the appalling odors—you can imagine the source, she added unnecessarily—for the dear merciful Cavaliere had insisted that some food be lowered to the courtyard twice a day, in the morning and in the evening, partly to win their confidence and partly because he could hardly let poor Luca, who was only fifteen, and Franco, the violinist, starve, and what with the foul odors and the frenzied shouts and insolent songs of the quarreling murderers, and the racket of the soldiers camped outside, with little to do themselves but drink and quarrel, so it went on, until on the sixth day—was it the sixth day, she looked over at the Cavaliere, asking him to help her with this least vivid detail of her story, thereby acknowledging that it was his story as well, that they had shared this daunting adventure together; and he said, smiling gallantly, the seventh day, actually; ah, the seventh day, she cried triumphantly—and on the seventh day the Cavaliere succeeded in persuading the bearded chief of the band of murderers to surrender the two hostages (both grey with terror and covered with lice) unharmed, and since their situation was hopeless, eventually they would have to surrender, they would only seal the worst of fates if they did not do it now, and he, the British ambassador, promised that he would speak to the soldiers and tell the soldiers not to beat them and that after he would appeal to the King for as much clemency as was possible, if they would give themselves up. And, she concluded, they did.

I trust the brutes were all executed, said a lady across the table. As they deserved.

Not all, said the Cavaliere. The King is a goodhearted man and much given to acts of clemency, particularly to members of the lower orders.

What an astounding story, someone said.

And entirely true, she exclaimed.

And so it was, the Cavaliere reflected, except that it had happened to him a quarter of a century earlier, to him and Catherine, soon after he arrived to take up his post and the city, with the famine barely over, was still in a state of near-anarchy: a story he had told the girl and that she was now telling as something that had happened to her. Of course, embarrassed as he was while listening to her tell it, embroider it so prettily, he was never tempted to interrupt and correct her, saying, no, when that happened you were not here with me. You were not even born. And once she finished, embarrassment was succeeded by anxiety that her fabrication would be exposed by someone at the table who would dimly recall having heard of the incident, which had happened so long ago, and she would be humiliated and he, her sponsor and lover, would look like a fool. But when it seemed that there was no one within earshot familiar with the story, his anxiety subsided and what he felt was a pang of disillusionment, for he had discovered that his darling was a vulgar braggart and a liar. And that feeling was succeeded by a quite different, more compassionate one: for then he felt alarmed, fearing for her reason, wondering if this meant that she often failed to know the difference between a story she had heard and an experience of her own. And then he felt annoyed and a little sad, taking the lie as evidence of her immaturity, no, her insecurity, supposing that she had appropriated his story because she felt she didn't have enough interesting stories from her own life to tell, at least stories that could be related in general company. And finally he felt neither embarrassed nor anxious nor disillusioned nor alarmed nor annoyed nor saddened . . . but touched, immensely, joyously moved by this sign of how much a part of him she felt, to the point of such total surrender of her dear person to his care and tutelage that she no longer knew where she left off and he began. It seemed like an act of love.

•

Like Ariadne, the Cavaliere's companion was to have a more glorious destiny than she had thought possible. Vigée-Lebrun was more right than she knew—which does not make the intention behind the portrait any kinder.

Never trust an artist. They are always different from what they seem—even the most conforming, who live themselves as courtiers. Vigée-Lebrun flattered the Cavaliere, accepted many favors from him, won commissions for portraits from other local notables and a considerable social success, largely thanks to his patronage and hospitality. She was a frequent guest at the mansion in town, and in July and August was often invited to be one of a small party driving out to the three-room cottage above the beach at Posillipo, where the Cavaliere and his companion spent the hottest hours of the day, returning home only when the first breezes rose in the late afternoon. She flattered the Fair One, who, credulous as always, thought the painter was her friend. Never trust an artist.

But never trust a patron either. The following year, the Cavaliere and his new life journeyed back to England—it was the Cavaliere's fourth leave home since his arrival in Naples with Catherine twenty-seven years earlier. It had been a difficult time for new acquisitions; his expenses were mounting; he had no great treasures to sell: just some "restored" (that is, heavily filled-in) statues, an assortment of armor, candelabra, phallic amulets, coins of dubious provenance, and two paintings supposedly by Raphael and Guercino. There was one other item in the Cavaliere's cargo. It seems that during a hot summer afternoon spent at the little house in Posillipo, Vigée-Lebrun had impulsively sketched two small heads in charcoal on one of the doors. Gift of the artist. Which the Cavaliere had seen no reason not to turn to profit, as she was to complain in her memoirs many years later—for he'd had the surface of the door sawn off and was carrying it back to England to sell.

•

The Cavaliere was ready to do the scandalous, the unthinkable. His royal foster brother's smile, when the Cavaliere alluded to the possibility of a marriage, was at best a tacit permission; he knew the daughter of Mrs. Cadogan could never be presented as his wife at the English court. Before leaving Naples, however, he had had a private moment with the Queen, who assured him that at the court of the Kingdom of the Two Sicilies there would be no obstacle to receiving this charming young lady of whom she, the Queen, was already so fond, once she was made a legitimate wife; and so there was no reason not to make her, and himself, happy.

Surely Charles, who has not married despite all his efforts (and never will), would understand. And as for the relations and friends who might laugh behind his back at an old man (he was sixty-one) giving his name to a notorious beauty of the humblest origin—let them go to the devil. He had been a rational voluptuary long enough. Too long.

Would Catherine, Catherine who understood him so perfectly, have recognized him now? No.

At first he told no one except Charles of his intention, though his sisters and oldest brother and all his friends had already concluded among themselves that this disaster was unavoidable. They stayed in a hotel. Mrs. Cadogan left to visit relatives. Then he, Charles, and the young woman went off to Wales, where he consulted with the steward of the estate and looked over the accounts. She gazed at Charles with maternal solicitude and placed flowers daily on Catherine's tomb. During the third week of their stay, she begged leave to visit her daughter in Manchester, whom she had not seen for so many years. And she asked the Cavaliere for some money to give to the family rearing the girl, and other small sums for a cousin and an ailing uncle and aunt in the village where she was born, which her mother would transmit. She had always kept in touch with her relations and sent them gifts from Naples; and the Cavaliere was gracious and would not think of refusing her, despite his money worries. So she went off . . . and wept and fell in love with her daughter and wept some more when she had to leave her. She dreamed of bringing the child back to Naples; nothing would have made her happier. But she did not dare ask this of the Cavaliere, though it was unlikely he would refuse her anything; she knew it would embarrass him (no one would believe she had been married before) and she knew, too, that if the child were there, she would love her more and more and perhaps love the Cavaliere less. She was shrewd enough to know her success with him required that he have her undivided attention.

So the child must be, was, sacrificed.

And for this the young woman never forgave herself; and, perhaps, not the Cavaliere either.

It was summer now and they returned to London. The Cavaliere decided to pay a week-long visit to the frail elderly Walpole, whom he feared he might be seeing for the last time, and show the amusing excesses of his friend's pseudo-mediaeval castle, Strawberry Hill, to his companion, who went into ecstasies over the painted windows and the dim religious light, in which she was moved to perform for their admiring host a spirited rendition of the mad scene from Paisiello's *Nina*. Back in the city, a letter for the young woman offering an engagement at the London Opera House at two thousand pounds a year was awaiting them. Tell Gallini you have already been engaged for life, the Cavaliere said with a smile, amused to hear himself say something so fatuous and so charming.

In their London life there were meetings of the Royal Society and the Society of Dilettanti for the Cavaliere, who could not resist also going to some picture auctions. And the young woman went to spend time with her old friend Mr. Romney, to tell him of her glorious life in Naples, and he listened gravely, and drew her as she talked; he would use her once more as a model, this time for a painting of Joan of Arc, while her station still permitted it. She babbled on, and asked him to give her regards to Mr. Hayley and to tell him that his book on self-control had been her bedside reading, she truly had become serene, and look at her now, she was a real lady, and could speak Italian and French and sing and everyone liked her, and the King of Naples flirted with her and squeezed her hands, but he meant no harm, but the Queen, oh the Queen, who was a wonderful woman, and such a wonderful mother, who had just given birth to her fourteenth child, though some of them had died—alas, the King would not leave her alone, she said, he was a man, so he did not have much self-control, and had his way too with the young peasant women employed in the royal silk factory on the grounds of the palace at Caserta, who were said to be his private harem—this dear Queen had become a true friend to herself—she came up the back stairs of the palace, for of course she could not be received officially because, she stammered, until, she corrected herself—what she meant was that she and the Queen had become true friends and she had a wonderful life and only felt a little sorry for Charles, who had not managed to marry the heiress, and was all alone, and it was not good for a man to be alone, even though Charles still had his seat in Parliament and his collection of stones and the management of the Cavaliere's estate to occupy him, and as he must be having money problems, she was going to ask the Cavaliere to help out with a gift or a little loan that might—

And Romney, busy drawing her luminous auburn tresses, looked up. He began to tell her of his trip last year to Paris, where he had met a virtuous painter named David, who had put his art at the service of the revolution (he, Romney, had recently done a portrait of a Mr. Thomas Paine, who was one of its sympathizers), and that he had to confess to his old friend, trusting in her discretion, that he was much impressed by the revolutionaries and by their ideas. For instance, Romney explained, the revolution wants to make inheritance divisible and divorce possible and slavery unlawful, all reforms that any right-thinking person would agree are much overdue. And the young woman, who would have been just, if all there were to justice was generosity, was promptly of his opinion. Why indeed should first-born sons inherit everything (condemning younger sons like Charles and the Cavaliere to lifelong anxieties about money), and why should people who make each other unhappy not be able to make themselves happy with someone else legally, and yes, what was more horrible than slavery: she had heard of the horrors of slavery, for instance in Jamaica, which abominable trade had made one of the Cavaliere's cousins, owner of most of Jamaica's sugar plantations, the richest man in England. All this she could not help agreeing to. And apart from the justice of the revolutionaries' ideas, as Romney explained them to her (she had never heard them described like this), the ardor with which he spoke of the revolution and the cleansing flame of liberty which would burn up the dry dead wood of the old society made her heart surge—ardor always inspired her—and everything Romney said was so convincing and so beautiful, and there seems little doubt that had she stayed in London the Cavaliere's beloved would have been a secret revolutionary sympathizer too, at least for a while.

In September she began to sit for a formal portrait by Romney to be titled *The Ambassadress*—the first time she was painted as herself, no longer a model but a subject, at last. In the background is a dark, fiery Vesuvius—signifying Naples, where her husband-to-be was the envoy; signifying the Cavaliere as well. And, to ratify the picture, the third day after the sittings began, there was a marriage ceremony at the small exclusive church of St. Marylebone in the presence of five of the Cavaliere's relations and friends and Mrs. Cadogan. When Charles arrived, paler than usual, he took his seat in the third row of the church. His mother, the Cavaliere's favorite sister, had refused to attend. This was not a marriage for England—the Cavaliere could not avoid seeing the condescending smiles—but for his other, second life, such as remained to him (another twelve years, if he believed the sibyl's prophecy), in Naples. Even the Fair One, who loved to please and thought she usually did, could not deceive herself into thinking the Cavaliere's relations were anything but disapproving of the marriage, however happy she made him. The only relation who seemed to like her was the immensely rich cousin whom the Cavaliere had told her was very eccentric and, as a result of his eccentricities (which the Cavaliere promised to describe some other time), was himself shunned by the rest of the family and unwelcome at court; and so, the Cavaliere explained, although he had been a great admirer of his dear Catherine, was perhaps a natural ally of their marriage, one of the few. For he had several friends, Walpole for instance, and his young cousin, who knew what it was to defy convention in the interests of happiness, and would not find scandalous the Cavaliere's seeking his happiness with her.

At the reception following the ceremony, this cousin, a young man hardly older than herself, was particularly gracious, taking her hands in his and looking into her eyes—he had fine curly hair and a full mouth—and said in his high, strange voice that he was glad to hear she had made the Cavaliere happy, and that in this life it was important to follow one's dreams. And the Cavaliere's bride said politely, a little timidly, that she hoped the Cavaliere's cousin would be moved to visit Naples again, where she could have the pleasure of entertaining him and coming to know him. And of course she extended an invitation to Charles, but really meant it, who knows when she would see him again. She said, roguishly, Now you can keep your promise to come to Naples.

On the following day, the very eve of their departure, she extracted a promise to visit them from several of the Cavaliere's friends. She felt fluttery about going back. It seemed odd to be the same person as the one who had gone abroad for the first time, sent to a faraway country to visit her lover's uncle, an innocent girl, already (unbeknownst to her) betrayed, and now a woman with everything a woman could want: a distinguished husband, life, world. Oh, please come and see it!

Once they had crossed the Channel, most of these London feelings vanished: the wish to include everyone in her happiness, her triumph—and the budding pro-republican sympathies Mr. Romney had inspired in her, for during their stop in Paris she had the unexpected honor of being presented to Marie Antoinette and entrusted by the queen with a letter to give to her royal sister. An instant re-convert to the cause of monarchy everywhere, the Cavaliere's wife devoutly carried the letter back to *her* Queen.

•

1793. They had been back a year. His contentment bloomed, unfolded.

Not that he hadn't been happy before. Not that he hadn't almost always been happy. But the Cavaliere's command of gratification had depended on his being able to take up the right distance from himself and from his passions. His happiness had had the self-consciousness of a view claimed at the top of a mountain, and the deliberate contrasts of one of those busy paintings of a scene, observed from a high angle, in which some people are sowing and tilling, others are bringing harvest to market, others are getting drunk in the village square, children are playing, lovers are fondling each other . . .

Of course he had known happiness! But his happiness had been composed of many small parts, like a portrait in mosaic that doesn't read as a face until you stand back. Now he could stand as close as he wanted and see both the tiny fragments and the large bewitching face. He still had the same tastes, still liked to read, fish, play the cello, climb the mountain, examine marine specimens, have a learned conversation, look at a pretty woman, acquire a new painting—the world was a theatre of felicity. But now it had one person at the center, unifying it. His heart's choice was as affectionate as ever—her warm flesh against his, she was ripening. And she was interested in everything. She accompanied him to the new excavations at Paestum (she had entirely concurred with his disparagement of the brutal, primitive Doric columns of the Temple of Neptune), she was studying botany so she could help him advise on the completion of the English garden at Caserta, she adored the life of the court, she seemed fascinated by his vases and rock collections. He had only to stretch out his hand to something and it was his.

He yielded gratefully to the experience of satiety. Inevitably, some of his collecting zeal began to abate. It was no longer the chase that obsessed him, but the sheer joy of ownership. He derived no less pleasure from looking at the things he possessed and showing them to others and seeing their admiration and envy. But his need to add to his collections had slackened. Financial interest more than desire now drove him to continue to acquire new pictures, vases, bronzes, ornaments. The collecting desire *can* be enfeebled by happiness—acute enough, erotic enough happiness—and the Cavaliere was happy, as happy as that.

Reports on the newlywed couple went back to England. The Cavaliere, people said, is as amorous as ever, his lady no less vulgar, with the accent and manners of a barmaid, braying, bawling, cackling. Few deigned to add that she seemed extremely goodhearted. They were a most improbable couple—the reformed kept woman and the unapologetic, elderly aristocrat with his exquisite manners and indefinitely expanding horizons of appreciation—and, thanks to the unique demands and generic permissions of this southern setting, a very successful one. She had become a wife without forfeiting the attentiveness and charms of a mistress. She helped him, not just as a wife (or not just as Catherine did) but as a collaborator. Her talents twinned with his. For he always had to spend a great deal of time with the King, and now she spent a great deal of time with the Queen. Their tasks are symmetrical: he to be first in the King's favor and she to be first in the eyes of the Queen.

The Cavaliere must keep up with the King's diversions. She must keep up with the Queen's burdens. Moderately intelligent, which makes her far more intelligent than her husband, the Queen has all the cares of an immoderate number of births and a partial understanding of political realities to add to her normal duties, frustrations, and distractions. The Cavaliere's wife, with her great capacity for taking in information and for identifying with someone, quickly became an ideal confidante. She and the Queen write each other every day. Rowing vigorously in the polyglot sea of the era, the Austrian-born Queen writes not in German or in Italian or in English but in an ill-spelled French. She signs herself Charlotte. There are visits several times a day as well as daily letters.

Secret Jacobin sympathizers in Naples added to their defamatory portrait of the royal couple the charge that the Queen and the Cavaliere's wife are lovers. And the charge has been vigorously denied by beauty snobs, who cannot imagine a physical relationship between the Cavaliere's wife and a woman of forty with a dramatically homely face and a body abused by fourteen childbirths—grounds of denial that are as much a cliché as the allegation. (The Queen had real power, and a woman in power, feared as virile, is often accused of being a slut. An ampler anti-royalist campaign in France had featured charges of incest as well as lesbianism against her sister.) The charge was false. The effusive sentimental temperament of the Cavaliere's wife rarely flowed into the erotic. But she did have a great need for the affection and friendship of women—indeed, she enjoyed the company of women more than of men. She loved being unbuttoned with women, as she could be in her bedroom with five or six of her maids on a hot afternoon, gossiping, trying on her clothes, having a glass or two, listening to their love griefs, showing off the latest dance or a new cap from Paris with white feathers. That was when she felt most like a woman, surrounded by her adoring maids and by the mother whom she kept by her side the older woman's entire life. Their prattle calmed her. And then she would make them fall silent and hold their breath, make their eyes shine and go moist—as hers would too—with a song.

•

Autumn 1793. The Queen, her dear Charlotte, cannot help conjuring up the scene.

Portrait of a woman condemned to death. In the cart transporting her to this, this, this . . . machine, this new machine, her hands tied loosely behind her, her hair cropped short to expose her nape. Portrait of a martyr. She is all in white: a simple dress, coarse stockings, a shapeless bonnet on her head. Her face is old, tired, and drawn. The only trace of her former glory is her strict and upright posture.

She blinks her eyes. They sting because she has been so many months in prison. The cart wheels rattle and bump. The streets are strangely silent. The sun is shining. The cart arrives, she mounts the ten rough wooden steps. There is her chaplain murmuring prayers, staring at his crucifix, tears streaming down his face. And a voice, someone else's voice, saying, It will not hurt, Your Majesty. It seems to come from the man with the hood. She averts her eyes from the ladder-like structure, some fourteen feet tall, with its ax-shaped blade rusty with blood, and she feels her shoulders being pushed down on both sides, making her lean over, no, lie down, her stomach and legs on the board, lie just so. Someone pulls her by the shoulders a little forward, so her throat rests in the trough of the bottom half of a wooden yoke, and then the upper part closes down on the back of her neck. She feels a strap squeezing her waist and another being affixed to her calves, binding her to the board. Her head is over the dark-brown plaited basket, the blood rushes forward to her face. She resisted the weight of her head pulling it down, held it out to see over the platform the bobbing heads of the crowd, lifted it up to lighten the painful contact of the edge of the board with her collarbone, the yoke against her gorge, which made her gag, which was starting to cut off her breath, saw a pair of large muddy boots advancing toward her and heard the bellowing of the mob go still louder, then go silent; here's some kind of strange creaking: something rising, higher, higher; the sun getting brighter, so she shuts her eyes; the sound, higher still, stops—

No!

The Queen tossed in her bed and groaned, then woke, parted the curtains of her bed, and stood up. She had slept only fitfully for weeks, waiting for news from Paris. Because of the worsening situation in France they were now at the mercy of the British—the only country strong enough and with the will to oppose the tide of revolution. The British naval commander who had anchored in the bay for five days, Captain Nelson, had won a great victory over the French, and been most encouraging about British resolve; but the Queen placed little trust in military solutions. Though the offer of a ransom had been refused, she dared to be hopeful. To kill a king was already unthinkable. And killing their king should have sufficed them. What could they want from a foreigner, a woman; surely they would not execute her young sister.

Would not, could not . . .

When the news came that Marie Antoinette had been executed, there was consternation at the court. The Queen retreated to Portici, her favorite of the royal palaces. It was feared she would go mad. She refused to see her children (she had just given birth a fifteenth time); she refused to bathe or change her clothes. She howled with rage and despair, chorused by her tribe of forty German-speaking maids. Even the King was moved by his wife's grief, though he had not much luck in consoling her, since every attempt at tenderness ended in his becoming aroused and trying to mount her. Her husband's embraces were the last thing the Queen desired. She was vomiting convulsively. Doctors wanted to bleed her. The Cavaliere's wife spent every day at the palace, joining her in shrieks and cries, bathing her head, and singing to her. Only her singing calmed the Queen. Music cures. When the King's grandfather, Philip V, had tumbled into the abyss of depression, the greatest voice of the earlier part of the century, that of Carlo Broschi, known as Farinelli, had brought relief.

Until the appearance of the wonder-working castrato at the Bourbon court in Madrid—where he would be detained at a vast salary for nine years—the stuporous monarch would neither eat, drink, change his clothes, nor rule. For nine years Farinelli would arrive at the royal bedchamber every evening promptly at midnight, and until five in the morning would sing the same four songs over and over, interposing the songs with elegant conversation. And Philip V would eat and drink and let himself be washed and shaved, and look over the papers that his ministers had left him.

So the Cavaliere's wife, with her beautiful voice, calmed the Queen. Day after day she went to the palace to sit with the Queen in a darkened room, returning home red-eyed to the Cavaliere late each evening. Never have I seen anything so piteous, she said. The dear woman's grief knows no bounds.

With her indefatigable gift for empathy, she was almost as grief-struck as the Queen. But the Queen became calmer, between bouts of tears, and the Cavaliere's wife did too.

The Queen returned to the city and took her seat at the Council of State.

She was a woman, said the Queen. Only a woman.

(Majesty!)

But I will have my revenge.

(How can the puny Kingdom of the Two Sicilies punish mighty France?)

God will punish France, and the English will help God, and we will help the English, said the Queen.

(You mean the English will help us, said the prime minister.)

Yes, said the Queen. Our friends.

And so they—he—did.

•

The Cavaliere's mazy backwater, so rewardingly isolated from transforming events, was being dragged into what passed then for the real world, the one defined by the threat of France. As was this fastidious spectator himself.

A club calling itself the Society for the Friends of Liberty and Equality began to meet in secret to draw up plans for modernizing the kingdom, and quickly divided into two clubs, one in favor of a constitutional monarchy and the other determined to go all the way to a republic. Someone was indiscreet, a plot to assassinate the King was discovered or concocted, and of those arrested, who included jurists, professors, men of letters, doctors, and scions of some of the oldest noble families in the kingdom, nine were sentenced to severe prison terms and three were executed. The Queen boasted bitterly of the extreme clemency of Neapolitan justice, in contrast to the carnage in France. The lava of the revolution was flowing, the Terror was just reaching its climax—and in June 1794, nature rhyming with history, Vesuvius erupted with a violence that had no precedent in the Cavaliere's experience. It was the worst, or best, eruption since 1631, and would be counted the third greatest in the nearly two millennia of the volcano's modern history.

The volcano was not to be patronized, after all, by such stale categories as grandeur and interest and beauty. This was terror —blackening day and bloodying night. In the evening sky, a roar of broad flame streamed sideways and upward, as if seeking to flee the thin diagonal orange slash of the descending lava. The inky sea turned red and the moon blood-orange. All night the swath of descending lava widened. In the brief interregnum of pale dawn, ropes of pitchy smoke were unfurling, climbing, fattening at the top into a sky-high funnel of smoke and fire, which became steadily more columnar, first materializing a stack of bulging rings of smoke around its stem, then widening to engulf them. By midday the sky had gone dark and the sun was a cloud-blackened moon. But the roiling bay was still blood red.

A paralyzing, silencing vista.

The greatest shock to the Cavaliere came when a more indifferent light had washed the sky and the customary distant view had returned. It was as painful as the sight of a leafy, many-branched, centuries-old tree gone diagonal, cleaved through the heart of its trunk. The mountain cannot fall, like a great tree brought down in a hurricane, but a mountain can be mutilated. And like the dismayed homeowner in her yard who has to admit that while winds of such velocity might have been enough to do in the tree, it was already in trouble, and points to the exposed innards of the fallen trunk, a repulsive, termite-rotted, crumbly brown, so the admirer of a shapely volcano has to think that some weakness in the volcano's retaining walls made this indignity inevitable. The force of the eruption had lopped off one-ninth of its height, slicing the summit flat at the top. The Cavaliere's wife wept with pity for the mountain, which had become ugly. The Cavaliere, feeling something not too different, professed to find in the mountain's new shape only a destiny—and a fresh reason for a quick ascent, as soon as the eruption had subsided.

Tolo, are you there?

Yes, my lord.

I should like to see.

Yes, my lord.

At the end of June, attended by a now bearded Bartolomeo Pumo, the sixty-four-year-old Cavaliere reached the top of the dramatically changed mountain he had been climbing for thirty years. The cone was gone. In its place there was now a huge jagged crater.

I would like to stand closer.

Yes, my lord.

But the ground was burning through his thick-soled boots, and he was choking from the noxious exhalations of sulphurous and vitriolic vapors.

Tolo, are you there?

Yes, my lord.

Shall we retreat?

Yes, my lord.

He should have been frightened, but he was not. The mountain had a right to explode. The destructive mission of the volcano inspired in him a satisfaction, an increasing satisfaction, that he would have found hard to acknowledge.

But what could be more apt for this great collector of valuable objects than to have also been collecting the very principle of destruction, a volcano. Collectors have a divided consciousness. No one is more naturally allied with the forces in a society that preserve and conserve. But every collector is also an accomplice of the ideal of destruction. For the very excessiveness of the collecting passion makes a collector also a self-despiser. Every collector-passion contains within it the fantasy of its own self-abolition. Worn down by the disparity between the collector's need to idealize and all that is base, purely materialistic, in the soul of a lover of beautiful objects and trophies of the glorious past, he may long to be purged by a consuming fire.

Perhaps every collector has dreamed of a holocaust that will relieve him of his collection—converting all to ashes, or burying it under lava. Destruction is only the strongest form of divestment. The collector may be so disappointed with his life that he wants to divest himself of himself, as in the novel about the book-besotted reclusive scholar with a legendary hoard of twenty-five thousand necessary, irreplaceable volumes (that dream, the perfect library), who pitches himself into the pyre he makes out of what he has most loved. But should such an angry collector survive his fire or fit, he will probably want to start another collection.

4

He was often described as little. Certainly he was short, a good bit shorter than the Cavaliere and his young wife, and thin, with an arresting tanned face set low on his large squarish head, thick brows, heavy-lidded eyes, a deep philtrum below his bold nose, full lips, a wide mouth already missing a fair number of teeth. When they first saw him, he had not fought any important battles. But he had the look, the hungry look that evinces the power to concentrate utterly on something, of one destined to go far. Mark him, said the Cavaliere—an expert on promise, or the lack of it, in younger men—he will be the bravest hero England has ever produced. The Cavaliere's spurt of recognition was not so remarkable. A star is always a star, even before the right vehicle has been found, and even after, when the good parts are no longer available. And the thirty-five-year-old captain was undoubtedly a star—like the Cavaliere's wife.

She, despite her large talent for effusiveness, had not seen *that*. Yes, his arrival had been thrilling, it was thrilling to stand with the Cavaliere at the window of the observatory room and watch the sixty-four-gun two-decker ship he commanded, the *Agamemnon*, sail proudly into the bay only seven months after wicked France had declared war on England. And his brief stay had been memorable—mainly because of the role she had played. He had brought urgent dispatches from Lord Hood for the Cavaliere. Neapolitan troops were needed to reinforce the coalition gathering to defend Toulon, where a royalist faction had seized power, against the advancing republican forces; and it was she who had got him his six thousand troops when the Cavaliere could get neither a yes nor a no from the frightened King and his advisers, got them by the route women use, the back stairs, taking the request to the bedchamber of the most powerful voice on the Council of State, who lay in seclusion, about to give birth to a sixteenth prince or princess, and securing her support. Invited to dine at the royal palace, he had the place of honor at the King's right, and the Cavaliere's wife, seated on his right, translated his attempts to converse with the King about the French menace and the King's long rambling anecdote about a giant boar he'd killed which turned out to have three testicles. She was satisfied that she had impressed him. His visit lasted five days. After came many other distinguished visitors. She did not single him out.

He left. History promoted him. It was a time for concentrated men of preposterous ambition and small stature who needed no more than four hours of sleep a night. Under the canopy of many skies, on the rocking sea and the lurching ship, he gave chase to the enemy. He had many battles to his credit now. War confiscated parts of his body. The *Captain*, mounting seventy-four guns, then another seventy-four, the *Theseus*, was his island, kingdom, vehicle, platform. Five years passed. He became a hero, *the* hero to the rulers of Naples, who lived in terror of the small concentrated man who had taken over a fractured revolution and transposed its energies into a seemingly invincible campaign for the French conquest of Europe and the dethroning of old monarchies everywhere. He will save us, only he can save us, said the Queen. The King assented. The British envoy, representing the extension of British power, could only agree. In the last two years he had exchanged many letters with the young captain, now an admiral, in which the Cavaliere described his efforts to win cowardly Naples to the British cause. The Cavaliere's wife had been writing him, too. She loved to admire, and here was someone really worth admiring. She needs her fix of rapture. She needs it more and more often.

Ricocheting around the Mediterranean, the lake of war, he kept them informed, succinctly, of his accumulation of fearful injuries.

Everything was simple, physical, painful, exalting. The world consisted of the four elements—land and water, firepower and distancing air. Of the many sail-of-the-line whose command he coveted, each with its resonant name, history, seasoned in sweat and blood, his was now the seventy-four-gun *Vanguard*, carrying more than six hundred officers and men. He spent as little time as possible in his large, luxuriously furnished admiral's cabin. Day and night he paced the deck. He had the privilege of always seeing the sun rise and set. He had unobstructed views. In the water you are always moving, even when you are still. Birds floated above like tiny kites and vertical canvas clouds unfurled, tilted, crumpled, pivoted, arched into the wind, dragging the ship forward into the weather; movement is always into the weather. Cycles of light, cycles of duties—he oversaw them all. When he grew very tired, he stood on the quarter-deck, immobile, and let himself be seen. He believed that the sight of him standing there had a certain magic—he had seen it work on his men, and not only at the height of battle—and he believed it frightened the enemy. It did.

Avenged, cried the Queen, when news reached Naples that the young admiral's fleet had destroyed the French fleet on the Nile. Hype hype hype ma chere Miledy Je suis folle de joye, she wrote to her dear friend, the English ambassador's wife, who had fainted when she heard the news, the joyful news of his victory. I fell on my side & I hurt myself but what of that, she wrote the admiral. I shall feal it a glory to dye in such a cause

—no I wood not like to dye untill I see & embrace the Victor of the Nile.

•

And the hero vaulted into their lives.

September 22, 1798. Leading the small flotilla of impressive boats swathed with emblems that came out in the midday heat to meet the *Vanguard* was the royal barge, piloted by the admiral of the Neapolitan fleet, Caracciolo, with the King and Queen and several of their children under its spangled awnings, followed by a barge with musicians from the royal chapel. The barge with the British flag carried the Cavaliere and his lady, sumptuous in blue and gold, the Bourbon colors: a blue dress with gold lace, a shawl of naval blue with gold anchors, and gold anchor ear-rings. The royal band had got the tune of "Rule, Britannia" right, and the Cavaliere was smiling, thinking of the words.

All thine shall be the subject main;
And every shore it circles, thine.

Close behind mingled some five hundred feluccas, barges, yachts, and fishing boats swaying and bumping into one another, filled with shouting, waving people. As the royal party and the Cava-liere and his wife started to board the ship, they cheered the King, and the hero took off the green eye shield he wore and put it in his pocket.

Our liberator, said the King. Deliverer and preserver, said the Queen. Oh, cried the Cavaliere's wife when she saw him, haggard, coughing, his hair powdered but too long, his empty right sleeve pinned to the breast of his dress uniform, a red gash above his blind eye where he had been struck by a fragment of grapeshot during the Battle of the Nile. Oh! And she fell against him.

She fell into my arm, it was a very affecting scene, the hero told his wife in a long letter describing the magnificence of his reception: the bay teeming with boats to welcome him, the banners, the gun salutes, the cannon booming from the ramparts of Sant'Elmo above the city, and the *vivas* of the crowds bedecked in velvet and braid reaching out to him when he landed, surging after him through the streets. Sunlight hurt his eye when he didn't wear the shield, and Naples was filled with sunlight. But blessed evening came, with its splendid display of fireworks that ended in the British flag and his initials limned across the sky, and bonfires and dancing in the steeply pitched squares. My greeting from the lower classes was truly affecting. In the Cavaliere's mansion three thousand lamps were ablaze for a banquet attended by the deferential Admiral Caracciolo, which he enjoyed and endured.

His right arm ached, the phantom arm that started high up near his right shoulder, he was racked with coughing spasms, he had a fever. He had been holding himself in, he hated to complain. He'd always been small and thin, but he was sturdy. He knew how to endure the unbearable. Feeling ill was like a wave. One had to hold on and it would pass. Even the agony of the amputation, without a swig of rum, and the additional agony, due to the surgeon's ineptness, as the stump suppurated for three months, even that was just a wave.

Like the waves rocking the boat of pain—the little boat that rowed the hero away from the battle he never had a chance to fight. The boat he had stepped out of a right-handed hero, drawing his sword to lead a nighttime amphibious assault on a Spanish fort; the boat that received his senseless body as he fell backward, his right elbow shattered by grape, and which his frantic men turned around and out into the bay, hoping to reach the flagship before he died from loss of blood. He had regained consciousness, clawing at the tourniquet near his shoulder, as they were passing one of his cutters, which had been hit below water and was sinking, and he had insisted on stopping to pick up the survivors—more waves, another hour before they reached the darkened *Theseus*, swaying at anchor. Raging at those who would have helped him, Let me alone! I have my legs left, and one arm!

he twisted a rope around his left arm and hauled himself on board, called for the surgeon to come and cut off the right one, high up, where the tourniquet was, and a half hour later was on his feet, giving orders to his flag captain in a severe, calm voice.

Now he was a left-handed hero.

And what was his bravery compared to that of the captain of the eighty-gun *Tonnant* last month at the Battle of the Nile, who lost both arms and a leg to British round shot. Refusing to allow himself to be taken below, this Dupetit Thouars called for a tub of bran to be brought up from the galley and directed that he be immersed in it to his collarbone, and went on issuing gunnery orders for another two hours until blood and consciousness drained out of him. The last words from the head sticking out of the tub of soggy red bran were to implore his crew to sink their ship rather than surrender. Now there was a gallant man! exclaimed the hero—whose hero-world had a large, necessary place for bravery, and abominable pain, bravely borne.

And for cowardice too: the crew of the *Tonnant*, after observing that the head of their captain would speak no more, moved the ship out of range, surrendering it to the British victor two days later. But is it not the aim of a hero to make cowards of his enemies?

A hero was stoical. And a hero was also candid about his thirst for glory. A clergyman's solemn son whose mother had died when he was nine, he had gone to sea at twelve, his head filled with noble models from books; he loved to quote Shakespeare and saw himself as Hotspur, without the miserable end: gallant, impetuous, warmhearted . . . and, therefore, covetous of honors. He did not see himself as gullible and vain. He admired valor, steadfastness, generosity, frankness. He wanted to approve of himself. He wanted not to let himself down. He intended to be a hero. He wanted to deserve praise, to be decorated, remembered, to figure in history books. He saw himself in history paintings, as a portrait bust, as a statue on a pedestal, or even atop a high column in a public square.

He had wished to be taller but he loved himself in dress uniform. He had a wife in England, a widow he had married for love and to whom he considered himself devoted, and whom he had last seen when he was sent home a year ago to recover from the botched amputation. He admired her dignified character and her taste in clothes and considered that she had honored him by agreeing to be his wife. He had taken his stepson Josiah, Fanny's only child by her first husband, to sea with him, and kept her informed in his weekly letters of the youth's progress and misbehavior. He no longer expected children of his own. His fame would assure the continuation of his name, his great deeds would be his progeny.

He had begun training himself to write rapidly and legibly with his left hand within two days after the amputation, though he found it hard not to keep watching that new animal, the back of his left hand—it felt as if someone else were writing his letters and dispatches.

He did not want to feel weak, and up to now he had never felt weak, not even in the boat, nor when the surgeon did as he was ordered. Perhaps he never felt weak because no one had ever really comforted him or treated him as a suffering person. He had announced as a child that he was not to be treated as a child, that he was strong and that no one should worry about him, he was there to worry about them; and ever since, his father, his brothers and sisters, his wife, had taken him at his word. People wanted to believe in him; that was part of being a star.

He protested to the Cavaliere and his wife that he wished to stay in a hotel. They would not hear of it. He was put to bed in the best, upper apartment in the British envoy's residence. He begged the Cavaliere's wife not to fuss over him. All he needed was to be alone for a little while, and he would recover. The house was very large in the Italian way, staffed with more servants than an English mansion of the same standing, as one would expect in a backward country, but she insisted on doing many of the nursing chores herself, assisted by her mother. He fainted soon after he was put to bed, and woke to the country voice and country ministrations of Mrs. Cadogan. 'Ere now, don't be feared, I'll not 'urt you, let me lift yer shoulder. . . . He remembered how his wife flinched when dressing his wound each day, how shocked she had been by the sight of the hot red ulcerous stump. Meanwhile, the Cavaliere's wife opened the windows wide and described to him the stupendous view of the bay and Capri and the smoking mountain in the distance, which, he knew, was of special interest to the Cavaliere. She told him court gossip. She sang to him. And she touched him. She cut the nails of his left hand and bathed his poor gashed forehead with milk. When she leaned over to wash and trim his hair, the smell from her armpits was like oranges or, sweeter, like lilies; he'd never known a woman could smell like that. He kept his eyes closed and breathed it in through his nostrils.

She seemed to admire him so much, and he enjoyed that.

Like everyone else, he knew her story: the fallen woman, taken under the Cavaliere's protection, who had become an irreproachable wife. But she had a warmth and directness that is never found in the world of courts. And sometimes she asked questions that no well-bred lady would have asked. For instance, she asked him about his dreams, rather an impertinent question, but he enjoyed it. The trouble was that he didn't have any dreams, none that he could remember, only memories—of battles, of the noise and the blood and the fear. There was one dream that he'd had several times recently: he dreamed that he had both arms. He would be on deck in the thick of battle, feelings clenched, holding the spyglass to his eye with his right hand and beckoning to Captain Hardy with his left; the scene was utterly lifelike, both exactly as it was and as it could be painted, except that since it could no longer be so (he didn't remember if he had his eye back, too), he knew that it must be a dream and would will himself awake. But he couldn't relate this dream. It would sound like a plea for sympathy.

He tried to make up some dreams. Dreams appropriate for

a hero. I dreamed, he said, that I was mounting a large staircase. Or: I dreamed, he said, that I was standing on the balcony of a palace. Or, fearing these sounded too vainglorious: I dreamed I was alone, in a valley, wandering in an immense field filled with flowers. And . . . (Go on!) . . . I dreamed of galloping on a horse, I dreamed I was crossing a misty lake, I dreamed I was at a great banquet—no, that sounded too insipid.

What the devil does someone dream? Had he forgotten how to converse with a beautiful woman? Hell and damnation! He was no better than a beast. All he'd thought about for so long was maps and tactics and the readiness of cannon and weather and horizon lines and lines of battle and sometimes the woman in Leghorn and always Napoleon and now the pain in his right arm, the missing arm, the ghostly pain.

Tired and feverish as he was, he would try again.

I dreamed I was in a theatre—no. I was dreaming that I had gained entrance to a castle and had found a secret room—no. I remember, yes, I was on a cliff, below me a raging flood—no. I was crossing a sea on the back of a dolphin and heard a voice calling me, the voice of a mermaid—no. I dreamed, I dreamed—

She must have divined he was making them up, to entertain her. He wouldn't have found these dreams convincing; they sounded like pictures. He didn't mind making them up. He only wished they were better inventions. He was looking for a poetical manner . . .

•

Sometimes it's acceptable not to tell the truth, the full truth, when relating or rendering the past. Sometimes it is necessary.

According to the norms of history painting at that time, the artist must preserve the larger truth of a subject from the claims of a literal, that is, inferior, truth. With a great subject, it is that subject's greatness which the painter must endeavor to depict. So, for instance, Raphael was praised for drawing the Apostles as noble in body and demeanor, not as the mean, lumpish figures he assumed that scripture was telling us they were. "Alexander is said to have been of low stature; a Painter ought not so to represent him," declared Sir Joshua Reynolds. A great man does not have a mean or vulgar appearance, is not maimed or lame, does not squint or have a bulbous nose or an unsightly wig—or if he does, these aren't part of his essence. And the essence of a subject is what a painter ought to show.

We like to stress the commonness of heroes. Essences seem undemocratic. We feel oppressed by the call to greatness. We regard an interest in glory or perfection as a sign of mental unhealthiness, and have decided that high achievers, who are called overachievers, owe their surplus of ambition to a defect in mothering (either too little or too much). We want to admire but think we have a right not to be intimidated. We dislike feeling inferior to an ideal. So away with ideals, with essences. The only ideals allowed are healthy ones—those everyone may aspire to, or comfortably imagine oneself possessing.

•

A mermaid!

What, dear sir?

He must have fallen asleep for a moment. She was looking at him tenderly.

Embarrassed, he murmured, Did I finish telling you?

Yes, she said, you were in a royal castle where the king and queen was giving a great banquet in your honor, such as we want to give in a few days if you be well enough, to celebrate your birthday and express the eternal gratitude of this drooping but fine country what has been picked up and saved by your valiant self.

Of course I am well enough, he said, and tried to stand up and groaned and fell back in a faint on the bed.

•

She loved to watch him sleeping, with his left hand between his thighs, like a child. He looked so small and vulnerable. Fighting back the ache in her womb, she was glad she could say "we"—my husband and I, the Queen and I: we feel, we admire, we care, we are so grateful, we will show you how grateful we are. Which she did.

Never had the Cavaliere's mansion seemed so splendid or been so brightly illuminated as one week later, on the hero's birthday, when it was turned into a shrine to the hero's glory.

It was like one of his boyhood daydreams, everyone calling his name and hailing him, and he raised his glass as toast after toast was offered to the savior of the royalist cause. Just as he imagined it—except that he was lifting his glass with his left arm, and his right arm ached, it burned, and he still felt feverish and a little queasy, perhaps it was the wine. He was normally very abstemious.

He took in the smiles and the gay dresses of the ladies, the Cavaliere's wife radiant in a gown of blue satin, and the flowery tributes; above all he saw his name, his initials, his face—on candelabra, vases, medallions, brooches, cameos, sashes—multiplying wherever he turned. His hosts had kept the local pottery works busy these last weeks. He and they and the English residents and the officers from his squadron anchored out in the gulf had dined on plates and drunk from goblets emblazoned with his initials. And when the eighty at table adjourned to the ballroom to join the two thousand more guests whom the Cavaliere and his wife had invited to dance and to take supper, ribbons and buttons decorated with his illustrious name were distributed to everyone. He slipped eight of each inside his right sleeve to send back to Fanny and his father and some of his brothers and sisters, to show how he had been honored.

How are you, dear sir, the Cavaliere's wife had whispered, taking his arm as they walked toward the ballroom.

Very well, very well.

He felt very faint.

Under a canopy in the center of the vast room stood something tall draped with the Union Jack and his own blue ensign. For a moment he had the absurd fancy it was a piece of one of the *Vanguard*'s masts. He approached it, the Cavaliere's wife still holding his arm. He wished he could lean against it for a moment.

Don't lean on it, she said. It was as if she could read his mind. It's a surprise, you see, but it ain't too steady. We wouldn't want it to fall down!

Then she left him to join the Cavaliere, who was standing near the musicians. The dancing was about to begin, and he wondered how he would negotiate that. He did not want to be seen sitting down. But the dancing was not starting yet, for the musicians had struck up "God Save the King," which the Cavaliere's wife stepped forward to sing. What a beautiful voice she had! She seemed to give new life to the familiar inspiring verses, and then, yes, he had heard correctly, his name. "First on the rolls of fame," she was singing.

Him let us sing;
Spread we his fame around,
Honour of British ground,
Who made Nile's shores resound—
God Save the King!

And he was blushing as the thousands in the great ballroom began to applaud and cheer, and when she repeated the new verse, beckoning to the whole assembly to join her, they all sang his name, his praise. Then she and the Cavaliere came toward him, and the hubbub subsided as she pulled the flags from the mast-like object under the canopy to unveil a column on which was engraved the conqueror's *Veni vidi vici*, and the names of the captains in the Battle of the Nile, his brothers-in-arms, almost all of whom were present, who came forward to clasp his arm and respectfully reaffirm their gratitude for the privilege of serving under him. The Cavaliere stood beside the column and made a short speech of welcome comparing him to Alexander the

Great, the close of which the Cavaliere's wife interrupted, crying that there should be a statue of him made of pure gold and placed in the middle of London, and would be if those at home understood how much they owed him—he felt quite aureoled. And then many others crowded around him, beaming at him, some pawing him, as people do here, and smiling, smiling. Oh, if only his father and Fanny could see him now!

He turned to the Cavaliere to make his speech of thanks for this magnificent celebration. The honor you do me, he began.

It is we who are honored, said the Cavaliere, and now it was he who took the hero's arm.

Then the musicians began to play and the hero, supposing that the Cavaliere's wife expected him to partner her in the quadrille, went toward her. No, no, not to dance, she would have to understand, but to try to express his thanks.

The Cavaliere, as besotted with the young admiral in his way as his wife was in hers, looked on fondly. How brilliant the occasion, as after an eclipse. All that was black now seemed resplendent, luminous. His house and all the bright and eloquent things in it which he feared he might soon have to abandon, his house—now the official quarters of the hero—harbors the future as well as shelters the past.

•

He had thought his expatriate paradise was foundering. In the earlier months of the year, as the international alliance against France seemed to be failing, Naples was bending to French will. First came the indignity of having to receive as the new ambassador none other than Monsieur Garat, the man who had read out the death sentence to Louis XVI. Then the influential anti-French prime minister had been dismissed and replaced by one favorable to an accommodation with the French. Meanwhile, Napoleon's armies advanced with impunity and the young British admiral was still roaming the Mediterranean looking unsuccessfully to engage the French fleet.

The Cavaliere didn't panic, that wasn't his nature. Still, suppose the French army should start advancing down the peninsula from the papal capital, which they already controlled, and one morning he learned that they were just up the coast, beyond the Campi Phlegraei. There would still be time for him and his wife and any of their English guests (there were always guests) to flee; he had no worry about that. But he did fear for the safety of his possessions. Things that are valuable are also vulnerable—to theft, fire, flood, loss, mistreatment, the negligence of servants and employees, the lethal rays of the sun, and war, which to the Cavaliere meant mainly vandalism, looting, confiscation.

Every collector feels menaced by all the imponderables that can bring disaster. Which is to say that every collection—itself an island—needs an island. And grandiose collections often inspire grandiose ideas of proper storage and safekeeping. An indefatigable collector in southern Florida, who travels about on his buying expeditions in the last private train in the United States, has acquired a gigantic castle in Genoa to store his vast assemblage of decorative objects; and the Nationalist Chinese, who in 1949 packed up in rice grass and cotton all the portable masterpieces of the fine arts in China then above ground (silk paintings, small sculpture, jades, bronzes, porcelain, and calligraphy) to take with them to Taiwan, keep them in tunnels and vaults hollowed out of a mountain next to a huge museum with room to display no more than a tiny fraction of their booty. Most storage places need not be so fanciful or fortress-like to be safe. But stored in a place that does not feel secure, the collection is a constant source of anxiety. Pleasure is haunted by the phantom of loss.

Who knows, it may not be necessary to flee Naples. But if it is, three decades of accumulation are not easily packed, crated, moved. (The Wandering Jew can't be a major collector, except of postage stamps. There are few great collections that could be put on someone's back.) The Cavaliere thought it wise to have on paper exactly what he has, to make—for the first time—a complete inventory.

This was hardly his first list: collectors are inveterate list-makers, and all people who enjoy making lists are actual or would-be collectors.

Collecting is a species of insatiable desire, a Don Juanism of objects in which each new find arouses a new mental tumescence, and generates the added pleasure of scorekeeping, of enumeration. Volume and tirelessness of conquest would lose some of its point and savor were there not a ledger somewhere with one's assorted *mille e tre* (and, preferably, a factotum to keep it updated), the happy contemplation of which at off-moments counteracts the exhaustion of desire that the erotic athlete is condemned to and against which he struggles. But lists are a much more spiritual enterprise for the athlete of material and mental acquisitiveness.

The list is itself a collection, a sublimated collection. One does not actually have to own the things. To know is to have (luckily, for those without great means). It is already a claim, a species of possession, to think about them in this form, the form of a list: which is to value them, to rank them, to say they are worth remembering or desiring.

What you like: your five favorite flowers, spices, films, cars, poems, hotels, names, dogs, inventions, Roman emperors, novels, actors, restaurants, paintings, gems, cities, friends, museums, tennis players . . . just five. Or ten . . . or twenty . . . or a hundred. For, midway through whatever number you settled for, you always wish you had a bigger number to play in. You'd forgotten there were that many things you liked.

What you've done: everyone you've gone to bed with, every state you've been in, country you've visited, house or apartment you've lived in, school you've attended, car you've owned, pet you've had, job you've held, Shakespeare play you've seen . . .

What the world has in it: the names of Mozart's twenty operas or of the kings and queens of England or of the fifty American state capitals . . . Even the making of such lists is an expression of desire: the desire to know, to see arranged, to commit to memory.

What you actually have: all your CDs, your bottles of wine, your first editions, the vintage photographs you've purchased at auctions—such lists may do no more than ratify the acquiring lust, unless, as it is with the Cavaliere, your purchases are imperiled.

He wants to know what he has, now that it may be lost to him. He wants to have it forever, at least in the form of a list.

For the Cavaliere it is a rescue mission. But despite this unpleasant incentive, he rather looked forward to the task. To look at each item he has collected, put the items in some sort of sequence, lay out the exact state of variety, profusion, excellence, and, yes, incompleteness of each of his collections: that would be a pleasure as well as a labor, a voluptuous labor, and one he would not delegate to anyone of his household.

Starting from the hall that led to the lower staircase, he went from room to room, floor to floor, memory to memory (it was all there), trailed by his pair of English secretaries, Oliver and Smith, who took down whatever he chose to say aloud, by Gaetano with a taper and a measure, and by a page who carried a stool. He had never seen his house in this unsettling light, as a stranger might—a servile curator, a taciturn assessor, or the bullying envoy of an art-coveting foreign despot. He was impressed. It took nearly a week to make the inventory; for he dallied, he doted. Then he retired to his study and spent a full day writing it up. Dated 14 July 1798, two months ago, set down in his careless but legible hand in many manuscript pages, then bound in reddish leather and laid in a drawer of his locked desk—excepting his collections of volcanic minerals, fish skeletons, and other natural wonders, it is all there: the more than two hundred paintings, including pictures by Raphael, Titian, Veronese, Canaletto, Rubens, Rembrandt, Van Dyck, Chardin, Poussin, many gouaches of Vesuvius in eruption, and the fourteen portraits of his wife that he owned, the vases, the statues, the cameos, down to the last candelabrum and sarcophagus and agate lamp in the cellar storerooms, leaving out items that would be immediately recognized as illegitimately acquired from the royal excavations.

That was the mood this summer, when Naples was waiting for the French to charge down the peninsula, and the Cavaliere, fortunate in being able to anticipate well in advance the end of the privileged life he'd known (this is not Pompeii or Herculaneum), made his inventory and started to think about how to evacuate his most prized possessions.

And now the danger had been turned back by the great victory his peerless friend had won against the French fleet, surely the beginning of the containment of the French incursion into Italy two years ago—which they were celebrating here on his birthday tonight. The Cavaliere had made arrangements for a major portion of his holdings to be sent back to England: his second collection of antique vases, much larger and finer than the collection brought back and sold to the British Museum on his first leave home. These were being meticulously packed by his agents and servants, and in a few days would be put in crates and then loaded on a British storeship lying in the harbor. It would be foolish to cancel these arrangements just because the menace of French occupation or (even worse) republican insurrection had receded. Let the vases go to England and be sold, he had decided. I need the money. Money, always a need. That was the base side of the collecting cycle—for collecting is a cycle, not a progress. The gallantry of it emerged at the nadir of the cycle, when the objects are gone and one started again from scratch. He consoled himself with thinking of the joy of making a new collection of vases, even greater than this one.

He looked forward to beginning again.

•

The Cavaliere is down at the quay supervising the loading of his crates of treasure aboard the *Colossus*. The hero is still in bed, but feeling stronger. Mrs. Cadogan brings him broth and the Cavaliere's wife sits with him while he works at his correspondence. To his brother, a parson like their father, he wrote to recount his victories and express concern that his services not be overlooked. Credit must be given me in spite of envy, he wrote. (He was hoping for a viscountcy for his victory on the Nile.) To Fanny he wrote letters even more frankly boastful. Like the Cavaliere's wife, writing to Charles all these years, artlessly repeating any praise of herself she heard, the hero repeated every word of praise to his wife. Everyone admires me. Even the French respect me. They were very similar, the mangled hero and the exuberant matron—with something childlike about both which the Cavaliere noted and was touched by.

People follow me in the streets and shout my name. He was up now, and it was the Cavaliere's wife who accompanied him to the royal palace for his parleys with the King and the ministers, to the harbor where his presence was needed to settle disputes between his sailors and the wily Neapolitans; I do all the enterprating for our grate guest, she wrote Charles. Her sympathies on behalf of his interests, his world, were tireless. She made friends with all his officers, and brought their concerns to the attention of their revered but distracted admiral. The avid learner having been supplemented by the indefatigable motherer, she helped the young midshipmen with letters to their sweethearts back in England and tried to teach Josiah the gavotte. When Josiah told her that it was he in the boat who had twisted the lifesaving tourniquet around his stepfather's arm, she leaned over and kissed the boy's hands. She sent presents and verses about the hero's glory to his wife, and when word came that he had only been made a baron, the lowest rank of the peerage, albeit with an annual pension of two thousand pounds, she dashed off a letter to Fanny to express her indignation at the Admiralty's ingratitude.

The Cavaliere, too, has written to the Foreign Office to protest the slight to the hero. They like nothing better than to be alone together. One evening in the Great Drawing Room, where forty of the paintings the Cavaliere owns are hung, they sketch out a homey routine. The Cavaliere plays the cello and his wife sings for the hero. At some point the Cavaliere tries to calm the hero's exasperation over the indecisiveness of the King, while the Cavaliere's wife watches with a deep feeling of happiness. One cannot expect such people to change, said the Cavaliere. By God, they *must* be brought to understand the disaster that lies before them, exclaims the hero, his left hand gesturing volubly and, as he becomes more agitated, the stump of his right arm visibly twitching inside the top of the empty sleeve. She gazes fondly at the Cavaliere, who is continuing his pithy exposition of the King's lamentable mental deficiency. She stares at the hero intently, her ardor covering him with its healing warmth. Then the three stroll out on the terrace to look at Vesuvius, which has been unusually calm of late. Sometimes the Cavaliere is in the middle and they are on either side, like his two aging children, which they could well be. Sometimes she is in the middle, the hero (shorter than she) on her left—she can feel the heat of his missing arm against her body—and the Cavaliere (taller) on her right. And the Cavaliere continues to recount some of the local superstitions about the mountain to the hero.

•

What is a hero supposed to look like? Or a king? Or a beauty?

Neither this hero, nor this king, nor this beauty have what Reynolds would regard as an appropriate appearance. The hero doesn't look like a hero; this king has never looked or acted like a king; the beauty, alas, is no longer a beauty. To put matters plainly: the hero is a maimed, toothless, worn, underweight little man; the King is a grossly fat man with herpes and a huge snout; the beauty, thickened by drink, is now large as well as tall, and at thirty-three looks far from young. Only the Cavaliere (aristocrat, courtier, scholar, man of taste) conforms to ideal type. He is tall, slim, fine-featured, intact; and, though much the oldest of these four future citizens of the universe of history painting, he is the one in the best physical condition.

Of course, it didn't matter to *them*. What is interesting is that we, who are so remote from the time when painting was expected to represent an ideal appearance, and who claim to find ugliness and physical imperfection humanizing, nevertheless find it worthy of explanation, and a little unseemly, when the out-of-shape and the no-longer-young are romantic with each other, when they (foolishly, as we say) idealize.

•

Their trio seemed so natural. The Cavaliere had a new young man in his life, more son than nephew. His wife had someone she could admire as she had never admired anyone before. The hero had friends such as he had never had; he was genuinely flattered by the admiration of the elegant old Cavaliere, overwhelmed by the warmth and attentiveness of his young wife. And, beyond the exaltation of ever more intense friendship, they were united in feeling themselves actors in a great historical drama; saving England, and Europe, from French conquest and from republicanism.

The hero felt quite recovered and was preparing to go back to sea. There were dispatches and letters to write, to ministers and influential titled friends in England and to other British commanders in the Mediterranean. There were meetings with Neapolitan ministers and with the royal couple and with the deposed but still powerful anti-French prime minister. The Bourbon government was perpetually in council about whether to stand up to the French, with the Cavaliere urging them to send an army to Rome and the hero eager for Naples to enter the fray, thereby becoming an open ally of (that is, military base for) England, adding his influential support to the plan. And once this ill-judged expedition had been approved, there were army maneuvers to review, and all this in an emotional brew of patriotism, feelings of self-importance, frustration, anxiety, and lively contempt for most of the local actors on the scene . . . as agents of a world empire always feel when struggling to have their way in a far-off southern satrapy rich in traditions of corruption and indolence, where they are trying to inculcate martial virtues and the necessity of resisting the opposing superpower.

His superiors sent word that he was expected with his squadron in Malta. Returning from a fruitless meeting with the Council of State, he had written Earl St. Vincent that he could hardly wait to sail away from this country of fiddlers and poets, whores and scoundrels. But he didn't want to leave the Cavaliere and his wife.

After three weeks of convalescence and adulation, in mid-October, a few days after the *Colossus* left for England with the Cavaliere's vases, the hero sailed for Malta in search of new engagements with the enemy. The King, knowing that he was expected to head an army and spend some time in his palace in the middle of stony Rome, went to Caserta to get some hunting in first. The Cavaliere removed to Caserta, too, after giving orders for the packing of his pictures to begin—just in case, just in case. And from the great lodge his wife wrote each day to the hero, telling him how much he is missed. In the evening the Cavaliere returned from a long day of exercise and the contemplation of gore, and added his postscript.

The daily killing of many animals raised the King's spirits, and he was looking forward to riding at the head of an army in a handsome uniform. The Queen, some of whose intelligence had survived the gradual wearing down of her spirits, began to have doubts about the wisdom of the expedition. It was the Cavaliere's wife, as she related to the hero in her letters, who persuaded the Queen not to lose heart. She had vividly evoked the alternative to taking the offensive now: the Queen, her husband, and her children led to the guillotine, and the eternal dishonor to her memory for not fighting bravely to the last to save her family, her religion, her country from the hands of the rapacious murderers of her sister and the royal family of France. You shood have seen me, wrote the Cavaliere's wife. I stood up & put out my left arm like you & made a wonderfull speach & the dear Queen cryed & said I was right. She often spoke frankly of his missing arm, for the hero was not one of those people who involve you in the obstinate ignoring of a mutilation or a disablement: the blind woman who tells you how well you look and admires your red blouse, the one-armed man who exclaims that he couldn't stop applauding last night at the opera. In the letters the hero retired to his cabin to write every evening, addressed jointly to both his friends, he spoke of it too. I have enough correspondence for two arms, he said. And it often fatigues me to write. But apart from the ultimate happiness of seeing you both again, there is nothing I can look forward to each day but the pleasure of writing you. He thanked the Cavaliere's wife for raising the martial spirits of the Queen. And he repeated how much he missed them both, how grateful he was for their friendship, his gratitude is more than he can express, how they had honored him beyond what he deserved—it's as if no one had ever before been kind to him—and that having lived with them and known their affection had spoiled him for any other company, that the world now seems a barren place when he is separated from them, that his dearest wish was to come back and never leave them. I love Mrs. Cadogan too, he added.

•

Ill again and in need of nursing, the hero returned three weeks later and joined his friends in Caserta. From there he and the Cavaliere's wife each sent letters to the hero's wife. She wrote about the hero's health, and sent more poems, more presents. He, in his weekly letter, told his wife that, with the exception of herself and his father, he counted the Cavaliere and his wife as the dearest friends he had in the world. I live here as the son of the house. The Cavaliere is kind enough to undertake my instruction in many interesting scientific questions, and his wife is an honor to her sex. Her equal I never saw in any country.

In another two weeks everyone was obliged to return to Naples, from which an army of thirty-two thousand inexperienced men—commanded by an incompetent Austrian general, nominally headed by the King, and including among its conscripts the Cavaliere's one-eyed guide, Bartolomeo Pumo—marched north to Rome. The Cavaliere and his wife are down at the quay with the cheering crowds seeing off the hero, who is to take four thousand more troops to seize neutral Leghorn and interrupt communication between Rome and the French armies occupying most of the northern part of the peninsula.

The hero noted with some concern that the Cavaliere looks rather frail, his back is stooped, and his wife is pale and clearly trying to be very brave. Come back to us soon, says the Cavaliere. With more laurels on your brow, says his wife.

A few hours ago she had given him a note which she'd made him promise he would not read until he was aboard the *Vanguard.* He had kissed the note and put it next to his heart.

He opened it a few moments after he stepped into the boat that would bring him out to his flagship.

There it was in her adorable hand: a torrent of wishes for his safety, protestations of eternal friendship, expressions of gratitude. But he was becoming greedy. He wanted more—something more. That she would tell him she loved him? But she told him that all the time, how much she, she and the good Cavaliere, loved him. Something more. Avidly he reached the last page, clasping the sea-sprayed pages he'd already read between his knees, as his men rowed him toward the *Vanguard.* Something more. Ah, there it was.

Do not spend time ashore wile in Leghorn. Forgive me dear frend if I say their is no comfort for you in that citty.

He winced. So she had heard the story of his only dalliance in all the years of his marriage; he knew it had been much remarked on. In Leghorn four years ago with the *Captain*, he had met a charming woman married to a cold, neglectful husband, a naval officer, and felt sorry for her, and then admired her, and then thought he might be in love with her—for five weeks.

He smiled. If his dear friend was jealous, then he knew he was loved.

•

Fools! Fools! That he had been a fool did not enter the Cavaliere's mind. Though he had been the first to believe the Bourbon government could create and field an army competent enough to take on the French, the Cavaliere was not used to blaming himself.

The hero had done his part, depositing his troops at Leghorn, where he remained for a chaste three days. But how could the hero have thought that France would permit Rome to fall to the Neapolitans?

Having signed a treaty of peace with France two years ago (Farce! Shame! Ignominy! raged the Queen), officially the Kingdom of the Two Sicilies was neutral, and the King and his advisers—astutely, as they think—have not declared war on France. This expedition, they announce, is not directed against France. It is only a fraternal response to an appeal from the people of Rome—suffering under the republican government imposed on them nine months ago by Jacobin fanatics—to restore law and order. The French general who had occupied Rome since February and under whose aegis the Roman Republic has been declared, prudently withdrew his soldiers to a few miles outside the city. After the Neapolitan army took Rome without needing to fire a shot, the King entered with the pomp he considered his due, went to his residence, the Palazzo Farnese, issued a call for the Pope, who had been banished by the republic, to return, and started to enjoy himself. Two weeks later France declared war on the Kingdom of the Two Sicilies, and the French army started back toward the city.

The evening of the day that the King heard the French were returning, he changed from his royal garments into an ill fitting disguise of commoner's clothes several sizes too small for his corpulent figure and left for home. That ignominious fiasco, the Neapolitan occupation of Rome, lasted barely another week. The hero had predicted that if the march on Rome failed, Naples was lost. His prediction was correct.

When most of the chapfallen Neapolitan army had reached home, after the King but ahead of the French, who were heading south in an orderly fashion, the Cavaliere sent for Pumo. He had worried about him. Had he survived his stint as a soldier, or was he lying somewhere in a ditch with a bullet in his head? Word came back that his guide had not returned. The Cavaliere was more incredulous than distressed. It was unthinkable that Tolo, his lucky Tolo, should not have known how to cope with this peril, as he had coped with so many others, but the rest of what was happening was exactly what he had feared.

The King was cursing and whining and crossing himself. The Queen, in fierce reaction against her fling with enlightened views, had lately become almost as superstitious as her husband, and was writing out prayers on small pieces of paper, which she stuffed in her stays or swallowed. To all about her, she declared that only an army of Neapolitans would flee from an enemy they outnumbered six to one, that she'd always known that these shiftless Neapolitans never had a chance to hold Rome. Anti-royalist slogans appear each morning on walls: the French are coming and, anticipating their protection, the kind of protection they had given the patriots in Rome, the Jacobin sympathizers were making themselves visible. The King's fiercely loyal subjects, the city's poor, paint the republican slogans out and gather in the great square before the palace to demand a denial of the rumors circulating that the royal family is about to flee to Palermo. They care nothing about their foreign Queen, but they want their beloved King to stay, he must promise them he will stay. Come out, show yourself, Beggar King! And the King was obliged to appear on the balcony, the Queen at his side, to show the mob that they are still there—that he will stay and fight the

French and protect them—while the Queen, gazing out at the square, blinked back her visions of the guillotine rising where the *cuccagna* used to be erected. The hero, to whom everyone looks for salvation, must evacuate them immediately. Life and death is in the hero's hands.

•

The Queen would not hear of entrusting the crown jewels and her diamonds and nearly seven hundred casks filled with bar and coined gold (worth about twenty million pounds) to anyone but the Cavaliere's wife. These were conveyed by night to the British envoy's residence, repacked with British naval seals, and then brought down to the port where they were taken out to the hero's flagship. And it was the Cavaliere's wife who found and explored a forgotten tunnel leading from the royal palace to the nearby small harbor, through which the rest of the portable royal assets, including the choicest paintings and other valuables of the palaces of Caserta and Naples and the best objects of the museum at Portici, as well as the royal clothes and linen, were carried on the backs of British sailors in trunks and crates and coffers, each consignment accompanied by a note from the Queen, and stowed on board the merchant ships in the bay.

The Cavaliere's wife, a torrent of energy and courage, was shuttling between the Queen and home, where she and her mother are supervising the sorting of clothes and linen and medicines—what women are supposed to know how to pack—while the Cavaliere gave orders for the crating of the cultural goods: his correspondence and papers, instruments and music scores, maps and books. Those servants who could be spared from the packing were sent off with notes in the hand of the Cavaliere's wife to all the British residents, telling them to start their own packing and be ready to leave on a day's notice.

The Cavaliere has retired to his study and reads, trying not to think about what is going on around him—one of the principal uses of a book.

Luckily, he had sent off all the vases two months ago, and most of the three hundred and forty-seven paintings were already packed. All of collecting Italy lived in terror of that insatiable art predator, Napoleon, who had obliged the cities he conquered to surrender paintings and other works of art as a kind of war tax. Parma and Modena, Milan and Venice, each had been assessed twenty selected masterpieces, and the Pope ordered to furnish one hundred of the Vatican's treasures, all for a "Triumphal Entry of Objects of the Sciences and Arts Collected in Italy" into the French capital staged this past July, two weeks after the Cavaliere had made his inventory, when a long procession of priceless artifacts, including the Vatican's *Laocoön* and the four bronze horses of San Marco, was paraded through the Paris boulevards, presented in an official ceremony to the minister of the interior, and then conveyed to the Louvre.

The French would have none of his pictures. But what about his collections of volcanic minerals, his statues, bronzes, and the other antiquities? Only some could be taken with him. What a burden it is, finally, to be a collector!

He had sometimes dreamed of a fire in which he stood paralyzed with indecision, unable to give the orders to his servants naming the few objects to be saved. And now the dream of loss has come true. But fleeing before the fire of war is still better than being caught in an eruption, in which he would have to rush into the street in his nightgown, carrying nothing, or attempt to carry out some of his things and be trapped by the descending lava. He can take a great deal. But not all. And everything is so dear to him.

•

The people are angry—and the hero has thought it prudent to move his ships farther out in the gulf, beyond the range of Neapolitan guns, where they are berthed now, rising and dropping in the turbulent water. On the cold rainy night of December 21st he landed with three barges, went to the palace, led King,

Queen, children, including their eldest son, his wife, the newborn baby and wet nurse, the royal doctor, royal chaplain, head gamekeeper, and eighteen gentlemen- and ladies-in-waiting through the secret tunnel to the harbor, and guided them across the craggy swell to the *Vanguard*. The Cavaliere and his wife and mother-in-law, to disguise their flight, had gone that evening to a reception at the Turkish ambassador's residence from which they slipped away and came on foot to the port. There they went aboard their own barge and were welcomed with shrieks of relief by those of their household chosen to accompany them. The Cavaliere's English secretaries seemed almost as overwrought as one expected the Neapolitans to be: the major-domo, two cooks, two grooms, three valets, and several maids in the service of the Cavaliere's wife. And Fatima, her new favorite—a beautiful black Copt, chastely held trophy from the Battle of the Nile which the hero had presented to her—broke down in sobs when she saw her mistress. Another barge carrying two ex-prime ministers of the Kingdom of the Two Sicilies, the Austrian ambassador, the Russian ambassador, and their dependents and servants, followed them out into the rising gale.

The hero hoped to sail early next morning: Neptune's trident was digging into his throbbing stump, there was going to be a storm. But the King would not permit the *Vanguard* to weigh anchor until seventy of his hounds were brought from Caserta and boarded onto one of the other British ships waiting to leave for Palermo. The King, who would not entrust even his hounds to a Neapolitan ship, stood on the deck of the *Vanguard* and chattered excitedly to the Cavaliere about the grouse hunting they would do in Sicily, while Admiral Caracciolo paced the deck of the *Sannita*, enduring his final humiliation. Not only had the royal family elected to be transported by the British admiral, but they had not confided a single crate of their belongings to the Neapolitan flagship. Finally, on the evening of the following day, the *Vanguard* was allowed to venture out of the gulf into the tremendous sea. It was following rather than leading a flotilla that included the two other warships in the hero's squadron; the *Sannita* and another Neapolitan warship, most of whose crews had deserted and which were now manned by British sailors; a Portuguese man-of-war; and the merchant ships, on which had been distributed two cardinals, a number of Neapolitan noble families, all the British residents, the French residents, many of them aristocrats who had fled the revolution, a vast number of servants, and most of the possessions of the Cavaliere and his entourage.

In all the many trunks that the Queen has insisted must accompany her, she had not thought to put bed linen. When this was noticed the Cavaliere's wife promptly gave up hers, Mrs. Cadogan made up a bed for the King, and he went to sleep. The Cavaliere's wife sat with the Queen on a portmanteau containing sixty thousand ducats in royal savings and held her hand. Her youngest child, six-year-old Carlo Alberto, lay on a mattress in a corner of the cabin in an unnatural-looking sleep, wheezing and sighing. Before leaving the Queen, the Cavaliere's wife brushed away the secretions of sleep from his eyes and wiped the clammy moisture from his pale face. The older royal children were out on the tilting decks, trailing the British sea-slaves as they frantically crisscrossed the ship to prepare it for the storm's attack, and getting in their way. They were fascinated by the tattoos and unhealed scurvy ulcers on the sailors' faces, necks, biceps, and forearms.

By the next morning the storm was at full strength, and each pitch of the ship seemed more extreme. The waves lashed the hull. The sky punched the sails. The oak of the hull cracked and groaned. The sailors cursed one another. The adult passengers did the mostly noisy things people do when they think they are going to die—praying, weeping, jesting, sitting tight-lipped. The hero, who avowed that he had never seen as fierce a storm in all his years of seafaring, remained on deck. The Cavaliere's wife went from cabin to cabin with towels and bowls, assisting passengers who were sick. The Cavaliere stayed in their sleeping cabin and retched until there was nothing left in his stomach. He tried to sip some water from a flask and noticed the tremor in his hand.

•

To the blind, every happening is sudden. To the terrified, every event is happening too soon.

They are coming for you, to take you to the firing squad, the gallows, the stake, the electric chair, the gas chamber. You have to stand up; but you can't. Your body, gorged with fear, is too heavy to move. You'd like to be able to rise and walk between them out the open door of your cell with dignity; but you can't. So they have to drag you away.

Or, *it* is coming, it is upon you, you and the others; bells or sirens have gone off (air raid, hurricane, rising flood), and you've taken shelter in this cell-like space, as out of harm's way as you can be, and out of the way of those trained to cope with the emergency. But you don't feel safer; you feel trapped. There's no place to run, and even if there were, fear has made your limbs too heavy, you can barely move. It's an alien weight that you shift from the bed to the chair, the chair to the floor. And you are shivering with fear or cold; and there is absolutely nothing you can do except try not to be any more terrified than you already are. If you remain very still, you pretend that this is what you have decided to do.

The Cavaliere wasn't sure what he minded most about the storm. Perhaps it was having to huddle in the semi-darkness of the cramped, clanking, clattery cabin—the smallest cabin in the world. Perhaps it was his sodden clothes and the cold; it was terribly cold. Perhaps it was the noise: the creaking of the ship, as wood shuddered and ground against wood, and that terrible crash, which could be a mast tipping over; that blast, which must be the topsails being blown to pieces; the screaming of the storm, and the cacophony of human shouts and cries. No, it was the revolting odors. All the portholes and hatches have been closed.

In the entire ship, which is a little wider than and twice the length of a lawn tennis court, with some fifty passengers added to its crew of more than six hundred, there were only four latrines, all unusable. He wants to breathe sharp, stinging, pure air. Instead, what assails his nostrils are rank intestinal smells.

If he were outside he could see it, brave it: the ship rising, pitching forward, and falling back between two high walls of black water. Was he afraid to die? Yes, like this. It would be better to go up on deck, if his trembling legs could negotiate the slippery passage. He had gone out of the cabin to try to find his wife, wandered down the narrow listing corridor sloshing in several inches of cold sea and excrement and vomit, and turned right. Then the candle he was holding went out. He was afraid of getting lost. He longed for his Ariadne to come and console him—hold out a thread. But he was not Theseus, no, he was the Minotaur trapped in the labyrinth. Not the hero but the monster.

Steadying himself by holding on to the slimy walls and rough guide ropes, he returned to his tiny cabin. The candle-lantern was still lit. As he shut the door, the ship dipped sickeningly and he was hurled against the wall. He slid to the floor and held on to the frame of the bed, then leaned against it, gasping at the shock, at the stinging pain in his breastbone. The lantern flickered. He rocked violently from side to side. Every piece of furniture was bolted to the floor but he was not. He closed his eyes.

What had the sibyl said? Breathe.

Recipe: When you are sad, when you are alone, when no one else comes, you can summon spirits to keep you company. He opened his eyes. Efrosina Pumo was sitting now in the cabin with him, nodding with concern. And Tolo was there too, so it was not true that he had been cut down by a French soldier on the retreat from Rome. Tolo is holding his ankles, steadying him, keeping him from slumping over. And Efrosina is stroking his forehead.

Do not be afraid, my lord.

I'm not afraid, he thought. I'm humiliated.

He had not seen Efrosina in many years. She ought to be very old, but she looks younger than when he first visited her so many years ago. He wondered how that was possible. And Tolo looks young too, not the bearded, brawny fellow with a half-closed eye who had accompanied him up the mountain for twenty years (growing a little less agile, even he), but again the delicate, vulnerable boy with the open milky eye he had once been.

Am I going to die, murmured the Cavaliere.

She shook her head.

But the ship is going to capsize.

Efrosina has told you when. You still have four more years.

Only four years, he thought. That's not so long! He knew he should be relieved.

I don't want to die this way, he said sullenly.

Then he noticed—why hadn't he noticed before?—that Efrosina was holding out a deck of cards.

Let me show you your destiny, my lord.

But he could barely read the card he picked. All he could see was someone upside down. Is that me? he thought. The way the ship pitches and turns, I feel as if I'm upside down.

Yes, it is His Excellency. Notice the expression of detachment on the face of the Hanged Man. Yes, my lord, it is you.

The Cavaliere a man hanging head down in the air with his hands tied behind his back, suspended by his right ankle from a wooden gibbet?

Yes, it is certainly His Excellency. You have cast yourself head first into the void, but you are calm—

I am not calm!

You have faith—

I do not have faith!

He studied the card for a moment. But this means I will die.

Not so—and she sighed. The card does not mean what you

think. Look with the eye of indifference, my lord. She laughed mirthlessly. Not only will you not hang, my lord, I promise you that you will live to hang other people.

But he didn't want to hear about the cards. He wanted Efrosina to distract him, to make the storm into a picture on the wall, make the dark walls white, draw back the space, raise the ceiling.

The storm swatted the ship again and he heard a crashing sound and shouts from the deck. Another mast fallen? It was tipping more strongly to one side. It's going over now, he can feel it. Tolo! The air will start to fill with water. Tolo!

The boy was still there, massaging his feet.

I cannot find my calm, he muttered.

Take out your pistol, my lord, you will feel safer. Tolo's voice. A man's counsel.

My pistol?

Tolo brought him the traveling case, which contained two pistols he always carried with him, while Efrosina wiped the sweat from his brow. He took them out. He closed his eyes.

Safer now?

Yes.

And it was thus that his two companions left him, with a pistol in each hand, trying, despite the swerve and smash of the storm, to hold as still as he can.

•

The Cavaliere's wife had just left the cabin of the Austrian ambassador, Prince Esterházy, who had been vomiting and praying, when she realized with a start that she had not seen the Cavaliere for several hours. She made her way down the heaving corridor to their cabin.

What relief she felt when she pushed the door open and saw him, sitting up on a trunk; and what fright, when she saw he was holding a pistol in each hand.

Oh, what's that!

Guggle guggle guggle, he said in a ghostly toneless voice.

What?

The sound of salt water in my throat, he shouted.

In your throat?

In the ship! In my throat! The moment I feel the ship sinking—he brandished the pistols—I intend to shoot myself.

Holding on to the shuddering door frame, she stared at him until he averted his eyes and stopped waving the pistols.

Guggle guggle, he said.

She was overcome with pity for his fear and misery. His mouth looked swollen. But she did not rush to comfort him, as she had been comforting so many others on the ship. For the first time she is not his. That is, for the first time she wishes he were other than he is—a doleful elderly man, weakened by vomiting, offended by stink and the proximity of too many human animals and the absence of all decorum.

The ship isn't going to sink, she said. Not with our great friend at the helm.

Come and sit by me, said the Cavaliere.

I'll be back in an hour. The Queen—

Your dress is stained.

In no more than an hour I'll be back. I promise!

And she was, and that night, it was Christmas Eve, the wind fell. She coaxed the Cavaliere onto the deck to watch a fine sight: the live volcanoes of the Lipari Islands, Stromboli and Vulcano, flaring and flaming skyward. They stood together. The wind slapped and salted their faces, and the volcanic fires lit up the star-speckled sky.

See, see, she murmured, and put her arm around him. Then she guided him back to the cabin, where the presence of Efrosina and Tolo still lingered.

She left the Cavaliere to sleep, having resolved not to enter a bed as long as she was needed. At dawn she came back to the cabin to wake him and brought him outside on the debris-strewn deck. The sea had gone flat, the red ball of the rising sun was burnishing the full-out sails with rosy light, and the ghosts of the two who had come to console the Cavaliere began to fade. She showed him a note she had received at four in the morning, while she was in the Queen's cabin trying to lull the fretful, squirming Carlo Alberto back to sleep. Addressed to her from the hero, it requested the happiness of having the Cavaliere, her ladyship, and Mrs. Cadogan take Christmas dinner with him at midday in the admiral's cabin. What a beautiful morning, she said.

The dinner was under way, with the exhausted hero not eating at all, the nauseated Cavaliere attempting to eat, and the two women (Mrs. Cadogan had slept only an hour) eating heartily, when they were interrupted by someone knocking, hitting, beating the door. It was one of the Queen's maids, who between sobs begged the Cavaliere's wife to come quickly to the Queen's cabin. Mrs. Cadogan excused herself and followed her daughter. They arrived to see the Queen and a doctor bent over the little boy. Look, cried the Queen. Il meurt! The child's eyes had rolled back in his head, and he was shaking spasmodically and clenching his quivering fists, thumbs inserted into the palms of his hands. The Cavaliere's wife folded the child in her arms and kissed his cold forehead.

Convulsions are a common effect of fear, said the doctor. When the young prince comes to his senses and realizes that the storm has subsided—

No, the Cavaliere's wife shouted. No!

She rocked the stiffening child, while the Queen railed against her fate, and Mrs. Cadogan wedged a piece of towel between his teeth and wiped the foam from his mouth. The shouts of sailors told them Palermo had been sighted. Palermo! As the intervals between one paroxysm and the next became shorter, the Cavaliere's wife held the boy more firmly to her breast, rocking him, breathing with him, as if she could make his breathing unite with hers, and crooning English hymns from her childhood. He died that evening in her arms.

Shortly after midnight the *Vanguard* dropped anchor, and

an hour later the drowsy weeping Queen boarded a small boat with two of her daughters and a few servants. The King refused to leave the ship until a proper welcome by his Sicilian subjects had been organized on the splendid marina; he had never before visited his second capital.

The Cavaliere's wife wanted to accompany the Queen, but worried that the hero might need her services as an interpreter in the morning.

She was depleted. It was all right to sleep now.

Toward noon the next day, to the cheers of a boisterous, inquisitive throng and a deafening salvo of cannon, the King went ashore. The admiral, flanked by his two friends, watched dourly from the quarter-deck. He was not in a good mood. Although everyone in his custody except the unfortunate prince was alive and safe, this did not feel like one of his triumphs. The other warships and the twenty merchant ships that had left Naples—transporting in abominable discomfort but without incident some two thousand refugees, the King's favorite servants and hounds, and the Queen's maids—had already arrived. The storm had ambushed only his ship, the flagship. Three topsails were split, the mainmast and rigging badly damaged. He felt needlessly buffeted. Perhaps he was simply very tired. The Cavaliere's wife was wide awake, pleased with her conduct during the emergency—she had behaved well, she had thought only of others—and enjoying the spectacle of the royalist crowd. She was having an adventure. She felt irresponsible. She wished they could remain a while longer on the ship. The Cavaliere stood between them—the ghostly trio of which he had been a member during the storm replaced by the real one, he with his wife and their friend. He felt light-headed, relieved not to be retching, impatient to put his feet on land again. They congratulated one another on their good fortune.

5

Another storm.

After leaving Naples in October, plodding nervily across the Mediterranean, past the ships of warring nations, through the Strait of Gibraltar and into the ocean, up the Iberian, then the French coast, clinging to the western ledge of Europe, the storeship *Colossus*, carrying two thousand rare antique vases in its entrails, had struck out for England and near the end of its two-month-long journey, off the Scilly Isles, ran into a merciless, protean storm, shuddered, rocked, took on water, fractured, foundered, and was wrecked. There was time to save all members of the crew. Time even to dump into a lifeboat one crate from the hold believed by the sailors to contain treasure—not one of the crates bearing the Cavaliere's seal. The roiling waters rose over real treasure, the second and greater collection of vases that the Cavaliere had assembled.

Water. Fire. Earth. Air. Four modes of disaster. Possessions lost to fire disappear. They change into . . . air. Possessions lost to fire's enemy, water, are not consumed, though they may break (if porous, like paper, bloat and rot). They still exist, possibly intact, but sunk, sequestered, out of reach. They are still there, decaying imperceptibly, encrusted by sea creatures, shifting aimlessly under the tides, buoyed up and sucked back in their little space—an unhappier fate than lying under the earth, for they are much farther down, much more inaccessible. What the ground covers is not so hard to bring up, and may have been uncannily preserved by earth-burial. Look at the cities doomed, then buried, by Vesuvius. But to be covered by water . . .

Having survived *his* storm, the Cavaliere still doesn't know his vases were already lost to water several weeks before the flight from Naples. The *Vanguard* has made it safely to the Palermo harbor. And the relief at surviving the humiliating, storm-tossed passage dulled his anguish at the precipitous departure, which had allowed him to take only a select number of cherished objects in addition to his pictures. He tried not to think of all that he had left behind in his magnificently furnished houses, which now lie unguarded, awaiting their plunderers. He thought of his horses and seven handsome carriages, and Catherine's spinet, harpsichord, and piano.

But surely he need not conclude that he would never see his abandoned possessions again. Never entertain guests at his Vesuvian villa. Never set out on horseback at dawn from the lodge in Caserta to the cries of beaters and hounds. Never watch beauty bathing from the rocks at Posillipo. Never again stand at the window of his observatory room, admiring the sweep of the bay and his dear mountain. No. No. Yes? No. The Cavaliere was as ill-prepared as any connoisseur of disaster for the real thing.

•

Temporarily then, for a short time only, they were to live in Palermo: the south of south.

Every culture has its southerners—people who work as little as they can, preferring to dance, drink, sing, brawl, kill their unfaithful spouses; who have livelier gestures, more lustrous eyes, more colorful garments, more fancifully decorated vehicles, a wonderful sense of rhythm, and charm, charm, charm; unambitious, no, lazy, ignorant, superstitious, uninhibited people, never on time, conspicuously poorer (how could it be otherwise, say the northerners); who for all their poverty and squalor lead enviable lives—envied, that is, by work-driven, sensually inhibited, less corruptly governed northerners. We are superior to them, say the northerners, clearly superior. We do not shirk our duties or tell lies as a matter of course, we work hard, we are punctual, we keep reliable accounts. But they have more fun than we do. Every country, including southern countries, has its south: below the equator, it lies north. Hanoi has Saigon, São Paulo has Rio, Delhi has Calcutta, Rome has Naples, and Naples, which to those at the top of this peninsula hanging down from the belly of Europe was already Africa, Naples has Palermo, the crescent-shaped second capital of the Kingdom of the Two Sicilies, where it is even hotter, more heathenish, more dishonest, more picturesque.

As if to test the stereotype, it was snowing in palmy Palermo when they arrived just after Christmas. During the first weeks of January they camped in a few vast rooms of a villa with hardly any furniture and no fireplaces; a southern city is never prepared for a cold snap. The hero was desk-bound, writing furious dispatches. Wrapped in quilts, the Cavaliere shivered, brooded, and endured a merciless bout of diarrhea. Only his wife, who could not bear to be unoccupied, went out often, mainly to be at the Queen's side as she supervised the installation of her large family in the royal palace. She returned in the evening to report to the Cavaliere and their friend on the slovenliness of the local servants, the Queen's understandably despondent mood, and the defection of the King, who was busy sampling the theatres, masquerades, and other pleasures of his other capital.

Whatever the weather, the Cavaliere and his wife and their friend knew they were farther south, therefore among even more untrustworthy people, rascals and liars, more eccentric, more primitive. The thought that follows is that it was important not to change the way they had always lived. They cautioned themselves as people do who know they are part of a superior culture: we mustn't let ourselves go, mustn't descend to the level of the . . . jungle, street, bush, bog, hills, outback (take your pick). For if you start dancing on tables, fanning yourself, feeling sleepy when you pick up a book, developing a sense of rhythm, making love whenever you feel like it—then you know. The south has got you.

•

The weather turned warmer by the middle of the month as the Cavaliere reluctantly agreed to the exorbitant sum being asked for renting a palace near the Mole belonging to a Sicilian noble family with a reputation for eccentricity, even by local standards. Imagine a prince whose coat of arms is a satyr holding up a mirror to a woman with the head of a horse! But the palace had a commanding location, and within its walls covered with colored silk and portraits of somber-looking ancestors was generously furnished; it would do as the temporary British embassy. Unfortunately, it was too fraught with its saturnine history for the Cavaliere to make it also a home: that is, a museum of his enthusiasms. Weeks after they occupied it, he still had not unpacked most of what he was able to bring away from Naples.

Here, in this unexpected and alarmingly costly exile, they were even more intensely a trio. A large woman and a small man who are full of feeling for each other, and a tall emaciated man who loves them both ardently and rejoices in their company. Though sometimes the Cavaliere was glad to see his wife and their friend go out, because their animation exhausts him, when they were absent for more than a few hours he longed for their return. But he wished there were not always so many at his table. A fair number of the colony of English residents in Naples who had become refugees with them found their way to his house each evening. These unpredictably large suppers for twenty, thirty, forty, fifty would end only when the Cavaliere's wife rose from the table, or fell, or knelt—she needed no props to initiate a sample of her Attitudes—or went to the piano to play and sing; she had already learned a few sad, graceful Sicilian airs. The evenings seemed very long to the Cavaliere. But he could hardly refuse to welcome his compatriots, none of whom were as well housed as he—in all Palermo there was only one overcrowded hotel up to their standards—and at the jumped-up rates exacted from these captive tourists, double or triple what they were before. Their discomforts required that the Cavaliere flourish the standard to which they were accustomed. Arriving from their makeshift lodgings in the rented carriages for which they had been disagreeably overcharged, they thought as they entered the British envoy's brightly illuminated residence: This is how we live. What we have a right to. This luxury, this extravagance, this refinement, this overeating; this obligation to amuse ourselves.

Following supper and the entertainment offered by the Cavaliere's wife, the evenings usually devolved into late-night card parties and relays of gossip and condescending observations about the wantonness of local manners. The refugees told their old stories to each other, and made light of the inconveniences of their new situation. Nothing should seem to impair their capacity for pleasure—their pleasures. They saved their complaints, their vehement complaints, for letters, especially those to friends and family back in England. But that's what letters were for: to say something new, and say it eloquently. Society was for saying something old—predictable, throwaway, offhand—which would not startle the auditor. (Only savages blurted out what they felt.) Letters were for saying—I confess, I admit, I must avow. Letters took a long time to arrive, which encouraged their recipients to hope that in the meantime the sender's misfortunes had eased.

Some were making arrangements to return to England. For the news was bad—that is, it was just what the refugees expected. Two weeks after the flight of the government from Naples, the French moved an army of six thousand soldiers into the city, and by late January a cabal of enlightened aristocrats and professors had engendered a monstrosity that called itself the Parthenopean or Vesuvian Republic.

Most of the refugees were inclined to consider Naples lost. A foreigner who has enjoyed the good life in a poor country, life before the revolution—such an expatriate is quick to see the direst outcome for the whole country when his privileges have been rescinded. Even the Cavaliere reluctantly began to think of retirement and returning to England. But he did not see how he could extricate himself from Palermo. Not yet. Their magnificent friend, on whom all depended, spoke no foreign languages and could not be expected to understand, like a professional diplomat, the doublespeak of a court. They could not leave the King and Queen, as long as the fate of the country still hung in the balance. He had spoken to the King, but the King, he reported with more asperity than he intended, had given in to inarticulate gloom—whenever obliged by fresh news from Naples to ignore how much he was enjoying himself.

In fact the King, whenever he remembered to forget his pleasures, was in a fury. None of this would have happened if Naples had remained neutral, he bellowed at his wife. It was all her fault—it was because of her partiality to the English; that is, to the Cavaliere's wife. The Queen heard out the King's tirade in silence, the dense silence of a woman who knows that, although more intelligent than her husband, she is still only a wife, subject to his whim. She—despite her undiminished mistrust of the people, for all their vaunted loyalty to the royal family and the Church—was convinced that the French occupation, and this charade of a republic which had come into existence under French patronage and protection, could not possibly last. The people were picking off French soldiers who were foolhardy enough to wander at night in the byways of the city. Two soldiers had been murdered in a brothel by some neighborhood customers, and a mob had attacked one of the French barracks, managing to butcher twelve of the sleeping soldiers. And then, said the Queen to the Cavaliere's wife, there is our ally, syphilis. In that time often rapidly disabling or fatal, the horrifying illness which the Italians called the French disease and the French called *le mal de Naples* could be relied on to deduct at least a thousand soldiers.

The activities of the hero, rather than the Cavaliere's affairs, had become the main concern of the household. Commanders of other ships arrived for consultation. There was the defense of Sicily to organize, lest Napoleon be tempted to launch an invasion of the island. And Cardinal Ruffo, who had come with them to Palermo, was volunteering to return and lead an organized armed resistance to the French occupation. He proposed to make a clandestine landing on the coast of his native Calabria, where he owned a number of vast estates. From his own peasants he would levy an army—he told the Queen that, with promises of a tax amnesty and the right of unrestrained looting once Naples was retaken, he expected to raise between fifteen and twenty thousand men. The Queen had given her support to Ruffo's plan even though, with one exception, she trusted none of her subjects. She was counting more on a British blockade of Naples, which would compel the already overextended French forces to withdraw. With the French gone, the republicans would be left defenseless before the righteous wrath of the people. Thank God—the Queen crossed herself—the people had found an appropriate target for their vicious energies.

So far the French had not moved farther south than Naples; it seemed unlikely that they were planning to cross the Strait of Messina. But fear of revolution had come to Palermo. Although no revolutionary voices were yet audible, the look of fellow travelers had already arrived: shorter hair for women, longer hair for men. Watch the evolution of hair styles among the educated class! The King gave orders that anyone who appeared in a box at the opera or theatre with unpowdered hair was to be expelled. Men who had grown their hair below their ears were to be seized and shaved; any among them who wrote articles or books were imprisoned, while their dwellings were searched for further proof of revolutionary sympathies. One proof was finding a book, any book, by Voltaire, whose work—ever since 1791, when his remains were borne to the Pantheon in a great ceremony of apotheosis—was now synonymous with the Jacobin cause.

Odd to think that possession of a book by Voltaire could procure a gentle reader three years in the galleys. What a churl this illiterate King was! The Cavaliere, in the privacy of his own study, still felt the greatest admiration for the sage of Ferney, who would surely have been appalled to find himself a patron saint of Revolution and Terror. Who could have predicted that Voltaire's delightful mockery of received ideas would one day be taken as an invitation to tear down lawful arrangements in the best interests of order and stability? Who, other than the naïve or the benighted, felt they must put into practice what they had enjoyed in a book? (Had his passion for the artifacts of ancient Rome led him to the worship of Jupiter and Minerva?) Unfortunately, some of his distinguished friends in Naples had done just that. He feared they would pay a heavy price for their naïveté.

No, to read was precisely to enter another world, which was not the reader's own, and come back refreshed, ready to bear with equanimity the injustices and frustrations of this one. Reading was balm, amusement—not incitement. And reading was mostly what the Cavaliere did in these first weeks while he was still feeling ill, including rereading an essay on happiness by Voltaire. It was the best way to endure the elsewhere of exile: to be in the elsewhere of a book. And as he became stronger, he could gradually be where he was.

Diarrhea and rheumatism still kept him too indisposed to join the King, who had removed to one of the royal estates in the countryside to hunt. But the sour-sweet charms of this city began to rouse him. The tawny palaces ringing the harbor with their hybrid fantasies (Byzantine–Moorish, Moorish–Norman, Norman–Gothic, Gothic–Baroque). The looming pinkish limestone mass of Mount Pellegrino: one can see mountains or the sea at the end of almost every street. The gardens of oleander, smilax, agave, yucca, bamboo, and banana and pepper trees. Palermo, he admitted, might be thought as beautiful in its own way as Naples, even though it lacked a volcano in the distance, smoking under the brilliant blue and cloudless sky. (Would that he were a few years younger and could look forward to an expedition to Etna, climbed but once and so many years ago.) His sense of beauty had reawakened—and with it the old habits that defined him as an acquirer of the beautiful. Being one of the most famous men in the kingdom and acquainted, at least by correspondence, with all the notables and learned people in the city, he was besieged by invitations to view, to examine, to purchase. Collectors hoped to excite his envy. Antiquarians paraded their treasures. He looked, he allowed himself to be shown, he felt flickers of desire. But he acquired nothing. It was not only alarm about his finances that inhibited him. There was nothing irresistible, there was nothing that he felt he had to buy.

•

The collector's temperament is fastidious, sceptical. The authority of the collector lies in his ability to say: no—not that. Though there is a vulgar accumulator in the soul of every collector, his avidity must be matched by the power of his refusals.

No, thank you. It's very fine, but it's not exactly what I was looking for. Almost, but not quite. The lip of the vase has a hairline crack, the painting is not as good as another of the same subject by this painter. I want an earlier work. I want a perfect example.

The soul of the lover is the opposite of the collector's. The defect or blemish is part of the charm. A lover is never a sceptic.

Here is a trio. The eldest member is a great collector who had become, late in life, a lover; and whose instinct for collecting has waned. A thwarted collector who has had to let his collections out of his custody—abandoning some, sending others far away (where they have met the doom the collector most fears), packing up the rest; and who now lives without his collections, without the comfort and distraction of beautiful objects, whose merit derives in part from their belonging to *him*. And who has not been moved to accumulate anything more.

The others are two people whose most cherished objects are those that adorn and announce their presence. Emblems of who they are, what they care about, how they are loved by others. He accumulates medals; she accumulates what beautifies her, and what trumpets her love for him. While the Cavaliere, with his finely tuned sense of objects—how they have to breathe, how they inevitably take over any space in which they are set out—found the prince's palace too saturated with its owner's personality to think of installing his own treasures, his wife, with the Cavaliere's approval, quickly distributed the hero's portraits, flags, trophies, and china, mugs, and glassware made to honor the victor of the Battle of the Nile throughout their new, temporary residence, making it one more museum of his glory. No space was too crowded for her.

The lover's involvement with objects is the opposite of the collector's, whose strategy is one of passionate self-effacement. Don't look at me, says the collector. I'm nothing. Look at what I have. Isn't it, aren't they, beautiful.

The collector's world bespeaks the crushingly large existence of other worlds, energies, realms, eras than the one he lives in. The collection annihilates the collector's little slice of historic existence. The lover's relation to objects annihilates all but the world of the lovers. This world. My world. My beauty, my glory, my fame.

•

At first he had pretended not to notice her staring, then stared back, too. Stares like long deep respirations passed between them.

Their readiness to give themselves to strong emotions, which makes them different from the Cavaliere and so like each other, didn't mean they understood what they were feeling or what they should do about it. The Cavaliere, who had not known passion until he met the young woman he had made his second wife, had been quick to acknowledge what he felt. But then, the Cavaliere was not interested in being understood. The hero wants to be understood—which for him means being praised and sympathized with and encouraged. And the hero is a romantic: that is, his vanity was matched by an inordinate capacity for humility when his affections were engaged. He felt so honored by the Cavaliere's friendship, by the friendship and then the love (he dared call it love) of his wife. If I am loved by people of this quality, then I know I am worthwhile. He is infatuated with them both, and reluctant to think beyond his immediate feelings of elation in their company.

The Cavaliere's wife knows what she feels, but for the first time in her life doesn't know what to do about it. She can't help flirting, it's as much a part of her nature as her gift for monogamy. Loyalty is one of the virtues she practices most effortlessly, not that she is averse to effort: she too had a heroic temperament. Neither wants to offend, humiliate, or hurt the Cavaliere. Both hesitate to injure their most cherished ideas of themselves. The hero is a man of honor. The Cavaliere's wife is a reformed courtesan whose genuine devotion and serene fidelity to her husband attested to her having entirely left behind her old identity. The hero wanted to continue to be what he had always been. She wanted to continue to be what she so spectacularly had become.

Everyone assumed they were lovers. In fact, they had not yet even kissed.

As if by mutual accord, they tried to exhaust their passion for each other through quite public and entirely sincere expressions of mutual adulation. On one occasion, a party for the Russian ambassador, she leaned over and kissed his medals. He did not blush. And he recounted to every new guest the stories of *her* heroic deeds which the others had already heard. All that she had done for him, for the British cause. Her courage during the stormy passage from Naples—she never went to bed during the whole trip—and her selfless attendance on the royal couple: She became their slave, he said. And pronouncing the word slave thrilled him in a way he did not understand. He repeated it again. She became their slave.

Saint Emma, he called her sometimes, with the most earnest expression on his face. The pattern of perfection! He wanted to admire himself, but he was even quicker to admire anyone he loved. He admired his father, he had admired Fanny, he admired the Cavaliere, and now he admired the woman who was the Cavaliere's wife. To say that he loved her more than he had loved anyone in his life is to say he admired her more than anyone. She was his religion. Saint Emma! No one dared smile. But the refugees were becoming restless. Gratitude to the hero who had shepherded their flight to Palermo had been replaced by grumbling. They were stranded, he seemed becalmed. Wasn't it time for him to rejoin the British fleet in the Mediterranean and win a new battle? Or return to Naples and take the city back from the French and overthrow the puppet republican government? Why did he linger?

Of course, everyone knew why.

Whenever she performed a suite of her celebrated Attitudes—the same repertory, the same entrancing art, which even her severest critics still judged admirable—he was there, watching raptly, his right sleeve twitching, a beguiling, beatific smile on his full lips. By God, that is splendid, he exclaimed. If only the greatest actresses of Europe could have been among us tonight, how much they could have learned from you.

The guests exchanged knowing glances. She was not just impersonating Cleopatra now, she was Cleopatra, ensnaring Antony; a Dido whose charms detain Aeneas; an Armida who has bewitched Rinaldo—the familiar stories from ancient history and epic everyone knew, in which a man destined for glory makes a brief stop in the course of his great mission, succumbs to the charms of an irresistible woman, and stays. And stays. And stays.

The influence of women on men has always been disparaged, feared, for its power to make men gentle, loving—weak; which means that women are thought to pose a particular danger for soldiers. A warrior's relation to women is supposed to be brutal, or at least callous, so he can go on being battle-ready, violence-primed, brother-bonded, death-resigned. So he can be strong. But this warrior really was battered, and needed time to heal and be cared for. It took time to refit and repair the *Vanguard*, badly damaged by the storm. And his presence in Palermo was useful. Though not well enough to go back to sea, he stayed busy, drawing up plans to send a squadron under the command of Captain Troubridge to blockade the harbor of Naples. And the Cavaliere's wife was helping him. It was his glory that she loved. Together they are moving toward a great destiny, for him. And she was not a woman with a lapful of hero but, in her own way, a hero too.

•

He wanted to please her. She wanted so desperately to please him.

Ambition and the desire to please—these are not incompatible, for a woman. If you please, you are rewarded. The more you please, the greater your rewards. This is why monogamy can work so well for a woman. You know whom you have to please.

Now there were two men, her husband and their friend, whom the Cavaliere's wife wanted to please.

The Cavaliere's money worries were accumulating. He had been obliged to ask for several loans from their friend, confident that he could repay the money as soon as his great vase collection was sold in London, and in the meantime was discreetly selling some cameos, gems, small statues, and other lesser loves among the antiquities he had rescued from Naples. His wife had a plan: she would try to win enough money for their current expenses at the gambling table. But what started as one more dash of intervention in response to someone's distress turned into a passion. Another passion. Gambling, drinking, eating—all her activities were unstinting, became cravings. And the heightened, doubled desire to please further turned up the volume of her personality, her appetites.

The Cavaliere knew what she was up to when she played faro and hazard late into the night and began to count on her success, which made it grueling for him either to watch her or to ignore her. He despised anything imploring in himself: on these evenings he usually retired early. The hero remained by her side, whispered in her ear, beamed when she won, staked her to another game when she lost. How brilliantly she played, win or lose, thought the hero. No one would even have a chance against her were it not for an endearing frailty that sometimes made her a bit muddled. He had noticed she became tipsy after the second glass of brandy. How odd, he thought. If he drank two glasses of brandy, he was not affected. As indifferent to drink as he was to cards (the hero was almost as abstemious as the Cavaliere), he didn't understand that the rapidity with which she became drunk was a sign not of an unusual susceptibility but of advanced alcoholism.

She *is* a gifted player, but sometimes continues after a steady run of good fortune, risking her precious winnings, so as to keep him near. For she is never so muddled as to forget his electric presence beside her, or behind her, or across a room talking, gesturing, and, in fact, as aware of her as she is of him.

Now that she knew how much she wants to touch him, her old freedom to touch him had become a self-conscious adventure of delicate, compensatory gestures. Pausing at the foot of the great staircase to bid good night to the evening's guests, she absentmindedly touches the empty sleeve pinned to his jacket to pick off a speck of lint: she has noticed a tiny deposit of sleep in his right eye, the blind eye, and wishes she could flick it away.

He imagines touch without his arm: when face to face, he feels sometimes he is falling toward her.

She watches his lips, slightly parted when he is listening; when he speaks, she realizes sometimes that she has not heard a word of what he said. His features seem so very large.

It is easier when they don't face each other but, side by side, try to be interested in others. Right and left have new inflections. Right is the side on which the hero is maimed—his immobile eye, his empty sleeve. She notices that he invariably sits to her right, so as to offer his intact side.

The usual alignments give rise to new, tremulous manipulations. Seated beside her at the gambling table, he becomes aware that she has been steadily scratching her left knee, and wishes she would stop before she leaves a mark on her lovely skin. (Her eczema has come back, as it does from time to time, but he cannot know that.) Without thinking, he leans nearer to her to look at the cards in her right hand, close enough to whisper some advice about her next bid, which—as he somehow divined it would—makes the hand under the table that has been scratching stop.

How mindful they are of each other's bodies inside their clothes. How mindful they are of the space that separates them.

At a banquet, she becomes aware that his left thigh cannot be more than six—no, seven—inches from her right thigh. They are in the middle of the fourth course. Although he manages quite well with his elegant gold eating utensil, a hybrid device with knife fused to fork (blade facing right, tines to the left) sent him by an admirer after the Battle of the Nile, she picks up her own knife and fork, leans her upper body toward him, nearer to him, offering payment for this boldness, born of intolerable yearning, by moving her right leg several inches farther away from him, squeezing it against her own left leg. And being careful that her shoulder not touch his as she takes over the cutting of his meat.

She is not the only person at the table this evening who has been rattled by the distance between one thing and another.

Am I—one of their English guests was holding forth on a

most unusual phenomenon she had observed—am I the only person in this gathering who has seen a little island of a picturesque form opposite the city, not much more distant than our beautiful Capri is from Naples?

An island?

But there is no island visible from Palermo, said another guest.

So everyone has assured me, Miss Knight said primly.

And when did you see this . . . island? Her cross-examiner was Lord Minto, former ambassador to Malta and one of the hero's friends, who was staying with them for several weeks.

It is not visible much of the time. When the sky is entirely cloudless, I cannot distinguish it.

But you do see it when the day is cloudy?

Not cloudy, Lord Minto, if by that you mean overcast. When there are a few light clouds on the horizon.

Lady Minto laughed. Surely what you have seen is a cloud that you have mistaken for an island.

No, it cannot be a cloud.

And, pray, why?

Because it always has the same distinctive shape.

The table was silent. The Cavaliere's wife hoped the hero would enter the conversation.

Quite logical, said the Cavaliere. Go on, Miss Knight.

I do not know if I am logical, she said. But I will not deny the evidence of my senses.

Quite right, said the Cavaliere. Do go on.

I daresay I am very persistent, she continued, and then seemed to falter, as if unsure whether she had described the trait she so admired in herself in an attractive or an unattractive way.

But were you seeing an island? A real island?

Yes, Lord Minto, she exclaimed. Yes, I was. For after seeing it a dozen times I sketched it, and showed my drawing to some of our officers. They immediately recognized it as one of the outermost Lipari Islands which lies—

Vulcano, interrupted the Cavaliere.

I do not think that was the name.

Stromboli?

No, I think not.

You can see as far as the Liparis, squealed the Cavaliere's wife. Oh, I wish I could see that far.

A toast to Miss Knight's stubbornness, said the hero. A woman of character, and character is what I most admire in a woman.

Miss Knight flushed so deep a red at this compliment from the hero that the Cavaliere's wife was moved to reach across the table and pat her hand. A relay of feeling, in which a compliment inspired by her but addressed to another brought her a chance to make substitute contact with the hero's hand.

It is quite impossible to see the Lipari Islands from here, declared Lord Minto.

Since Miss Knight, after being alternately attacked and flattered by the most important men at the table, seemed adrift in feminine feelings of the self-silencing kind, the Cavaliere took the opportunity to volunteer an account of the scientific basis of mirages and other optical abnormalities—he had been reading a book about them.

I think we must allow Miss Knight's claim to have seen an island, he said, his voice gleaming with authority. Would not Lord Minto himself say that he has seen his own face? I mean, of course, with the aid of a mirror. So Miss Knight has seen a faraway island on motionless water in the bay of Palermo, the reflection of the island, projected in the same way a camera lucida delivers the image of an object on a plane surface but using clouds, when at a certain angle, instead of the camera lucida's three- or four-sided prism. Many artists of my acquaintance find this ingenious apparatus quite useful in making their drawings.

The Cavaliere's wife pointed out to the company that her husband was an expert on every scientific question. No one, she said firmly, knows more than him.

I cannot wait until the next day with light clouds to see Miss Knight's ghostly island, said Mr. MacKinnon, a banker. Perhaps, if the clouds are lying right, we shall see our Naples—

Oh, I would not want to see our Naples now, said old Miss Ellis, who had lived there for thirty years.

Perhaps the Cavaliere will be able to see Vesuvius, said the hero gaily. I'm sure he misses his volcano.

The Cavaliere's wife was thinking it is not true that she would like to see far. Everything she wants to see is right here.

•

How can not one but two fascinating men dote on her? Both be so blind to her vulgarity, the shameless way she flatters them?

The hero seemed ever more besotted, the Cavaliere more withered and passive, she more hectic and eager to exhibit herself. In their former life, in Naples, the wife of the British ambassador would not have considered adding a dance, much less a folkloric dance of erotic abandon, to her edifying repertoire of living statues. She dances the tarantella now before their guests, in Palermo. To their Sicilian acquaintances, her tambourine-shaking and foot-stamping and whirling about seemed nothing worse than odd. Or Neapolitan. But their British guests—the refugees from Naples and others who came to stay with them, such as Lord Minto on his way back to England and Lord Elgin going out to take up his post as ambassador to Turkey—were appalled, and found her manner increasingly coarse and vulgar.

Her dress: too ostentatious. Her laugh: even louder. Her chatter: more relentless. Indeed, she was incapable of the withholding that people think of as elegance. Not only was she by nature garrulous, she thought she was always supposed to say something, and the art of understatement was as alien to her as the art of hoarding feelings. She was constantly preening herself, or flattering her husband and their friend.

Of course, the hero flattered her just as outrageously. The finest actress of the century. The greatest singer in Europe. The cleverest of women. And the most selfless. A paragon. But however matched they were in the throw of their effusions, it was she, being a woman, who was judged more harshly. She, they assumed, who had seduced him; her unremitting flattery that had won his heart, and made him her slave. Were she still the most celebrated beauty of the era, as she had been a decade earlier, the hero's pitiable infatuation would have seemed all too understandable. But to be at the feet of—this?

Her demerits mounted. But for nothing was she judged more harshly than her failure at what is deemed a woman's greatest, most feminine accomplishment: the maintenance and proper care of a no longer youthful body. Visitors from abroad reported that the Cavaliere's wife was continuing to put on weight; most said she had entirely lost her looks; a few allowed that she still had a beautiful head. Though it was still several decades before the Romantics inaugurated the modern cult of thinness, which was eventually to make everyone, men as well as women, feel guilty about not being thin, even then, when it was uncommon for someone wellborn to be thin, *she* was not to be pardoned for becoming fat.

Odd that people judged vulgar are invariably presumed also to be lacking in self-awareness, with the implication that if only they knew how they looked or behaved they would immediately cut it out: upgrade their diction, become reticent and subtle, go on a diet. This may be the kindest form that snobbery can take, but no less obtuse for being kind. Try talking a good-natured, self-confident adult of plebeian origin out of a rich array of mannerisms called vulgar, try it—and see how successful you will be. (The Cavaliere has tried, and long ago stopped trying, or minding: he loved her.) So, it was assumed she was unaware of the change in her body. But the seams of her favorite clothes need to be let out every few months, an activity that now occupies a good deal of the energies of her dear mother, assisted by Fatima: how could she not know it? And if she overdresses now, it was precisely to say: don't look at me, look at my satin gowns, my rings, my tasseled sash, my hat with the ostrich plumes—a strategy of self-effacement not unlike that of the collector, but considerably less effective. Her detractors looked at both.

No letter back to England failed to make some cruel comment on her appearance. Impossible to describe how awful she looks. Her person is nothing short of monstrous in its enormity and is growing every day, wrote Lord Minto. I had been led to expect someone of undeniable physical charms, wrote Lady Elgin, but alas, no. She is indeed a Whapper!

The reports about the loss of her beauty were as extravagant, as hyperbolic, as the reports of her beauty had once been. It was as if people had been made to praise her, and overlook her low birth and disreputable past, because she was so beautiful. Only because she was so beautiful. But now that she was no longer the epitome of beauty, all the suppressed judgments—the snobbery and the cruelty—reemerged. The spell was broken, and everyone joined in an extraordinary chorus of scorn and spitefulness.

•

One spring day, the Cavaliere announced that he had arranged an excursion to a villa belonging to the prince whose palace in town they were occupying.

It lay on the plain east of Palermo, where many other noble families had been building country houses throughout the century; out of consideration for the hero's defunct eye, which was hypersensitive to light, they were going out in the afternoon, when the sun would be behind them. The Cavaliere's wife kept changing her place in the carriage to get a better view of the lush orange and lemon groves. Both men sat quietly, the hero toying with his eye shield and relishing the feeling of being taken care of, the Cavaliere anticipating the pleasure of sharing what he had gleaned from several descriptions of the villa in books by British travelers to Sicily. But he knew he must not say too much now, which would spoil the surprise in store for his companions when they reached their destination. And what a surprise it would be.

No eccentric like a southern eccentric. Even the astonishing, cathedral-like country retreat that the Cavaliere's rich cousin William was building back in England could not rival in insolence the villa built by the Sicilian prince's late half brother. The large two-storied edifice of flesh-pink and white stone which the trio saw from the carriage at a distance gave no inkling of the residence's singular contents. Its singularity was announced only when they reached the gates, which were guarded by two squatting, neckless, seven-eyed monsters, and saw before them a broad avenue lined on both sides with pedestals bearing more grotesque beings.

Oh. Oh, look.

Time for the Cavaliere to begin his commentary. To his wife he directed the information that Goethe had seen the villa twelve years ago, when he left Naples to go to Sicily, a year before the death of the prince who is responsible for the statues they were passing (there are more, there are more), and he took some pleasure in observing that the great poet's reaction had been quite conventional: he had thought the villa dreadful, and presumed its owner to be mad.

What was that, exclaimed the Cavaliere's wife.

They were driving rapidly past the horse with human hands, the Bactrian camel with two women's heads for humps, the goose with a horse's head, the man whose face sprouted an elephant's trunk and whose hands were vulture's claws.

Some of the late prince's guardian spirits, said the Cavaliere.

And that!

That being a man with a cow's head riding a wildcat with a man's head.

Let's stop the carriage, said the hero.

We shall see much more than this, said the Cavaliere. He pointed to the orchestra of monkeys with drums, flutes, and violins looking out at them from the edge of the villa's roof. Let us continue.

Lackeys were waiting to help them from the carriage, and a podgy man in black livery, the chamberlain, stood at the threshold of the great entrance to greet them.

I never before saw black livery, whispered the hero.

Perhaps he still wears mourning for his master, said the Cavaliere's wife.

The Cavaliere smiled. I should not be surprised, my dear, if you were right.

Outside the entrance door (warped, splintered) a dwarf with the laurel-crowned head of a Roman emperor sat astride a dolphin. The Cavaliere's wife patted the dwarf's head. There is more inside, said the Cavaliere, though the villa is already much despoiled. They followed the chamberlain up a rather filthy staircase and into the first floor above ground level, through halls and anterooms, past more composite creatures and odd couples.

Oh, look!

A double-headed peacock riding an angel on all fours.

Lordy!

A mermaid with a dog's paw coupling with a stag.

And look at this!

The Cavaliere's wife had stopped before two seated, sumptuously garbed figures playing cards, one a lady with a horse's head, the other a gentleman with a griffin's head dressed in a full-bottomed wig and crown.

I should like to have a horse's head for a day, she exclaimed. And see what it would feel like.

Oh, said the hero. I'm sure you would be a most beautiful horse.

I should like to see the faces of our guests when you sat down to play faro with such a head on your shoulders, said the Cavaliere. No doubt you would win every game.

The Cavaliere's wife gave a robust imitation of a horse's neigh, and both men broke into laughter.

The Cavaliere was ready to join in the mockery of the late prince's affectations, to be at one with his wife and their friend. But he wanted to make sure that their amusement was as saturated with knowledge as his own. Wherever he was, the Cavaliere was prone to cast himself in the role of the guide or mentor. At a funeral he would have lectured a fellow mourner on the history of cemetery monuments. What a deft antidote to anxiety or grief one's own erudition can be.

Stimulated by the prince's penchant for horses with limbs or the head of some other creature and humans with horses' heads, the Cavaliere began to recount the stories of Chiron, Pegasus, and other horses in ancient mythology with extra parts. He thought it worth pointing out that these mutants were always semi-divine creatures. Recall Achilles' wise tutor, who was half horse, half human. Or the hippogriff, whose father was a griffin and whose mother was a filly, and in Ariosto is a symbol of love.

Love. The Cavaliere's wife heard the word resound in the sepulchral silence of the villa. *She* had not pronounced it. Nor their friend.

The Cavaliere is not really thinking about love, but the word seems as good a talisman as any against the unsettling violence of feeling expressed in the grotesque inventions with which the prince had populated the villa and its grounds.

Their friend was dodging the thought of love too, and ventured a small contribution of his own to the learned discussion. In Egypt, said the victor of the Battle of the Nile, I was told of an immense statue that is a creature with the head and bosom of a woman and the lower limbs of a lion. She must be an awesome sight, crouching in the sand.

Yes, yes, I read about that! She waits for passing travelers and she makes them halt and then she kills them. Except those that can solve a riddle, them she spares.

That's another cruel creature, my dear, said the Cavaliere gently. But I would not be surprised if we were to come across either your Sphinx or the Egyptian one, or something resembling, here in these very rooms, among the prince's stone companions. Shall we look for her?

And we'll think of a riddle to ask her, cried the Cavaliere's wife.

They passed into another drawing room, calling out to one another as they came across more tableaux of the deformed and ill-coupled, the chamberlain trailing behind, a silent reproach to their gaiety and their wish to condescend to what they were seeing.

The human imagination has always been entertained by the fantasy of biological misalliances, and by the reality of bodies that don't look as bodies are supposed to look, which can endure ordeals bodies are not supposed to be able to endure. Painters loved to invent such creatures when they had the pretext. Circuses and fairs display them: freaks, mutants, odd couples, animals doing stunts that violate their nature. The Cavaliere may not have been familiar with Bosch and Bruegel on the subject of hell or the torments of Saint Anthony, but he had seen somewhat less inspired depictions of those anatomical assemblages called demons or monsters. Were it only a question of these freakish beings in every corner, the contents of the prince's lair would not have been so original. Even more astonishing was the profusion of whimsical, threatening—no, freakish—objects.

Lamps in the shape of a human or animal limb.

Tables constructed of shards of tile and made too tall to be of use.

Columns and pyramids, at least forty of them, made of different kinds of china and pottery; one column has a chamber pot for its plinth, a circle of little flowerpots for its capital, and a four-foot-long shaft composed entirely of teapots that diminish gradually in size from plinth to capital.

Chandeliers whose many-tiered components, suspended like drop earrings, were the bottoms, necks, and handles of broken bottles and barometers.

Candelabra, more than three feet high, jerry-built out of

pieces of caudle cups, saucers, bowls, jugs, kettles, and tilting ominously. Examining one of the candelabra more closely, the Cavaliere saw to his surprise that among the shards of humble crockery stuck together at random were segments of exceptionally fine porcelain.

Vases, each of which disgorges a mutant creature or a scroll from its belly or base.

The Cavaliere was starting to feel queasy, finally, as the impression of the grotesque was replaced by the impression of an immense sarcasm. He had been prepared for the grotesque. He had not been prepared for the recognition that the prince's temperament was a demented variant of the collector's—though what this fellow collector had amassed were not objects found or purchased but made, according to his designs. To piece together fragments of costly porcelain with chunks of kitchenware—was this not merely a mocking echo of the democracy of objects found in many aristocratic collections, such as the Duchess of Portland's, which displayed exquisite paintings alongside branches of coral and seashells. Like any collector, the prince had surrounded himself with things for people to pay attention to, marvel at when they visited him. They defined him. He was, above all, the proprietor of these objects—which spoke for him, which announced the way he saw the world. They did not say what the Cavaliere, like all great collectors, wished to say with objects: look at all the beauty and interest there is in the world. They said: the world is mad. Ordinary life is ridiculous, if you take some distance from it. Anything can turn into anything else, anything can be dangerous, anything can collapse, give way. An ordinary object can be made from . . . anything. Any shape can be deformed. Any common purpose served by objects balked.

How many of them there were! As the trio followed the chamberlain through room after room, their ability to respond to what they were seeing began to buckle under the emotional weight, the sheer profusion of assertive objects. Like any obsessed collector, the prince could not get enough of what he coveted.

Like a collector, he lived in a crowded space—the objects accumulated, multiplied. And the prince had devised a way to make them multiply further.

They had been brought into the great salon, one of the many rooms whose ceiling, walls, doors, even locks were covered with mirrors.

Where are the monsters, said the Cavaliere's wife. There's no monsters here.

The Cavaliere explained that some of the late prince's more fanciful creations had already been taken away and destroyed by his half brother, the present head of the family, who did not enjoy the villa's continuing notoriety.

Servants were bringing in tea and setting it on a great sideboard with panels made from hundreds of sawn-off pieces of antique gilt frames in different styles of carving. The black-garbed chamberlain had become more animated since they had entered the room.

Ah, if you could have seen the villa in the days when my late master was alive, the chamberlain broke out. The chandeliers ablaze, the room full of His Highness's friends dancing and enjoying themselves.

Did the prince give balls? asked the Cavaliere sharply. I am surprised to hear it. I should have thought a man of his tastes and temperament would have preferred seclusion.

True, Excellency, said the chamberlain. My master preferred the villa to himself. But his wife sometimes longed for company.

His wife, exclaimed the Cavaliere's wife. Did he have a wife?

Did they have children? asked the hero, who could not help wondering if a pregnant woman confined in these surroundings would not give birth to a monster.

My master lacked nothing that makes a man happy, said the chamberlain.

One would hardly suppose that, thought the Cavaliere, who had begun to examine the room.

May I humbly suggest, said the chamberlain, that Their Excellencies not sit—

Not sit?

He was pointing. There.

Oh. Indeed, one would have little incentive to do so. Not on chairs with legs of different lengths, ensuring that no one could sit on them.

Nor there, observed the hero, waving his arm at some normally constructed chairs grouped with their backs to one another. Most unfriendly, wouldn't you agree?

Nor there, continued the chamberlain solemnly, indicating three handsome ornate chairs arranged in the proper way, so that those conversing could face one another.

Why not, hooted the Cavaliere's wife, rolling her eyes at her husband in the familiar language of marital complicity.

If her ladyship will touch one of the chairs . . .

She went toward it.

Carefully, my lady!

She ran her beringed hand over the velvet-cushioned seat, and burst out laughing.

What is it, said the hero.

There's a spike under the cushion!

Perhaps, said the Cavaliere, we will forgo tea and venture out into the park. It is a fine day.

So my master would have wished it, said the chamberlain.

The Cavaliere, displeased with the chamberlain's tone, which since their arrival had seemed to him slightly impertinent, turned with a reproving stare to make the gesture that dismissed him (one of the rare occasions for looking closely at a servant's face), and only then observed that the man had a steely blue eye and a lustrous brown one—rhyming as it were with the hybrid objects the late prince had designed.

The Cavaliere's wife, trained by years of womanly solicitude to read every shift of her husband's attention, instantly saw what the Cavaliere was noticing. As the chamberlain bowed gravely and backed toward a door, she murmured something to the hero, who smiled, waited until the chamberlain had left, and then said he would be happy to have a brown and a blue eye if he could see with both of them. The Cavaliere's wife exclaimed how handsome he would be with eyes of different color.

Shall we go out, said the Cavaliere.

Forgive me if I do not join you both for a while, said the hero, who was looking a little wan. He was tired, he was often tired. It seemed an exertion even to have to put the shield back on his poor eye, to protect it from the roasting effulgence of Sicilian sun.

Please remain with our friend, said the Cavaliere to his wife. I shall enjoy looking by myself.

Before leaving them, however, he could not resist providing one more observation, to make sure that they fully appreciated the originality of the room in which they stood.

Looking up at the irregular panes of smoky mirror on the ceiling, he explained that the prevalence of mirrors is what he regarded as most novel in the prince's conception. I myself had once thought, he said—then paused, recalling with vexation the mirrored wall and lost vistas of his observatory room in Naples.

And note, he continued, stifling the pang, note how skillfully it is done. Taking sheets of mirror and breaking them into a multitude of little mirrors, each a different size, then ingeniously fitting them together, creates effects that are undoubtedly bizarre. Since each of them makes a small angle with the other, the effect is like that of multiplying glass, so that the three of us walking below make three hundred of us walking above. But I find this abundance of effects preferable to the monotony that would result from covering so vast a room with unbroken expanses of glass.

The Cavaliere's wife and the hero were listening attentively, respectfully. They are both genuinely interested in what the Cavaliere had to say. At the same time they see each other—they spy on each other—while the Cavaliere goes on talking. A room with mirrors is a fearful temptation. Even more so a room with a canopy of broken mirrors, as faceted as a fly's eye, in which they see themselves multiplied, superimposed, deformed —but deformities created by mirrors only make them laugh.

And when the Cavaliere went off to look at some other rooms and tour the park, and they realize it is just the two of them now, when father has gone and the children are left alone in the fun-house, they stand there in silence, the fat lady and the short man with one arm, and try to look only at the mirrors, but a gust of happiness that seems to have no borders, bliss without an edge, envelops them, and exhausted by the stress of desire, hilarious with happiness, they turn toward each other and kiss (and kiss and kiss), and their turn, their kiss, was shattered, multiplied in the mirrors above.

•

In these surroundings, which bespeak reclusiveness, refusal of ordinary sentiments, whose only romance is with objects, two people who have long loved each other have given way to the most ordinary and powerful of passions, from which there is no turning back.

For the Cavaliere another revelation had been in store. He had been gone for almost an hour, long enough to let his wife and their friend fully savor the force they had unleashed, and, embarrassed by its strength, to want to go look for him. They found him in the park seated on a marble bench, his back to the scarlet hibiscus and crimson bougainvillea climbing over a low wall crowned with more monsters, and listened to him describe in an oddly subdued voice another curious figure he had noted on the way to the park: the Atlas whose broad muscular back bends under the weight of an empty wine barrel. They could not help wondering, guiltily, if the somberness of his mood meant that he had divined what has just happened. But the Cavaliere had not been thinking about his companions at all for some time.

When he had descended one side of the monumental double-flighted external staircase and made his way to the rear of the villa, he was still thinking about them. Then something he had seen had made him lose himself, and so he lost them too.

It was in the prince's chapel. As soon as the Cavaliere entered the dank interior, he was stopped mid-stride. Something, he sensed, was moving high above his head. Probably a bat—he hated bats. Then he realized it was too large, and merely swaying; there was something hanging from the high gilded ceiling which had been agitated by the spring breeze he had let in with him when he opened the door. He could make it out now above him. It was the life-size carved figure of a man kneeling, on nothing, in prayer. As the Cavaliere's eyes became more accustomed to the dimness, he saw that the man was dangling in the musty void from a long chain fastened to the crown of his head. And this chain continued up to a hook that had been screwed into the navel of a large Christ nailed to his cross, which was fixed flat to the ceiling. Both the Crucified One and the suppliant suspended in the air were painted in disturbingly realistic colors.

Blasphemy could not distress this fervent atheist. But fear could, his own stab of fear at the sight of the hanging man, and the expression of inconsolable fear in another. The prince's congeries of grotesque persons and objects did not mean that the prince had been mad. What they signified is that he had been afraid.

He was more daring than I, thought the Cavaliere as he fled the chapel to wait for his wife and their friend to join him. The prince had taken the curiosity and avidity of the collector to its terminal stage, where the attachment to objects releases an ungovernable spirit of raillery. He had every reason to be afraid, and therefore to want to mock his fears. Weighed down with his objects, he had lowered himself, he had floated down, he had plummeted deep into his own feelings and naturally, because he had descended far enough, he had arrived in hell.

•

The Cavaliere has finally learned from Charles of the loss of his vases on the *Colossus* last December 10th. His collection was already under the sea when he was making his own perilous crossing. If they could have saved a few of his chests, only a few! For he learns that the one chest the sailors chose to rescue from the hold, thinking it contained treasure, was found when opened to contain a British admiral preserved in alcohol, who was being shipped home for burial. Damn his body, the Cavaliere wrote to Charles.

The death of objects can release a grief even more bewildering than the death of a loved person. People are supposed to die, hard as that is to keep in mind. Whether one lived with boring prudence, as the Cavaliere now did, or courted death, as his glorious friend did every time he went into battle, the end is the same, inevitable. But objects as durable and as ancient as the Cavaliere's magnificent antique vases, especially such objects, which have survived so many centuries, offer a promise of immortality. Part of why we become attached to them, collect them, is that it is not inevitable that they will some day be subtracted from the world. And when the promise is broken, by accident or negligence, our protestations seem pointless. Our grief a mite indecent. But the mourning, which amplifies grief and thereby eases it, still needs to be done.

Incredulity is our first response to the destruction of something we cherish profoundly. To begin to mourn, one must get past the feeling that this is not happening or has not happened. It helps to be present at the disaster. Having witnessed Catherine's diminishing, having leaned over her for the last breath, he had seen that his unhappy wife had ceased to exist; he had mourned, he had forgiven her for dying, and stopped mourning. Had his treasures gone in a fire in his own house, had they been devoured by lava, whose onrush he had seen with his own eyes, he would know how to do the mourning appropriate for beloved objects; mourning would do its work—and end, before he was irreparably wounded by the unfairness of the loss.

Whatever does not happen before our eyes must be taken on trust. And trust, for the Cavaliere, is becoming scarce. To learn that his treasures had been lost months ago, and so far away, was no different from learning of the death, similarly distant in time and geography, of a beloved person. Such a death bears a peculiar imprint of doubt. To be told one day that someone who has gone off to the other side of the world, and with whom you expect momentarily to be reunited, has actually been dead for many months, during which you have been going on with your life, unaware of this subtraction that has taken place, makes a mockery of the finality of death. Death is reduced to news. And news is always a little unreal—which is why we can bear to take in so much of it.

The Cavaliere mourned for his treasures. But a mourning that begins so posthumously, and under such conditions of doubt and disbelief, can never be fully experienced. Because he could not really mourn, he raged. His powers of recuperation, his resilience, had already been sorely tested, tested as they had never been, in the dispiriting weeks after his arrival in Palermo. But he had managed to pull himself together and reassemble, on a smaller scale, some of his old enjoyments. The loss of his treasures was a defining blow. He felt an accrual of bitterness, this man who had never before entertained the idea that he might be unlucky.

The Cavaliere's world is shrinking. He longed to be back in England, though such a retirement was not likely to be tranquil: he owed his bankers fifteen thousand pounds which he had expected to repay in large part by the sale of his vase collection. (He would have to borrow more from his friend, who has far less money than he but is so generous.) But, he felt, he could not yet extricate himself from Palermo. If there was a chance that their first capital could be returned to the King and Queen in the coming months, it would be worth waiting. His life in Naples could never be restored, but at least those who disrupted his felicity and set into motion all these losses would be punished.

Distance has betrayed him. And time is his enemy. His view of time, and of change, has become that of most elderly people: he hates change, since for him—for his body—any change is for the worse. And if there is to be change, then he wants it to happen quickly, so it does not use up too much of the time remaining to him. He is impatient to discharge his rage. He follows the news from Naples, and confers often with the royal couple and their ministers. The diplomat's virtue of patience, of waiting for events to season and ripen, has quite left him. He wants everything to happen soon, so he can be free, free to leave this dreadful Palermo and return to England. Why does everything happen so slowly?

For the Cavaliere's wife and the hero the world has shrunk, too, but in the most exalting sense. To each other. Any change from their present situation is fraught with the likelihood of separation. And the Cavaliere's wife is starting to like Palermo, but then she is the only one of the trio with something of the south in her.

Don't change anything!

In May the hero left Palermo for the first time since their arrival five months earlier, taking his squadron off the western tip of Sicily, to see if he can detect any new movements of the French fleet. He reassured his friends that he would be gone only a week. The waters are calm. The weather is excellent. The no-sharper-than-usual pain in the stump of his right arm tells him there will not be a storm.

The Cavaliere was cheered by this sign of their friend's recovery. And the woman supposed responsible for the hero's inaction also rejoiced in this evidence of his renewed health. By making him happy she had been making him well, and that was the point, too; so that he would be able to go back to war and win even greater glory for England, even greater victories. Still, she found his departure unbearable. The daily letters they wrote each other rapidly crisscrossed the space between them. But sending precious things away, out into the world, is always a little sad, even when there is hardly any chance they will be lost. It confirms distance and separation. It was not fully real to her that he had gone until the first time she wrote him, a few hours later. Then the awareness that he was not that far away, that he would not be gone for very long, lost all its power to console. Indeed, it is knowing how soon he would be holding the letter, reading it, that is painful. She stared at the letter, this bird that will fly to his breast. She ought to surrender it to the shiny-faced lieutenant waiting deferentially at the threshold of the drawing room, who will gallop west across the hundred miles that separate them and put it in his hand. But she didn't want to give it up, she didn't want to lose the letter, which could be with him tomorrow, while she is here and can't be with him; and overcome by such a dizzying sense of loss, she burst into tears. Suddenly space and time make no sense to her. Why isn't everything right here? Why doesn't everything happen at once?

•

The Cavaliere had been infatuated with the woman he made his wife, had been enthralled by her talents and her charms, had loved her, still loves her deeply; but he did not, as the hero did, worship her. As she passed into her thirties, he desired her less. They had not made love for nearly two years. The Cavaliere wondered if she minded very much. Women often were not sorry when a husband's lust ended. She never reproached him; and on his part there was no diminishment of trust, admiration, dependence—all the things that go by the name of love—nor of his pleasure in being kind to her. But it was her beauty, her unrivaled beauty, that he had desired.

The hero loved her as she was. Exactly as she was. And that made his love the one this former great beauty had always wanted. He thought her majestic.

Out there, in the world, they have both put on brave fronts about their less than ideal appearance. In here, inside their love, honesty becomes possible. They have had their tender moments of confessing the embarrassment they feel over their bodies. He said that he worried she found his stump repulsive. She told him his injuries made him more dear to her. She confessed that she was embarrassed to be so much bigger than he, that she hoped he did not mind, for she would do anything to please him, for he deserved the most beautiful woman in the world. He told her he considered her his wife. They pledged their eternal love. As soon as divorce or the other *d* word (it couldn't be pronounced) freed them, they would marry.

The hero had never before known sexual bliss. And she too experienced an unprecedented happiness in his embrace. She made him tell her about all the women he had slept with; there weren't many. A man who has to admire in order to desire is likely to have led a modest sexual life. He, even more prone to jealousy than she, could not bear to ask her about the men before the Cavaliere. (She had not yet told him she had a daughter.) He confessed that he was jealous of the Cavaliere. He is haunted by the fear of losing her. She makes him shudder.

Everyone was caught up in some kind of deception.

The ending of his sexual life had not made the Cavaliere so insensitive to the erotic currents which flow between others that he had failed to take in what has happened between his wife and his friend. In fact, like everyone else, he assumed they were lovers several months before the excursion to the villa of monsters. He'd always known, a man who marries a beauty thirty-six years younger than himself would have to be a fool not to know, that this would happen one day. And he cannot acquit himself of sexual neglect of his wife in the past few years, though it is not really his fault, he tells himself. He can only congratulate himself that his wife has never, until now, given him the slightest cause for jealousy or occasion for public humiliation; and that, after so many years of marriage, her affections have wandered toward the person to whom, after her, the Cavaliere is most attached in all the world.

The Cavaliere is not someone, like his wife or their friend, who is inclined to shirk the burden of lucidity. He is quite lucid about them. What he is deceived about is his own reactions. He was not aware of being jealous or resentful or humiliated. Since such feelings would be altogether unreasonable, how could he be? He thinks he ought not to mind. Therefore, he does not mind. But he does, for he knows that his wife feels an emotion she has never felt for him. This self-deception—this tendency to live beyond his psychological as well as his financial means—is part of the Cavaliere's abraded talent for happiness, his wish not to be discouraged by anything other than the terminally undesirable. Someone of the Cavaliere's temperament is already keeping at bay a great deal of anger, and fear. He was an expert in dismissing dangerous feelings.

Because he is deceived about his own feelings, it is easier for him to be mistaken about how he can deceive others. With the curious innocence of the obsessed, the Cavaliere imagines that as long as he pretends not to know he can silence the speculation of others. He is banking on his reputation as a judicious man of the world: if such a husband seems convinced there is nothing illicit in his wife's friendship with another man, then they will believe his dissembling, at which he knows himself to be an expert, rather than their own suspicions. A life spent among rulers has given the Cavaliere a rich experience of the powers of lies to distract from a disgracing reality, of denials to prevail over disagreeable truth. This will be just one more appearance, in which he pretends not to know some inconveniencing fact. It doesn't occur to him that the more he denies what is going on, the more he will seem like a dupe.

The Cavaliere does not see how he is already viewed, will be regarded for the rest of his life, and beyond: as a famous cuckold. Neither is the hero able to see what he has become in the eyes of others, and how he will be judged: part Lawrence of Arabia, self-appointed rescuer of incompetent native rulers; part Mark Antony, self-destructive lover of his own ruin.

Unlike the Cavaliere, at least he knew what he was feeling. But he had difficulty in understanding the feelings of others when they were negative about his own person. The only negative attitudes he could understand were neglect and indifference. Usually the last to know when someone was critical of him—he had such a strongly developed sense of his own righteousness—he doesn't realize that he is mocked and pitied; that his officers and his men consider their adored commander has been bewitched by a siren. Nor did he realize how displeased his superiors at the Admiralty were with his conduct: authorizing the preposterous Neapolitan march on Rome, diverting resources to evacuate the royal family, and delaying reentering the war against the French, remaining in Palermo, giving priority to setting the King and Queen back on the throne. Misjudgment? No, abandonment of judgment, for the personal reason that everybody gossiped about.

Even the Cavaliere's wife, although the most clear-sighted of the three, was in her way also self-deceived. Having had such a profound experience of the Cavaliere's generosity, she cannot believe it will not all work out. They both loved the Cavaliere. He loved them both. Why should they not always live together, with the Cavaliere as the good father. They will be an unusual family, but a family still. (The hero's wife back in England didn't enter the equation.) She even dared to hope that she could become pregnant, after all the unfruitful years with Charles and the Cavaliere.

She had had a dream recently in which she was accompanying the Cavaliere up the side of a volcano, as in the old days. But it did not look like Vesuvius. No, it must be Etna. It seemed they already knew that a minor eruption had started a few hours earlier; and after a while the Cavaliere suggested that they stop to eat and rest, and wait for the eruption to subside. She removed her sweaty blouse to dry, how delicious the wind felt on her skin; and they ate pigeons cooked on an open fire the Cavaliere had built, how succulent they were. Then they continued up the slope, their laboring feet crunching the hot cinders, and she began to feel apprehensive about what she would see when they reached the top. Wasn't it dangerous if the volcano was still erupting—

which it was, despite the Cavaliere's reassurances. They were pinnacled now, and the crater's baleful opening lay before them. The Cavaliere told her to stay where she was and moved closer. He seemed to be getting too close. She wanted to call out, to tell him to be careful. But when she opened her mouth no sound came, though she strained until her throat hurt. The Cavaliere was at the very brink of the crater. He was turning into something black, like the burnt pages of a book. He looked back at her and smiled. And then, as she found the voice to scream, he leapt into the fiery chasm.

Ejecting herself from the horrifying scene, she punched her way up through the roof of sleep and surfaced on the bed, panting, drenched in sweat. Then I would be a widow. The dream was so vivid. She had an impulse to dress and go to the Cavaliere's room and reassure herself that he was all right. And realizing what she was imagining, she was shaken, shocked, ashamed. Did this mean that she wished the Cavaliere's death? No, no. It would all work out.

•

Another night—late, very late. The guests must have departed by now, thought the Cavaliere, who had long been in his quarters, enduring the insomnia of the aged, and of the aggrieved. He has so much to think about, and even more not to think about: the loss of his treasures, his debts, his uncertainty about the future, the vague aches and pains in his brittle body, a vaguer sense of humiliation. His life, once so full of choices, offers no acceptable choice now.

He had already been in bed, and sought a comfortable sleep-inducing position, for more than an hour. On the balcony outside the great window, framed by silhouettes of palm trees, he gazed into the heavy scented air. The moonlit clouds were very low, the sky luminous, almost pink. The night itself augments his testy feeling that the hours do not advance, the night seems suspended. It is pure night, it could be night forever. There is not even a movement of clouds to show him night passing. He heard a man's voice singing a little out of tune, no doubt some caterwauling local complaining about the pains of love; the rumble of a distant carriage; a night bird; and very faintly the voices of British sailors in a vessel crossing the bay, singing hymns. And silence.

His anger keeps him from going back to bed. Though it might seem childish to imagine Naples being devastated by a volcanic eruption, the Cavaliere is not above having such fantasies sometimes as he is drifting off to sleep. If only he could punish those who had wronged him, if only he could find an event that would answer to his sense of grievance and loss. Then he would return to England. After all, he has to live somewhere. How angry he feels. And how inconsolable.

The Cavaliere was correct in supposing the guests had departed. Indeed, the servants had almost finished cleaning up in the great salon. His wife and their friend had gone to their separate quarters, and then the Cavaliere's wife joined the hero in his room at two in the morning. She had brought him some figs of Barbary, pomegranates, and Sicilian cakes covered with white sugar and lemon peel. She worried that he did not eat enough, he was so thin, and that he slept so little. Their hours together —usually from two until five in the morning, when she would return to her own quarters—were the only time they could be alone; she could sleep late, but he always rose at dawn. And they too stood on the balcony and breathed in the warm air scented with laurel and blossoming orange and almond trees, and admired the clouds that had been lowered from heaven, steeped in orange and pink. But there was no longing for what was absent or left behind. Everything was here, complete.

She loved to undress him, as if he were a child. He had the most beautiful skin of any man she had known, soft as a girl's. She pressed her lips to the poor scorched stump of his arm. He flinched. She kissed it again. He sighed. She kissed his groin and he laughed and pulled her onto the bed, into their position—they already had habits. She lay her head on his right shoulder, he held her with his left arm. That was the way they always lay: it was so comforting. It is your place. Your body is my arm.

She stroked his wavy hair, easing his head toward her so her face could receive his breath. She touched his cheek, with its beautiful stubble. She clasped him to her, her fingers scribbling down his back, her palm sliding upward to erase it. Their languid lying side by side began to quicken. She threw her leg over his hip and locked him to her. He groaned, and fell into her body. The work of pleasure began: the drop and push of pelvis, bone sheathed in flesh dissolving, blooming into pure fall. How deep it was. Touch me here, she said. I want your mouth here. And here. Deeper. Pressing, squeezing, at first she had feared she might overwhelm him with the intensity of her desire for him; he seemed so fragile to her. But he wanted to be dominated by her, he wanted to be flooded by her with emotion.

Weight against weight; fluid with fluid; inside against, filled, packed with outside. He felt she was swallowing him, and he wanted to live inside her.

She shut her eyes, although she loved nothing more than to watch his face, over hers, under hers, and see him feeling what she is feeling. She can feel him brimming and flooding. She never imagined a man could feel as she did. She always wanted to lose her body in the throes of pleasure, to become pure sensation. But that, she knew, is not the way a man feels. A man never forgets his body the way a woman does, because a man is pushing his body, a part of his body, forward, to make the act of love happen. He brings the jut of his body into the act of love, then takes it back, when it has had its way. That was the way men were. But now she knew that a man could feel as she did, in his whole body. That a man could allow himself to groan and cling, just as she did when he mounted her and pierced her. That he wanted to be taken by her as much as she wanted to be taken by him. That she did not have to pretend to feel more pleasure than she did; that he yielded to her as much as she yielded to him. That they both embarked on the adventure of pleasure with the same slight anxiety about their ability to please or be pleased, and the same ease, the same trust. That they were equals in pleasure, because equals in love.

Meanwhile, the world is still out there: the inexhaustible mystery of simultaneity. While this is happening, that is also happening. Meanwhile, both Vesuvius and Etna flamed and smoked. The members of the trio prepared to drift off to sleep. The Cavaliere in his bed, thinking of his drowned treasures, of the volcano, of his lost world. And his beloved wife and beloved friend interlaced in another bed, thinking of each other in the fullness of satisfied desire. They kissed delicately. Sleep, my love. Sleep, she repeats to him. He says he cannot sleep, he is too happy. Talk to me, he said. I love your voice. She begins to muse astutely about the latest news from Naples: the slow effectiveness of Captain Troubridge's blockade, which had begun in late March; the surprising progress of Cardinal Ruffo's Christian army, now seventeen thousand strong; the difficulty of. . . . He fell asleep while she was talking. The hero loves to sleep now.

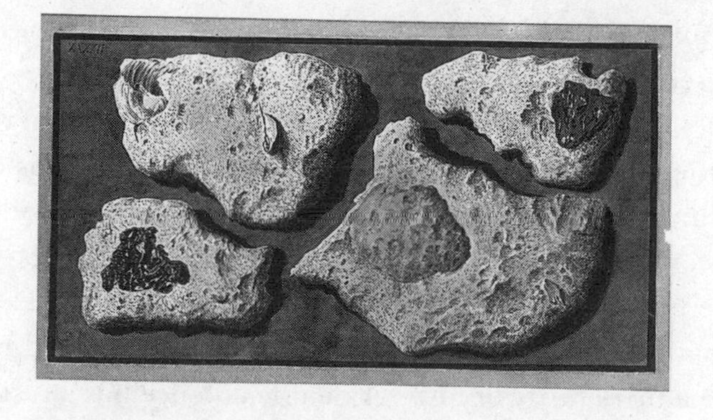

6

Baron Vitellio Scarpia was an exceptionally cruel man. Five years ago he had been put in charge of suppressing republican opposition in Naples by the Queen and, as if his pleasure in dispensing punishment were not credential enough for this appointment, was reputed to be one of her lovers (who close to the Queen was not?). Scarpia pursued his task with zeal. He was glad to concur in the Queen's view that every aristocrat was probably harboring revolutionary sympathies; a Sicilian himself, and only recently ennobled, he hated the old Neapolitan aristocracy. And of course not only aristocrats but also theologians, chemists, poets, lawyers, scholars, musicians, doctors, indeed anyone, including priests and monks, who possessed more than two or three books, were also suspect. Scarpia estimated there to be at least fifty thousand real or potential enemies of the monarchy, about a tenth of the city's population.

That many? exclaimed the Queen, who had to speak to this uncouth baron in Italian.

Probably more, said Scarpia. And every one of them, Majesty, is under surveillance.

The vast private army of informers Scarpia had recruited

were everywhere. A café might be the site of a secret Jacobin debating club or some other discussion; recent decrees had banned all scientific and literary meetings, as well as the reading of any foreign book or journal. A botanist's lecture room might be the setting in which someone passed a revolutionary signal, with eyes or hands, to another auditor. A performance at the San Carlo might be the occasion for sporting a scarlet waistcoat or distributing a clandestinely printed republican broadside. The prisons burgeoned with the most respectable—that is, the richest and the best educated—inhabitants of the kingdom.

That was the only mistake. The only mistake had been to execute a mere thirty or forty. A death sentence has a result, one which closes that particular file. A prison sentence has a term. Most of Scarpia's files were still open. After doing three years in the galleys for possession of two books by Voltaire (a single forbidden book being worth three years, it should have been six), the Marchese Angelotti had transferred his perfidious activities to Rome, where he had joined in the uprising there against law, order, and the Church. All too rarely did the rigors of imprisonment have a calming effect. The brother of the Duke della ***, after a much shorter term (unpowdered hair, six months), had come out of prison deranged and had withdrawn to the family palace, which he'd not been seen to leave since; one of Scarpia's informants in the household, a footman, reported that the duke's brother was sequestered on his floor, had ordered the shutters nailed shut, and spent most of his time writing unintelligible poems. And as the malefactors were released, others had to be locked up. That Portuguese lady at the court, Eleonora de Fonseca Pimentel, who used to write sonnets in praise of the Queen, had shown an Ode to Liberty she had composed to a friend and Scarpia had been able to put her away this past October for two years.

Poets!

When the royal family fled Naples in late December under the protection of the British admiral, Scarpia had stayed, charged with the duty of being the Queen's eyes in her absence. He prowled the city in a black cloak, like those worn by lawyers, watching the Queen's predictions come true. The Marchese Angelotti had hurried back from Rome to rejoice in the anarchy that succeeded the flight of legitimate government in Naples. A mob had stormed the Vicaria to rescue some common criminals. Unfortunately, this was the prison where he had put away Fonseca Pimentel, who had come out head high, prating about liberty and equality and the rights of the people. Hadn't she looked at the face of the mob that inadvertently liberated her? They thought they were speaking for the people, these poets and professors and liberal aristocrats. But the people had other ideas. The people loved the King (they were too ignorant to love the Queen), and admired the distance between the inordinate luxury and frivolity of the court and the misery and servitude of their own lives. Like the King and Queen, they hated the cultured aristocracy. The French were advancing down the peninsula, and the populace, enraged by the departure of the King, held the aristocrats responsible. Well, they were right. Let the conflagration come. Let Naples be cleansed of these damned malcontents with their atheistic books and French ideas and scientific conceits and humanitarian reforms. Scarpia gave himself over to an ecstasy of vengeful imaginings. The people were pigs but the people were preparing for the return of royal government. He did not have to do all the work. The people did it for him.

•

Baron Scarpia was an exceptionally passionate man. He understood much about human passions, particularly when they lead to wicked conduct. He understood how sexual pleasure is enhanced by debasing and humiliating the object of one's desire; this is how he experienced pleasure. He understood how fear, fear of change, fear of what is or seems foreign, therefore threatening, is relieved by banding together with others to harass and injure those who are defenseless as well as different; this is what he saw happening around him. Passion for Scarpia was vehemence, aggression. What he could not understand is a passion that finds happiness in a retreat from vehemence, which makes one self-withdrawn. Like the passion of the collector.

Numerous as were the converts that enlightened opinion had made among the upper classes, an even greater number were collectors, and collectors have a hard time accepting the consequences of revolutionary upheaval. Their holdings are an investment in the old regime, no matter how many volumes of Voltaire they have read. A revolution is not a good moment for collectors.

To collect is by definition to collect the past—while to make a revolution is to condemn what is now called the past. And the past is very heavy, as well as large. If the collapse of the old order makes you decide to flee, it's unlikely you can take everything with you—that was the Cavaliere's plight. It's unlikely you can protect it, if you have to stay.

•

This is one of the sights the baron saw.

January 19, 1799. Three weeks after the flight from Naples, and something terrible was happening to one of the Cavaliere's acquaintances and fellow collectors. This man, whose main interests were painting, mathematics, architecture, and geology, was one of the most erudite and studious inhabitants of the kingdom. And far from sharing the republican sympathies of some of the other cultivated aristocrats such as his brother, he was, like most collectors, of a conservative temperament; indeed, this collector was particularly averse to the novelties of the day. He had proposed to follow the King and the Queen to Palermo. But he had been refused permission. Stay in Naples, learned duke! And see how you like the rule of the godless French.

Surely the approaching French soldiers could not be a greater threat than the pillaging mobs roaming the streets, thought the duke, who remained in his palace in order to deliberate, to make a plan, to announce a plan. At a family council which lasted late into the night of January 18th perhaps the duke, who was recovering from a severe catarrh, did not preside as forcefully as he might have. The crosswinds of peril fractured the usual hierarchies of utterance. The duke's younger son shouted at his mother. The duke's young daughter interrupted her father. The duchess angrily contradicted both her husband and her venerable mother-in-law. But the decision that was finally reached as to who among them was to be removed from danger, no, do not call it flight, reinstated the violated hierarchies. The duke and his two sons would retire, that is the word, retire for a while to the villa in Sorrento—leaving behind in the safety of the palace the duchess, their daughter, his aged mother, and the brother who had come out of prison mad.

The duke was to leave the capital with his sons the next day, after a meeting of nobles in which he was expected to take part. To conserve his strength for the trip he sent his older son, who was nineteen, in his place. The young man sat politely through the many speeches of the nobles reaffirming their loyalty to the Bourbon monarchy in exile in Palermo, after which they agreed they had no other choice but to welcome the French, who would at least bring some order to the city; and at one o'clock he returned through the strangely deserted streets to make his report to his father. During the four hours he had been gone, he learned, his uncle tried to hang himself in the library but was cut down in time and had been put to bed. Three servants were stationed in the room to prevent another attempt.

The son was sent to bring his uncle, still in his nightgown, to join the family for dinner. As they eased him into his chair, the major-domo brought the news that a mob had gathered at the entrance to the palace and was demanding to see the duke. Against the advice of his wife and mother, the duke, accompanied only by his secretary, went down to talk to them himself. Among the fifty or so bronze-faced people in the courtyard he recognized a flour merchant, his barber, a water seller on the Toledo, and the wheelwright who repaired his carriages. The flour merchant, who seemed to be the hubbub-master, declared that they had come to break up the banquet the duke was giving for his Jacobin friends. The duke smiled gravely. My dear visitors, you are mistaken. It is only I and my family who are at dinner, and it is no banquet.

Again the flour merchant demanded entrance. Impossible, said the duke, and turned to go inside. A clanking volley of people wielding sticks and knives seized the duke, pushed past the servants, and rushed up the stairs. The family fled to a higher floor, except for the duke's stuporous brother, who remained at the table crumbling a piece of bread in his hand. The two brothers were dragged down and out of the palace. Some men were sent to stand guard over the family, while the looting began.

People went from room to room, pulling pictures off walls, opening chests and cupboards, emptying drawers and throwing their contents on the floor. Into the picture gallery, where most of the duke's magnificent collection of paintings were hung; into his library, which housed myriad valuable papers and documents, the splendid hoard of rare books and priceless manuscripts accumulated one hundred and fifty years ago by an illustrious ancestor, a cardinal, and a great number of modern works; into his study, where his collection of minerals was arrayed in a row of glass-fronted cabinets; into the duke's chemical laboratories, where dozens of mechanical instruments were kept; into his watchmaking studio, where the duke, who had been instructed in the watchmaker's art, enjoyed relaxing from his learned pursuits. The windows on the upper floors were flung open and down came paintings, statues, books, papers, implements, and instruments into the courtyard. Meanwhile, people were carrying downstairs all the rich furniture and plate and linen, and leaving the palace. Gradually the doors, windows, balcony railings, beams, and banisters were stripped and carted away.

A few hours and many bribes later, the duke's family was allowed to leave the palace, after being searched to make sure that they had not pocketed any of their possessions. Their pleas to be allowed to take the duke and his brother with them were met with jeers. At least allow my son who is ill to come with us, cried the old duchess. No. At least allow me to say goodbye to my father, cried the duke's young daughter. No. Are you not yourselves husbands, fathers, sons? cried the duke's wife. Have you no pity? Yes to the first. To the second: No.

The weeping family was led out a back entrance and shoved into the street.

Throughout this time the duke and his brother, shivering in his nightgown, had been kept under guard in the stable. When the bonfire was lit, they were brought out into the courtyard and roped to chairs so they could watch.

All afternoon the burning went on. The Raphael, the Titian, the Correggio, the Giorgione, the Guercino, and all the other sixty-four pictures . . . into the fire. And the books, works of history, travel, and science, and on arts and manufactures; the complete Vico and Voltaire and d'Alembert . . . into the fire. Into the soaring bonfire, what does not burn: his collection of Vesuvian rocks—taken from fire, returned to fire. The delicate watches, the pendulums, the compasses, the telescopes with platinum mirrors, the microscopes, the chronometers, barometers, thermometers, odometers, graphometers, echometers, hydrometers, vinometers, pyrometers . . . broken, melting. The light darkened. The fire went on burning. Night fell. The stars came out. And the burning burned. The brother cried for a while and begged to be untied and then fell asleep. The duke watched, his eyes stinging. He coughed convulsively, he said nothing. When there was no more to hurl in the flames, members of the mob gathered near the chairs to shout insults at them. Jacobins. French-lovers. Then several men took courage and laid hands first on the duke, pulling off his stockings and shoes, then severing the rope that tied his arms behind his back so they could take his silk coat, waistcoat, cravat, and linen shirt. The duke writhed as they pulled off his clothes, not to oppose what was being done to him but rather to make it easier for them, so he could more quickly resume his stiff posture of uncomplaining rectitude, the sole reproach he deemed consonant with his dignity. Torso bared, he lifted his head again. Still he kept silent.

More courage, more cruelty. A barrel of tar, which stood in a corner of the courtyard, had been rolled near the fire. A few men dipped wooden bowls into the barrel and threw the scorching tar on the brother, who woke up with a cry and then flung his head back as if he had been shot. Then someone shot him. They untied the body and heaved it onto the bonfire. The duke screamed.

•

At the entrance to the courtyard someone was watching the scene: a man in a black cloak and handsome powdered wig flanked by several municipal soldiers in uniform. Those in the crowd who became aware of him, even if they did not recognize him, regarded him with fear.

The man in black was staring fixedly at the duke, not at his face but at the pale, heavy abdomen swelling and contracting with his sobs. His feet were red—he had been shot in both legs—but he still kept himself upright in the chair, his arms again tied behind his back.

Neither the man in black nor his guards moved to intervene. But the duke's tormentors had paused. Though they seemed to know he would not stop them, they were not sure they could go on. Everyone was afraid of the man in black—except for the barber, who was one of his informants.

The barber stepped forward, his razor in hand, and sliced off the duke's ears. As they fell from his head, an apron of blood appeared on the lower part of his face. The crowd yelled, the bonfire trembled, and the man in black hummed with satisfaction and left, so the drama could go on to its end.

•

You saw when I left, said Scarpia the next day in a tavern by the harbor to a member of the mob in his employ. What happened then? Was he still alive?

Yes, said the man. Yes, that's what I'm saying. He was crying and the blood was running down from his face and head.

Still alive?

Yes, my lord. But you know how, when sweat runs down your chest—

(The man was a sedan-chair carrier, an occupation that would make him particularly familiar with the vagaries of sweat.)

—you know, when sweat runs down your chest, and sometimes it collects in the center—

(The immaculately garbed baron didn't know; but go on . . .)

—you know how, well, the blood was collecting in the center, and he was trying to make it run down.

The sedan-chair carrier stopped his narrative to mime the action, lowering his chin on his chest and blowing through pursed lips toward an imaginary spot above his larded waist.

Blowing, he said. You know. He just kept blowing. Blowing air. That's all he did. To make the blood run down. Then one of our fellows thought he was trying a magic spell, blowing on himself to make himself disappear, and shot him again.

And was he dead then?

Nearly dead. He'd lost so much blood.

Still alive?

Yes. Yes. Then more of our people came up and went at him with their knives. Someone slashed at the front of his breeches and cut off . . . you know, and held them up to the crowd. And then we dumped the body in the tar barrel and threw it on the fire.

•

When news of these heinous events reached Palermo, the Cavaliere shuddered and fell silent. He had liked the duke, and admired his collections. Much of what had been destroyed was irreplaceable. Besides the paintings, in the duke's library there were several unpublished works by the prolific Athanasius Kircher. And, the Cavaliere recalled, the manuscript—he feared it might have been the only copy—of his friend Piranesi's autobiography. What a loss. The Cavaliere grimaced. What a terrible loss.

The Cavaliere's wife and the hero talked of little else for days. They saw in the fate of the duke and his brother the propensity of all undisciplined crowds to relapse into savagery, and the need to protect the sanctity of property, the property of the privileged. These were of course also the Cavaliere's convictions, but he held them less volubly, with less indignation. Although a collection is far more than just a special, particularly vulnerable form of property-holding, the collector's rue is difficult to share, except with other collectors. And to the vulnerability of the state and of the flesh, the Cavaliere had become almost resigned.

The Queen was neither indignant nor rueful. When she read the long description by her most trusted agent left behind in Naples of the gory fate of the duke and his brother and of other nobles at the hands of the mob, the Queen had been taking tea with her most trusted agent here in Palermo. After finishing Scarpia's letter, she passed it to the Cavaliere's wife. Je crois que le peuple avait grandement raison, said the Queen.

Even the Cavaliere's wife flinched.

The Cavaliere's wife did not like Scarpia. Nobody liked Scarpia. But she tried, as she always did, to see matters from the Queen's point of view. The Queen had explained to her dear friend that she did not trust Prince Pignatelli, the regent they had appointed before leaving—and, as she was soon able to point out, she was right, for Pignatelli abandoned the city a few weeks later. Neither did the Queen trust that Calabrian, Cardinal Ruffo, who was preparing to return in secrecy to lead the resistance against the French. But she did trust Baron Scarpia, she told the Cavaliere's wife.

Vouz verrez, ma chère Miledy. Notre Scarpia restera fidèle.

•

In the days following the murder of the duke and his brother, mobs continued to sack and pillage the aristocrats' properties, and the patriots, as they called themselves, took refuge in the sea-fort of Ovo, from whose battlements at night they could see the fires of the French encampments outside the city. When General Championnet's army entered Naples, Scarpia went into hiding. Of the three days of murderous combat between the populace and the French soldiers, and the moment when the tricolor was hoisted over the royal palace and the revolutionaries emerged from the fortress, he could not give an eyewitness account to the Queen.

His hiding place, in the chambers of a bishop who was one of his informers, was a secure one. But, of course, no hiding place is entirely secure; he would have known how to track himself down (the right bribes, the right application of torture). He knew the revolutionaries must be looking for him. Wasn't he responsible for the deaths of some of the premature conspirators? Hadn't he persecuted many of those now leading the republic? Jurists, scholars, defrocked priests, professors of mathematics and chemistry—the twenty-five men appointed by the French general to serve as a provisional government were like a roll call of the kind of cosmopolites and subversives Scarpia had been putting in jail whenever he had a pretext. But apparently they didn't know how to find him. Unstimulated by fear, Scarpia felt the acrid essence of himself each day more diluted by the bishop's tiresome I-always-knew and But-never-did-I-expect and, not least, by this unaccustomed stint of celibacy. The first time he ventured out, to get a woman, he was sure he was recognized. The second time, to exhibit himself watching the curious crowd watching a large pine tree being planted in front of the ex-royal palace, he was not so sure. He spent a few more days with the bishop and then went home, wrote a long report to the Queen, and waited to be arrested. And waited. His enemies, it seemed, were too high-minded for anything like revenge.

Now he was biding his time while these protégés of self-styled enlightenment put on their ridiculous floppy red Phrygian caps and addressed each other as Citizen and made speeches and took down royal emblems and planted their Tree of Liberty in squares throughout the city and went into committee to write a constitution modeled on that of the French republic. They were dreamers, all of them. They would see. He would have his revenge.

You can always count on the gullibility of the benevolent. They go along, marching ahead, thinking they have the people behind them, and then they turn around and . . . nobody there. The mob has peeled off, looking for food or wine or sex or a nap or a good brawl. The mob is unwilling to be high-minded. A mob wants to fight or to disperse. The Jacobin lords and ladies with their sentimental ideas of justice and liberty—they thought they were giving the people what they wanted, or what was good for them. Which, in their sonorous naïveté, they believed to be the same thing. No, the lash, and punctual displays of pomp glorifying state and ecclesiastical power, that's what the people want. Of course, these professors and liberal aristocrats thought they understood the people's need for pageantry, and were planning a festival celebrating the Goddess of Reason. Reason! What kind of spectacle is that! Did they really expect the people to love reason—no, Reason—as they loved the King? Did they really expect the people to take to the new calendar that had been decreed, with Italianized versions of the names of the French revolutionary calendar?

Scarpia noted with glee that the republicans were soon forced to recognize that these borrowed rites and nomenclature were not enough to inspire loyalty in the ignorant masses. An article in the revolutionary newspaper edited by Eleonora de Fonseca Pimentel on the value to the revolution of a successful performance of the city's famous biannual miracle was the first sign of realism. But such open patronizing of the people's faith showed how far these prisoners of Reason were from the understanding needed to dominate the people. Scarpia, cleverest of manipulators and bigots, knew that once you cease talking about faith and start talking about religion—even more indiscreetly, about the role of religion in upholding order and maintaining public morale—faith is being discredited, and the true authority of the Church compromised, fatally so. The value of religion! That was a secret never to be mentioned in public. How guileless they were.

And impotent. For the traditional rites and local omens that alarmed or pacified the superstitious masses were not under the control of the republicans. Take the miracle of the liquefaction of the ampule of dried saint's blood: the republicans were right to worry that, to demonstrate the withdrawal of heavenly protection from the city, the royalist archbishop would prevent the miracle from taking place. And of course no one could control Vesuvius, all-purpose omen and supreme expression of the force and autonomy of nature. True, the mountain had been behaving well recently. The republicans hoped the people would notice that even if San Gennaro withheld his benediction, the mountain was on the patriots' side. Vesuvius, quiet ever since 1794, sent up a placid flame, as of rejoicing, on the evening of the fireworks celebrating the proclamation of the republic, wrote the Fonseca woman. More poet's fancies! But the people were not reassured so easily, although they could always be made more fearful than they already were. What a pity, thought Scarpia, that there is not some way to bring about an eruption. A big eruption. Now.

How much more to the point was the Queen's appeal to the people's faith. She had entrusted her fellow exile and closest confidante, the wife of the British minister, with the task of diffusing packets of the fake republican proclamations she had devised. EASTER ABOLISHED! ALL VENERATION OF THE VIRGIN HEREBY PROHIBITED! BAPTISM AT THE AGE OF SEVEN! MARRIAGE NO LONGER A SACRAMENT! All the English had to do was throw them in the post at Leghorn for Naples, the Queen had told her friend. The Cavaliere, when informed of the plan by his wife, inquired if the Queen expected the English, that is, himself, to pay the postage. No, no, said the Cavaliere's wife, she pays, out of her own purse. I wonder how many will arrive, said the Cavaliere. Oh, the Queen don't care if they all arrive or not. She says some will arrive. Some did arrive; Scarpia had seen them passed from hand to hand. Proclamations that flattered the people and praised their courage would be less convincing, he knew, than those that incited fear. People, look what these agents of the French Antichrist have in store for you! For the better-off, money is more effective: the large sums from her own purse the Queen was sending him to retain the loyalty of aristocrats who might have concluded they had no choice but to cooperate with the self-styled patriots.

Their fairy-tale revolution was under siege from the beginning but, Scarpia saw, although they knew they would be obliged to take up arms, they would never understand the necessary role of state violence. While their constitution invokes the martial spirit of ancient Greece and Rome, they hadn't a clue how to organize a militia, let alone an army. And what kind of police, thought the former head of the secret police in Naples, was a citizens' police? No police at all. In fact, their revolution was defenseless.

•

Alas, Scarpia's predictions were correct.

A revolution made by members of the privileged classes in the metropolis, lacking any support in the countryside or among the urban masses, now further pauperized by the exit of capital with the flight of the old regime and the loss of revenues brought in by tourism . . . a revolution led by the honorable and the scrupulous, who are not only unwilling to use force to suppress popular discontent but have no ambition to increase state power . . . a revolution threatened with imminent invasion and already encircled by a naval blockade of the capital city (worsening the food shortages) mounted by the great empire of the counter-revolution supporting the government in exile . . . a revolution protected by occupying troops, hated by the people, of the continent-conquering rival empire . . . a revolution challenged by a large guerrilla insurgency in the rural areas financed by the government in exile and commanded by a popular émigré grandee . . . a revolution subverted by the smuggling to its potential supporters among the privileged classes of large cash gifts from abroad, and by a disinformation campaign devised by the government in exile to persuade the people that their most cherished customs are about to be abolished . . . a revolution immobilized because its leaders, who fully recognize the need for economic reform, include both radicals and moderates, neither of whom gains the upper hand. A revolution without the time to work it all out.

Such a revolution doesn't have a chance. Indeed, it is the classic design, confected in that decade, reused many times since, for a revolution that doesn't have a chance. And will go down in history as naïve. Well-intentioned. Idealistic. Premature. The sort of revolution that gives, to some, a good name to revolution; and to everyone else confirms the impossibility of a governance that lacks an appetite for repression.

Of course the future will prove these patriots right. The future will make of the doomed leaders of the Vesuvian republic heroes, martyrs, forerunners. But the future is another country.

In the country that is the only one the revolutionaries have, there is dearth and unfamiliar kinds of disorder. The revolutionaries have not exactly inherited a balanced economy. Everything had to be imported except silk stockings, soap, tortoiseshell snuffboxes, marble tables, ornamental furniture, and porcelain figure groups, the kingdom's principal manufactures. The silk and ceramic factories offered paid drudgery to a select few; many were servants or artisans; and a large portion of the city's population was accustomed to subsisting on beggary, theft, and tips for menial services rendered to nobs and to tourists. But the robbery of the entire treasury by the King and Queen, which had left the kingdom without any money, had shriveled patronage, halted the construction boom that had begun with the arrival of the Bourbon monarchy in 1734 (the building of new public works, of palaces and residences for the rich, of churches and theatres, had been one of the few steady sources of employment), and suspended tourism (there was no Grand Tour of revolution). Food prices soared. Hardly anyone had work now.

The necessity of eliminating corruption—indeed, of reorganizing the whole society on a natural, rational basis by the science of legislation—was obvious to all the leaders of the new government, who were not so naïve as to think that there was no more to governing than educating. But the rift widened between moderates and radicals, with the moderates advocating the taxation of the rich and the reduction of Church exemptions, and the radicals urging the abolition of titles and the confiscation of all aristocratic and ecclesiastical property. When one of the government committees proposed public lotteries as a way of replenishing the empty treasury, the proposal was denounced as inadequate or impractical or immoral, the last argument being advanced by Fonseca Pimentel in the pages of her newspaper. The instruction of the people and their conversion to republican ideas—propaganda—was the only one of the revolution's tasks on which everyone could agree. New, uplifting names—Modesty, Silence, Frugality, Triumph—were given to the Toledo, the Chiaia, and other principal streets. Fonseca Pimentel proposed bringing out a gazette and almanacs for the people in Neapolitan dialect. She wrote an article about the need for theatre and opera reform. The people were to have open-air puppet shows with more edifying escapades for their Punchinellos, and at the San Carlo—already renamed the National Theatre—the educated classes would have operas with allegorical subjects such as those being staged in France: *The Triumph of Reason*, *Sacrifice on the*

Altar of Liberty, *Hymn to the Supreme Being*, *Republican Discipline*, and *The Crimes of the Old Regime*.

The whole thing lasted five months. Five renamed months: Piovoso (rainy), Ventoso (windy), Germile (budding), Fiorile (flowering), and Pratile (meadowed) . . .

The first acts of resistance were in outlying villages and small towns—there were more than two thousand settled villages and small towns in the kingdom. The patriots in the capital were astonished at the unrest, and went back into committee to discuss their plans for appropriating great estates and distributing them to landless peasants.

The news worsened. The republican forces sent to the provinces proved no match for the small landing parties from English frigates they encountered. Ruffo's self-styled Christian army was taking village after village. It now included thousands of convicts released by royal order from prisons in Sicily and transported in English ships to the Calabrian coast. Besieged from without and confronting increasing disaffection and civil disturbances in Naples itself, the republic redoubled its efforts to win the hearts and minds of the people.

There were food riots. More French soldiers were ambushed. Trees of Liberty burned at night in the public squares.

The Tree of Liberty is an artificial plant, Scarpia wrote the Queen. As it has taken no roots here, it does not need to be uprooted. Even now it is being shaken vigorously by Your Majesty's loyal subjects, and without the protection of the French it will topple on its own, as soon as the enemy departs.

In May, France, defeated in a number of battles with the newly formed Second Coalition in the north of Italy, withdrew its forces from Naples. British frigates occupied Capri and Ischia. A few weeks later Ruffo and his army of sullen peasants and country bandits poured into the city, merged with crowds of the witty urban poor chanting slogans such as "Whoever has anything worth stealing must be a Jacobin," and embarked on an extraordinary spree of pillage and atrocity. The rich were hunted down in their mansions, the young medical students with republican sympathies in their hospitals, the prelates of conscience in their churches. Nearly fifteen hundred patriots managed to regain their refuge in the sea-forts of Ovo and Nuovo.

The liquid crowd poured into every crevice of the city, sucking into its lethal embrace anyone who did not belong to it. A hunting crowd, looking for the telltale signs of Jacobin identity (apart from having something worth stealing): a soberly dressed man with unpowdered hair; someone with trousers; someone with spectacles; someone who dared to walk on the street alone or seemed to panic at the sight of the crowd surging round the corner. Oh, yes, and since every male patriot had a Tree of Liberty tattooed at the top of one thigh, those not immediately killed or seriously wounded were stripped and then paraded through the streets, to be mocked and reviled by the clothed. It didn't matter that no one had ever found such a tattoo on the naked captives. Don't they invite a pinch, a blow, a jeer. A baiting crowd, loudly enjoying itself. Here comes another Jacobin! Let's look for his tattoo! And here comes a woman strapped in a cart with a sheet barely covering the upper part of her limp naked body in rough allusion to some ideal antique dress: Look, another Goddess of Reason!

The crowd doesn't torment like Scarpia. The work of the true torturer is guided by the fact that, in order to register pain, consciousness is necessary. The crowd is no less gratified if the person being tormented is already unconscious. It is the action of bodies on bodies, not bodies on minds, which the crowd enjoys.

A rock through the window, the hand tightening around the wrist, the crack of the staff to the head, the blade or the penis intruding in soft flesh, the ear or nose or foot in the gutter or sticking out of someone's pocket. Smite, stomp, shoot, throttle, clobber, stone, impale, hang, burn, dismember, drown. A full debauch of homicidal modes whose purpose is much more than just to exact revenge or express a sense of grievance. The revenge of the country against the city, the uneducated against the educated, the poor against the privileged—these explanations don't name the deeper energy released in such havoc. The river of tears and blood that is swamping, carrying away, engulfing the revolution menaces the restoration as well. For this is something like nature—which, notoriously, does not act in its own interest or make judicious discriminations. Even before this energy exhausts itself, it will doubtless be reined in by the rulers who have sanctioned it.

Ruffo was appalled by the butchery he had unleashed. A moderate amount of looting, battery, rape, and mayhem was what he had in mind. But not wholesale slaughter: that is, the clubbing, knifing, shooting, and burning of several thousand of the inhabitants whom, because of their rank and distinction, he was obliged to regard as individuals. But not so much rape. And not cannibalism, no. He had not envisaged the pyres of bodies, dead and still dying, the smell of burning flesh, the sight of two young boys feasting on the pale arms and legs of a duchess whose confessor and lover he had once been. It was time to rein in this energy. The final act of Ruffo's royalist hordes, just before the cardinal called a halt to the killing and looting, was to attack the royal palace and carry off its contents. Even the lead from the windows was taken.

•

Now the masters must assume control of what the people have impulsively, justly, but crudely begun. And not shrink from the task that masters must perform.

When the news of the French evacuation and the retreat of the patriots to their Masada reached Palermo, the Queen feared that Ruffo would not treat the rebels with the necessary, defining severity their crimes deserved. She summoned the hero to the royal palace and requested that he go to Naples to receive their unconditional surrender and mete out justice—that is, punishment—in the King's name. She says, said the Cavaliere's wife, who was rendering the Queen's French into English for the monoglot hero, You should treat Naples like it was an Irish town in a similar state of rebellion.

Ah, said the hero.

Ireland had had its French-inspired revolution the year before, and the Queen had been most impressed by the thoroughness with which it had been crushed by the English.

Of course, it was inconceivable that the hero undertake this mission without the aid, counsel, and language skills of the Cavaliere and his wife.

For the Cavaliere's wife, it was an ideal mission, one in which she would prove herself indispensable both to the Queen and to the man she adored. For the Cavaliere, it was a duty he could not refuse. But he wanted nothing to disturb the beautiful images he preserved of Naples. He certainly hoped to be spared the sight of the horrors reported to be taking place in the city. We can force ourselves to look, squirming a little, at a great painting of the flaying of Marsyas, or look with equanimity, especially if we're not women, at a lively rendering of the rape of the Sabine women . . . these were canonical subjects for painting. And Piranesi had made images of the most unspeakable tortures taking place in corners of ingeniously vast prisons. But it would be something else to see a real flaying, or the mass rape that had been going on in Naples, or the sufferings of the thousands who survived their humiliations and wounds at the hands of the crowds and lay penned in the stifling granaries, without food, sleeping in their excrement.

On June 20th, having shifted his flag from the disabled *Vanguard* to the eighty-gun *Foudroyant*, the hero left Palermo with a squadron of seventeen sail-of-the-line, three more than the number under his command at the Battle of the Nile. Four days later the flagship entered the Gulf of Naples, and Mars in full regalia with all his decorations paced the quarter-deck beside his Venus in a dress of fine white muslin with a long tasseled sash around her waist and a broad-brimmed hat trimmed with ribbons and crowned with ostrich plumes. The Cavaliere, dozing in his cabin, felt the walls shudder as the *Foudroyant* dropped its anchor into thirty fathoms of the turquoise water. What a calm trip, he said, as he joined them. There was the dear geography, the familiar splendors of the cityscape—give or take a few new details. Fires were still burning in the city. Flags of truce were flying from Ovo and Nuovo. Plumed Vesuvius, the Cavaliere noted, was smoking benignly. And there was not a French ship in sight.

The next day the hero received Ruffo in the Great Cabin, as his headquarters in the rear of the ship was called, and through the Cavaliere informed the cardinal that he, he alone, now represented the monarchs in Palermo. Ruffo made his case for the need to halt the bloodshed and restore order. What started as a frigid interview soon turned into a shouting match. The Cavaliere knew Ruffo, he knew his friend, he would explain each to the other. But the room was so hot, he felt staggery—his wife and the hero begged him to retire to his cabin. The Cavaliere's wife was acting as the interpreter when Ruffo explained the treaty he had made with the rebels barricaded in the sea-forts. As the Queen feared, he had accepted a capitulation with terms. The rebels were to be allowed several days to put their affairs in order, and then have passage out of the country into permanent exile. Fourteen transports lay in the harbor, and many of the rebels had gone aboard with their families and possessions. The first ship, already loaded, was to leave for Toulon tomorrow at dawn.

Ruffo stood while the British admiral looked up from his desk and asked the Cavaliere's wife to tell the cardinal that the arrival of the British fleet has completely destroyed the treaty. When the cardinal protested that it had already been signed and solemnly ratified by both sides, the hero replied, agitating the stump of his lost arm, that he would have Ruffo arrested if he persisted in his treachery. Then the hero ordered the transports boarded, the rebels taken off in chains and put in prison to await speedy punishment for their crimes. And summoned Captain

Troubridge and issued orders for the deploying of British troops to retake the last French strongholds in Sant'Elmo, Capua, and Gaeta.

We must set an example, the hero said later to the Cavaliere.

Setting an example meant being merciless—the Cavaliere knew that.

The first example was to be Admiral Caracciolo, who in early March had returned to Naples and offered his services to the republic, and when Ruffo's army arrived and the republic fell had gone into hiding on one of his estates in the country. The hero ordered Ruffo to deliver the admiral to him; Ruffo refused. We are awaiting news of Caracciolo, who will be executed as soon as he is captured, the Cavaliere wrote to the Foreign Office.

The Cavaliere hardly recognized as the forty-seven-year-old Neapolitan admiral and prince the old man with the grey face and long beard and peasant clothes worn to disguise himself, who had been abducted the following day by British soldiers, returned to the city, and immediately taken aboard the *Foudroyant* in shackles and brought before its commander.

Caracciolo thought his rank—he belonged to one of the most ancient and public-spirited noble families in the kingdom—as well as his decades of faithful service to the Bourbon monarchs might count in his favor. And his good friends the British minister and his wife would surely intercede for him with the gallant victor of the Battle of the Nile. Never could he have imagined that there would be no trial, that he would have no counsel, that no evidence would be admitted, and that the verdict would be the ignominious sentence of death reserved for common sailors. Caracciolo pleaded for a proper trial (no), implored to be allowed to introduce testimony in his favor (no), begged to be shot (no). And never could the Cavaliere have imagined, as he sat in the Great Cabin writing another dispatch, how quickly it would all go. Sometimes everything goes so quickly. It seemed only minutes since Caracciolo had been pulled into the next room for the travesty of a court-martial ordered by the hero. When the verdict the hero had requested was announced, the Cavaliere took his friend to the long bay window to suggest that it might be well to follow custom and defer the execution for another twenty-four hours. The hero nodded and returned to his desk. Caracciolo was brought before him, head bowed. Sentence to be carried out immediately, said the hero. Already a living corpse, sweat pouring from his armpits, Caracciolo was hurried onto the deck and lowered into a small boat which took him to a Sicilian frigate, where he was pulled on board and hanged. At the British admiral's orders, the Neapolitan admiral's body dangled from the yardarm into the evening. Only when the June sun set around nine o'clock did the hero give the order that iron weights be attached to each foot, the rope be cut, and the body let drop, shroudless, straight down into the sea.

By the rules of war the hero had no right to abrogate Ruffo's treaty with the rebels, no right to abduct and execute the Bourbon monarchs' senior naval officer or even to receive him on board an English ship as a prisoner; but this was not war. This was the administration of punishment.

I wish we could hang Ruffo, he exclaimed to the Cavaliere. The Cavaliere counseled prudence. But there were plenty of other prisoners, at least twenty thousand of them now languishing in the forts and state prisons, who would have to be vetted to see who needed punishment. After lynching comes judicial murder, which involves a good deal of paperwork. In the Great Cabin the Cavaliere's wife sat at a desk near the admiral's, drawing up lists of prisoners to submit to the Queen for her verdict.

We are restoring happiness to the Kingdom of Naples, and doing good to millions, the hero wrote to Mrs. Cadogan, whom they had left behind in Palermo, of the work initiated from his headquarters in the bay in June 1799. Your daughter is well, but she is very tired with all she has to do.

When the Cavaliere's wife is not busy assisting the hero, and writing the Queen three times a day, she receives the Neapolitan grandees who have come to pay their homage and ask her to transmit their professions of loyalty to the Queen. I am the Queen's deputy, she wrote to Charles. Unfortunately, the Cavaliere could not lay claim to a symmetrical role. He could hardly call himself the King's deputy. The King wrote no letters. Indeed, the King, as the Queen reported to *her* deputy, had gone out to one of their Palermitan country palaces and, though he knows that he must soon make an appearance to receive the allegiance of his subjects, does not want to be bothered with any news from Naples. But what does the King really think, asked the hero earnestly. Laughing, the Cavaliere's wife translated a line from the Queen's morning letter. As far as the King is concerned, the Queen had written, the Neapolitans might just as well be Hottentots.

•

More examples.

Public executions, which were held in the large market square of the city, began on a Sunday, July 7th, the day before the arrival of the King.

Neither the hero nor his friends witnessed any of the executions. They were not slaughter-minded, merely implacable. And distance distances.

And yet sometimes something comes close that you don't expect. It was two days after the public executions had started, and a day after the King had arrived from Palermo on a Sicilian frigate, wearing a dried heron's leg in his buttonhole as a charm against the evil eye, and had taken up residence on the *Foudroyant*. The King had laboriously climbed the quarter-deck ladder to complain to the Cavaliere about how boring Palermo was in the summer, when a shout from some of the sailors drew him to the railing to see what the commotion was about. A fish. It must be a very large fish. There below him, about thirty feet off the stern, the spume-ringleted head and upright water-flayed torso of his old friend Admiral Caracciolo was weaving and lolling, his beard floating in front of his ghastly rotted face. Had the shouting sailors been Neapolitans, they would have been crossing themselves. The terror-struck King crossed himself, cursed, and fled below. The Cavaliere found him, whimpering and giggling to himself in the dark 'tween deck, surrounded by his apprehensive attendants.

Is he there, is he still there? the King bellowed. Push him under!

It will be done, Majesty.

Now!

Majesty, a boat has been lowered to tow the body to shore for burial in the sand.

Why is he doing this to me? screamed this incurably childish man.

The Cavaliere had his last inspiration of the great courtier he once was.

Though Caracciolo may have been a traitor, he explained to the King, he means you no harm now. But having repented he still cannot rest. So he has come to ask your pardon.

•

You are a passenger. We are all, often, passengers. The boat, history, is going somewhere. You are not the captain. But you have excellent accommodations.

Of course, down there in the hold are famished immigrants or enslaved Africans or press-ganged tars. You can't help them —you do feel sorry for them—and you can't control the captain, either. Cosseted though you may be, you are actually quite powerless. A gesture on your part might relieve your bad conscience, if you have a bad conscience, but would not materially improve their situation. How would it help them to give up your own spacious cabin, with the room you require for your copious belongings, since, although those below have very few belongings, there are so many of them? The food you are eating would never be enough to feed all of them; indeed, if prepared with them in mind as well, it would no longer be as refined; and of course the view would be spoiled (crowds spoil a view, crowds litter, etc.). So you have no choice but to enjoy the excellent food and the view.

Nevertheless, assuming you are not indifferent, you think a lot about what is going on. Even if it is not your responsibility, how can it be your responsibility, you are still a participant and a witness. (First- or second-class passengers, these are the points of view from which most accounts of history are written.) And if those being persecuted are those who might have had accommodations as agreeable as your own, people of your own rank or who have your interests, you are far less likely to be indifferent to their present distress. Of course, you cannot prevent them from being punished if they are in fact guilty. But, assuming you are not indifferent, that you are a decent person, you will try to intervene when you can. Counsel leniency. Or at least prudence.

The Cavaliere had tried to intervene for someone, his old friend Domenico Cirillo. One of the most eminent biologists in Italy, eminent enough to have been made a Fellow of the Royal Society, official physician to the court and personal physician of the Cavaliere and his wife, Cirillo had welcomed the republic's invitation to carry out much needed reforms in the organization of hospitals and medical care for the poor. There is something to be said in the case of old Cirillo, said the Cavaliere to the hero. I can testify to his benevolence. Unfortunately, we cannot interfere with the course of justice, said the hero. Which meant that Cirillo would be hanged.

•

Their passenger life continues, at anchor. For the time being, they are not going anywhere.

Relieved of the stress of war, the flagship is entirely devoted to command, to its own maintenance, and to the diversions of its leading passengers. The hardest to keep diverted is, of course, the King. When the sailors sluice the decks under the hot dawn sun and hoist a rose-colored awning over most of the quarter-deck, where the King will hold his levee in the middle of the morning, they usually find the King already up and somewhere on the deck shooting sea gulls or fishing in a boat a few hundred yards from the ship. During the levee, from time to time he breaks away from his courtiers and, belly to the railing, shouts down at the victualers from the city in their small boats below. He is thinking about the lavish dinners each day at noon in the admiral's cabin with the hero, his old friend the British envoy, and his charming wife with the long white arms, who vies with him in appreciating the heaps of excellent fish and game he has chosen for their repast. She is not made logy by the meal, as he is, and afterward provides some delicious entertainment. When she leaves the table to play the harp and sing, he knew she was singing for him. And certainly she was performing for him when she sang "Rule, Britannia" one moonlit night on the poop, with the *Foudroyant*'s whole crew as chorus. The inspiring verses and the singer's beautiful voice seemed to dulcify the King. I like her better fat, he thought sleepily, as his Brava, brava, brava! subsided into snores.

Since they did not go to the city, the city must come to them. Heads of noble families arrive in barges to pay their respects to the King and the hero and the Cavaliere and his wife, and explain that they had never cooperated with the republic, or only cooperated under duress. The city's tradesfolk keep the ship surrounded with their motley craft: butchers and greengrocers and vintners and bakers offering the day's fare, clothiers with bolts of silk and milliners with new hats for the Cavaliere's wife, booksellers with old books or the latest volumes on the natural sciences to tempt the Cavaliere. He was easily tempted; it had been hard to procure new books in Palermo. Among the books he was offered were rare folios which the Cavaliere recognized, he had perused them in the libraries of friends who were now languishing in prison, awaiting—but it was not certain what would happen to them. Distressing to think of how the books had become homeless, though this was not a reason not to purchase them.

No, he was not the kind of collector who without any pangs of conscience scoops up what other collectors have been unjustly dispossessed of or had confiscated. Still, wasn't it better that *he* buy the folios, he who knows their worth and will treasure them, than that they disappear or be broken up for their plates.

The bay is a forest of ships—the hero's have hulls freshly painted black with a yellow streak along each tier of ports and white masts, his colors. And everywhere white, white sails that go pink each evening with the sunset over Capri. Gaily decorated small boats bring musicians out each evening to play for the trio and the King; plainer boats carry out parties of whores for the sailors (everyone knows not to tell the hero). The King's sexual amusements arrive at any hour.

Some days the fidgety King has himself taken farther out in the bay, to shoot African quail on Capri. The Cavaliere never went with him. His legs are no longer strong enough for the island's steep, rocky slopes. Nor did the Cavaliere ever accompany the King when he went to harpoon swordfish out in the gulf, or fish on his own (much as he loved fishing), but spent his afternoons on the shaded quarter-deck reading and met his wife and the hero again at supper. Sometimes they went up to the poop afterward to look at the night sky and the phantom ships rocking nearby. Although the Cavaliere knew perfectly well why only the *Foudroyant*'s poop has three lanterns—it is the mark of the flagship—he sometimes imagined for a moment, and then chided himself for thinking such a fond, foolish thought, that the three lanterns stand for his wife, the hero, and himself.

Each has a reverie of self-importance and an experience, perhaps enhanced by living on water, of the ego's boundlessness. The hero considers his activities on behalf of the Bourbon monarchs another theatre of his own glory. The Cavaliere's wife regards it as theatre and as glory. And as the unremitting adventure of love. One night when she sat with the hero in his quarters, she took his eye shield from the shelf beside the bed and put it over her own right eye. Shocked, he begged her to remove it immediately. No, let me keep it on for a while, she said. I wish I only had one eye. I want to be like you. You *are* me, he said, as lovers have always said and felt. But she was not only he. Sometimes, when they were alone, she was many others, too. She could waddle like the King, and mime him attacking his food, and render a sample of his wayward patter in singsong Neapolitan (which the hero could appreciate without understanding a word); she could do the wily Ruffo with his hooded eyes and aristocratic accent (Yes, exactly! exclaimed the hero); she could make herself British-solemn and naval-officer-masculine like his faithful Captain Hardy and the ambitious Troubridge; she could change mien, shape, and voice to mimic the shouts and rolling gait of his illiterate tars. How she made the hero laugh. And then she paused, and somehow the hero knew what she was going to do, and she became the Cavaliere, perfectly imitated the stiff, careful way he walked, his near-reproachful, watchful silences, then it was exactly his voice going on about the beauties of some vase or painting, slightly rising in pitch as he tried to keep his enthusiasm under control. The hero was startled, and wondered if it was cruel for the woman he loved to mock the man he revered, and condescended to, as a father—he, the man who every day was issuing orders to kill, worried about being cruel to someone behind his back—but finally, after a moment's earnest examination of his conscience, decided that it was all right for her to imitate the Cavaliere, to make innocent fun of the way he walked and talked. That they were not cruel, not cruel at all.

•

The hero and the Cavaliere's wife have more than enough to divert them. The hero spent most of his time in the Great Cabin, conferring with the captains of his squadron. For his parleys with Neapolitan officers he needed the Cavaliere's wife at his side. My faithful interpreter on all occasions, he called her in public. And there are moments when they can be alone, even there, and kiss and beam and sigh.

I hope this country will be happier than ever, the hero wrote to the new commander in chief of the British fleet in the Mediterranean. Lord Keith replied, summoning the hero and his squadron (a sizable portion of all the British ships available for warfare against the French in the Mediterranean) to Minorca, where the British were expecting an engagement with the French fleet. The hero wrote back insolently that Naples was more important than Minorca, that the mission he had undertaken in Naples made it impossible for him to bring his fleet to the rendezvous, adding that he hoped his judgment would be respected but knew he could be tried for disobeying orders and was prepared to take the consequences.

There was still so much to do! For the sake of the civilized world, and as the best act of our lives, the hero said to the Cavaliere, let us hang Ruffo and all those cabaling against our English king of Naples.

A week later, Keith summoned the hero once again, once again the hero refused, though this time he did let four ships in his squadron depart to join the engagement, which, as it happened, never took place.

•

The hot wind of southern summer, and the hot wind of history.

The ship, like the Cavaliere's observatory room, gives a commanding view.

From the ship, Naples is like a picture. Always seen from the same point of view. Orders issue from the ship, cross the water, are put into effect; travesties of trials take place in which the accused is sometimes not even present; the condemned are brought to the market square and mount the scaffold. There was no single method of execution. Hanging, the ugliest and most humiliating, had preference. But some were shot. Others were beheaded.

If those who were responsible for their deaths wanted to set an example, those who went to die wanted to show an example. They too saw themselves as future citizens of the world of history painting, of the didactic art of the significant moment. *This* is the way we suffer, surmount suffering, die. Showing an example meant being stoical. Although they could not control the paleness of their faces, the trembling lips and shaking knees, their insubordinate bowels, the head was held high. When they were about to die, they made themselves brave by thinking (and they were not wrong) that they were becoming an image. An image, even of the most lamentable events, should also give hope. Even the most horrifying stories can be told in a way that does not make us despair.

•

Because an image can show only a moment, the painter or sculptor must choose the moment that presents what the viewer most needs to know and feel about the subject.

But what does the viewer need to know and feel?

Take the doom of the Trojan priest, Laocoön, who protested the decision to draw the wooden horse inside the city's walls, sensing a trap set by the Greeks, and whom Athena punished for his astuteness with a terrible death inflicted on him and his two sons. Take the representation of their death agony in the famous sculpture from the first century which Pliny the Elder had considered superior to any painting or any bronze for its technical virtuosity, and which tastemakers in the Cavaliere's era admired for its discretion—because it evoked the worst without showing us the worst. This was the reigning cliché about the achievement of classical art: that it showed suffering with decorum, dignity in the midst of horror. Instead of depicting the priest and the children as they might have looked, transfixed by the two giant serpents slithering toward them, their mouths torn open with screams—or worse still, in a tableau of disfiguring death, faces bloated, eyes bulging from their sockets—we see manly strain and heroic resistance to enveloping death. "As the bottom of the sea lies peaceful beneath a foaming surface," Winckelmann wrote, evoking the standard offered by the *Laocoön*, "so a great soul remains calm amid the strife of passions."

In the Cavaliere's day, the significant moment for the depiction of an intolerable situation was before the full horror had reached its apex, when we can still find something edifying in the spectacle. Perhaps what lies behind this curious theory of the significant moment, and its prejudice in favor of moments that are not too upsetting, is a new anxiety about how to react to or represent deep pain. Or deep injustice. A fear of minding too much—of unappeasable feelings, feelings that would cause an irreparable rupture of protest with the established social order.

You can look at the most appalling things in art. Even a *Laocoön* more to our modern taste, with our identification of truth with painful feelings, would happily still be only marble. The coils of the two serpents cannot tighten any further around the Trojan priest and his children. Their agony is forever fixed at this moment. Whatever art shows, it is not going to get any worse. The flute-playing satyr Marsyas, who had had the temerity to challenge Apollo himself to a contest in music, is just *about* to be flayed. The knives are out; the goofy look, readying himself for (or not fully taking in) his coming martyrdom, is in place around the eyes and mouth; but his tormentors haven't started yet . . . to cut. Not even one tiny morsel of flesh. His monstrous punishment is forever only seconds away.

•

What people admired then was an art (whose model was the classical one) that minimized the pain of pain. It showed people able to maintain decorum and composure, even in monumental suffering.

We admire, in the name of truthfulness, an art that exhibits the maximum amount of trauma, violence, physical indignity. (The question is: Do we feel it?) For us, the significant moment is the one that disturbs us most.

•

There are many kinds of quiet, of calm.

The defiant hero to Lord Keith: I have the honor to tell you that no capital is more quiet than Naples.

And then there is the calm inside the Cavaliere's heart.

The Cavaliere says to himself: Be calm, be calm. You cannot help. It is out of your hands. You no longer have power. You never had real power.

Seeing from afar. We are here, they are there.

It is June, July, then August—high summer. In the interior of the *Foudroyant*, whose floors as in all British warships are painted red to mask the blood shed in casualties, there was little light by day; and nothing to dry out the dampness between decks, where, year round, fires are never allowed except in the galley. At night, and even with the portholes open, the sleeping cabins are stifling. The lovers sweat in each other's embrace, and the Cavaliere shifts restlessly in his bed, eventually managing to block out the pain in his rheumatic knees, the food smells real or imaginary from the galley several decks below, the relentless cracking of floors and oozy walls produced by the gentle roll of the ship.

It would have been much more comfortable for them to have taken up residence in the conquered city. One of the sacked palaces could have been quickly fitted up for their comfort: either the former mansion of the British envoy or the gutted royal palace itself. But for the King and the trio there was no question of moving ashore. Naples has become untouchable, a heart of darkness.

You might have thought that Naples belonged to the imperial center, to ever cherishable Europe, because it had a renowned opera house and glorious museums and brilliant humanitarian reformers and a monarch with the thick Hapsburg lower lip. But no, it had been abandoned by its rulers and redefined as a refractory colony, or a country on Europe's margin—to be disciplined, mercilessly, as colonies and rebellious provinces are. (Scarpia says: Cruelty is one of the branches of sensibility. Stripping people of their liberty amuses me. I like holding captives. . . . But this is not Scarpia in action. This is not personal cruelty, this is politics.) Naples was to be dealt with as a colony. Naples became Ireland (or Greece, or Turkey, or Poland). For the sake of the civilized world, said the hero. They are doing the work of civilization—which always means: the work of empire. Unconditional submission! Lop off the rebellion's head. Execute anyone who balks at this policy.

Ruffo was never hanged. But the friend and physician of the Cavaliere and his wife, old Domenico Cirillo, was; and the celebrated jurist Mario Pagano, leader of the moderates; and the gentle poet Ignazio Ciaja; and so was Eleonora de Fonseca Pimentel, de facto minister of propaganda, two weeks after the trio set sail in August and returned to Palermo. And many, many others.

If they were a mob, one would have said that the beast had had its fill of blood. Since they were individuals, claiming to be acting for the public good—My principle is to restore peace and happiness to mankind, wrote the hero—one says that they did not know what they were doing. Or that they were dupes. Or that they must have felt guilty after all.

Eternal shame on the hero!

•

They stayed on board the *Foudroyant* six weeks. Six weeks is a long time.

Strange seeing Naples day after day in reverse shot, from the sea—instead of as observed by the Cavaliere for so many years from his windows and terraces, looking out into the great view. With Capri and Ischia behind them now, and Vesuvius to the right rather than to the left, a ghostly grey cutout in sunset light, and the sea-forts and the palaces on the Chiaia goldenly vibrant, three-dimensional, taking the light off the sea.

And strange, too, seeing the hero in reverse. From another view, the view of history, the judgment that posterity—along with many of his contemporaries—was to pass on the hero and his companions. The hero not chivalrous, high-minded, but vindictive, self-righteous; even if a dupe, proving himself capable of hardening his heart against the most obvious claims of mercy. The Cavaliere not benevolent, detached, but spiritless, passive. The Cavaliere's wife not merely exuberant and vulgar, but cunning, cruel, bloodthirsty. All three giving themselves over to a terrible crime.

A new face for each of them. But of the three, the one thought most culpable was the Cavaliere's wife.

They were a family—a family doing wrong. And family was the model of rule, mostly misrule, that was being challenged by revolution. One consequence of the old model, in which eligibility for rulership was conferred by being born into a ruling family, was that women, a few women, had a visible and very real share in power. Occasionally monarchs themselves, often advisers to the monarch, who was a son, husband, brother—whatever the degree of their subjection, women cannot be entirely banished from family life. (The new model of rule, which revoked whatever legitimate claim women had to governance, was the assembly—composed only of men, since it derived its legitimacy from a hypothetical contract among equals. Women, defined as neither fully rational nor free, could not be a party to this contract.)

They were a family—a family that had gone wrong, in which the influence of a woman had become predominant. Part of the scandal of their misdeeds was that a woman played so visible a role in them. It became another household drama of the old regime, featuring a powerful woman—that is, a woman exercising inappropriate power—who, having ventured out of the sphere appropriate to women (children, domestic duties, some talented dabbling in the arts), had become power-hungry, depraved, and through her sexual wiles had enslaved a weak male and corrupted a righteous one.

•

Stories were told, and invented, about the Cavaliere's wife to illustrate the new reputation she acquired for vengefulness and heartlessness.

For instance, the persecution of the liberal aristocrat Angelotti, whom Scarpia had picked up for possession of forbidden books, was remade into a story about the implacable pursuit by the Cavaliere's wife of a man who years before had mortally offended her by referring in public to her sordid past.

It was in 1794, the year of the Terror, when Scarpia had received his commission from the Queen to round up republican conspirators and fellow travelers of the French Revolution. During a grand party at the British envoy's mansion, his wife was going on in her usual clamorous way about the dear, dear Queen, the horrors of the French, the infamy of the revolution, and the perfidy of certain aristocrats who dared sympathize with the murderers of order, decency, and the Queen's sister. These traitors, she said, no mercy should be shown them.

Although the Marchese Angelotti, who was one of the guests, could not have felt it was he who was being singled out for attack, since at that time he was not yet an anti-monarchist, he decided to take her remarks personally. Perhaps he was simply put off by her vulgarity and aggressiveness, as more and more people were now. Or perhaps he didn't like a woman talking so much. Whatever the reason, the story goes that he was so incensed by her ferocious tirade against the republicans that he clapped his hands and raised his glass. I wish to toast our hostess, he cried, and to acknowledge the pleasure I have in seeing her in such good spirits and occupying so exalted a station, so different from the one in which I first encountered her.

Whispers around the table. All eyes turned to the Marchese.

Where was that, you may well ask, he shouted.

Avid silence.

In London, he continued loudly. At Vauxhall Gardens, some dozen years ago. Yes, I suppose I may claim the honor of having known the Cavaliere's wife longer than anyone else at this table, including His Excellency, her husband.

The Cavaliere cleared his throat. He alone continued to eat.

Yes, continued the Marchese, I was walking with two friends, the Count del *** from here and an English friend of ours, Sir ***, when I was accosted by one of those creatures who roam the public gardens in the evening looking for a meal and willing to pay for it. This one was no more than seventeen, and irresistible, from her bonnet to her pale stockings, and she had the most beautiful blue eyes. I suppose we Neapolitans are always enthralled by blue eyes. I took leave of my friends and must have found the company of this delightful creature even more agreeable than I expected, though being a foreigner I could not understand everything she said in her charming country accent. She loved to talk, but fortunately that was not the only thing she loved to do. Our liaison lasted eight days. She could not, I think, have been too long in her profession, for she still had a flavor of country innocence, which often adds a certain piquancy to what might be considered one of the more facile pleasures of a great city. As I said, our liaison lasted eight days, leaving me with recollections no more intense than the encounter deserved. Imagine my delight after so many years, on meeting her again, to see her quite transformed, transposed to another life, and set down among us here to be the ornament of our local musical society, the delight of the distinguished British ambassador, and the dear friend of our Queen—

It is told that the Queen ordered Angelotti's arrest a few days later at the Cavaliere's wife's request, and the Marchese was promptly sentenced to three years in the galleys, where he converted from the cause of constitutional monarchy to republicanism. Of course, the tellers of tales could as well have said that he was arrested at the request of the Cavaliere, so infatuated was the old man with his wife. But the blame always fell on the Cavaliere's wife. After it was all over, it was said that the hero would never have done what he did had he not been under the influence of the woman with whom he was so abjectly in love, who was the closest friend of the Neapolitan Queen. On his own, it was thought, the British admiral would never have consented to become the Bourbon executioner.

Not only were the men in the story seen as a woman's dupe, but so were the women. After it was all over, and their actions were the scandal of Europe, some said that it was the Cavaliere's vicious wife who had influenced the excitable Queen and persuaded her to order the judicial murder of the Neapolitan patriots—though others insisted it was the vicious Queen who had made a pawn of her doting, credulous friend. Either way, the Queen herself was to be more censured than the King. One of despotic Maria Theresa's hellish brood, didn't she have complete mastery over her ignorant, passive husband? (On his own, it was thought, the King would never have authorized such cruelties.) The woman can be blamed for being at the scene of the crime, even if it is only to cheer the men on. And also blamed when, being less than all-powerful, she is absent. For when it had been decided that a royal presence in the Bay of Naples was needed to confer full legitimacy on the restoration's sanguinary course, the Queen had wanted, wanted very much, to accompany her husband, to join her friends on the *Foudroyant*. But the King, who longed for a vacation from his overbearing wife, had ordered her to remain in Palermo.

Letting the woman, or women, in the story take the rap is a resourceful way of occluding the full coherence as politics of what was decreed from the hero's flagship. (This is often part of misogyny's usefulness.) Accounts of the Queen invariably reflected the perennial disparagement of women rulers and dominant female consorts—objects of mockery and condescension (for being unbecomingly virile) or of double-standard calumnies (for being frivolous or sexually insatiable). But the Queen's role did fit a familiar mold—governance by a household—and she had the right credentials. The participation of the Cavaliere's wife in the White Terror that followed the suppression of the Neapolitan Republic seemed entirely gratuitous and far more reprehensible. Who was this social upstart, this drunk, this femme fatale, this posturing, exuberant, overdressed . . . actress? A soubrette who has insinuated herself in the heart of a public drama but then goes off on her own tangent—is she not a woman? therefore, not fully responsible?—whenever she wants.

•

Probably it would have been regarded as yet another proof of her heartlessness were it known that the Cavaliere's wife, she alone of the trio, did visit the martyred city during the six weeks the *Foudroyant* lay anchored in the bay. It could not be the hero, whose role required him to keep to his floating command post, the better to administer the sentence passed on the gleaming, despoiled city. Nor the Cavaliere, who whenever he went on deck could not help picking out in the amphitheatre of buildings and gardens above the port the mansion where he had lived for more than thirty-five years, over half his life; the prospect of going ashore, and succumbing to the temptation to inspect his ravaged and muck-strewn dwelling, filled him with anticipated grief. But one scorching July day, the Cavaliere's wife went ashore for a few hours, laughing away the pleas of her husband and her lover, who were beside themselves with worry over this foolhardy adventure.

But she will be in disguise, she told them gaily. Fatima, Julia, and Marianne, the three maids she had brought with her from Palermo, were sewing her costume as they spoke. At Palermo, hadn't she frequently accompanied the hero on nocturnal rambles through the city, dressed in sailor's clothes. For the excursion to Naples she will wear widow's weeds, which will permit her to cover herself entirely.

A carriage with attendants in the employ of the British met the small boat that brought the Cavaliere's wife to a landing at a safe remove from the harbor's swarm of beggars, vendors, whores, and foreign sailors. Nearby in a second carriage were four officers from the *Foudroyant*, dispatched by the anxious hero with instructions never to let her ladyship out of their sight and to guard her life with their own. They saw her stumble as she stepped from the boat, then totter while she paused to cover her face with a black silk shawl. Must have started early today. God almighty! I say, do you think we should help her? No, look, she's recovered herself. Everyone knew that the admiral's siren abused her wine. But they were mistaken. It was not the wine she had been sipping on the boat but the dizzying shock of firm ground under her feet, after nearly four weeks aboard the swaying ship.

She told the driver her destination, was helped by the footmen into the carriage, and settled back in the harrowing heat to peer from behind the curtain at the strip of buildings, people, vehicles unwinding alongside her. The streets were as crowded as ever, but there seemed to be more than the usual number of women entirely swathed in black, as she is. She made a stop to acquire an enormous bouquet of jasmine and cameo pink roses.

The Cavaliere's wife uncovered her face and entered the cool cavernous church. It was between masses and very quiet, with a scattering of dark figures in prayer framed between the soaring columns. She dipped her fingers in the stoup, genuflected, and crossed herself, afterward kissing the tips of her fingers as people do here. Before penetrating farther into the church she hesitated, for she could not help expecting that she would be recognized, that people would rush toward her, as in the old days, and touch her dress and beg favors and alms from the second most powerful woman in the kingdom, the wife of the British envoy. When no one took notice of her, she was a little disappointed. A star, as opposed to an actress, always wants to be recognized.

In the last year in Naples she had come on many afternoons to San Domenico Maggiore, pretending to study the inscriptions on the old tombs of the Neapolitan nobility; in fact, to watch people pray and imagine the comfort of some kind of benevolent protective presence, always on call. Now she wanted to protect someone else. The hero was in pain, many kinds of pain, not just in his arm and eye. He spoke of a tightening around his heart, and in the middle of the night when she lay beside him and he was already asleep, he groaned so piteously. She had begun to pray silently for his health—she had never prayed as a child, but it comforted her to pray in this foreign religion—and the Madonna often came into her mind. She became convinced, lying beside him, listening to the ship's bell tolling the hours, that if she could visit this church again, and make an offering to this statue of the Madonna, her prayer would certainly be heard. She did not want protection for herself, she wanted it for the man she loved. She wanted to take his pain away.

She went to a side altar, set her flowers in an ornate gilt vase at the Madonna's feet, lit a bank of candles, knelt, and murmured a long effusive entreaty to the statue. When she finished, she looked up at the Madonna's painted blue eyes and imagined she saw compassion. How lovely she was. I suppose I am being very foolish, she thought, and then wondered if the Madonna heard what she said only to herself. She placed her offering of a large sum of money in a velvet pouch beside the flowers.

Though no one approached her, she now had a distinct impression that she was being observed. Yet the moment she turned and saw a broad-shouldered man with a fleshy mouth standing by a column at the rear, and recognized him, he was not looking at her. Perhaps he wanted her to approach him.

He smiled and bowed. He told her what a surprise it was to see her. He did not say: and here. Of course it was no surprise at all. Scarpia's spies on the *Foudroyant* had informed him of the impending visit ashore of the Cavaliere's wife. He had been at the port when she landed, and had followed her to the church. Though she could not appreciate the recent alteration in Scarpia's appearance, that he was no longer wearing his sinister black cloak but had reassumed his nobleman's finery, Scarpia did not fail to note the further changes in the woman who stood before him, this once great beauty who had managed to turn the gullible British admiral's head. There must have been a lot of guzzling in Palermo. But she had a beautiful face and beautiful feet.

Her ladyship's courage is admirable. Still, the city is not without its dangers.

I feel quite safe here, she said. I like churches.

So does Scarpia. Churches remind Scarpia of what attracts him in Christianity. Not its doctrines but its historic concern with pain: its palette of inventive martyrdoms, inquisitorial torture, and torments of the damned.

No doubt your ladyship has been offering prayers for the well-being of Their Majesties and the rapid restoration of order in this unfortunate kingdom.

My mother has been poorly, she said, annoyed that she found it necessary to lie to him.

Was she planning to visit her former home, Scarpia inquired.

Certainly not!

I have never cared as much for this church, so dear to the nobility, as for the one where I am a communicant, the Church of the Carmine, in the market square. There is an execution scheduled for two o'clock.

The church with the Black Madonna, said the Cavaliere's wife, as if she had not grasped what Scarpia was suggesting.

You can witness the just punishment of several of the principal traitors, Scarpia said. But perhaps your ladyship does not feel up to this spectacle, which so rejoices all Their Majesties' faithful subjects.

Of course she could watch, if she had to. Part of being brave was having to look at gore. What did it matter? She could look at anything. She was not squeamish. Not a silly, trembly, sentimental woman like Miss Knight. But she could not bring herself to accept Scarpia's dare.

Scarpia waited a moment. In the silence (which became her reply) a Te Deum had begun.

Or we can do whatever would give you pleasure, Scarpia continued in his taunting, ingratiating voice. I am at your ladyship's disposal for as many hours as you like.

The church is starting to fill, and they are being observed now.

It might be worth accepting this opportunity to spend an hour with Scarpia, thought the Cavaliere's wife. The Queen would be interested to have her firsthand assessment of the police chief. But she knew that even as she would be making a report on him, he would be making a report on her. All her instincts said: be careful! And, because she was a woman: be charming!

He dipped his fingers in the stoup and offered her some holy water. She nodded gravely, touched his fingers, and crossed herself. Thank you.

They walked out into the searing heat, and at a food stall in the square she bought a packet of grimy sugar cakes, which Scarpia warned her against. Oh, I have a very good digestion, the Cavaliere's wife exclaimed. Everything agrees with me.

He repeated his offer to escort her, and once again she refused. Perhaps she would have liked to do a bit of tourism, clandestine tourism, in the city in which she had spent one-third of her life. But not with him. Why was he always smiling? He must think himself very attractive. He did. Scarpia knew the effect he had on women, not because he was handsome (he was not), but because of his strong look, which made women turn away, then turn back; his hoarse, deep-toned voice; his way of slowly shifting his weight as he stood; the refinement of his apparel; and his perfect manners, flecked with rudeness. But the Cavaliere's wife was not attracted to blatantly virile men. She did not want to think of what he would be like as a lover. She also found it hard to imagine someone who, as she surmised, did not seek the good opinion of others, indeed cared nothing about what others thought of him. It must be true then, what people said of Scarpia, that he was very wicked. But she did not like to think about that either. Among the many things she preferred not to think about now, one was human wickedness. Evil is something like space. All the space there is. When you imagine reaching the end, you can only imagine it as a boundary, or a wall, which means there is something on the other side; when you think you have reached the bottom, there is always something knocking from below.

She wanted to get into the cool carriage and eat her pastries.

I cannot tempt you with my company?

No longer abashed, she said airily she must forgo that pleasure because—

You would disappoint one of your most faithful admirers?

—because I must regain the *Foudroyant* as quickly as possible, she continued evenly. They were standing next to her carriage.

How dare she rebuff him! But perhaps he could provoke her. Wasn't there a story about this vixen and Angelotti, that they had been lovers? Hoping to revive an unpleasant or embarrassing memory, he informed her that Angelotti, who had fled to Rome, had just been arrested.

I'm sure this news is gratifying.

Oh, yes, Angelotti, said the Cavaliere's wife.

It's not that she had forgiven Angelotti. But his insult has been buried under so many other emotions and events, so much triumph, so much happiness. The Cavaliere's wife prided herself on not holding grudges. If she wishes the death of all the conspirators, it is because the Queen wishes their death. Lack of sympathy (for Cirillo) was sympathy for someone else (the Queen). She is no more cruel than the hero or the Cavaliere. She seems the cruelest only because she is the most emotional

—what women are expected to be. And emotional women who don't have power, real power, usually end up being victims.

As a flash-forward may serve to recall.

•

June 17, 1800. The Queen of Naples, who had continued to live in Palermo, never once visiting her first capital although it is almost a year since the restoration of royal government, has arrived for a short visit to Rome on the eve of what is expected to be a decisive engagement with Napoleon.

Tonight she was giving a party to celebrate the news, received that morning, of Napoleon's defeat by the Austrian forces at Marengo. This false good news (Napoleon had in fact won the battle) was followed in the early afternoon by a small piece of genuine bad news. Angelotti, who was about to be sent in chains back to Naples to be hanged—though not, as slander has it, for the delectation of the Cavaliere's wife, who is at this moment on her way back to England with her husband and her lover—Angelotti has escaped from the prison in the papal fortress of Sant'Angelo, where he has been held for more than a year. The Queen was furious with Scarpia, whom she had summoned from Naples and installed in one of the upper floors in the Palazzo Farnese. She expects infallibility in vengeance from her most trusted servant. Find him today or else, she said. Your Majesty, said the baron, it is as good as done.

The guard at the prison who helped Angelotti escape has already been identified, Scarpia told the Queen, and before he died (the questioning had been a bit peremptory) had revealed the fugitive's first destination, a church in which his family has a chapel. Although Angelotti had already left by the time Scarpia reached the church, evidence had been found incriminating a man who is probably an accomplice. Another patrician Jacobin, said Scarpia. But of course they call themselves liberals or patriots. This one is worse than the usual kind. An artist. A rootless expatriate. Not even really an Italian. Brought up in Paris—his father, who married a Frenchwoman, was a friend of Voltaire. And the son was a pupil of the French Revolution's official artist, David.

I don't care who he is, exclaimed the irate Queen.

Scarpia hastened to inform the Queen that the young painter is now under arrest. I guarantee we will know Angelotti's whereabouts within a few hours. Scarpia smiled.

The Queen knew what the police chief meant. Torture is still legal in the Papal States as well as in the Kingdom of the Two Sicilies, though reformers have succeeded in abolishing it elsewhere. It is no longer legal in the more civilized Hapsburg domains, nor in Prussia and Sweden. She regrets Scarpia's methods, though one must be realistic. In spite of her delight at the fate met by the Neapolitan rebels, the Queen would be shocked to learn that there are those who consider her a bloodthirsty woman. Though she is always for executions, she is against torture.

Angelotti must be recaptured tonight, do you understand?

Yes, Majesty.

Scarpia takes his leave to return to his headquarters upstairs in the palace, where the painter will be interrogated.

The Queen, having vented her fury on Scarpia, is resolved not to let this little piece of bad news spoil her party.

As they speak, the great Paisiello is bent over a keyboard somewhere in the palace composing a cantata in celebration of the victory, which will be performed this evening. The composer will conduct, and it will be sung by the sensation of the current season at the Argentina. The Queen has a weakness for women who sing. The opera star reminded her of her beloved friend, the British envoy's wife, who has an even more beautiful voice.

The opera star, like the Queen's friend, is also impetuous, warm, effusive, and knows how to give herself in love.

The diva arrived at the great ballroom where the party is in progress and made her reverence to the Queen. She has looked over Paisiello's score and feels confident (she never feels anything other than confident) about her part.

She hears the guests talking about politics. She doesn't know anything about politics, nor does she want to. All this talk about France, she barely understands it. Her lover had tried to explain it to her. He had tried to get her to read one of his favorite books, by Russo—something like that, but the writer was French, not Italian. She could make nothing of it, and wondered why he was pressing the novel on her. Although he has friends like the Marchese Angelotti, a Neapolitan aristocrat who was locked up for being one of the six consuls of the godless but short-lived Roman Republic, she knows her lover hardly cares about politics either. He is an artist, too. As she lives only for her art and for love, he thinks only of her and his painting.

She was watching the play at one of the gaming tables when her maid, Luciana, handed her a note. It was from Paisiello, who has not quite finished the cantata and requests that she distract the Queen's attention from this delay by beginning the evening's music without him. Of course, he hopes that she will sing an aria from one of his own operas; he had written nearly a hundred. Furious at being kept waiting, the diva began her improvised recital with an aria by Jommelli. Then the Queen requested another aria, remarking that this was one that her friend, the wife of the British ambassador, sang so beautifully. It is the mad scene from Paisiello's *Nina*. The diva, who had no intention of complying with the wish of a composer, can hardly refuse a royal command.

When Paisiello finally appeared with the score of his victory cantata, the performance was a great success. It was such a success that the Queen wanted her to go on singing. She sings and sings . . . about eternal love, and the stars, and art, and jealousy. She knows a lot about jealousy.

She was eager for the evening to be over as quickly as possible. Unfortunately, before she can join her lover, she had something unpleasant to do. She has promised to call on the notorious Neapolitan chief of police, whom she had met that afternoon at the church which had commissioned from her lover a large painting of the Madonna. When she had stopped by earlier her lover had seemed distracted, and she was surprised that he was not there when she returned; instead, she had found this professed admirer of hers, prowling near the scaffolding. So this is the man before whom all Naples trembled! And he was attractive, she could not help noticing that. The police chief, flirting with her in a rather overbearing way, had tried to convince her that her lover was interested in another woman. She had been foolish enough to believe him when he had shown her among her lover's dirty brushes a woman's fan, a fan that did not belong to her.

The diva is a woman who knows how to take care of herself. She knows how to fend off lecherous men. Like the Cavaliere's wife, she is capable of giving herself only for love. She will find out what the police chief wants to tell her. Then she will join her lover, and they will go out to his country villa for the weekend. She has reason now to think that he has probably not been unfaithful to her; but jealousy is one of the few weapons a woman has. After all, she is an actress. Perhaps he will confess that he did find attractive the woman in the church whose face he used as a model for the Madonna's; and she will be cold to him for a few minutes, and then she will forgive him, and they will be happier than ever.

The diva is not a vengeful woman. And she has seen operas and plays extolling clemency. Many dramas about merciful monarchs have been staged in this past decade, the very decade in which hitherto clement autocrats discovered that the iron fist and the gallows had their uses too. The diva thinks there is nothing more beautiful than clemency. Why can't it always be as in the operas of Mozart, like the one about the abduction, which contains the sublime line: Nothing is more hateful than revenge. Or the one about the mercy of the Roman emperor—written for the coronation of the Queen of Naples's brother, the Hapsburg emperor, as King of Bohemia—in which Titus discovers a plot against his life by those dearest to him and, declining to execute the conspirators, declares: It seems that the stars conspire to oblige me in spite of myself to become cruel. No, they shall not have this victory!

True, the opera's Titus, whose day, in A.D. 79, began with his announcing that Vesuvius has erupted and directing that the gold allocated by the Senate for a temple in his honor be used to succor the volcano's victims, and ends with his pardoning the friend who sought to murder him, is also history's Titus, scourge of the Jews and destroyer of the Temple. But perhaps we need every model of magnanimity we are offered, including the invented ones. Even the diva knows that, innocent of history though she may be.

Perhaps life is not the way it is in an opera, thinks the diva as she prepares to go upstairs to see the police chief, but it ought to be. Nothing is more hateful than revenge.

•

We know about evil people. Like Scarpia. Baron Scarpia is truly wicked. He exults in his wickedness and his intelligence. Little pleases him more than practicing his skills of deception. An excellent judge of character, he understands the diva is rash as well as naïve. To the wicked, a person understood is a person manipulated. It was all too easy to convince her that her lover is carrying on with another woman, which has led her to commit an indiscretion that dooms the fugitive Angelotti. Further, there is the sheer love of inflicting pain. When she arrived upstairs, he had her lover brought in and tortured within her hearing —partly because he likes to torture, partly because torture may produce the information he seeks, and partly because he enjoys watching what happens to her face when she hears the screams coming from the next room. Your tears were like lava, burning my senses, he says. After the torture has made her speak, he declares that if she yields to him he will spare her lover's life (the firing squad's bullets will be blanks) and allow them to leave Rome. Of course, he has no intention of doing anything of the kind. To the wicked, a promise made is a promise to be broken.

We know about good people—and their reputation for being not very astute. The diva is warmhearted, generous. But to be as easily manipulated as she is, is not without its share of fault. Were the diva just a bit more sceptical—that is, a little less proud of being passionate—perhaps Scarpia could not so promptly have turned her into a decoy; for his brandishing of another woman's fan had sent her rushing out that afternoon to her lover's country villa, where she discovered him not with another woman but with Angelotti, whom he was hiding there, so that she now possessed the knowledge her lover had wanted to keep from her, which she can then divulge when Scarpia confronts her with the unbearable choice of betraying Angelotti or letting her lover die. While her lover would never, never have betrayed Angelotti's whereabouts no matter how excruciating the torture became (or so he believes), the woman who loves him cannot bear his screams. Perhaps she is not more emotional than a man. Scarpia, too, is ruled by his emotions. But the combination of emotions with power creates . . . power. The combination of emotions with powerlessness creates . . . powerlessness. Already too late for poor Angelotti, who swallowed poison as Scarpia's men reached down to haul him out of the well. But the diva thought that by agreeing to let Scarpia rape her, she had saved her lover's life. She saw the police chief give the order for a sham execution at dawn; then, when they are alone, he wrote out the passes that will allow them to leave the city. But although the diva seizes a sharp pointed knife from the table just as Scarpia is about to pounce—nothing would seem more powerful than a murder—her courage cannot halt what her credulity has set in motion, her lover will still be mowed down in his fake fake-execution before her eyes, and she must jump from the parapet of the Castel Sant'Angelo, adding to the three other deaths her own.

We know about the very bad and clever, and the very good and gullible.

But what about all the others: those who are neither wicked nor innocent. Just normal important people, going about their important business, wanting to think well of themselves, and committing the most atrocious crimes.

Take the Cavaliere and his wife. Why weren't they moved by the cries of their victims? Of poor Caracciolo, who, like Angelotti, had been found cowering at the bottom of a well. But unlike Angelotti he didn't choose to kill himself immediately. Unlike Angelotti, he didn't think he had the certainty of death before him. Caracciolo thought he had a chance. He was wrong.

•

You can plead for your life, and it doesn't do any good. The diva pleading with Scarpia to spare her lover. The elderly doctor Cirillo writing a few days after his arrest from his cell, in irons, to the Cavaliere and his wife: I hope you won't take it ill if I take this liberty to trouble you with a few lines, in order to make you recollect that nobody in this world can protect and save a miserable being but you . . .

You can go with preternatural courage. The young aristocrat Ettore Carafa, sentenced in September to be beheaded, who asked to be placed on the block looking up instead of face down, and kept his eyes open as the ax descended. Or with inspired dispassion and foresight. Eleonora de Fonseca Pimentel, who, turning to her fellow prisoners as they were waiting to be taken to the cart that would bring them to the gallows, uttered a line from Virgil: *Forsan et haec olim meminisse juvabit*—Perhaps one day even this will be a joy to recall.

Dignity or wretched groveling, nothing will affect what implacable victors decree, turning themselves into a force of nature. As immovable by pity as the volcano. Mercy is what takes us beyond nature, beyond our natures, which are always stocked with cruel feelings. Mercy, which is not forgiveness, means not doing what nature, and self-interest, tells us we have a right to do. And perhaps we do have the right, as well as the power. How sublime not to, anyway. Nothing is more admirable than mercy.

7

Politics is all very salient and absorbing. Alas, you have to care about politics, even if you don't want to. But there are many other important things to care about. For instance, the choice of what to wear may be of great import. What to wear to flatter obesity —no, to hide pregnancy. A pregnancy best hidden, since everyone will correctly assume that the father is the lover, not the elderly husband. A voluminous gown? A loose dress? And perhaps a shawl arranged over it, several shawls despite the heat, since their wearer is the mistress of the art of draping shawls.

And what to wear to respond to disgrace already made public, to show that you don't acknowledge what people whose opinion you care about are saying behind your back. If you are a hero, you wear your ribands, orders, stars, and medals. All of them. Sometimes you wear the ankle-length sable-trimmed scarlet pelisse presented to you by the Turkish ambassador. Your diamond aigrette with its rotating star, another gift (they call it a chelengk) from the Grand Signior in Constantinople. And the gold sword with hilt and blade set in diamonds which the King has given you, along with a Sicilian dukedom, to express his gratitude for the actions that have brought disgrace on your head. And always, next to your heart, a lace handkerchief belonging to the woman whose influence is reputed to have made you commit the actions that have brought disgrace on your head.

It is important, too, how any representation of you is outfitted. For the party the Queen gave in the vast park of the country royal palace to which five thousand were invited, a small Greek temple was erected, inside which were placed life-size wax effigies of the trio garnished with chaplets of laurel. The Queen had requested that the originals of the statues contribute their own clothes. The slender effigy of the Cavaliere's wife wore the purple satin gown of the last opera gala in Naples on which had been embroidered the names of the captains of the Nile; the youthful-looking effigy of the Cavaliere was in full diplomatic dress with the star and red sash of the Order of the Bath; between them stood the hero-effigy with two bright blue agate eyes, his admiral's regalia a field of gleaming medals and stars and *his* Order of the Bath. On the temple roof a musician crouched behind the statue of Fame blowing a trumpet, and when the ceremonies began her trumpet seemed to blow. The Cavaliere received a portrait of the King in a frame encrusted with diamonds; the Cavaliere's wife was presented with the Queen's portrait set in diamonds and crowned by the Queen with the laurel chaplet from her effigy; and the King gave the hero a bejeweled double portrait of Their Majesties and inducted him into the Order of Saint Ferdinand, whose members have the privilege of not removing their hats in the King's presence. The orchestra began to play "Rule, Britannia." The sky began to thunder: a grand display of fireworks representing the Battle of the Nile which concluded with the spectacular blowing up of the French tricolor. Who could resist such flattery? They gaze at the statues of themselves. Quite lifelike, says the hero, for want of something better to say.

•

The hero's shameful role as the Bourbon executioner was the talk of Europe, the Europe of privilege. Hang the country's best poet? Most eminent Greek scholar? Leading scientists? Even the most fervent opponents of republicanism and of French ideas were shocked by the butchery of the Neapolitan nobility. Class solidarity easily overrode national enmities.

Then make the hero a villain? But heroes are useful. No, easier to find some influence on the hero that had warped his judgment, that had corrupted him. The good do not become bad, but the strong may become weak. What has made him weak is that he is no longer separate, solitary—what a hero must be. A hero is one who knows how to leave, to break ties. Bad enough when a hero becomes a married man. If married, he cannot be uxorious. If a lover, he must (like Aeneas) disappoint. If a member of a trio, he must . . . but a hero must not become a member of a trio. A hero must float, must soar. A hero does not cling.

•

Disgrace, disgrace, disgrace.

Triple disgrace. Three united as one.

The hero, who has in effect gone AWOL, could not be replaced, discarded by his superiors back in London—though this was considered. But those who abetted him, whose pawn he had become, could feel the weight of official displeasure. The Cavaliere's role in the savage retaliation against the Neapolitan patriots had made him, at the very least, controversial. Some said he was a dupe of his wife; others, of the Bourbon government. Of course, no one expected a diplomat to be a paragon, as they did the hero. But he should not be controversial, either. A diplomat who has become an open partisan of the government to which he is posted has fatally impaired his usefulness to the government that dispatched him and whose interests he is supposed to promote. It is only a matter of time before he is replaced.

One morning the Cavaliere received a letter from Charles, who regretted having to inform his uncle that he had learned from that damned Whig newspaper the *Morning Chronicle* that a new envoy to the Kingdom of the Two Sicilies, young Arthur Paget, had been named. The Cavaliere could no longer conceal from himself the extent of his disfavor. Not only was he dismissed after thirty-seven years in his post instead of being allowed to retire, after being consulted about the choice of his successor; they did not care if he was the last to know. The document from the Foreign Office followed a month later, with a curt subscript informing him that his successor had already left London. Upon hearing the news, the Queen tearfully embraced her dearest confidant, her sister, the ambassador's wife. Oh what will I do without my friends, she cried. It's all the fault of the French.

Fatal Paget, as the Queen calls him, has arrived in Palermo, and after five days was received by the Cavaliere. Here is a young man—Paget is twenty-nine, a full forty years younger than the Cavaliere—to whom the Cavaliere felt no avuncular attraction whatsoever.

And you come from what post, said the Cavaliere coldly.

I was envoy extraordinary in Bavaria.

But not minister plenipotentiary?

That is correct.

I have heard you held this post only one year.

Yes.

And before that?

Bavaria was my first post.

Of course you speak Italian, said the Cavaliere.

No, but I will learn. In Munich I learned German quickly.

And you will need to learn Sicilian, for who knows when Their Majesties will return to their first capital. And the Neapolitan dialect as well, even if you never see Naples, for the King does not speak Italian.

So I have heard.

Some moments of silence followed, during which the Cavaliere inwardly berated himself for saying too much. Then, clearing his throat nervously, Paget found the courage to say that he was ready to present his credentials letter to the King and Queen as soon as the Cavaliere presented his letter of recall.

The Cavaliere replied that since he had no intention of remaining for even a single day in the Kingdom of the Two Sicilies as a private person, and has already made plans for a month's sightseeing trip, he will attend to the matter when he returns. And off he went with his wife, Mrs. Cadogan, and the hero on the *Foudroyant*, water-borne once again, this time not to engage with history (though the hero must make a stop at Malta) but to float out of history, out of the schedule of their lives.

His superiors and erstwhile friends at the Foreign Office had dismissed him? He would dismiss them for a while from his mind. Take a larger, more mobile view. Watching the coastline unfold, when majestic cloud-crowned Etna came into sight, thundering a little, the Cavaliere recalled the astonishing view from the summit in the blue-tinted dawn, with the whole island of Sicily, Malta, the Liparis, and Calabria outlined below him as on a map. Yes, I have done that. I am the only one here who has done that. What a rich life I have had.

Passing near Etna, the *Foudroyant* was not far from Brontë, the fief attached to the hero's new Sicilian title. The Cavaliere's wife was eager to go ashore, but the hero said he preferred to inspect the estate, whose volcanic soil yielded revenues, so he had been told, amounting to three thousand pounds a year, when his visit had been properly prepared for. The Duke of Brontë, he declared, should not simply appear, unheralded, on his own domain. The Cavaliere, who suspected some prankishness in the King's choice of a dukedom to bestow on his British savior, Brontë being the name of the cyclops who forges Etna's thunder, thought it best to keep this bit of information to himself. The one-eyed hero, who seemed so proud of being a Sicilian duke, might not be amused by the jest. The Cavaliere thought it rather droll.

The Cavaliere has reached the zero point of pleasure, where pleasure consists in being able to put unpleasant thoughts out of one's mind. His dismissal, Paget, his debts, the uncertain future awaiting him in England—these erupted in his mind and then were blown backward into the wind, like the sea birds over his head streaming from stern to prow. The relief of not dwelling on what preoccupied him was so pleasurable that he had the impression he truly was enjoying himself. This ship was his home. When they stopped in Syracuse for two days to visit the ruins of the Temple of Jupiter and the celebrated quarries and caverns, the Cavaliere's wife, despite her morning sickness, refused to remain on board with her mother. She did not wish to miss even one of the Cavaliere's enthusiastic on-site lectures, and she did not want to be separated for even an hour from the hero. His wife and his friend seemed so happy. Neither a naïve nor a complaisant husband, he really loved his wife and he really loved the man close to his wife's age, whom she now loved, and they really loved him, so he hadn't lost a wife but gained a son, isn't that how it was working out?

As in the palace in Palermo, as on the flagship during the six weeks anchored in the Bay of Naples, they behave with perfect correctness in the Cavaliere's presence. That is, they don't fawn on each other any more than they did before they became lovers. That is, they lie. He has no idea when or how often his wife goes to the hero's quarters late at night, or he to hers. Nor does he want to know. His wife, with her unassailable intestinal tract and proven resistance to seasickness, now complains at breakfast of having digestive problems and being made queasy by the movement of the ship. Of course, he would not want them to allude openly to their relationship or her to mention the nausea of pregnancy—that would be painful. And yet, perversely, he minds that they are playacting in front of him. It makes him feel excluded, condescended to. It makes him feel ignored, since he is the one with the weak digestion, he is the one who is sometimes seasick, though one could not hope for a more tranquil sea.

•

And what to wear now that they will almost immediately be traveling again, for the hero is eager to return to England, and the Admiralty is impatient for their greatest weapon against Napoleon to conclude his stint as the Bourbon paladin and yacht captain to the discredited, now former British ambassador and his irresistible wife; and of course, they will go with him. What to wear, for this will be a long, complex journey. First by sea, on the hero's flagship, as far as Leghorn; then overland in many wheeled vehicles (carriage, state coach, post chaise), going from south to north, heading from heat and long days into a more modest summer, traveling through many states, stopping for many festivities, for each of which one must appear at one's best.

There was never any question of their not leaving together. The only question was how many others would depart with the trio and Mrs. Cadogan, besides Miss Knight, who will not hear of being left behind, and Oliver, one of the Cavaliere's two English secretaries, who had been seconded to the hero, plus the usual passel of servants. How big the cavalcade would be.

Upon their return in early June from the month-long cruise, the Cavaliere submitted his letter of recall and Paget was allowed to present his credentials at court. The Queen ground her teeth and did not once look at him. Much more than the imminent loss of her loyal friends was on the Queen's mind, for she understood that the replacement of the Cavaliere with a new envoy signified British displeasure with *her*. Slighting Paget and showing solidarity with her friends is one of her reasons for resolving to leave Palermo, for Vienna, to visit her daughter (as well as her nephew and son-in-law)—her first-born, Maria Theresa, is now the Hapsburg empress. (The other reason for a departure: her bitter awareness of how much her influence over the King has waned.) The hero had hoped to return by sea to England with the Cavaliere and his wife, their entourage, and all their belongings, which would permit him to bring the Queen and her train of ladies-in-waiting, chaplains, doctors, and servants as far north as Leghorn. When his request to take the *Foudroyant* to England was refused, the hero saw no reason for them not to make it a long journey through Europe, and accede to the Queen's desire that her friends escort her all the way to Vienna.

When they arrived in Leghorn, where the irate Lord Keith at last recovered the wayward *Foudroyant* for the military purposes for which it was intended, and while arrangements were being made to continue the journey, there was news of an impending engagement of the Austrian forces with Napoleon at Marengo, and the Queen impulsively decided not to proceed to Vienna directly but to go for a short stay at the Palazzo Farnese in Rome (she sends word for Baron Scarpia to join her there) to await the outcome of the battle. She will join her British friends in Vienna in a few weeks.

On then, in seven carriages followed by four baggage wagons, onto which have been loaded all the Cavaliere's pictures and other possessions saved from Naples. The bone-bruising ride on the road along the Arno proves more strenuous than the Cavaliere anticipated. He was unable to read, he could only close his eyes and try to shut out the pain in his back and hips and knees, while Mrs. Cadogan held a damp cloth to his forehead. At Florence they stopped for two days of receptions and calls. The Cavaliere had wanted to stay longer. It was not only because he is not feeling well at all. He would like to visit the Uffizi again, whose treasures have unaccountably been spared by Napoleon —one can't stop in Florence and not see the pictures—but his wife and his friend will not hear of it. If you are so ill and tired, then surely you aren't strong enough to go around and look at pictures. I am always strong enough to look at pictures, he said weakly. How I feel does not matter. It gives me pleasure.

No, no, said his wife. You are ill. We are worried about you. You must rest. And then we will continue the journey. And so he rested dispiritedly, efficiently, without the stab of pleasure he had been anticipating. How boring just to be a body. And then in Trieste, where there are very few notable pictures, they stopped for almost a week. The Cavaliere could not understand the delay.

The disconsolate Queen arrived a week after they reached Vienna, having cut short her visit to Rome upon hearing the news of Napoleon's victory. The stay of the hero, the Cavaliere, and his wife was prolonged to another month of parties and balls in honor of the hero. The Cavaliere's wife has her triumphs, too. One night she won five hundred pounds at the faro table. Their four-day stay on the Esterházy country estate ended with a festivity for which the prince's celebrated composer-in-residence produced a musical tribute to the hero; the composer was at the keyboard, and it was sung by the Cavaliere's wife.

A few days later she sang Haydn's *The Battle of the Nile* again, accompanying herself, for her royal friend, who was living in resentful seclusion at Schönbrunn Palace. Très beau, très émouvant, exclaimed the Queen, who could not help recalling a voice she had heard in Rome almost as beautiful as that of the Cavaliere's wife. Unfortunately, describing this voice would mean mixing her opinion of the fortunate Haydn, author of a cantata celebrating a victory over the French that actually took place, with the memory of the boring Paisiello and *his* cantata. It might necessitate mentioning that the diva, a woman of great charm, had committed suicide under the most melodramatic circumstances the very morning after the performance, after murdering the clearly incompetent police chief.

Baron Scarpia est mort, Miledy, vous l'avez entendu.

How terrible, exclaimed the Cavaliere's wife. I mean, how upset you must be!

The Queen denied she was upset. After all these deaths, what was one more. And then she began to weep, and to say that all the terrible events she had had to endure had made her insensible to human feelings—that is, she felt she was no longer a woman. And then the whole story came out, backward. Apparently the diva was offended by the attentions of the highly sexed baron. Isn't it amazing, exclaimed the Queen, wiping her eyes, how these Italians overreact to everything? The Cavaliere's wife, as much a champion of the histrionic reaction as the Queen, said she knew all too well what the Queen meant. My husband has always said that Italians lack common sense, she said to the Queen, judging that disaffection with all things Italian would accord with the Neapolitan Queen's mood since she had returned to her native city.

The Queen, a distinctly lesser star in the Hapsburg firmament in Vienna, had been relegated by her nephew's ministers to quarters in Schönbrunn that she interpreted (not wrongly) as a slight, but the sympathies of the Cavaliere's wife were no longer as focused on the Queen's grievances. And the Queen was beginning to learn that her friends were not as esteemed in Vienna as she had thought. More than a few members of the Hapsburg court were relieved when the British party, having exhausted the entertainment and the ovations of the hero that Vienna could provide, had no further excuse not to continue their journey, though the Queen seemed quite distressed at the farewells, adding to the jewelry and portraits of herself she had already given to her friend, as well as presenting a gold snuffbox set in diamonds to the Cavaliere.

Then whorling through central Europe to Prague, the city where legends are told of statues that come to life, the city once ruled by that multi-obsessed collector Rudolf II, who purchased a long-coveted Dürer in Venice and then couldn't bear—the Cavaliere recalled as he jolted along in the badly sprung carriage—couldn't bear to think of his treasure being jolted and jarred across the Alps, and had the thickly sheathed painting walked through the mountains by four hardy young men taking turns holding it upright all the way. In Prague, the reigning duke, another nephew of the Queen, gave a tremendous party to celebrate the hero's forty-second birthday. Then along the Elbe to Dresden, where they viewed the Elector's porcelain collection and went to the opera, at which the hero and the Cavaliere's wife were reported as wholly enwrapped in each other's conversation; and where, at one of the balls given for the hero, he lost a diamond from the hilt of his gold sword (they advertise, offering a reward, but it is not returned). There, as on other stops, the hero's appetite for tributes, gifts, and fireworks was amply satisfied. In each city, the diplomatic community and resident English have enough gossip and malicious observations about the trio to enliven many diary entries and letters. He is covered with stars, ribbons, and medals, wrote one of their hosts, more like the prince of an opera than the Conqueror of the Nile. And no one failed to deplore the slavishness of his attendance on the Cavaliere's wife, whose own outsized presentation of herself, whether in the form of flamboyant performances, appetite for food and drink, or sheer girth, was also caustically noted.

The one indulgence that the Cavaliere requested on the journey was a detour to Anhalt-Dessau to call on its prince, who had visited him in Naples several times and had been one of the early subscribers to the volumes of his volcanic writings, and ten years ago had constructed his own Vesuvius on an island in a lake at his country domain. Three hundred yards in circumference at its base, rising to a height of eighty feet, it could send out real fire and smoke (when combustible material inside the hollow cone was ignited), and emit its version of molten lava (actually, water pumped over the rim of the cone and streaming down the volcano's sides past red-tinted glass ports illuminated from within). Unlike the fifty-four-foot-high structure of glass, fiberglass, and reinforced concrete in front of the hotel in Las Vegas—a generic volcano, which goes off every fifteen minutes (between dusk and 1 a.m.)—the Prince of Anhalt-Dessau's volcano was specifically Vesuvius and went off only on grand occasions for distinguished guests. Six years ago it had performed for Goethe. The Cavaliere wished it to perform for him. (After all, it was his Vesuvius as well as his volcano viewing that had inspired the prince, who had also built on the island a replica of the Cavaliere's villa near Portici.) That would be amusing, said his wife, who was not averse to a stop at the court of another petty German principality. The Cavaliere sent word ahead to the prince that they intended to pay him a visit. But, unfortunately, the prince's private secretary wrote back that his master was away and the machinery could not be activated in his absence. The Cavaliere missed his last volcano.

Perhaps it is just as well, said the Cavaliere's wife, who realized that the hero was tired and eager now to reach Hamburg and its festivities. They traveled by river; when they left Dresden, every bridge, every window commanding a view of the Elbe was filled with cheering spectators. From Hamburg, where he also signed many Bibles and prayer books, the hero sent word to the Admiralty that he expected a frigate to come and pick them up and bring them to England. There was no answer to his request.

•

And what to wear for England, where the hero has not set foot for nearly three years. The worshipful crowds who are there to greet him when the hired packet lands at Yarmouth, and turn out for the hero everywhere he and his party stop on the carriage journey to London, can't know of their rulers' displeasure with the hero and the life he has been leading for the past year. They have not read the mocking accounts of the hero's triumphal progress (only ten thousand people in the country read newspapers). Nor do they know the difference between the Neapolitan stars and the star of the Order of the Bath pinned to the breast of his uniform.

For the crowd, he was still the greatest hero England had ever known. As for Fanny, he was still her husband. Fanny and the hero's mildly senile father, who have come from the country to London and taken rooms in a hotel in King Street, have been waiting for more than a week. The hero embraced his father with genuine fervor and his wife with pained reserve. The Cavaliere's wife, who was wearing a white muslin gown with the hero's name and BRONTË embroidered round the hem in gold thread and sequins, embraced the wife and the father of her lover. They dined together in the hotel—a painful performance. The Cavaliere's wife imitated the huzzahs of the acclaiming crowds on their various stops during the three-day trip to London, as well as the ringing of town bells. The morose hero, who was wearing, as he would until his death, a miniature of the Cavaliere's wife around his neck under his shirt, bit his full lip every time Fanny spoke. The Cavaliere observed on Fanny's face her soaring arc of dismay and humiliation.

To pay his respects at the Admiralty the next day, the hero was in half-dress: naval coat, white naval breeches with naval buttons at the knees, silk stockings, shoes with large buckles. That was prudent, and his old friends at the Admiralty, bent on reprimand, softened as they listened to the hero earnestly lecture them on his plans for the defense of the Channel coast should Napoleon be so foolish as to attempt an invasion, and his wish to return to active service as soon as possible. But the hero made a serious miscalculation on the following day when he appeared at the palace for the royal levee with the Grand Signior's chelengk in his hat, his three stars on his breast (one for the Order of the Bath, two for Sicilian honors), and the bejeweled portrait of the King of Naples hanging from his neck. No wonder he was snubbed by the British king, who barely acknowledged his presence, merely asking him if he had recovered his health, and then turned away to converse animatedly with General *** for some thirty minutes about his desire that the army play a larger role in the war with the French. The British monarch has not acknowledged the hero's Sicilian title, as its recipient knew perfectly well. (And will not do so until two months later, when the hero receives a new command and goes off to win another famous victory.) Had the hero engaged his sovereign's attention even for ten minutes, he would no doubt have used some of the time to laud the Cavaliere's wife and her indispensable patriotic services in Naples and Palermo, which merited remuneration and public thanks. But it was not the hero's praise of the woman who was ruining him, nor an effusive testimonial letter from the discredited Queen of Naples, that would make her less of a pariah. These only confirmed what everyone already thought.

The newspapers had been speculating whether the Cavaliere's wife would even be deemed presentable at court, and her absence when the Cavaliere made his own impeccable appearance unleashed the relentless evocation of a physical disgrace. If some realized her obesity also concealed a pregnancy—her ladyship has reached these shores just in time, the *Morning Post* noted tersely—it was less the scandal of her pregnancy that fascinated society than the loss of her beauty. COMPLEXION. So rosy and blooming is her ladyship's countenance that, as Doctor Graham would say, she appears a perfect Goddess of Health! (A double sneer: both an allusion to the pregnancy and a reminder of her brief employment half a lifetime ago by the once fashionable healer and fertility therapist.) FIGURE. That for which she was particularly celebrated and in consequence of which her reputation commenced, and now so swollen that it has lost all its original beauty. ATTITUDES. Her ladyship is fitting up a room to display her Attitudes and is planning to give Attitude parties. Attitudes will be much more in vogue this winter than shape or feature.

The caricaturists did not spare her or the Cavaliere. Gillray showed him as a withered old grotesque absorbed by an array of ugly statuettes and a damaged vase; above his head are portraits of a bare-breasted Cleopatra holding a gin bottle and a one-armed Mark Antony wearing a cocked hat, and a picture of Vesuvius in full eruption. But there were no full-scale caricatures of the hero, who is sitting for many busts and portraits, and has been introduced in the House of Lords—only tattle. Rumor has it, and the rumor was true, that the hero now paints his face. Rumor exaggerates, and says he weighs no more than eighty pounds.

The House of Lords is a stage, the court is a stage, a dinner party is a stage—even a box in a theatre is a stage. The two couples went to the Drury Lane together, and when they took their seats the entire audience stood and cheered, the orchestra struck up "Rule, Britannia," and the hero had to rise and bow his thanks. The next day the newspapers reported that the hero's wife appeared in white with a violet satin headdress and small white feather, and the Cavaliere's wife wore a blue satin gown and headdress, with a fine plume of feathers. In the drama they saw, the leading woman's role was played by Jane Powell, whom the Cavaliere's wife told her husband she had known oh so long ago, even before she met Charles—meaning, the Cavaliere supposed, when she was, when she was a . . . he did not like to think of it. In fact, she had known Jane when she was a servant in the household of Doctor *** at the age of fourteen, when she came to London. Jane, another underhousemaid, had been her first friend. They shared the same room in the attic. They were both going to be actresses.

Acting is one thing, being civilized (which includes acting) is another. The Cavaliere wished the hero would keep up appearances—as he does. He can understand that the hero is galled by the stubbornness of Fanny's love, by her pathetic belief that if she is patient and behaves as if nothing is changed, her husband will be content to live with her and his father in the furnished house in Dover Street. But that is no reason for the hero to show what he feels, as he apparently did at a banquet in his honor given by Earl Spencer within the precincts of the Admiralty. While he was explaining to Countess Spencer on his right the four principal weaknesses of French gunnery, Fanny, seated on his left, was taken up by her self-appointed task of cracking walnuts for him and when finished had put them beside his plate in a little glass, which he slapped aside. The glass broke, and Fanny burst into tears and left the table. Continuing to train both dim fixed eye and mobile eye rightward on the wife of the First Lord of the Admiralty, stump thrashing in his empty sleeve, the hero went on being brilliant, original, inimitable, on the subject of naval tactics.

The pretense of being two couples was over. The hero moved into his friends' house in Piccadilly, offering to assume half of the Cavaliere's annual rent of one hundred and fifty pounds; the Cavaliere refused. Soon after, Fanny returned with the hero's father to the country.

The Cavaliere felt obliged to economize his energies. Time that he might have spent attending meetings of the Royal Society was now spent conferring with his bankers, who were attempting to create a reasonable schedule for settling his debts. The bounty and novelty of goods in the shops astonished him. London, after nine years of absence, struck him as extraordinarily modern, energetic, opulent—almost a foreign city. He watched a few auctions, though he was in no position to buy anything. He visited his vase collection in the British Museum. Charles was often with him, Charles is always available. With Charles, and without his wife, he made a trip to his estate in Wales, now mortgaged for thirteen thousand pounds. The Cavaliere had submitted to the Foreign Office an accounting of his losses in Naples (furniture, carriages, &c: thirteen thousand pounds), and the enormous expenses (ten thousand pounds) incurred during the year and a half in Palermo. While just managing to keep his creditors at bay, he has applied for an annual pension of two thousand pounds, a modest request. Everyone tells him, especially Charles, that he has a right to expect a peerage as well. But he doubts that he can have both. He would rather have the money than be a lord. It is too late for titles. Charles asks him if he is glad to be back in London. He replies, I shall be at home here as soon as I feel well.

•

They were rescued from an end of December in London with its plethora of status-evaluating parties by an invitation from William, the Cavaliere's reclusive, scandal-shrouded kinsman, to spend Christmas week with him in his Palladian country mansion, and see the stupendous building project William has undertaken in the woods of Fonthill.

He calls it an abbey, which means its architecture is inspired by the Gothic, said the Cavaliere. Pointed arches and painted windows, he added for the hero's benefit.

Like Strawberry Hill, cried the Cavaliere's wife.

Don't let William hear you say that, my dear. He is our late friend Walpole's greatest rival and detractor, and despises his castle.

They had stopped at nearby Salisbury, where the hero was received by the mayor and presented with the freedom of the city, and their carriage—going slowly, to minimize jolts, in consideration of the delicate condition of the Cavaliere's wife—was being escorted by a detachment of yeoman cavalry as far as the gates of Fonthill.

No, said the Cavaliere after a long pause, this is something far more grandiose.

What's grandiose, said his wife.

The Abbey! exclaimed the Cavaliere. Wasn't he being clear? We are talking about the Abbey, are we not? Its tower, William tells me, will be higher than the spire of Salisbury Cathedral.

It was snowing, and the Cavaliere felt immured in cold. This is the first English Christmas he has had in, how many years? For when he was last in England, he had started the journey back to Italy in September. Yes. Two days after the wedding. And the time before, when he brought Catherine's body back and sold the vase, it had been October when he returned. The previous leave home—but that was almost twenty-five years ago, when there was war with the American colonies—hadn't he and Catherine left before Christmas? He was sure they had left before Christmas. And he busied himself, making the calculations in his head, the numbers and faces slipping in and out of his mind, but it seemed important to get it right. The last Christmas in England, how many years was it? How many?

How many, said the Cavaliere's wife.

The Cavaliere, startled out of his reverie, wondered if his wife could read his mind.

How many feet, she said. Its height.

Height?

How high is the Abbey tower to be?

Nearly three hundred feet, murmured the Cavaliere.

I know nothing about architecture, said the hero, but I am sure that without immoderate ambition nothing fine is ever accomplished.

Agreed, said the Cavaliere, but William's ambitions are not as well supported as they might be. Eight months ago, at still less than half its eventual height, the tower collapsed in a gale. Apparently he is allowing his architect to build not with stone but with stucco and compo-cement.

What folly, said the hero. Who would not build to last?

Ah, but he believes it will last, replied the Cavaliere, and has had it rebuilt in the same material for our visit. I would not be surprised if my kinsman does not intend one day to live in the tower, so he can look down on the world, look down on all of us, and see how small we are.

•

William, Catherine's William, the slightly plump, wistful youth now a lean, startlingly juvenile-looking man of forty-one, was still a gifted musician. On the first evening, he played for his guests in the large drawing room for nearly an hour (Mozart, Scarlatti, Couperin). Then, with summary politeness, he ceded the right of musical performance to the Cavaliere's wife, who offered a Sicilian air, arias by Vivaldi and Handel, and "Ooody Oody Purbum," a Hindu song she had learned for the occasion, knowing of William's excessive infatuation with the Orient. She concluded with several martial songs in honor of the hero.

The three men had moved to the blazing fireplace while the Cavaliere's wife remained nearby at the piano, softly touching the keys. It was William, speaking with clenched teeth, who broached the subject of happiness, turning first to his celebrated guest for a contribution.

Happiness! exclaimed the hero. Happiness for me lies first and last in serving my country, if my country still has need of, or even wants, the services of a poor soldier who has already sacrificed health, sight, and much else for her glory. But if my country has no further need of me, nothing would make me happier than a simple rustic dwelling by a little stream, where I may spend the rest of my life with my friends.

And the lady?

The lady called out from the piano that she was happy when those she loved were happy.

How absurd you are, my dear, said the Cavaliere.

You may be right, she replied, smiling. No doubt I have many faults—

No! said the hero.

But, she went on, I have a good heart.

That's not enough, William said.

The Cavaliere's wife continued to strum at the piano. Ooody oody purbum, she sang out teasingly.

And what would make the Cavaliere happy?

I have noticed that many persons have lately expressed concern for my contentment, said the Cavaliere. But I do not seem to content them with my replies. Absence of strife. Freedom from disquiet. Firmness of nerves. At my age I do not expect ecstasies.

They all joined in telling him he was not *so* old.

And William? Who had been waiting impatiently for his turn.

I think I have found the recipe for happiness, said William. It is never to change, always to remain young. Being old is just a state of mind. One grows old because one allows oneself to grow old. And I pride myself that I am, give or take a few lines on my face, no different from when I was seventeen. I have the same dreams, the same ideals.

Ah, thought the Cavaliere, to be young forever. Not to

change. That is perfectly possible if you don't care about anyone but yourself. If he could live his life over again, that is exactly what he would do.

•

The second day William took his guests on a carriage ride through a portion of the vast estate, much of which he has enclosed with a twelve-foot wall topped with iron stakes to protect the wild animals in his custody, and to deny his hunting neighbors the use of even one of his two thousand acres for the pursuit of their helpless prey.

To be sure, William said, my neighbors cannot fathom someone who objects to the slaughter of innocent animals and believe that I have erected the wall to shield the orgies and satanic rites which I am reputed to conduct here. I am not liked in the neighborhood, nor would I think well of myself if I were.

In the afternoon, following dinner, while the Cavaliere was lingering in William's picture gallery (Dürer, Bellini, Mantegna, Caravaggio, Rembrandt, Poussin, &c &c, as well as many paintings of a tower), his wife and the hero had slipped off to be alone for a moment, hoping to elude the servants and find some corner where they could embrace. Like mischievous children, they looked into William's sleeping chamber with its azure Indian hangings, and the hero avowed that he had never seen so large a bed. For the Cavaliere's wife it was the second largest bed she had ever seen, the largest being Doctor Graham's Grand Celestial Bed—twelve feet by nine feet, constructed on a double frame so that it could be converted into an inclined plane, supported by forty pillars of brilliant richly colored glass, and covered by its Super Celestial Dome of precious wood inset with highly scented spices, mirrored on the underside, and crowned by automata playing flutes, guitars, violins, oboes, clarinets, and kettledrums. Guaranteed to produce fertility in any hitherto barren couple. Fifty guineas a night.

Oh, it's almost as big as the Celestial Bed.

What is that, said the hero.

That is the bed I am in whenever I lie with you, his beloved replied without missing a beat, and went on to muse astutely: I wager he usually lies alone in this bed, even though he have such a reputation for debauchery. Poor William!

He seems most disdainful of society, observed the hero.

Meanwhile, the Cavaliere was pursuing a similar line of reflection. After admiring the glorious paintings, the books, the rococo porcelain, the Japanese lacquer chests, the enameled miniatures, the Italian bronzes, and all the other treasures he was shown, he was now marveling at the fact that he was the first person not in William's employ to see them. The Cavaliere had never thought of collecting as the operation of an enraged recluse.

They had settled in William's study, whose ebony tables inlaid with Florentine mosaic were piled high with books he was reading. Unlike most bibliophiles, William read every volume he acquired, and then, with a finely sharpened pencil and in tiny script that with age had become meticulously legible, filled its inside covers and end pages with numbered glosses and a judgment, favorable or dismissive, of the book. The desk was covered with annotated lists from booksellers and auction catalogues, several of which he passed to the Cavaliere, indicating what he had already instructed his agents to purchase.

I gather that you do not enjoy browsing in bookshops or attending auctions, said the Cavaliere, citing two of his own favorite activities.

Being in attendance at something is an ordeal for me, as, indeed, is having to leave Fonthill for any reason, exclaimed William, who had spent years in peripatetic exile on the Continent before settling back on his domain to build his collections and his Abbey. But when I have properly housed the rare and beautiful objects I possess, I will not need ever to go out, ever be obliged to see anyone again. Thus fortressed, I can cheerfully contemplate the destruction of the world, for I will have saved all that is of value in it.

You do not want to give others the opportunity to admire what you have collected, the Cavaliere said.

Why should I be interested in the opinion of those less intelligent and less sensitive than myself?

I take your point, said the Cavaliere, who had not ever before thought of collecting as excluding the world. He had no quarrel with the world (though lately it seemed to have struck up a quarrel with him) and his collections had been a profitable, as well as pleasurable, connection to it.

Clearly, his kinsman did not give a damn about the improvement of public taste. But, the Cavaliere ventured, could William not envisage his collections open to view and prized at their true value by connoisseurs of some future age with the wit to appreciate what he had—

Nothing is more odious to me than thinking about the future, William interrupted.

Then the past is your—

I do not know if I love the past either, William again interrupted impatiently. In any case, love does not enter into it.

This was the Cavaliere's first experience of collecting as revenge. Revenge facilitated by the immensest privilege. His kinsman never had to think whether he could afford what caught his fancy or whether it would be a good investment, as the Cavaliere had always had to do. Collecting, like all of William's experiences, was a venture into the infinite, the imprecise, the not needing to be counted or weighed. He had none of the collector's inveterate pleasure in the making of inventories. These described only the finite, as William might say. There could be no interest in knowing that he possessed forty maki-e lacquer boxes and thirteen statues of Saint Anthony of Padua and a Meissen dinner service of three hundred and sixty-three pieces. And all six thousand one hundred and four volumes of the splendid library of Edward Gibbon, which he had purchased upon learning of the great historian's death in Lausanne—William had despised his *Decline and Fall*—but had never had sent over. For not only did he not have to know exactly what he had but sometimes he bought things in order *not* to have them, to sequester them from others; perhaps even from himself.

In some instances, William mused, it is the idea of possession that suffices me.

But if you do not see and touch what you possess, said the Cavaliere, you do not have the experience of beauty, which is what all lovers of art—all lovers, he was about to say—desire.

Beauty! exclaimed William. Who is more susceptible to beauty than I am? You need not praise beauty to me! But there is something higher still.

Which is . . . ?

Something mystical, William said coldly. I fear you will not understand it.

You may tell me, said the Cavaliere, who was enjoying this exchange with his contentious relation, and enjoying, too, the feeling of clarity in his own mind. Perhaps, he thought, the reason it wandered so often lately is that he no longer ever had a conversation that challenged him or that touched on any learned subject. All had become anecdote. Do tell me, he said.

To go as high as possible, proclaimed William. There. Have I truly made myself clear?

Perfectly clear. You refer to your tower.

Yes, if you will, my tower. I will retire to my tower and never come down.

Thereby you escape the world which you reproach for mistreating you. But you also confine yourself.

As does a monk who seeks—

Surely you would not say you live as a monk, interrupted the Cavaliere with a laugh.

Yes, I will be a monk! You do not understand me, of course. All this luxury—William waved a slender hand at the damask hangings and rococo furniture—is no less an instrument of the spirit than the whip which the monk hangs on the wall of his cell and takes down nightly to purify his soul!

•

To surround oneself with enchanting and stimulating objects, a superfluity of objects, to ensure that the senses will never be unoccupied, nor the faculty of imagination left unexercised—this the Cavaliere understood well. What he could not imagine is a collector-lust pledged to something higher than art, more ravishing than beauty, of which art, as well as beauty, is only one possible instrument. The Cavaliere was a seeker of felicity, not of bliss. Never, in all his musings on felicity, had he sighted the chasm between a happy life and one that covets ecstasy. Ecstasy does not only make, as the Cavaliere might say, an unreasonable demand on life. It has to turn brutal, too.

Like sexual feelings, when they become a focus of dedication or devotion, and are actually lived out in all their vehemence and addictiveness, so the feeling for art (or beauty) can, after a while, only be experienced as excess, as something that strains to surpass itself, to be annihilated.

To really love something is to wish to die of it.

Or to live only in it, which is the same thing. To go up and never have to come down.

I want that, you say. And that. And that. And also that.

Sold, says the amiable dealer.

If you are rich enough to buy anything you want, you will probably be moved to shift your engagement with insatiability, with unattainability, to a building—a unique, intricate dwelling for you and your collections. This dwelling is the ultimate form of the collector's fantasy of ideal self-sufficiency.

So now you say to your architect: I want that. And that. And that.

And the architect provides the obstacle. The architect says: That's impossible. Or: I don't understand.

You try to explain. You use the impure word Gothic, or

whatever the retro style of the moment is. He seems to understand. But you don't really want him to understand. I'm thinking of the Orient, you say. And you don't really mean the Orient but the decor of the Orient, which you have always found conducive to losing yourself in what you call your visions and prophetic trances.

The architect does do what you want: difficult as you may be, you are the best client he has ever had. But no matter how faithfully he executes your fantasies, he cannot fully satisfy them. You keep asking for changes and additions to the structure. New fantasies come to mind. Or, rather, new elaborations of the old fantasy that has driven you to undertake the building in the first place.

I want more, you say to the harried, servile architect, who has by now started to disregard some of his eccentric patron's instructions or to cut corners with the building materials. More, more. Such a building has the open-endedness of a collection. You think you want to finish it, but you don't.

•

It is only because it is not finished (in fact, it was never finished) that he can show it to them, stage it for them. For once this is not their theatre. No one, not even the hero, can upstage William.

He had ordered flambeaux hung from miles of trees and stationed bands of musicians along the newly cut carriageway, and farther back to provide the solemnity of echo, in order to enchant them as they rode at dusk through the woods. When the first carriage broke into open terrain, there was still enough light to make out the hero's colors flying from the octagonal tower of the prodigious cruciform building, already burgeoning with turrets, gables, oriels, and smaller towers. The flag was William's only concession in all this theatre to the presence among his guests of the most famous man in England.

He led them into the building from an entrance on the west

transept, through the Great Hall, to a room he told them was called the Cardinal's Parlour, where a banquet was laid out on a refectory table lined with silver dishes. When they had finished dining, the Cavaliere's wife offered a pantomime of an abbess welcoming novices to her convent. It seemed a good subject, she confided to William after the performance.

Most of the interior was lined by scaffolding spotted with shadowy figures of the five hundred local artisans, carpenters, plasterers, and masons whom William employed on round-the-clock shifts. Giggling nervously in his tense, high-pitched voice, cursing the slowness of the architect and the dilatoriness of the laborers, and then forgetting his annoyance and succumbing to a rapturous vision of what will be, William led his guests along the groined corridors and galleries lit with silver sconces, and up and down circular stairways which the Cavaliere's wife, only a month short of her confinement, gamely negotiated. The Cavaliere smiled to himself at the hooded figures with muscular bare arms holding large wax tapers to illuminate the way.

A cathedral of art, William explained to his guests, in which all the strong sensations our limited sensory organs crave will be amplified and all uplifting thoughts of which our slender spirit is capable will be awakened.

He showed them the Gallery, three hundred fifty feet long, which would hold his pictures. The Vaulted Library. And the Music Room, where he would make resound on his keyboard instruments all the music worth playing.

A few rooms, provisionally readied for inspection, were paneled and had peacock blue, purple, and scarlet hangings. But William seemed more and more worried that the company would not understand what they were seeing.

This is my Oratory, he said. They were to imagine it filled with golden candlesticks, enameled reliquaries, and vases, chalices, and monstrances studded with jewels. Its fan vault will be in burnished gold.

Here, you must imagine doors of violet velvet, covered with

purple-and-gold embroidery, said William. And for this room, I call it the Sanctuary, windows with lattices like those of confessionals.

I am rather cold, murmured the Cavaliere.

And for each of the sixty fireplaces, William continued imperturbably, there will be gilded filigree baskets heaped with perfumed coal.

The dark, the cold, the flickering light from the torches—the Cavaliere was beginning to feel ill. His wife wished there were a chair or a prie-dieu for her heavy body. The hero's eyes were stinging from the smoke of the torches.

He showed them his Revelation Chamber, which would have a floor of polished jasper, where he would be buried.

He showed them what would be the Crimson Drawing Room, to be covered with crimson silk damask, and his Yellow Withdrawing Room, to be covered with yellow &c.

Last, he brought them to the immense room under the central tower.

The Octagon Hall. Here you must imagine the oak wainscot and stained glass in all the soaring arches, with a great central rose window, William said.

Look, exclaimed the Cavaliere's wife. It really is like a church.

I estimate the altitude to be nearly a hundred and thirty feet, said the hero.

You must use your imagination, continued William irritably. But, when completed, my Abbey will leave nothing to the imagination. It will *be* the imagination, given tangible form.

He wanted so much for them to admire it.

So in the end—for William was not unique among collectors, as he imagined—he was disappointed. He expected nothing from this minister's son, this wraith bulked out in an admiral's uniform, whose only interest, apart from the Cavaliere's wife, was in killing people. Neither did he expect anything from the hero's inamorata, who belonged to that deplorable race of people who are effusive about everything. But perhaps he had expected something from her husband, Catherine's husband, his fastidious elderly relation with the gaunt face and absent look. There was nothing. Nothing. I vowed when I was twenty that I would always remain a child, thought William to himself; and I must bear with having a child's vulnerability, a child's absurd desire to be understood.

He would never have house guests when work on the Abbey had gone far enough for him to inhabit it. It was not a cathedral but a temple, only for the initiated: those who shared his dreams and who, like him, had undergone great ordeals and disappointments.

It will turn out, however, that the future use of these grandiose monuments to sentimentality and self-regard invariably defies the pious restrictions of their builders. Judged by posterity to be enchanting, berserk exercises in bad taste, they are destined to be gawked at on the guided tour by generations of tourists, who reach over the velvet ropes when the guards are not watching to finger the megalomaniac's precious objects or silk hangings. But William's Abbey, the mighty forerunner of all the aesthete palaces of surfeit and synesthesia and indoor theatrics of the next two centuries (both those built and those evoked in novels), did not survive to suffer the Disneyesque fate of Ludwig II's Neuschwanstein and D'Annunzio's Vittoriale. Incompetently built, the Abbey was from the beginning a ruin in the making. And since this cathedral of art, with all its gaudy arenas for self-dramatization, was principally an excuse to build the tower, it seems right that the tower's fate be the fate of the building. The tower did not fall again for another twenty-five years, soon after Fonthill was sold, but when it did, the tumbling cloud of rotted stucco and mortar took much of the Abbey with it. And no one saw any reason not to tear the rest of it down.

•

Things decay, crash, vanish. Such is the law of the world, thought the Cavaliere. Wisdom of age. And those few deemed worth reconstructing or repairing will forever bear the marks of the violence done to them.

One February mid-afternoon in 1845, a young man of nineteen entered the British Museum, went directly to the unguarded room where the Portland Vase, one of the museum's most valuable and celebrated holdings since its deposit on loan by the Fourth Duke of Portland in 1810, was kept in a glass case, picked up what was later described as "a curiosity in sculpture," and started beating the vase to death. The vase broke, fractured, shattered, was decreated. The young man whistled softly and sat down in front of the heap to admire his handiwork. Guards arrived at a run.

The constables were summoned and the young man was taken to the Bow Street Police Station, where he gave a false name and address; the director of the museum set out to break the unpleasant news to the duke; the curators went to their knees to gather up all the little pieces. Careful not to miss any!

The malefactor, discovered to be an Irish divinity student who had dropped out of Trinity College after a few weeks' study, was considerably less jaunty when brought before a magistrate. When asked to explain what had possessed him to commit this senseless act of vandalism, he said that he was drunk . . . or that he was suffering from a kind of nervous excitement, a continual fear of everything he saw . . . or that he heard voices telling him to do it . . . or that he envied the maker of the vase . . . or that he had found himself aroused by the figure of Thetis, recumbent, awaiting her bridegroom . . . or that he thought the vase's depiction of erotic longing a sacrilege, an offense to Christian morals . . . or that he couldn't stand to see such a beautiful thing be so admired while he was poor and lonely and unsuccessful. The usual reasons given for destroying objects of incalculable value, admired by everyone. These are always stories of a haunting.

Self-defined outcasts and solitaries, almost always men, begin to be haunted by a supremely beautiful building, like the Temple of the Golden Pavilion, or by representations of a languorous female beauty, like Thetis on the Portland Vase or the *Rokeby Venus* of Velázquez, or of ideal, naked male beauty, like the *David* of Michelangelo—begin to be haunted, continue to be haunted, rise to a state of congested, fabulous misery, the inverse of the goal of nonstop ecstasy, and become convinced that they have a right to be relieved of this feeling. They must strike out, smash their way out of it. The ravishing object is there. The object is provoking them. The object is insolent. The object is, ah, worst of all, indifferent.

Torch a temple. Pulverize a vase. Slash a Venus. Smash a perfect ephebe's toes.

Then lapse back into a shame-ridden, baleful torpor: from now on, the malefactor is likely to be a danger only to himself. For this is not a crime one commits more than once. This form of obsession with an object, the obsession to destroy it, is monogamous. We know Mr. *** won't come back to the British Museum and take a thwack at the Rosetta Stone or the Elgin Marbles—nor is it likely that anyone else will either, for it appears there are no more than ten or fifteen works of art in the whole world that create obsessions (this recent estimate, probably low, by the Superintendent of Fine Arts in Florence, whose city has the honor to harbor two of these, Michelangelo's statue and Botticelli's *Birth of Venus*). The Portland Vase is not on the list.

No one can repair Mr. ***, whom the magistrate sentenced to a fine of three pounds or two months' hard labor. Having only ninepence in his pocket, he was taken to prison, and released a few days later when someone paid the fine. (His benefactor, it was rumored, was a clement aristocrat, none other than the Duke of Portland himself, who declared that he did not wish to appear to be persecuting a young man who might be mad.) But the vase, in one hundred and eighty-nine pieces on a table in the museum's basement, being examined with tweezers and loupe, was put back together by one intrepid, skillful employee and assistant in seven months.

Can something shattered, then expertly repaired, be the same, the same as it was? Yes, to the eye, yes, if one doesn't look too closely. No, to the mind.

Back inside its glass case, this new vase, neither replica nor original, was enough like its former incarnation that no visitors to the museum observed it had been broken and restored unless it was pointed out to them. A perfect job of reconstruction, for the time. Until time wears it out. Transparent glue yellows and bulges, making seamless joints visible. The jeopardous decision to attempt a better reconstruction of the vase was made in 1989. First, it had to be restored to its shattered condition. A team of experts immersed the vase in a desiccating solvent to soften the old adhesive, peeled off the one hundred and eighty-nine fragments one by one, washed each in a solution of warm water and non-ionic soap, and reassembled them with a new adhesive, which hardens naturally, and resin, which can be cured with ultraviolet light in thirty seconds. The work, checked by electron microscope and photographed at every stage, took nine months. The result is optimal. The vase will last forever, now. Well, at least another hundred years.

•

Some things can never be put back together again: someone's life, someone's reputation.

In the first weeks of January, the hero was made second in command of the Channel Fleet—he still had a moment more to linger under the shadow of official disapproval of his reprehensible conduct during the last two years—and given a new flagship. Gillray celebrated the hero's return to his hero's destiny with an etching entitled "Dido in Despair." Dido is an unsightly mountain of a woman starting up from a bed, her gargantuan legs asprawl, her mammoth arms and meaty paws flung wide to a window that opens onto the sea and a squadron of departing warships.

Ah, where, & ah where, is my gallant
Sailor gone?
He's gone to Fight the Frenchmen, for
George upon the Throne,
He's gone to fight the Frenchmen, t'lose
t'other Arm & Eye,
And left me here with old Antique, to lay
me down & Cry.

And indeed, in a dusky corner of the bed, one can just make out the wizened head of a small, sleeping spouse.

There are a few people, such as the hero, whose lives and reputations are like the Portland Vase, already in a museum and too valuable to be allowed to disappear.

He is a warrior, the best that his bellicose country, about to become the greatest imperial power the world has ever known, has produced. Everyone admires him. The creation of his reputation has gone too far. It cannot be allowed to be destroyed.

But who cares about this fat vulgar woman and this emaciated weary old man. They can be destroyed. Society will not be the loser. Nothing important has been invested in them.

So, from now on, nothing they do will be right.

Disgrace, disgrace. Double disgrace.

And for the hero, soon, immortal glory.

Of course, the hero's reputation has a crack. Nothing can efface it. Not the great victory he won a few months later, the second of his three great victories, in which he broke Napoleon's control of the Baltic; not even the final, the supreme victory when, having ignored advice not to make himself a target by wearing all his stars and decorations on deck during battle, he was shattered by a musketball fired from the mizzentop of a nearby French warship. Everyone who relates the story of his life must take a position on the period of misconduct in the Mediterranean, if only in the form of declaring it not worth discussing. One has to maintain the right velocity of narration, as one has to keep the right distance from the dashed and rebuilt Portland Vase. Slow down, or move in for a closer scrutiny, and one cannot help but see it. Speed up, describe only what is essential—and it's gone.

•

And what to wear to disguise the reason for a sudden loss of weight, for that is the problem of the Cavaliere's wife two weeks after the hero sailed off for the Baltic. Luckily, it is early February and extremely cold. Answer: the voluminous clothes of the last months of pregnancy, but padded out a little, in the hope that, as layers are gradually discarded, the change in silhouette may appear the result of a remarkably effective crash diet.

And what to wear at night when, in the greatest secrecy, you convey your week-old daughter out of the house in Piccadilly and into a hackney carriage to Little Titchfield Street, where she must be left with a wet nurse until you can figure out how to reclaim the baby as another's offspring who has been committed to your care. Answer: a fur muff.

News has come of the great victory won at Copenhagen, won by your true husband, the father of your precious daughter, your first child as far as your beloved knows, who is mad with grief that he could not be present at his daughter's birth, mad with joy at being a father, he tells you, he writes you once or twice a day; you write him three or four times a day. He writes mostly about the child now, how she must be christened, there is no question of his not acknowledging her paternity, how worried he is about her health. That and his jealousy. He does not seriously believe that you will be unfaithful to him, but he is convinced that every man in London is attracted to you. And the truth is that several are. You may not be presentable at court, and Miss Knight, warned the very evening of the return to London that any further contact with you will tarnish her reputation, has never once called on you. But others do. You are received, you entertain, there have to be parties and musical evenings, if only because your husband, whom you now regard as the father you never had, you were a girl when you married him, but you really are a woman now, your father-husband must show he is still well-off, with no pressing need to sell his collections. There are plans for a party which the Prince of Wales will attend. And a friend of the hero was delighted to be able to inform him that the prince is saying around town that you have hit his fancy. He will be next to you, telling you soft things, wails the hero. He will put his foot near yours! For you have been exchanging crazy hectic letters, you are both being driven mad by the separation. You make him promise that he will never go ashore whenever his ship is in harbor, no matter how long, or allow any woman to come aboard. He keeps his promise. He makes you promise that you will never allow yourself to be seated next to the Prince of Wales at any party (you didn't keep this promise), but when the prince did press a leg against yours under the table, you swiftly pulled your leg away, and with the excuse of preparing your performance left the table. He hasn't made you promise that you won't exhibit yourself.

And at the grand dinner party celebrating the news of the hero's great victory at Copenhagen, after giving a short sedate recital on the harpsichord, you start to dance the tarantella, and then pull toward you Lord *** to dance with you, and when he seems unable to follow you, you seize the hand of Sir ***, and after a few minutes recall that you should have first asked your husband, poor old soul, who gallantly joins you for a few steps, you can feel the trembling of his bandy legs. Then you beckon to Charles, but he refuses. And when you have exhausted the few possible partners in the room, you are still not tired, of course you have been drinking, how else to get through the evening, perhaps you have drunk too much, as you often do, you know that. But you don't want to stop. You go on dancing for a while by yourself. As an exhibition of Neapolitan folklore, which you thought would impress your guests, you have danced the tarantella many times in Palermo, but this is the first time you dance it in cold grey London. It doesn't matter, the tarantella is inside you. You always had a pretext for performing, you were a living statue or a painter's model, reproducing the postures and demeanor of some figure of history or poetry, you impersonated, or Attitudinized, as those who pillory you are now wont to say, you sang, with another's cry or gaiety in your mouth. Now you have no pretext, no mask. There is just the feeling of joy, now, dancing to this music in your head, here, in London, in your own house, with your old husband sitting over there, not looking at you, looking away, while everyone else is looking, staring, you are making a fool of yourself, it doesn't matter, you feel so alive. You know you are not as graceful as you once were, but it is you, it is what you have become, you are starting to put on weight again, your mother and your maids are taking out the seams again, and you call for your black Fatima and your blond Marianne, who are standing with some of the other servants in a far doorway watching the masters' pleasures, to join you in the tarantella. They both come forward shyly, and begin to dance with you, but Marianne has gone all red, and says something you don't hear, and slips away, while Fatima is dancing as ardently as you are. Perhaps it is the wine, perhaps it is Fatima's glossy black skin, perhaps it is your elation over Copenhagen, and you now dance holding Fatima's sweating black hand—faster, your heart thumping, and your engorged, unmilked breasts bumping against your chest. You have no pretext now, you always had a pretext for performing. You are just you. Pure energy, pure defiance, pure foreboding. And you hear the strange cries and screams coming from your mouth, sounds of a most peculiar nature, even you can hear that, and you can see you are creating a scandal, your guests look quite startled. But this is what they wanted. This is what they think of you anyway. You wish you could rip off your clothes and show them your heavy body, the mottling and stretchmarks on your belly, your pale blue-veined huge breasts, the eczema on your elbows and knees. You pull at your clothes, you pull at Fatima's clothes. This is who they think you really are, twirling, screeching, shrieking, all mouth, all breasts, all thighs, vulgar, unrestrained, lewd, lascivious, fleshy, wet. Let them see what they think they see anyway. And you pull Fatima toward you, receiving in her breath, you imagine, all of Africa, and you kiss her on the mouth, tasting the spices, the scents, all the faraway places, you want to be everywhere, but you are only here, with something filling your body, and you dance faster, faster. Something is bursting out of you, almost like when the child was pushing out of your fundament, it is frightening, as that was, you thought you were going to die, a woman always thinks she is going to die when the contractions come faster, and it seems impossible that you can pass this huge thing out of your body. Like that, it is frightening though not painful, not painful as giving birth to life is. No, it is joy, the aliveness of being alive, you have become a figure of scandal, but you are feeling how happy you are, how proud of him you are, and then how big the world is—he is far away and may have to stay away for months, he may be wounded, he may be killed at any time, he will be killed one day, you know that—and how alone you are, and how always alone you are, not so different from this docile Fatima, a stranger in this world like you, a woman, a helot, who must be what others want her to be. And it is so big, the world, and you have lived so much, but everyone blames you, you know it. But there is his glory, his glory, and you sink to your knees, and Fatima follows, and you embrace and kiss once more and then you both rise and Fatima, her eyes closed, is uttering strange ululating cries, and they pour out of your throat too. And the guests are very embarrassed, but for a long time you have been an embarrassment, you always embarrass people now. You've seen it in their eyes, you are anything but unobservant, you just pretend you don't notice. Let them all be embarrassed even further. It feels so good to sing and stamp and twirl. Why do they criticize you and mock you? Why do you embarrass them? They must sometimes feel as you do now. Why are people always trying to stop you? You've tried to be what they wanted you to be.

•

My dearest wife, the hero writes to the Cavaliere's wife. Parting from you is literally tearing one's own flesh. I am so low I cannot hold up my head.

In February, the hero got three days' leave and saw his daughter in Little Titchfield Street. He wept when he took the infant and held her against his breast. They wept together when he left to go back to sea.

She had always meant to tell him about the other daughter, now nineteen, to whom she had given her own first name. But the right moment had never come, and now it was too late. The other daughter was herself, whereas this child bore the hero's first name, with the feminine *a* ending. So this tiny babe was her only child.

Whenever the Cavaliere was out for the day with Charles, she had the baby brought from Little Titchfield Street. She would go back to bed and sleep beside her. It was kind of him never to allude to the child's existence, she was grateful to him for that. He could have reproached her. No, he will not reproach her. Her mother would knock when the Cavaliere returned. She does not want to impose the child on him, she told herself. The truth was, she did not want to share the child with him, but one day . . . surely not too far off . . . he will be . . . she will no longer be . . . she will not have to send her child away!

•

The Cavaliere reproached his wife only about money—the expenses of their entertaining, for instance; a wine bill of four hundred pounds, in particular. But she was as unmercenary as she was extravagant. She volunteered to sell all the presents from the Queen, the diamond necklace given her many years ago by the Cavaliere for her birthday, and the rest of her jewelry. There was a glut of diamonds on the London market (too many penniless French émigré aristocrats selling their jewels); valued in Italy at the equivalent of thirty thousand pounds, they fetched only a twentieth of that. But at least the sum paid for the furnishing of the house in Piccadilly.

Now he had to sell what he had to sell.

The inventory had already been made two and a half years ago, a lifetime ago, before they left Naples. The few paintings which had been uncrated and hung in the house in Piccadilly were repacked; and the fourteen cases of pictures and the other boxes were taken out of the house in Piccadilly and conveyed to the auctioneer.

What's hard is choosing. I'll keep this, but I'll let that go. No, I can't give that up. *That's* hard.

But once you decide to let everything go, it isn't so hard. One feels rather reckless, giddy. The important thing is to hold nothing back.

A collection is, ideally, acquired piece by piece—there is more pleasure that way—but that would be the most unpleasant way of selling it. Instead of the death of a thousand cuts, one clean lethal blow. When Mr. Christie informed him of the result of the first two days of sale, entirely devoted to his pictures, he barely glanced at the breakdown. He did not want to dwell on the fact that the Veronese and the Rubens had gone for more than he had expected, the Titian and the Canaletto for less. The important thing is that he had got far more than he had paid for them, nearly six thousand pounds.

Though away at sea, the hero had instructed an agent to bid for two of the fifteen pictures of the Cavaliere's wife. Go to any price. I must have them. And to the Cavaliere's wife: I see you are for SALE. How can he, how can he part with pictures of you? When I think that anyone can buy them. How I wish I could buy them all! The one the hero would most like to have acquired was

Vigée-Lebrun's salacious Ariadne; but, unfortunately, it had never been in the Cavaliere's collection.

Two more days of sale in early May yielded another three thousand pounds. Then the Cavaliere made his will, the will he always thought he was going to make, and which he had no reason to change now. He felt himself lighter, relieved of a burden.

•

And what to wear at home, the home you have always wanted, a real home, which means a property in the country, a farm, with a stream running through it. Even when doing the honors of the table, a simple suit of black. And when pacing your property, looking at your livestock, supervising the pruning of trees, a crumpled hat and a striped brown overcoat thrown round your shoulders.

The summer's invasion scare had passed without Napoleon's fleet making its expected appearance in the Channel. The hero had written yet one more letter to the Admiralty. I beg their lordships' permission to go ashore, as I want repose. And he had asked the Cavaliere's wife to look for a house where he can settle when he returns, as he expects, in October. She found a property with a two-story house in unspoiled Surrey countryside only an hour's drive from Westminster Bridge. Against the advice of friends, who thought the century-old brick house and acreage too modest and, at nine thousand pounds, overpriced, the hero borrowed money to purchase it and requested the Cavaliere's wife to ready it for his return. With her mother, she set about fitting up the house. It was to be beautiful, and needed to be plastered, painted, mirrored, furnished (neither a piano nor flags, trophies, pictures, and china celebrating the hero's victories would be lacking). It was to be up-to-date: she installed five water closets and put modern stoves in the kitchens. And it was to be something of a farm, with sheepcotes, pigsties, and hen coops.

I am as much amused with sheap & pigs & hens as ever I was in the court of Naples, she wrote the hero. I hope I do not bore you with these detayls.

My dearest, the hero replied, I would rather read and hear you on the subject of pigs and hens, sheets and towels, saltcellars and ladles, carpenters and upholsterers, than any speech I shall hear in the House of Lords, for there is no subject which you do not enlighten with your wit and eloquence. I agree to African parrots on the veranda. Assure Fatima that I hope to be home in time for her christening. Please remember to instruct Mr. Morley to put some netting round the edges of the stream and on the bridge to prevent any possibility of our child's falling in when she comes to live with us. You will have the kindness to remember that I do not want anything in the house but what is my own, and to tell me everything that you and Mrs. Cadogan are doing. You are speaking of our paradise. I do not know how I can bear our separation much longer. How the Conqueror longs to return and become again the Conquered.

Since his wife and her mother were always at the house in Surrey once the hero returned, the Cavaliere had no choice but to live there too, although he still kept the house in London. They had not forgotten him. It was for him that the stream, which his wife had renamed the Nile, had been stocked with fish. But he had not been allowed to bring his books from the house in London or his French cook. His wife pointed out that he had the library and the servants at the hero's house at his disposal. He could not explain why he needed the French cook. He was weary of giving things up.

You give up this, and this, and this. And there is always more.

The covering of the coach-box was stolen from his carriage while he stopped at an inn for refreshment after a day of fishing in the Wandle. The Cavaliere came out and immediately saw it gone, and the postilion dozing on his perch. Tears nibbled his eyes. On the drive back he could not stop thinking about it. He told his wife as soon as he returned and could get her attention. She said, Oh those are stolen all the time.

The Cavaliere felt very foolish about minding so much the loss of the cloth on his carriage. Its value was insignificant. But it was not a question of money. Sometimes one becomes attached to things that are worth nothing at all. Sometimes, especially when one is old, it is such things to which one is most attached. The loss of a pen or a pin or a ribbon hurts, hurts unforgettably. He insisted on placing an advertisement for the stolen cloth.

It's a waste of money to advertise for it, his wife said. It isn't like the diamond we lost in Dresden.

"Lost off a Gentleman's Coach Box, a Crimson Coffoy Hammer Cloth, trimm'd with white Silk Lace about it, embroidered with white and blue."

It will never be returned, said the Cavaliere's wife.

And, of course, it was not. He often dreamed of the cloth. He might have said that its loss affected him more than anything else with which he had recently parted.

•

To lie in bed, to give way to the counterforce of an immense fatigue, to float between dream and waking, to remember the past, to have nothing in your mind, to have everything in your mind, to see the faces bent over you, looking worried, there's my wife, there's her mother. Someone puts a wet cloth to his lips. What's that strange raspy sound? Someone in the room is having trouble breathing.

There are endless passages through which he must walk, until he realizes he no longer has the use of his legs. There are things he has left undone. It is spring and the window is open, there are voices. They ask him many questions. How are you, how do you feel, do you feel better? Surely they don't expect him to answer. He hadn't been able to say, though he meant to say, that he had to piss. He won't tell them the sheet is wet. They might be angry. He wants them to stay as they are now, with their smiling, intent faces—her face, his face. They are holding his hands. How warm their hands are. They have taken him in their arms. He hears the crinkling of cloth. That is his wife on his left. He can feel her bosom. And that is his friend on the other side. He is in his friend's left arm. He hopes he is not too heavy for them. There is a big hollow space inside his chest where the pain used to be.

He has escaped the dungeon of thought. He feels elated. He is climbing. It is a laborious ascent. But now the mountain no longer has to be climbed. He has climbed. By a kind of levitation. He was looking up for so long, and now he can look down from this high place. It is a big panorama. So this is dying, thought the Cavaliere.

PART THREE

AVGVSTO·PIO·FELICI
P·P·
GVLIELMVS·HAMILTON
MAGN·BRITANN·NEAP
LEGATVS·EXTRAORDIN
L·C·N·D

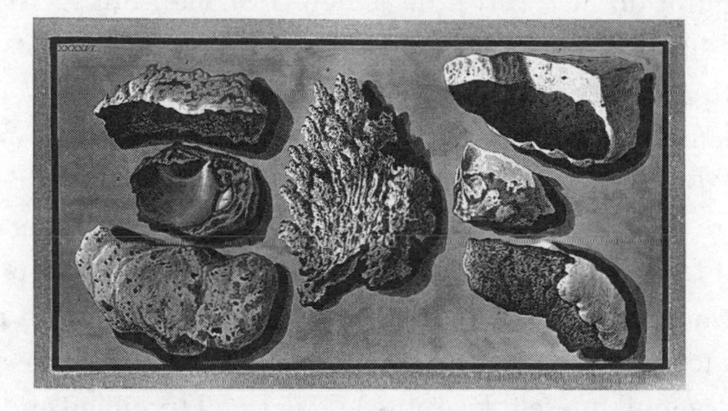

6 April 1803

Just because I have closed my eyes and am lying quite still they suppose I cannot hear what they are saying, though I hear perfectly well. But it is better thus, the chamber is so large, the curtains fluttering on the windows are afflicted with a nervous disorder, everything cannot be brought into one view. The light closes my eyes. Softly, someone said, it cannot last much longer. And I heard everything they said earlier while I slept, while I did not want to wake. Not yet. To awake is to be surprised. I have never cared much for surprises. Tolo and my wife are pressing against me. They have made peace since I became ill. In Naples Tolo comported himself with her like a surly retainer, looking down at the ground whenever she addressed him, but they have been conversing quietly, then pausing, like old friends, and just now I felt their heads lean toward each other over my breast and their lips touch. How odd that my faithful Neapolitan cyclops should be wearing a British naval uniform. Perhaps he has donned this costume to amuse me. He understands me very well. It would sometimes happen that I took fright, as when he drew me over the river of lava and my heart thundered in my breast, but I did not show it, it was not fitting that I show fear. He may suppose, mistakenly, that I am afraid or dejected now. He is very fearless, Tolo. He has won many battles. Everyone admires him. Though of obscure birth, he is now a Sicilian duke. The King would like to make him the thunder-cyclops who lurks inside Etna, but I am sure that Tolo still prefers our Vesuvius, as I do. We cannot climb Etna together. There was no peerage for me. But allowing myself to be cast down by this provides no remedy, as there is nothing to be gained by agitating oneself when in the grip of fear. Better to hold very still. Thus giving the impression one is not afraid, which reassures the others, because it is necessary to set an example for others, and in this fashion becoming more tranquil oneself. En route to Palermo I trembled and shook with the shaking and trembling of the ship, and Tolo came to sit with me and hold my feet, as I wish he would do now because they are quite cold, I wish he would rub them. And foolish as it may seem to have taken up my pistols, what did I imagine I could do with them, execute the storm, I was able to sit quite calmly after that, when Tolo had to return to the deck, because he too had to set an example of calmness. I sat still and closed my eyes and the storm subsided. And I know if I lie here without moving I will not be frightened. They are speaking now. It cannot last much longer. Perhaps Tolo is fearless because he sees only half of what others see. Half-blind he won his greatest battles. And if I keep both eyes closed I will see no danger at all. Where true danger lies is altogether unpredictable. My friends here imagined me in constant peril from the volcano, and told me how displeased they would be to hear that I had perished in an eruption like Pliny the Elder, but they were wrong to fear for my safety. No calamity ever befell me, at least not on the volcano. The volcano was a haven. Naples itself was very salubrious. I felt so well. The air. I do not feel well now. And the sea. When I swam from my boat, the delicious sensation of the water supporting my limbs. I am glad they are holding me because my limbs are very heavy. I detect some impediment to my breathing. I would not be ill if I were still in Naples. The air was considerate to

Catherine. If Pliny had not been fat and always short of breath, he would not have died when Vesuvius erupted. He did not divine, no one knew then, that it was a volcano. How surprised they must have been. When he took a ship to rescue some of the victims of the eruption, those who accompanied him did not perish. He alone succumbed to the volcano's mephitic fumes. Perhaps the volcano was harmful to Catherine. I recall that she was very sorry to die and asked me to see to it that she not be buried. She was very tired. I believe she is resting now in her room. Many persons want to rest. After reaching the shore, Pliny felt tired and a sheet was spread on the ground for him to lie down for a brief rest, from which he never recovered. One cannot know when one is going to die, but one can take reasonable precautions. While avoiding unreasonable precautions. For, now I remember why, I was holding the pistols so as to shoot myself when I would feel the ship about to go down. I was more afraid of the water filling my throat, choking off the air, than of metal opening my head. I shall not panic again. How absurd if I had killed myself because I heard too loud a noise, because the vessel tipped too far to one side. A noise may subside, an oblique object may right itself. And then I would have died before I am supposed to die. Tolo's mother said I would not die then in the storm, and she proved correct. She reassured me that I would live to the age I have now attained, which I cannot remember, though it will come to me in a moment. I do not care for predictions. Any number makes one's life shorter than it ought to be. At twenty-two, yes, events of one's youth are easier to recall, the month was September and the year 1752, when the calendar was changed, I saw a crowd following a sign inscribed GIVE US OUR ELEVEN DAYS, because the ignorant thought the eliminated days were being subtracted from their lives. But nothing is ever subtracted. And one will never convince the ignorant that they are ignorant, nor fools that they are fools. However, it is natural to wish to prolong one's being, wretched though it may be. It cannot last much longer. In Naples aged persons are knocked down every day by the darting calashes with their insolent drivers crying to all and sundry to get out of the way. One of these, I saw it, was an old fellow, very old, very thin, the merest skeleton, a skeleton in rags, who would carry each foot to the ground not forward and obliquely but perpendicularly and with a kind of stamp, setting down the entire sole at once. This was not fearlessness but obstinacy. I would not want to walk if I could not remain vertical. But lying here, even if I no longer have the use of my arms and my legs but have only my reason and my sadness, I can still enjoy watching events unfold. Who would wish to have the curtain fall on the play before it is finished. Who said it cannot last much longer. Even if no story ever finishes, or rather one story turns into another, and that into another, &c &c &c, I would like to know when and how damned Bonaparte gets his comeuppance and, ah, someone has closed the window. I heard carriage wheels. I believe they are planning to take me on a journey. But at least I have lived to see the collusion with revolutionary infamy subside in England. Human nature is so perverse that it is absurd even to hope, much less to desire, that society can ever be translated to another, better plane. The most one can aspire to is a very slow uplifting. Nothing conical. For what rises too high will tumble down. It is difficult for anything to stand for very long. My body is leaving me. I wonder if I could stand now. I should be practicing standing if we are about to go on a journey. I would surprise them if I stood up with my cold heavy legs. Tolo will come when this little fellow in the admiral's uniform goes away, and he will rub my legs. But I want my wife to stay. She need not always go with him. She can stay with me and sing to me. For her I would even open my eyes. She is being very kind now. Lately she has not been so kind to me as I would have wished. I trust she is not being kind because I am ill, for I intend to become tolerably well again. There are persons who become protective of something only when it is endangered or damaged or nearly gone. The ignorant laborers at Pompeii and Herculaneum had no thought of what they were sundering and burying with pick and shovel, until Winckelmann visited the excavations and denounced the utter lack of method and care with which they were being conducted, and a more cautious method was adopted. And then soon after he was murdered by a horrible young man, no Ganymede I was told but an ugly brute with pockmarks, whom my susceptible friend invited to his hotel room and had the imprudence to show some of the treasures he was conveying to Rome. I should have thought Winckelmann would fancy only youths with faces and bodies like the Greek statues whose beauties he extolled, but there is no single standard of taste despite all the eager legislators, and then if one is to be murdered, if such is one's destiny, one cannot anticipate who the murderer will be. Never, not once, did I fear the flash of a knife while living for thirty-seven years among a violent and intemperate people. But in the safety of my bed, of my England, it cannot last much longer, night terrors are one of the infirmities I now have to bear, which I trust will pass when I have recovered, I wish I were not thinking about them now. My own mother advances toward me while opening her robe and making lewd signs. A circle of men and women sit feasting on dead bodies, softly smacking their lips and spitting out bits of white bone, like the pumice stone I have collected on the volcano. And a bloated man floating in the water and a pregnant woman dangling from a gibbet. In dreams I have been taken to be hanged, most disagreeable, even though I protested that I was unable to walk, in dreams a band of men with knives were closing about me while I lay helpless in bed. I often dream now that I am about to be murdered. Usually I can master myself when I awake, although these phantasms prolong themselves for some minutes into my waking state, but if necessary I pull on the bell rope and bring old Gaetano to sit by me until I fall back to sleep. And once, I believe it was the other evening, I heard myself cry out, most piteously I fear, and my wife and my cyclops entered the room and inquired if I was in pain. No, there is no pain, I replied. It was only a dream, but I am surprised how vivid it was. Let me not dwell on it. I prefer, I have always preferred, to dwell on what is pleasant, and fortunate, of which I have much to recall. First of all, my good health. In all the years in Naples I was hardly ever ill. An occasional disorder of the stomach, nothing more. My distinguished physician often remarked on my strong constitution and firm state of nerves. An excellent man, Cirillo. I enjoyed listening to him discourse on recent discoveries in the science of living beings. I had only to maintain nature's endowment, eschewing excessive drink and food, especially highly seasoned dishes, which turn the body's fluids thick and viscous, sluggish and torpid, and narrow the channels through which they circulate. And to practice a moderate and continual stimulation of the animal functions by riding, swimming, climbing, and other forms of exercise. Bodily action invariably restored me to myself. And if when indoors I suffered from lowness of spirits, I had only to read or take up my violin or my cello and I was immediately cheerful again. I was not difficult to console. Nature made me even-tempered. Age has made me phlegmatic. Nothing disturbs me. I cannot be much of a bother to those who are caring for me now. If they would call Simon to shave me, my face would not feel so stiff. I was always fortunate. Beauty surrounded me. I surrounded myself with beauty. Each enthusiasm a new crater of an old volcano. To enter a shop or an auction room or a fellow collector's sanctum, and be surprised. But not to show it. It could be mine. As one passion begins to fail it is necessary to form another, for the whole art of going through life tolerably is to keep oneself eager about anything. Although the King's enthusiasms, billiards and fishing excepted, were conducted immoderately, and he himself was exceedingly repulsive in his person and altogether lacking in wit and discernment, I preferred his company to that of the intelligent Queen. Women are often discontented, I have observed. I think many of them are bored. I am never bored as long as I have an enthusiasm to share or observe. I have appreciated every enthusiasm except the religious ones, and while in Vienna I enjoyed fishing in the Danube. Catherine hoped that I would become a believer, but it is not my nature, which is sceptical. While I would hardly deny that illusions are necessary for human life to be supportable, the sour sad tales of Christianity hold no charm for me. I do not wish to be indignant. My mouth is very dry. The first principle of the science of felicity is not to succumb to indignation or self-pity. Or water. I would like some water. They do not hear me. The pressure of a hand. But the affections stray. A Venus cannot remain faithful. And I am not Mars. But I refused all opportunities to avenge myself. I did not sell my Venus. Faithful in spite of myself, for I did try to sell her. But I never loved a painting quite as much as my Correggio. I am surprised that Charles is not in the room, it is not kind, for I did not forget to make him my heir. I know he is despondent because I do not have more money. Charles is not as happy as he expected to be. There was no Venus for Charles. He loves his gems and scarabs and ring bezels. And he is much older now. I believe he has envied me. First in the arts of happiness. While satisfying myself, at the same time I have been useful to others. I have never overestimated my abilities. While there are more exalted destinies, I maintain that to discover what is beautiful and share that with others is also a worthy employment for a life. Art must not be merely the object of fruitless admiration. I said that. A work of art must inspire the leading artists and craftsmen of one's own time. It was I who brought the vase back to England which Wedgwood now puts out in many copies. Plumpity dumpity. Who said that. When one has lived as long as I have, one is bound to mix everything up, but I am endeavoring to get it right now. It is to be expected that many subjects come to mind at the same time, because I have had a very long life. But I do not need to touch them or handle them. My arms and legs are heavy and I am not sure where my back is. The heavy baggage, the burden of every journey, could not feel as heavy as my body does now. Something pressing down on me. Everything very close. A child had been buried for weeks under the house after the earthquake, after

Catherine died. I wonder if she knew enough to hope that she might be rescued, or did she believe that she was buried alive forever. I mean the child, the child who had been pressing her fist to the side of her face and emerged from the ground with a hole in her cheek. Men do not like to acknowledge the finality of catastrophe. Pagano wrote an essay in which he made the earthquake in Calabria an emblem of the dissolution of society and a return to primitive equality. I cannot remember why he advanced such a preposterous notion. He was very intelligent, Pagano. But something happened to him, I do not remember what it is. I have noticed that authors are capable of raising up any event to the height of a lesson or a warning or a punishment, but it is my view that a man of sense, why are the voices becoming softer, I trust they are not leaving me when my mouth is dry, my tongue is stiff, it is my view that a man of sense will observe the unrolling of events with calm, with measured detachment. Even under this weight. When a catastrophe occurs, one should try to save oneself and the others. That estimable Roman Pliny the Elder felt obliged to try to rescue the victims of the volcano. He was reared to be a gentleman. But then there are those who teach themselves how they must behave. This is common in the age I have lived to see, where the gifted may rise from the lowest station in life. The meanly-born learn to surpass themselves. When Vesuvius erupted again, Tolo landed in his boat and rescued the King and Queen and brought us all to Palermo. But he lost the vases. There was a storm and they went to the bottom of the sea. I have the impression that I am not reasoning with the same clarity and equanimity that have always been mine. Voices crying *bella cosa è l'acqua fresca*. Tolo should tell me why his men chose to save the admiral in the coffin instead of my vases, which would have brought delight and instruction to many. My bankers expected them to be saved. An admiral is not worth very many guineas. I refer to the admiral in the coffin, a man of no great distinction or accomplishments. But there is much glory to be won at sea. Who does not laud the intrepid commander whose name I have forgotten but it is on everyone's lips. No, not Pliny the Elder but another admiral, who is anything but corpulent and does not suffer from asthma. But that was Catherine. No, both. It is perfectly possible for two human beings to resemble each other. Were that not the case how could we understand anything about our fellow creatures, for it is only by assiduous comparison of the various types of, yes, the admiral, my great friend, our country's savior. So the King of Naples hailed him. His words. But I mean this country, England. And this admiral, who has become as a son to me, and whose well-being and peace of mind mean more to me than my own, for it has not been easy for me these past five years, I must admit, the world in which I felt at home is greatly altered. Old customs thrown down. New sentiments which I do not understand and can only deplore, for alas I do understand them, and therefore shall not assume a dullness of comprehension which has never been mine. To others I am a fool. She should be punished for making the others think of me as a fool. May I have some water, I wonder if they hear me. I can hear them perfectly well.

•

I feel clearer now. To sleep was refreshing. I cannot hear Tolo and my wife anymore, though I can still feel them. Their clothes. If I were not so cold, I would be very comfortable. It was always very cold at the summit of the volcano when it was abominably hot below. I do not see why even the timorous would not want to climb the volcano, what do they fear. I could never persuade Charles to make the ascent with me, and Catherine was too frail. And Pliny too fat. It is unwise to let oneself become corpulent, although I have perhaps become too thin. I should have insisted that they climb with me, it is an exhilarating effort, especially during an eruption. While I advance fearlessly, the guides will pull them up with thongs. Everyone should climb the volcano and observe for himself that the monster is quite harmless. I can smell its hot sulphurous breath. And the odor of roasted chestnuts. No, it might be coffee, but if I ask for a spoonful of coffee I suspect they would not give it to me, they would tell me it will keep me awake. The light is keeping me awake now. A current of orange-red light. To lure the sedentary, tender, and decayed to the summit, I shall offer them a musical assembly after their efforts. Catherine will play the piano, and she who no longer loves me will sing. Rule Britannia. And I will play the cello, for one does not forget the skills of one's youth. After making sure that walls have been erected to protect us from the wind, there is a great deal of wind inside my head, the wind must not get out and tip over Catherine's piano. Thus protected, thus protected, Tolo is squeezing my hand, *al fresco*, most original, everything is here, carried in strong arms, on strong backs, up the slopes of the mountain. All gathered in one site. I observe that most of my guests are examining my pictures and vases. A few would be interested in my samples of volcanic rocks. And what do you think of all this, Jack. The monkey has thrown me a look I cannot but think mischievous, Jack has lowered his head to his little red prick, Jack is whispering to me. Though all evils are burdens, yet an erected spirit may bear them, but when the supports are fallen, and cover the man with their ruins, the desolation is perfect. A most remarkable creature. He understands me very well. I shall write a communication to the Royal Society, which is the most important scientific academy of Europe and of which I have the honor. Fortitude, patience, tranquillity, and resignation. And a shimmering. A cold musty smell like a *mofetta*. Oh beware. It is possible to be too fearless. Jack has darted behind a rock. Someone must watch that the rascal does not approach too closely the brink of the crater. I shall save him. He is here. He is sitting on my breast. I can feel the weight, I can smell the stench of his animal bowels. I shall not breathe in any more with my nostrils. And when the guests have departed I shall return to bed, for it is permitted to rest if one has greatly exerted oneself, one need not be elderly to tire after a great exertion. My breath. I always found the energy to do what pleased me. And the more I exerted myself, the livelier I felt. It is staying so long in bed that has enfeebled me. Being an antiquarian has not made me old. Rather, the objects I have loved have kept me young. My principal interest was always the extraordinary times in which I have lived. I do not like what is said about me now. The friends who understood me are all dead. Even to them I seemed eccentric, although perhaps I was not eccentric enough. But a man in my position does not defend himself, like a common author, and every day I can see the happy results of my endeavors in the improvement of taste and increase of knowledge throughout the room. I meant something other. I do not mean the room. Among people of fashion. Like a ship, rocking. Admiral. Admirable. I was always clear about what I admired and wanted to explain to others. I could see that I held their interest. The light is white. They respected my judgment. My enthusiasms made me visible, that is why I do not have to open my eyes. I was expected to fall into excess. Only what is excessive makes a lasting impression. But then they learned to mock me. Taste is fickle, like a woman. Are they still here? A woman's arms cradling my head. My wife I think how comforting. Yes, about that for which I am renowned. Approbation may wobble but I have exerted considerable influence. I would like to place my hand in front of my mouth, the air is leaving my head. But my wife who means well is grasping me too tightly. The air is streaming out of my mouth. Let me see if I can draw some of it back in. Then I will hold it. Little sips. There. Fortunate to have lived at the same time as and enjoyed the friendship and esteem of so many great men, I can take pride in my role in devotion to energies on behalf of. Air. No, influence. Still inside my mouth. I wager I will be remembered. But history teaches us that one does not always live on in the minds of men for that for which one desires to be remembered. One applies oneself diligently, one's achievements mount, genuine achievements, and then, alas, a story becomes attached to one's name, everyone hears it, everyone tells it, and that is all finally which anyone recalls. Such was the fate of Pliny the Elder. I will let some of the air out now. He who never wasted a moment, never stopped studying and collecting facts and writing his hundred books, what would be Pliny's thoughts could he have known that all his vast labors would be overrun, swallowed, absorbed, the air is still coming out, that his knowledge was nothing, because knowledge sweeps forward, devouring, burying the hard-won knowledge of the past. Enough breathing out. That he would be remembered only for one story, his end. That only because of Vesuvius does everyone still pronounce his name. Now I will take some of the air back. I think he would be quite disappointed. Only a little air is returned to me, I have given too much away, but I will make do. Well, well, if one is to live on in history for one story only, one event of a long crowded life, I suppose there are worse fates than being remembered as a volcano's most famous casualty. I was luckier. The volcano never did me any harm. Far from punishing me for my devotion, it brought me only pleasure. This time I will not let any more air out of my mouth. I have had a happy life. I would like to be remembered for the volcano.

PART FOUR

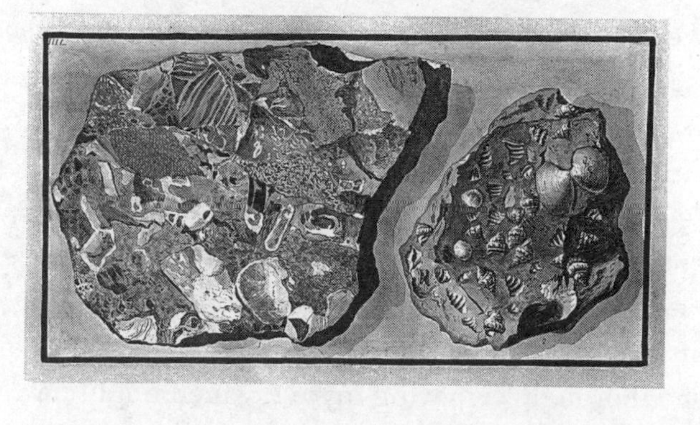

I

I cannot speak of myself without speaking of him. Even when I do not mention him, he is present by omission. But I will speak of myself, too.

I was his first wife.

I was plain. I was often unwell. I was devout. I loved music. He married me for my money. I fell in love with him after we were married. My God, how I loved him! He grew to love me, more than he had expected.

He had not had much affection from women. His mother, lady-in-waiting to the Princess of Wales and the mistress of her royal husband, was rather hard on him. And in the eyes of his severe father he was only a fourth son, almost a stranger, since as a child he was taken by his mother to live at court. How unlike my own dear kind parents, who lavished affection upon me and shed tears when I departed to live in a heathen land, fearing that they would never again see their only child, who might be killed by bandits or perish of the plague. And I, ungrateful daughter, was so happy to leave.

We left England, as I say, for my husband had become a diplomat. He had hoped to be posted to a more influential capital, but had decided, as he always did, to make the best of it. For the salutary climate alone, and the resulting improvement in my health, he would be reconciled to the disappointment. Soon after we arrived, he discovered many other advantages, advantages for himself, in his new situation. He was incapable of not enjoying himself, whatever he did, and incapable, too, of not pleasing and impressing others. He allowed me to contribute to his ascendancy by being a perfect wife.

I would have liked to be perfect. I made an excellent ambassador's wife. I was never lax or inattentive or ungracious, but—this was thought becoming in a woman—neither did I appear to be thoroughly enjoying myself, which might have led me to want to enjoy myself more, in a fashion incompatible with my duties. He knew I would never fail him. He hated failure, bad temper, grief, anything difficult, and apart from being sometimes ill, I made sure that he had nothing to complain of me. What I liked best about myself was that he had chosen me, and that I did not disappoint him. What he liked best about me was that I was admirable.

I was regarded as far superior to the generality of my sex because of my solemn demeanor, my dull plumage, my appetite for reading, and my attainments at the keyboard.

It was an exceedingly companionable marriage. We both loved music. I knew how to distract him when he was exasperated by some vile or tedious business at court or made anxious by a protracted negotiation for a painting or a vase on which he had set his heart. He behaved toward me with the utmost attention, with the result that I was constantly reproaching myself for a want of gratitude or an encumbering predisposition to melancholy. He was not the sort of man to wring a woman's heart, but mine was a heart that could not help but be wrung; and mine the fault, for rising to a pitch of unseemly fierceness of attachment.

Talking with him was like talking with someone on a horse.

I felt yearnings, which I thought were for God, or heaven's

mercy. I do not believe they were for a child, although I regret I never had any children. A child would have been another soul to love, and would have helped me to mind his absences less.

I am grateful for the consolations of faith. Nothing else makes any response to the awful darkness which, at one time or another, we discern around us.

As a child one of my favorite books, given me by my excellent father, was Foxe's *Book of Martyrs.* I thrilled to its stories of the wickedness of the Church of Rome and the inspiring courage of the noble Protestant martyrs, who were beaten and scourged, whipped and bastinadoed, whose flesh was torn with red-hot pincers, whose nails were pulled off and whose teeth were wrenched out, whose extremities were doused with boiling oil, before they finally received the mercy of the stake. I saw the faggots being kindled, the mantle of flame enveloping their garments, and the backward arc of their necks and shoulders, as if they wished to toss their heads to heaven, leaving their poor bodies to burn below. With pity and awe I mused on the glorious doom of Bishop Latimer, whose body was forcibly penetrated by the fire, and whose blood flowed abundantly from the heart, as if to verify his constant desire that his heart's blood might be shed in defense of the Gospel. I longed to be tested as they were and prove true to my faith in a holy martyr's death. The dreams of a foolish, presumptuous girl. For I was not brave, I think, though I never had the opportunity to give proof of bravery. I do not know if I could have borne the stake, I who could not even bear to look down from a safe distance into a volcano's fire!

My husband fondly described me to others as a hermit. I do not have the temperament of a recluse. But I could not overcome my distaste for the ignoble, dull-minded court, and he was often in attendance at court, and I preferred his company to that of anyone else.

I took pleasure only in him. What music gave me could not be described as pleasure, for it was more bracing than that. Music stretched my breath. The music held me. The music heard me.

My harpsichord was my voice. In its lucent sound I heard the pure, thin sound of myself. I composed delicate tunes, which were neither original nor very ambitious. I was bolder when performing the music of others.

Since regular attendance at the opera was required of everyone attached to the court, indeed everyone of condition, I professed to enjoy it, as he truly did. I do not like theatre. I do not like what is false. Music should not be seen. Music should be pure. I told none of my companions at the opera of these scruples, not even William, the ardent unhappy young man who came into my life toward the end and gave me a taste of what it was like to feel understood and to understand myself. With William, I could speak of my cravings for purity; in his company, I dared to acknowledge fancies incompatible with my destiny. I was often called a paragon, an angel—ludicrous compliments—but when William spoke these words, I heard them as the genuine effusions of a thankful heart. I thought he meant he was very fond of me. I had been kind to him. He was my friend, I thought, and I his. Then I understood he did regard me as an angel, I who brimmed with unruly humors. Once, after we played a four-hand sonata, he left the piano to recline on a sofa and close his eyes. When I cautioned him against too sensual a reaction to our music-making, he replied: Alas, it is very true that music destroys me —and what is worse, I love being destroyed. I fell silent when I might have continued my homily, for I realized that I was capable of an utterance no less extreme. I would have said not that music destroys me but rather that I destroy others, with music. While I was playing, even my husband did not exist.

I was younger than my husband, but I never felt young. I cannot imagine that I could have had a better life. A woman's weakness bound me to him. My soul clung to his. I did not respect myself enough. I am surprised that I find so much to complain of, since it is my belief that a wife's part is to excuse, to pardon, to bear with everything. To whom would I have disclosed my chagrin? I was not blinded by the partiality of love, but it strained me to judge him. I was never angry. I never had any harsh or base feelings. It is a relief to admit to them now.

I suppose I must acknowledge that I was unhappy, or lonely. But I do not ask for pity. I should scorn to cry about my lot when there are so many truly unfortunate women, such as those deceived or abandoned by their husbands, or those who have borne a child only to lose it.

I suppose he might be described as selfish. It is not easy for me to say this. As soon as I begin to find fault with him, I recall how a man of his background is reared to view his pleasures and obligations, and how a man of his temperament would seek to lose himself in them, in all the variety of their claims on his attention, and my old fondness rises up to obscure my sense of grievance. I know he was capable of unease, for he often held forth on the subject of felicity. When I heard him sigh, I could bear anything.

I suppose I must allow that he was cynical. He would have scorned as women's foolishness the notion that in this brazen, prearranged world one could comport oneself otherwise. Perhaps I must even allow that he could be cruel, for I suppose it might be said he was not a man of tender feelings. You may reply, he was a man, and tender feelings are the domain of the weaker sex, which is spared the battle with adversity. But I do not believe this to be true. Our undefended sex, the greatest number among us, meet adversity in as unprotected a form as does any man. And there are many men of tender hearts, I am sure, although I have met only one, my own dear father.

A woman is first a daughter, then half of a couple. I am described, I describe myself, first of all, as one who was married to him. He would not be described, first, as married to me, though he is most often remembered—unusual destiny for a man—as the one who was married to his second wife.

He disliked my leaving him. The grief that I felt, during my last illness, is unutterable. And I knew he would miss me more than he anticipated. I hoped he would remarry. I imagined he would marry a respectable widow a little younger than himself, not necessarily with fortune, who loved music. And he would think fondly of me. We women cannot imagine how different from us men are. There is something imperative men feel, which makes even the finest of them prone to lewd and indecent conduct. He loved me, as much as he was capable of loving anyone, and then he truly loved a woman who was as unlike me as one could be. But it often happens that the good wife, marooned with the desiccating virtues she has cultivated in order to be beyond reproach, is abandoned for a woman who is livelier, younger, more distracting. At least I was spared that common indignity, the indignity suffered by the wife of the man who captured the love of my husband's second wife. I had all that my husband could give to someone like me.

I regret that I could not help desiring more from him. If he left me alone too much, and was more entertained by himself than by me when we were together, who behaves otherwise to a wife? Did I expect the fervor he might show a mistress? It seems unchristian of me to reproach him for not being what he could not be.

I should be able to imagine a life without him, but I cannot. If I even imagine that he might have died before I did, my mind darkens. We never lived separately. I had the pleasure of seeing him near and far in many brilliant rooms, in which he was ever the most radiant presence of all, and I had his picture to gaze at when he was called away, a small painting of no great distinction to which I was greatly attached. It was this picture which I bore on my body into the tomb.

2

I'm her mother. You know who I mean: *her* mother. Many has always taken me for her ladyship's maid. I know how to hang back. But I am her mother.

In a church I was married to old Lyon the blacksmith, her father, who perished of fever two months after my darling was born. As he was Mary's only husband, she was Mary's only child, so you can imagine how fond this Mary was. Furthermore I was still young and fair-looking and had ideas above my station, so folk in the village was always telling me. It must be she inherited some of her boldness from me, we're very resembling, almost like sisters. I was only happy when I was with her. We always were.

I did go first up to London, following my heart, it was Joe Hart the brewer, as soon as she went into service as a nursemaid to Mrs. Thomas in the village. I didn't think it wrong to leave her, she had already turned thirteen, while being a mother was not yet all for me. Just for that time I left her, and lived without her with Hart, London was like another country, what revels we had, I was still young myself. But she came up before long, being about fourteen and much grown, for my clever darling had got herself engaged as underhousemaid by a doctor who had a whole house in a fine square near Blackfriars Bridge, where when the riots came later that year the soldiers threw all the bodies in the Thames. It was a drunken mob, looting and burning the houses and shops of their betters for a week, but they were cut down before they reached the doctor's house, with everyone inside, she said, nearly deaf from the musket fire. It's terrible to be poor. But still worse is to have no other idea of bettering yourself than VIOLENCE.

She held back from meeting me with her mistress and she never would visit the alehouse where I stayed with my Joe. We used to meet in secret like lovers, to share the odd glass or walk arm in arm in Vauxhall, listening to the birds. I suppose she told Doctor Budd a story about where she come from, less common, with no place for Mrs. Hart as I called myself then, and he was teaching her to read. But then one day she told me the son had took her. A mother is always sad to hear such news when it is the first, but I told her what could she expect being so beautiful. I begged her not to leave Doctor Budd, as she could have a good situation there, but she said she never did plan to be a proper housemaid, she was going to be an actress, a famous actress, she and her best friend, also underhousemaid at Doctor Budd's. And that anyway she had heard of another doctor who was taking on young women, but not to be maids, it was more being an actress, but why does a doctor need actresses, I asked. It was in a cure for people of quality, she said. And then she went into service with Doctor Graham until she met Sir Harry by Drury Lane Theatre, and he said he would help her become a real actress, for he went to the theatre all the time. My poor innocent darling, but who would know more at fifteen. And he, a real baronet with a tasseled cane hanging from his wrist, invited her to his estate in Sussex for the summer. What a change of fortune, and only the first! She knew enough to nick that there would be a rackety crew, Sir Harry's friends, and she bid me come with her. Like a lady already she was, who would have her companion. Only for the summer, she said. And after, I asked. God will provide, she said gaily. I can't resist her smile. Indeed we lasted to the end of the year. So I had to quit my Joe, just for a time, but it was for good, Cadogan came later, and since then no one did part us. She was more than a daughter to me. She looked after me. She told me everything. She took me wherever she went and she had to go where the man went, but she always took me. And when she set up with her gentleman it was my task to manage the household, so I was like a servant, but I am her mother.

How proud of her I was. To have such a beautiful daughter, admired by so many. When she was little I already knew men would not be able to resist her. But she wasn't born to be empty-headed as Sir Harry wanted her to be. He was the first, and he was the worst, perhaps it is always like that. He and his friends were all day out shooting and fishing and racing in phaetons down the muddy roads, and every evening was cards and dice and charades and jugs of port and punch. The charades, that always ended with someone taking off his clothes and led straight to bed. But still my darling did her best, and watched with those beautiful bright eyes what the rich did and how they dressed. And Sir Harry did teach her to ride, and she was so handsome and right on a horse. And sometimes there was Charles for a week, and she liked to talk to him. And so many servants, I was not her servant, but stayed in our room. I was her mother.

After the sixmonth with Sir Harry, she wrote a desperate letter to the other one, Charles, for we needed help. Sir Harry had seemed better than Charles because he was richer. But soon as he found a child was coming, he could only think of turning us off. And as there was no way we could keep Sir Harry's bastard, I did not want her to cling to her babe as a mother can do. What a pain there was in my heart when my darling wrapped her tiny hand round my finger and pulled me to her. A child is the best happiness a woman ever knows. I'm not taking against men, I've known men, and had my good times, and some was fond of me. But a child's love and the love a mother feels for a child is the best of all.

We had to wait a while, already back in London and near starving, and I knew what the next step for a woman is, oh that my darling should come to that. But then Charles answered her letter and our state was changed. He wanted her to live with him, but she wouldn't go without me, and he did not make objection. This was a long time, years. And I got on with her Charles, I always made a point to get on with the man who was appreciating her, and he wasn't like Sir Harry at all, though he was one of Sir Harry's friends. For he wasn't as rich and he hardly touched the bottle and he was always with a book in his hands. He wanted my darling to learn to read books and write letters, and pour tea and receive guests with him just like a wife. And I was there, I was there, so he saved the wages of a servant, for he had not much money, he said. He taught her to write a book of her own, in a neat hand, with all the words on the left side going down the page, the Bread, Leg of Mutton, Wood, Sugar, Pins and Thread, Pork, Mop, A Nutmeg, Mustard, Mold Candles, Cheese, Pint of Porter, and such, and then a line. And on the right side the sums, and he would go over them with her every week and said he was glad with how thrifty she was. But after he let me do it for her, I wanted her to be free to be more with him, so she could improve herself more by copying him and his fine friends, so she would talk more like them than like me. And one of the friends took a fancy to her, and asked her to sit for him, for a real painting, and after he said he would use no other model again. Mr. Romney he worshipped her, he said she was a genius and there was no woman in the world like her, and they weren't even lovers. My daughter was very particular.

And so we had a fine life, I could imagine no better, with Charles in a big house that was warm in the winter, and I had my own room, and she was improving herself all the time, and I was happy too, with her, that's all I wanted, except that I met

Cadogan and lost my heart. He was devilish handsome, and after a week I told her Charles I was called to the village to see my sister, the one who was dying of scrofula and had nine young children. But the truth was, as my darling knew, for I never kept secrets from her, that I was going with my Cadogan. And we went in a wagon to Swansea, where his brother kept a tavern and I slaved there seven months, sleeping in the attic, and then he went off with a hussy he met in the tavern, disappeared, and his brother turned me off. I walked back, having many hard times on the road from men in fields but no matter, I reached London safely, and my darling was very angry with me but forgave me, she was so happy to see her mother. We told Charles that I had got wed to someone in the village thinking I would have to stay there, then my sister didn't die, so I come back to London because I missed my daughter too much. Which in a way was the truth.

I don't know why I chose Cadogan for my married name that I had to tell Charles, it being the name of that Welshman who broke my heart. I could have told him I married a man named Cooper. But my heart was too fond. So Cadogan I said, and Cadogan it was to be. We women always have more than one name. A man who changed his name four times in his life, you would think he had something to hide. But not a woman. Imagine a man who changed his name each time he married a woman or said he did. It makes me laugh. That would be a topsy-turvy world.

Anyway, that was my last name, my last man, I was so glad I was back. And from then on this fond old soul, for though I was not so old then I let myself look old, it is men that keep a woman young, and I was done with men, I would think only of my darling and help her. And never was I happier, because this is the greatest happiness. Men are bad, there I have said it. They think only of their own pleasure, and they can hurt a woman when they are drunk. I never hurt anyone when I was drunk, and I wager I have liked my gin as much as any man. But women are different. Men are bad, I will say it one more time and then hold my peace, but we can't do without them, and I am glad I did not have to do without them, like those poor girls in Ireland who are locked in convents and can never come out. The Romish church is so wicked, I never understood why my darling late in her life . . . but that is another story, I was saying about men. And how we poor women need them, and go to them as an insect to the flame, we can't help ourselves, but the best part is the child. That is true love, the mother for a child.

Though a mother can't expect her child to love her as fierce, specially when the child be grown, it's enough that she needed me and wanted me always to be with her.

Life, as I say, could be no better, except that Charles was always glooming about money and making us watch every penny. He could go out and buy an old picture for himself, in a big gold frame that must have cost many guineas, and then he raised his voice at my darling when in her book in between fourpence for Eggs and twelve shillings for Tea he saw tuppence for Poor Man. But still he was very kind to her, he called her his dear girl, and she came to love him desperate and think only to please him and he was fond of her, I could see it in his face, I know men. And he gave us money to go for two weeks to sea bathe for the nettle rash on her pretty elbows and knees. And he paid a family in the country for the keep of her infant, which was kind of him, since it was not his but Sir Harry's who would hear nothing of her.

So all was well, except that Charles was not so fine a character as he seemed. For he decided to give this priceless girl up so he could marry money, but did not have the courage to tell, and lied to her, and though it all turned out for the best, first my darling's heart had to bleed until she be used to it. For Charles had a rich old uncle, and he wanted the uncle to pay his debts. He was always writing letters to his uncle, and Charles truly looked up to him, and he was very tall, but so was Charles, because they both come from the same family. They did look alike, both fine men, except the uncle did not seem always so worried like Charles. He was in England now for he had lost his Welsh wife, and had to bring the poor woman's body back so she wouldn't be buried in heathen ground. And after that he came often to visit us. I don't think he had an eye on my beautiful girl, I believe it was all Charles's idea, but you never know, men can turn ruttish so quick. And the next thing you know, the uncle had gone back to where he lived, where he was very grand, Charles said, and Charles wanted us both go visit him, so my darling could speak Italian and French and learn the piano and all that which make a lady. And my darling, who never could resist a chance to better herself, said yes. She was so happy to go to foreign parts and see what was in books, but she mainly did it so Charles would love her more and be proud of her. I know she thought nothing but still she made Charles swear over and over he would come soon, in just a few months. I was not so keen to go, being a little feared of the travel, and having my old bones bumped over so many roads and high places. I heard that we would cross the Alp, which I thought then was just one mountain, and that the countries are very dangerous, and a body can starve from not eating the food, which is full of hot pepper. But if my darling wanted to go, I said, then I would be happy. And she kissed me.

It was a very long journey, I did not know any place could be so far away, but very enjoyable for me because we were seeing new sights all the time, which is natural because we had not come this way before. My darling was hanging out the coach from morning to night, so joyful to see everything she had not seen. With us we had a painter who was a friend of Charles and lived in Rome and he was going back, and he said that all good painters had to live in Italy now. And she said to him, Mr. Romney don't want to live in Rome, which was a bit forward of her, because she meant Mr. Romney is a better painter than you, but she didn't say that. But he knew it. My darling loved Mr. Romney so much, like a father. She was almost as grieved to quit him as Charles, though she thought it only for a year at most before she would see her painter again, and five months before seeing Charles. Little did she know it would be five YEARS.

Even if it was less time, these changes and being apart are hard to bear if you are truly fond. How happy I am that after Cadogan, God take his black Welsh heart, I never was parted with my darling again.

When we reached Rome she wanted to see the buildings, but the uncle had sent a steward to fetch us and we went on the rest of the journey with him in the uncle's carriage. This steward told us his master had seven carriages, and this was the least good of them. Seven carriages. How does one man need seven carriages, even if he be a fine gentleman, since his wife is gone now, and I suppose a rich pair want to travel separate, but even if his wife was still alive that would only make a need for two. So what did he do with the other five? While I was breaking my skull over these foolish questions, for foolish they were as I was soon to find out, for the rich always find a use for their luxury, one need not worry about them, my darling was taking in the sights to be seen from the carriage window, which was real glass by the way. She had her questions that she put to the steward Valerio, who spoke a bit of the King's English. She was asking the names of the flowers and the trees and the fruit in them, and writing on a tablet what he told her. And she asked him to say very slow some words in his language, good day and farewell and please and thank you and how beautiful and I am so happy and what is that. She wrote these down too. She was always learning.

And when we arrived where we were going, this great house where Charles's uncle was ambassador in, that was truly a surprise. I never saw such a house, and more servants than you could count, and the uncle gave us four big rooms and servants for my darling all for herself. And I was so happy for her, for I could see the uncle looking at her, and I thought why not. But she, poor darling, she didn't see it at first. She thought his being so kind to her was because he loved his nephew so much. My daughter had such a good heart, she could be very innocent. I had to tell her what was as plain as the nose on the uncle's face, and Charles sent us here for that, and she fell in a rage. It was the first time my own child ever raged against her own mother, and it was cruel to bear. She threatened to send me back to England the next day to beg forgiveness of her dear Charles for insulting him, but I didn't take it personal. She said it was her own mother who was trying to sell her to the uncle. Mr. Romney had told her about a picture of someone like me, she said, by a French painter that showed an artist and a model and an old woman in the corner who could have been the mother and was really a bawd, and how this may be the custom in other countries like France or Italy, but it wasn't like that in England. Look at Mr. Romney, she had gone to his studio so many times alone, without any chaperone, and he never laid a hand on her. And her Charles was his friend and could not be base. How could I suggest Charles would pass her on to his uncle for money. Then tell me, I said, why you have never had one letter from him since we come here, and you writing him fond letters every day. And then she looked so sad, and cried, oh, he must come, I will make him come and fetch me. How I wished I was wrong, but I was right. I don't say a mother is always right, but sometimes she is when she don't want to be.

But then everything came out for the best, as it always did for my darling, when she was young. There was the lowest time of all, after she told Sir Harry she was with child, I told her not to tell him, but she wouldn't mind me. And he turned us off and we came back to London, she with child, though it didn't show, and soon we had not a farthing, owing rent in the doss house, and she took herself off and was gone for eight days. How drear I felt while I waited, thinking all those men, under bridges, against alley walls, you know how men are. But when she came back, to spare me, for she was always thinking of my feelings, she told me it was just one man the whole time, and a gentleman, walking with his fine friends in Vauxhall Gardens though he was a foreigner, who gave her all that money, enough to feed us a month. And just as that was running out was the letter from Charles and we were saved. And now it was the same with Charles's uncle, with us living now as we never did before, much better than with Charles.

His house seemed so small to me now. How quick this old Mary got herself used to being waited on. One day in a doss house, the next day in a palace! That is life, I always say. Or the other way round. It was a handsome city, I liked to see the sea, though I couldn't understand what nobody said, and she told me, you will have to learn to speak the language. But I never did, which must be one reason people thought I was my darling's maid. But I was her mother.

As I said, the uncle was really a high person there. He was close with the King and Queen, who was the first king and queen we had ever met, so we felt very curious. The King had an awful big nose and the Queen had a big lower lip that stuck out. This was a surprise. But it was still a wonder to see them in their gold carriages.

I do not say my darling was happy at first. She had to get over the other one for she had a tender heart, and she loved Charles so much. She cried and cried, for finally a letter come from Charles who told her to go with his uncle. I did not see why she hated the notion so much. The old man was giving her lessons in French and Italian, and he was taking us in his carriage and showing her off to everybody. He couldn't move his eyes off her, you could see he would give her anything, but she said no. She had to find her own way. But to be sure she got fond of him, he being so kind and she so good-humored, she could not help being grateful to anyone who loved her, and so, finally, all was well, and she went into the old man's bed.

I breathed a sigh of relief because I knew that meant we could stay on here awhile, maybe even a twelvemonth longer before we would have to go back to England, and no point to worry on what would happen then. Let her enjoy herself, I said to myself, she is still young. She had a teacher come three times a day to sing with her, and in the neighbor room sometimes I could not tell who was singing. When I asked Valerio how a man could sing so high, he laughed at my ignorance, and said because the teacher had his thingums cut off when just a lad, and that was the custom here to make a good singer, though forbid by the law, but the churches used all such boys they could get. And he touched his own thingums and crossed himself. And when I told my darling, thinking she would be as surprised as me, she said she knew it, and I should accept that we be now in a foreign country where they do things different than back in dear old England, and that he was a great singer, who had told her she had a wonderful voice. But then he is not a man, I say. Is he a woman. No, she said, he is a man, and some of them do fancy women and women chase after them. But what do he do if it don't rise, I asked. And then she shook her head and said she was surprised to learn I knew so little of the arts of bed as to not imagine what. And I had to own that I never met a man who wanted anything but one thing and that very quick, but she told me there were some men, not too many, who studied to please a woman just like a woman studied to please a man. I never heard of that, said I. And she said she was sorry I had not known that with men. But I told my young lady I had jolly times with her father, rest his soul, and Joe, and some others, and that Welsh thief of my heart, Cadogan. And to watch her tongue and not take on airs with her old mother now she was living like a fine lady, but remember the simple folk she come from. And she said she never did forget who she was, and was just teasing me. But I could not help wondering what man had been such a fancy lover. It could not have been Sir Harry, who was always drunk, or Charles, always washing his hands, that is not a good sign in a man. And the old uncle, much as he doted on her, seemed not such a man for bed. But I did not ask. We always told all, but I did not care to see her too clear in my mind lying with men. To me she would always be my little girl, with her pale skin and wide, wide eyes. I am glad she knew men, for what would a woman be without a man, especially a woman like her who hopes to better herself, to go up in the world. It can't be done no other way. And yet I wish sometimes the world were topsy-turvy. I mean that a woman did not have to please a man if she is such a bold clever girl as my darling. But this is only my view.

And I said to her, how long do you think it will last. And she said what, and I said with the uncle, and she laughed and laughed and said, forever. And I said, don't be foolish, you know how men are, surely by now you understand, after what Charles did to you. And she said, no he is different, he really loves me and I mean to love him and make him as happy as I can.

I think she was happy with the old man. For certainly she made him very happy, and he just doted on her more and more. And he was good to me too, and gave me a little pocket money. And I always ate with them and was asked to stay when the guests came. He had many rocks and statues and paintings and such, the house was full of them everywhere you turned, I am certainly glad I did not have the dusting and polishing of them. And she learned the names of them, and could follow anything he said. When he had clothes made for her, some was so she could look like a lady on one of his old red-and-black vases which he had everywhere, and she dressed up like in the vases and would pose for the guests and everyone admired her. I would sit in one of the first chairs, but the guests did not talk to me. Some was from all over Europe at his parties, even Russia. And wherever they came from they thought my darling was the most beautiful woman they had ever seen, and the old man was so proud of her. It was almost like what I felt, as if he was her father, though you could see he was a healthy man and could not wait to put his hands on her, but then many fathers are like that with their daughters. Who knows if she would not have had a hard time with old Lyon, who died when she was only two months, if he lived for another ten years. Men have their ways, and many cannot leave a woman alone even if she is their own flesh and blood. The only pure love is between a mother and a child. But best if the child be a daughter, for a son grows up and becomes another man. But a daughter can be yours all your life.

And so we had many years of happiness in this foreign land, though I always found it hard to believe in happiness, but my darling did. Whenever matters took a bad turn I would see the worst, and she would say no, it will all work out. And she was always right, for such a long time. She said she would be her ladyship one day, and I told her she was daft. And she was right and the old man did marry her, and that made this old Mary his mother-in-law, and he older than me. But he was very proper and always called me by my name, Mrs. Cadogan. I wager my Welshman would be sorry he had not kept me if he could know how well I would turn out to be.

It was when we went back to England that he married my darling, which his family did not like it at all and it was hardly a wedding with so few people, though in a rich church. It did me good to see the look on Charles's face. But my darling never held anger against him, all those years she sent letters, she being the kind who always loves one she loved even if she was used ill, women are like that, as I still think with fondness of old Lyon, my darling's father, and God help me, my handsome Cadogan. I don't think now of Joe Hart, who drifted from mind, so perhaps I did not love him so much.

While we stayed in England I went back to the village and saw the relations that had not died, which my poor sister with scrofula had, and I gave them money and presents from my darling. She never forgot her family. She pined to see her daughter, who was a big girl now, and I was vexed she would not let me go with her. I went everywhere with her, she always wanted my company to talk things over when it was done. But she said she had to be alone for this. I could see she was in for a sore visit, I was sorry I couldn't protect her, as I always did.

When she came back to me she said, my heart is aching. We had not met since she was four years old, and now she found me again and grew to love me, and I have left her. And the fond mother wept, which was the first time since when we come to the uncle's house, who was now her husband, when she found Charles was not coming to fetch her, Charles had sold her to the uncle. It is not my destiny to be a mother, she said. I may be married to him now, but he still expects from me to be like a mistress. And she cried again. But imagine, I said as I dried her tears, imagine a woman has not shed a tear once for five whole years, how many women can say that, you should count your blessings.

Then we went back, and we saw a balloon go up in Paris with a man in it, and my darling met the French queen, but she was used to meeting royalty now. And now she was her ladyship, and I was madam her ladyship's mother, madam mother of the ambassador's wife. And men took their hats off to me, although many still took me for a servant or her chaperone. I never learned Italian. I don't have a mind like my daughter's. I was the woman in a black dress and white bonnet nobody took mind of, except when they was told who I was. I was her mother.

Now my darling had what she wanted, we could be easy and just enjoying ourselves when we ate and drank and laughed. I taught one of the cooks some dishes like we had in the village, and I would save them for her, and she would come to my room late at night after one of those grand evenings she and her husband had to go to or the opera. Guttling, we called it, it was our secret. And we could have a bit of good English gin, none of your outlandish wines.

Her husband said I was always welcome at the opera, for sometimes they went almost every night, but I had no aim to go after the first time. I told my darling, what was the use since I can't catch what they say, and she laughed, I like to make her laugh at me, and said I was very foolish, and didn't have to understand the words, it was like a play, only with music. And the music was so beautiful. So I did go some but didn't take much from it, but my darling and her husband would sit very quiet and listen. But then they could both speak the language, while all about us was eating and drinking and playing cards and from the noises I heard and the sound of a falling chair even you know what, and the King used to carry on very loud in his box, so what do you expect from the rest of them. I never could tell what was going to happen down on the stage, where not all of them was really in the play. My darling explained this to me. One of them there she said was to remind the singers in case they forgot their lines, so I guess they didn't understand what they was saying either. And the singers was free to behave on the stage as they pleased, just like the fine folk in the boxes. In one opera was a fat lady in a corner with two men dressed up very fine by her chair that my darling told me was the mother and two admirers of the prima donna, right there on the stage! The mother had a little table by her chair with vinegar and mirrors and sweets and gargles and combs which her daughter might suddenly have need, while somebody else was having an aria.

That's me, I told my darling. That's what I'll always be for you. And she hugged me, and I could see she had a little wetness in her eyes, she knew how much I loved her. How she was THE LIGHT OF MY LIFE, if I can speak like they do in plays. I would never leave her, never let her down. If she wasn't always so happy, she wanted so much to be happy, she loved to enjoy herself, and we had good times ourselves when we were alone or with her maids. They loved her so much too, laughing and singing and getting tipsy and telling naughty stories. What a beautiful life she had. How lucky I was to share it with her.

To be sure, nothing good lasts forever, although all this lasted a very long time. I never saw or heard a husband so in love with his wife as the ambassador with my daughter, he worshipped her. And I saw some guests winking and nodding at how he fussed on her, this being years after they begun together and been married. They took him for a fond old fool for loving her so much, but he could not never love her enough far as I was concerned. He wasn't worth half her, for all his Sir This and Knight of That. Any man could count himself blessed to be loved by her. My daughter was a treasure.

And he was so much older, so it was natural a man more her age should take her fancy. It was well done with him and he made her easy, but she was still a healthy young woman full of spirit, and who could resist the little admiral, everybody cheered him coming fresh from his great victory in Egypt against Boney's fleet, he sunk all the ships himself, but now he was all sick and weak. It gave me something to do. For what did I have to do except sit about and watch myself grow old, until the old man died, and then we would go back to England. But then it turned out we were living in stirring times, it made me proud to be English, which I never forgot I was, and the admiral came to live with us, and he could not stop staring at my darling. He looked so hard at her all the time I could swear he saw her with his poor blind eye too. The first days he was in bed, and I was helping my darling nurse him, and I could see clear as I saw that old volcano from the window that he was going to love her and she would love him, and we would have a whole new life before us with the admiral. So we would be going back to England sooner than I thought. Because even though the admiral was married, once he discovered he was in love with my daughter and had found the best woman in the world he certainly would never have anything more to do with his wife again. That's the way men are.

Also I guess as how I still had a bit of fire in me myself, for I liked to see my darling's heart woke again. And it would give me something to do, once they found out they were in love, though that took longer than I expected, he being different, whoever heard of a man being faithful to his wife. But he was, my darling told me he had only fallen once with some woman in another port in Italy a few years ago, but a gentlewoman and not a whore. I certainly never heard of a seagoing man like that who was a real man, but then I never heard my darling say fallen. She had her serious spells now, she even went to one of the churches sometimes and prayed in the Romish way. As I say, they took their time about it like two innocent young girls, just looking at each other and looking away, but I knew what was going on.

And then everything happened at once, and the French was coming, and we had to pack up everything, and the old ambassador was all broken and quiet for quitting his house and his furniture, we left in the middle of the night in a dreadful storm. My darling's suitor rescued us and the King and Queen and everyone, but the crossing was terrible, with five and six in a cabin, all sleeping on cots and mattresses or on the floor. And we never went to sleep. I put the King to bed, what a big baby he was, he was holding a little holy bell and crossing himself. And my darling put the Queen to bed, the Queen and her was best of friends, for she went every day to the palace to see the Queen. And then we just went around the boat helping people vomit and cleaning up a little. I wasn't feared, and my darling wasn't feared at all. She was the bravest, a true heroine. Everybody admired her. And we did pass safely, though the Queen lost her little boy, that was the saddest sight to see, my darling holding that child to her breast and trying to keep it alive. I think I knew then she was meant to be a mother, and would have a child after all, that would really be hers by this little admiral who loved her so much. A mother knows this sort of thing.

I was so happy for her, to see her happy so, the way she was never happy before. And all those years being madam the mother of the ambassador's wife I didn't have much to do except hand her her combs and sweets and gargle like the prima donna's mother on the stage, but now I could help her, I could watch the old man, when he was coming and going, when the two lovers wanted to be together. The admiral was like a little boy with her. I could see he wanted me to like him, for he lost his mother when he was a lad, even before he went to sea, my darling told me. He wasn't like most men. He really liked to be with women and talk to them.

So we were closer than ever, and the only time apart was when they had to go back to Naples and stop the revolution after the French had left, they couldn't take me, they left me behind in Palermo for six weeks. That was the longest time I ever was separate from my darling after she was sixteen. We were always together, she knew she could count on me.

After they came back we went on his boat to see the sights, and had a party for her birthday on the boat, but she was not such a good sailor this time, being with child now, just as I knew she would. Her husband did take it very well, better than some might, never saying a word, but then he was old and where was he going to find another woman like my daughter. No such woman ever existed. Both of them knew that. So the old ambassador wasn't too sad, except that he could not be ambassador anymore, and everybody was glad to go back to England, we had a fine journey, though all those carriages tired out my old bones, and those cannons booming everywhere we went for the admiral was a little hard on my ears. And when we got home safe, he was greeted the same way but more, it took us three days to reach London. And then there was something of their own to go through, my darling had warned me, with the admiral's wife herself waiting in a hotel in King Street. So when we entered London they put Miss Knight and me first in Albemarle Street, where we was to stay. Miss Knight was with us for a long time, she truly admired my daughter. I was so weary I took straight to my room, but the next morning when I went to look for Miss Knight if she wanted breakfast, I found she had not ever spent the night there. She had left an hour after we arrived the hotel-keeper told me, and run to the house of a friend, for someone had come to the hotel and told wicked stories about my darling, as that she was not fit company for a respectable woman. And so, hard as it is to believe, this Miss Knight we had been so kind to, my daughter insisted on taking her in when her mother died, we had her with us one of the family for near two years, we never saw her again.

It seemed there was many in London jealous of my darling, how could they not be, because the most famous man of all was at her feet! But you can be sure we all paid them no mind and went ahead, and there was plenty of work for old Mary, with a new house in London, and soon the admiral came to live with us when his wife saw she would not rival with the charms of my darling. And then the child was born. And I was there, I held her hand, I suffered the pain with her, she was so brave she hardly cried out, but it was not a hard birth, it being her second child, but we never spoke of the first one, who would be a woman now. She did not want the admiral to know about it, because he was so proud she was with child for the first time by him. I was there, I was all she had, for he was called back to sea two weeks before. The poor man had lost his teeth and his eye and his arm and they still could not do without him, and made him go off and fight the Danes, because he was the bravest. He missed my darling so much, I don't think ever a man doted on a woman as him. The letters he wrote her! And in April his whole fleet had to celebrate her birthday and all his officers drink toasts to her, and he hung her picture round his neck. And in a port when one of his officers started to bring his own wife aboard, the admiral would not let him because he said he promised my daughter he would never let a woman on the boat, but I don't think she meant him to go as far as that. But he was so eager to prove how much he loved her. And then they still wouldn't let him come home, for that was the summer everybody heard that Boney would come and kill us all and plant the Tree of Liberty and take away our English freedoms. But I wasn't feared. And my daughter wasn't either, we knew who was guarding our shores, and we were looking that summer for a house in the country for when the nation's savior and my darling's beloved would come home and be allowed to rest his poor bones.

Now there was something for this Mary to do. A fancy life with servants, I don't detract it, but I was happier choosing ducks to stock in the admiral's canal and keeping watch over the grooms and gardeners. And my darling was having a gay time too, for she knew all about everything new, I don't know how but she did, she knew everything. It wasn't a large house after all we had known, only five bedrooms, but that's what he wanted. So she put in each a water closet and a washstand and bowl with a lead tank and tap, and a bath to be filled by servants. It was all very well in Italy with those big palaces with more rooms than a body can count, but we were back in England now, which may not have ruins and art but people know how to make themselves cozy and comfortable. And the admiral was overjoyed when he saw what we did, when they let him come home, to the home we made for him. And the ambassador had his place too, for I could see he felt a bit lost back in England. I didn't, it was as I had never left, all those years in Italy and hearing a foreign language faded away. But the man missed his glory, and money fretted him, even worse. He was always tight with a penny, and when he came to live with us in the country, because he couldn't let his wife live there without him and make a scandal, he offered to pay half the household expenses. But it made me smile to see the two great men, the admiral and he almost blind who won all those battles and this old knight who was brought up with our king, there at a table in one of the sitting rooms, leaning over the bills from the fishmonger, the brewer, the baker, the butcher, the milkman, the chandler, counting out pounds and shillings and pence, and then writing their famous names at the bottom of the book after they approved it. Men get so grand and make you never forget it, that it makes me laugh when they get just like women too.

It went on with the admiral, he was a man who didn't change. I never saw one worship a woman as he did, he still couldn't take his eyes off her. And his face lit up when she came into a room even if she left it a moment before, but it was just the way

I felt when she came into a room all my life. But I was her mother. There's no love like what a mother with no husband has for her only child. No man feels that for a woman, no woman for a man. But I have to say that the admiral came close to what this old mother felt. But then we both loved the same person, who was the finest woman in the world. And I had the joy of knowing her all her life, and he only knew her for seven years.

It was sad when the old husband died, even though they had been expecting it and hoping for it, that was natural, because then they could have their child with them, and we could be a proper family, if only the admiral's wife would die too or let him divorce her. The old man didn't suffer too much, he just stopped fishing, that was the first sign. And then he didn't talk much, and then he took to his bed in February and at the end when it got worse asked to be taken back to the house in London, which was a fine house, full of rich furniture paid for by my darling selling all her jewels. I did most of the nursing. He trusted me because I was old like him, though not as old, and I still was full of spirit. I rubbed his feet. And he died there in April very peaceful, with my darling and the admiral right there on both sides of the bed holding him.

I got a shock when the will was read. It was a heartless mean will. But my darling said it didn't matter, that she always knew Charles was his heir, already when she was with Charles, before she ever met him. But think of all that happened after that, I said. Shh, shh, she said. She wouldn't let me talk of it. And Charles put us out of the house a month later. But we found another though it was small, and that should have been the beginning of a new life, but then the war started again and my darling's love had to go back to sea and he stayed away a year and a half! They were desperate. He was sent all over chasing Boney, to the West Indies and in the Mediterranean again, he even stopped at Naples. It seems, my darling told me he wrote her this, our old house there was now a hotel, and not a very clean hotel either. We were glad the old ambassador didn't live to hear that, for it would have cast him down, but it didn't bother us too much, at least not me. You have to know when to let the old life go, and go on and not look back and have regrets, I always say. Otherwise you will always be sad, because you are always losing something. That's the way life is, if you let misfortunes strike you too hard, you won't see the new chance coming. If I didn't know this I would not have had such a GOOD LIFE. And the same for my darling, because on this point she had the same opinion as me.

So we remained hopeful, and the following year her beloved came home and—

But it didn't come true as we hoped. My poor, poor darling. They only had eighteen days together, and the house the whole time was full of his officers and people from the Admiralty.

I kept telling her all would be well, he had come back each time, he would come back again. But this time, she said, there will be a great battle. That's why he goes. I told her he was better than the French, that she was born under a charitable star, that everything had always turned out, but it didn't this once.

And after he died, Captain Hardy told her with her name on his lips, everybody turned their back on us except the creditors. The old man had left her something a year and three hundred pounds to pay debts, but she had many more than that. And we moved to a smaller house, and then still smaller, we had the child with us now who had his name, but there was nothing from the crown, no pension as she was supposed to have, even to bring HIS child up properly. She had to be generous, and have some pleasures, which make more debts, and servants and a governess for the child, and be drinking a bit too much but so was I, what else was there to do when everybody becomes so cruel. But I said to her, you'll see things will not always be thus, we have each other, and some man will help you. And there was a neighbor in the country who sent us money, a kind man, I think he had sympathy for us because folk scoffed him too. And I said what about Mr. Goldsmid, and she laughed, but now her laugh was bitter, and said Abraham Goldsmid is quite happy with the wife and the fine family he has. And I reminded her that no man could resist her, no matter how fine his wife, but she made me promise never to speak more of my notion about her and Mr. Goldsmid, and so nothing came of that. But the good man did send us some money from time to time, and I hope he will be let into heaven for it.

So in the end it was not to be better. For everyone deserted her, even the one she loved most, though he did not mean to die, but why go about the boat in his admiral's frock coat and his stars so a French sharpshooter could find him easy and kill him, if he wanted to stay alive to come back to her. Men are so foolish. Women may be vain, but when a man is vain it is beyond believing, for a man is willing to die for his vanity. Everyone deserted my poor darling, even I deserted her four years after when the little admiral was killed, and I wanted so much to be with her and take care, she needed caring so, and she could count on me. I do not want to tell what happened to her after. My daughter was very unhappy when I died.

3

There was some magic about me. I knew it from the way others responded, had always responded to me, as if I were larger than life. Then there are all the stories told about me, some false, most of them true.

Only thus can I explain why I was once so praised, why so many doors were opened to me. I was very talented, as a performer. But it could not have been only my talents. I was intelligent, curious, quick, and though men do not expect a woman to be intelligent, they often enjoy it when she is, especially when she applies her mind to what is of interest to them. But there are many intelligent women. And do not suppose I underestimate the power of beauty—how could I, since I was so scorned when I lost it. But there are many beautiful women and why, I ask, is one, even for a time, named the most beautiful. Even that part of my reputation, my celebrated beauty, testifies to something I had that was more inclusive, that compelled attention, like a ring of light.

I can describe what it sometimes made me do. I recall myself when still a small child lingering on the road in my village one winter day, lingering, looking about me, and feeling the look flowing out of my eyes. It took in this one, and that one, all shivering and sour-faced in their toil and their idleness. I already felt myself to be different, and it came to me that I could warm them with my look. So I started walking along the road, warming them, drawing them to turn toward me. It was a foolish child's fancy, to be sure, and I soon put it behind me. But when I was grown, whenever I walked on the street or entered rooms or gazed out of the windows of houses and carriages, I still felt: I must find with my look as many as I can.

Wherever I went, I felt chosen. I do not know from where I drew such confidence. I could not have been *that* extraordinary, and yet I was. The others appeared so easily satisfied, or resigned. I wanted to awaken them and make them see how glorious this existence was. The others were usually trying to be calm. I wanted them to appreciate themselves. I wanted them to love what they loved.

It was better when they were obsessed. I was not obsessed, but I was always eager. Even when beautiful, I was never elegant. I never withheld. I was not snobbish. I was effusive. I craved the exaltation of fervent affection. I didn't have to embrace. Bodies didn't have to rub and sweat together. I loved to pierce and be pierced with a look.

I heard the sound of my own voice. It embraced the others, it encouraged them. But I was even more skilled at listening. There is a moment when one must be silent. That is the moment when you touch the other's soul. Someone who is pouring out feeling—whom you have helped bring to that point, perhaps by the display of your own feeling. And then you look deeply into the other's eyes. You make a little mmmm or ahhh, an encouraging, sympathetic sound. For now, you just listen, really listen, and show that you take what you are hearing into your heart. Hardly anyone does this.

It is true that I labored without stint to become what I could become, but I also had the impression that success was easy, prodigiously easy. Within a year after I was given my first singing lessons in Naples, with the allowance given to my mother and me for all our expenses set at one hundred and fifty pounds a year, the Italian opera in Madrid wanted to make me its prima donna at six thousand pounds for three years. And there were several such offers of contracts from European opera houses, all of which I refused without regret.

If I wanted to sing, I could sing well. When I needed to be brave, it was easy for me to be brave.

Whatever I did not do well, I had not tried to do well—sometimes because I had understood that a higher attainment would have obliged me to alter my character and contain its overflow. Thus, I was adept at the piano, but I never played as Catherine did, I am sure. I lacked the necessary melancholy, the inwardness. But I could represent emotions with my body, with my face. Everyone marveled at my Attitudes.

I could not help it if I had an actress's talent. If I liked to please. What could I do if I understood so quickly what others desire. And who would have protected me if I had not schooled myself to triumph over my temper. But I used my heart to draw others to me. More than once I saw the Queen, in order to get her way with the King on some matter of state, take herself into his presence and then smooth a pair of long white gloves over her arms. The King loved women's arms and their gloves. I didn't use tricks like that. I had no need. It is really very easy to please. It is no different from learning. In the world which scrutinized me, my accent was noted with disapproval, as well as my spelling, which I did improve. But had I not loved my mother so much, I do not doubt I would have shed all traces of my rustic origins, and spoken an English pure as moonlight. As I said, for a long time I could always do what I really wanted to do.

It was said I flattered everyone shamelessly—my husband, and then the Queen, and other people who could be useful to me in Naples, and finally my beloved. I flattered, yes. But I *was* flattered. Mr. Romney told me that I was a genius, a divinity, that I had only to pose and the painting was done; the rest was mere transcription. My husband thought I was all his vases and statues, all the beauty he admired, come to life. My beloved sincerely thought me superior to all womankind. He called me a saint, and told everyone I was his religion. My mother always told me I was the finest woman in the world. And I was regarded as the greatest beauty of the age.

This could not have been good for my character. But it is not my fault such things were said.

Even when I was thought the most beautiful I did have one defect, or was it my beauty that had the defect: my small receding chin. Then, while still young, my body thickened. I drank, not to counter lowness of spirits but because I was sometimes angry and knew I would be rebuked, perhaps abandoned, were I to show it. I was often hungry. I saw my chin become heavy. One sultry night as I turned in my bed, I felt my belly, and I thought, something has happened to my waist, my body is changing. Without my beauty, my shield, everyone could mock me.

Everyone said how coarse and monstrous I had become. It was always thought that I talked too much. I own that I always had something to say. My life had great velocity. Then it was spent. My detractors would no doubt be pleased to know I was quite silent at the end.

I do not have as much to say now as you might suppose.

Had he lived, I would have been happy. But he died, winning the great victory expected of him. He died with my name on his lips and in his will left his daughter and me as his bequest to his king and country. I received no pension. I and his child were not even invited to the funeral, the most glorious ever staged in England. The whole nation was in tears. But I can't help thinking some were relieved that he died at the summit of his destiny, that he did not survive to live as an ordinary man, having an ordinary life, with me, in my arms, with our child, and more children. For I would have gone on having children, as many as I could, his gifts of love to me and mine to him.

I did not beg and plead and complain until after my beloved

died. Then I discovered that no one would help me—that my destiny was to be an embarrassment, an encumbrance to everyone.

After my beloved left my arms to go to Trafalgar, I never embraced another man again. How my detractors must regret being unable to charge me with lustfulness. Nor were there grounds for describing me as mercenary, though they would have liked to spread that calumny, too. I never cared about money, except to spend it or buy presents. My affections were never guided by the desire to lead an easeful life: I would have been content to live in modest circumstances or even in poverty with the one I loved. Sometimes I think of a quite different life that might have been mine. I would not have minded being less beautiful, as long as I was not plain. I would not have minded being a fat old woman hobbling up the church steps at the end of a life that was not so sad.

People will be very sorry they spoke so cruelly of me. One day they will see that they were abusing a tragic figure.

What am I charged with? Drunkenness, debts, vulgarity, unattractiveness, a siren's lures. Oh yes, and complicity in murder.

I will mention one of the stories told about me which is not true. I am said to have felt guilty afterward for not intervening to save Doctor Cirillo, and to have known at the time that innocent blood was being shed at Naples. It was told that I had nightmares until the end of my life and, on some nights, like Lady Macbeth I would walk in my sleep and cry out and raise my hands to look for the blood. I do not believe I felt guilty. What was I supposed to feel guilty for?

In the end, everyone repudiated me. I wrote to the Queen, my friend. She did not answer. I was sent to debtors' prison. As soon as I was let out conditionally, I packed two trunks of clothes and a few pieces of jewelry and mementoes and bought passage on the packet for Calais that left from the Tower for myself and my child—who knew no more than that she was her father's daughter and I, his friend, was her guardian. In Calais I took the best rooms in the best hotel for two weeks and spent half the money I had brought with me. Then we moved to a farm a few miles beyond the town. Since there was no school for her, I gave the lessons, teaching her German and Spanish—her French was already acceptable—and reading Greek and Roman history with her. And I hired a woman in the village to take her for rides on an ass, so she would have some exercise.

My daughter was fourteen when we fled England. I was fourteen when I came up to London from my village, so eager and happy to begin my life and rise in the world. I was born of nobody. She was the daughter of the greatest hero and the once-greatest beauty of the age. I had a mother who always praised me, whatever I did—an ignorant fool of a mother whose company and whose love afforded me great pleasure and comfort. My daughter had a mother who never praised her, who told her constantly to be mindful of who her father was, that he was looking down from heaven on her, and must at all moments see only what could make him proud of her—a sharp-witted mother whose presence terrified and appalled her.

No one crossed from England to see us. I had become so repulsive I never looked in a mirror. I was orange with jaundice and bloated with fluids. When I became too ill, we returned to town and went into a dark room in a miserable pension. My bed was in the alcove. I sent the child to the pawnbroker each week, first with a watch, then with a gold pin, then with my dresses, so there was food for her and I could go on drinking. I taught her to play backgammon with me. I slept much of the time. My one visitor was a priest from a nearby church.

There was no one but a child to tend to an ill-smelling, weeping, snoring, dying woman, no one but she to empty bedpans and wash out the sheets. I was quite cruel to her and she was very dutiful.

At the very end I asked my daughter to fetch the priest from the Church of Saint Pierre for the last rites. Only then, and for the first time, did the solemn oppressed creature, who would grow up to marry a vicar and remember the terrible last six months in France with grim charity, try to oppose my will.

You will not deny me this consolation, I shouted. How dare you!

I will go for the priest if you tell me who my mother is, replied the wretched girl.

Your mother, I hissed, is an unfortunate woman who wishes to remain unnamed. I shall not betray her trust.

She waited. I closed my eyes. She touched my hand. I pulled it away. I began to sing to myself. I felt the acrid stream of vomit run down the side of my mouth. Nothing, not even the certainty of losing heaven, could have made me tell her the truth. Why should I have consoled her when there was no one to console me. I heard the door close. She had gone for the priest.

4

I could see their ship in the bay from the window of my cell.

My friends and I had already boarded one of the transports leaving for Toulon when they arrived on the 24th of June and annulled the treaty that had been signed with the Cardinal Monster: we were dragged off the transport and taken to the Vicaria. As one of the few women in the prison, I was allotted a scummy cell of my own, ten steps by seven, with a cot to sleep on and no chains. Two of my friends spent the summer shackled to the wall by iron collars, and others were hunched five in a cell, and slept body to body on the floor. Some of us went through the farce of hearings called trials, but our guilt had already been decided.

Day after day I watched the black ship riding the water. I would not send them a letter greasy with sweat or tears. I would not beg for my life.

At night I saw the lanterns and the white masts gleaming in the moonlight. Sometimes I stared for so long at the ship that I could make the swaying masts stand still and feel the prison move.

I saw the small craft coming to and fro which brought them food and wine and musicians for their evening's entertainment.

I could hear the shouts and the laughter. I remembered the many sumptuous repasts at their table. I remembered the assemblies for which the British ambassador and his wife were celebrated. On several of the evenings that she had performed her Attitudes, I read my poems. In my cell I wrote several verses, two in Neapolitan and an elegy to the blue sky and the gulls composed in homage to my master Virgil in Latin.

How glorious to be a ship cleaving the thick summer sea. How glorious to be a gull soaring in the blue summer air. As a child, I often gave myself in fantasy the power to fly. But the body acquires gravity in a prison. Although quite diminished by the meager ration of bread and soup brought twice a day to my cell, I had never felt so earth-bound. My spirit wanted to climb, but I could not even daydream myself into flying with the body I had become. I could only imagine that, no sooner aloft, I would plummet—aside their ship, their ship—directly into the sea.

At dawn on the sixth of August, when I went to my window, I saw that the flagship was gone. Their work of authorizing and giving legitimacy to the murder of the Neapolitan patriots having been concluded, they had sailed back to Palermo. The hangings and beheadings were to continue until the following spring.

I was executed two weeks later.

When I saw that I could not escape execution, I demanded to be beheaded rather than hanged. It was the only right pertaining to my class I would have liked to exercise. My request was denied by the Junta of State on the grounds that I was a foreigner. And I was a foreigner. I was born in Rome and had lived in Naples since the age of eight. I had been naturalized when my Portuguese father received a Neapolitan patent of nobility and assumed Neapolitan citizenship. I had been married to a Neapolitan noble and officer. Yes, I was a foreigner.

For the performance of my death, I had chosen a long black gown which narrowed at my ankles, last worn four years ago to my husband's funeral. I chose this garment not to present myself as in mourning for our dashed hopes, but because my monthly flow had started and I preferred to wear something that would not show any stain when I stood at the foot of the scaffold.

I spent my last night trying to master my fear.

First, I was afraid I would lose my dignity. I had heard that those about to be hanged often lose control of their bowels. I was afraid that my knees would buckle as I was led through the square to the platform on which the gallows and its ladder stood. I feared a convulsion of unseemly terror at the sight of the hangman advancing toward me with the blindfold, and his assistant holding the long rope with a noose. The crowd's shouts of Long Live the King had provoked some of my friends to make their last words Long Live the Republic. But I wanted to go to my death in silence.

Then, I was afraid of being choked before they hanged me. For I knew that after the hangman tied a dirty rag around my head, he or his assistant would drop a heavy hairy ring of rope over my head onto my shoulders. Unseen hands would pull it tighter, and where it tugged I must go, to the foot of the ladder, and then upward—I would have to follow the rope. I imagined the ladder sagging with the weight of three. The hangman above me, pulling me up by the head. His assistant below me, holding my ankles and guiding, thrusting them from one rung up to the next.

Then, I was afraid I would not die after the hangman scrambled onto the crossbeam to make fast his end of the rope, and his assistant, tightening his grip on my ankles, pushed off into the air, taking me with him. Could I still be alive when there were two of us swinging in the air, his weight stretching downward from my feet? Still alive when the hangman leapt from the crossbeam to straddle my shoulders, and we became a dangling, swaying chain of three?

Dawn came. I dressed. I was brought from my cell to a room near the office of the director of the prison, and my joy at seeing my friends again—I was to be hanged in good company, with seven of my fellow patriots—suddenly gave me the impression that I was not afraid to die.

The air was already torrid. We were offered water. I asked for coffee. A guard went to the director of the prison and he gave his permission. But my coffee arrived scalding, and while I waited for it to cool, those at the door were waiting too. They told me I had no more time. I told them that I was allowed to have my coffee first, and that they would have to grant me a few minutes more. There was a poet among us, only twenty-three years old, who used this delay to take out a scrap of paper and write. I wondered if it was another poem, or some words he was preparing to say at the foot of the scaffold. The coffee still burned my tongue when I tried to sip it. I put it down, ignoring the ferocious stares at the door. The poet was still writing. I was glad to afford him these few words more. The bishop was on his knees with his rosary. It was as if I had made time stop—but it would be I who made it go forward again. For meanwhile my coffee was inexorably cooling. The moment I could drink it, the spell would be broken, and we would go forward to our deaths.

I did not move. Any movement on my part, I felt, would have broken the spell. I was famished, and had slipped between my breasts a piece of roll saved from the scant repast of the night before. I could have eaten the roll while waiting for my coffee to cool. But the guards might have said I had permission to take coffee, not to eat.

I lifted the bowl to my lips once more and, alas, the coffee was tepid enough to drink.

I thought—a woman's thought, perhaps—I should offer a word of consolation to the others, for I saw they were at least as weakened by despair as I was. Some words from the *Aeneid* came to mind: *Forsan et haec olim meminisse juvabit*—Perhaps one day even this will be a joy to recall. I saw a smile cross my young poet's face.

We were escorted out of the prison and, before being put in the cart, our arms were bound tightly behind our backs. I realized then that my arms would never be unbound again. How I regretted not having been braver and eaten the piece of roll.

The cart brought us under the carefree cloudless sky; through streets crowded with those habituated to the repeated, corrupting spectacle of suffering; to the market square with its gallows-stage and vast audience assembled to watch us dance in the air. These impatient spectators were themselves observed, surrounded by soldiers from regular units and the Cardinal Monster's army, and two regiments of cavalry. We were taken inside the walls of the Church of the Carmine, where other troops stood in reserve in case of any tumult, and put into a windowless guardhouse.

They took our cavalry officer first. Twenty-four years old, and the scion of one of the great ducal families, he had been second-in-command of the National Guard. It seemed to take no more than twenty minutes. We listened to the shouts of the crowd.

Then they took the seventy-three-year-old priest, a fine hale old man.

As I had watched my friends go one by one, I wondered if—perhaps because I was the only woman—I would be saved for last.

When only the young poet and I were left, I said to him: I hope I do not embarrass you by this request, but since our bodies are shortly to be mangled and defiled, perhaps we can be released a few minutes earlier from the scruples of modesty that ordinarily bind us. I am painfully hungry and have a small piece of roll inside the bodice of my gown. Would you have the kindness to attempt to extract it. Think that you incline your head to the breast of your mother.

I incline my head with reverence to a fellow poet, he said.

I had forgotten how a man's face felt buried in my breast. How beautiful it was. He lifted his head, the piece of roll between his teeth. He had tears in his eyes as I had in mine. We brought our faces together so we could share the bread between us. And then they took him.

I heard the shouts of the crowd. That meant my poet was

hanging. I wished I could use a water closet. Then it was my turn—and, yes, it was exactly as I had imagined it.

•

My name is Eleonora de Fonseca Pimentel. This is the name I was born to (my father was Don Clemente de Fonseca Pimentel) and the name I am known by (I resumed my family name after the death of my husband)—or some version of it. Usually I am referred to as Eleonora Pimentel. Sometimes as Eleonora Pimentel Fonseca. Occasionally as Eleonora de Fonseca. Often just as Eleonora, when historians go on about me at some length in books and articles, while my colleagues in the Neapolitan revolution of 1799, all men, never are referred to by their first names alone.

I was precocious: prodigies were not rare among the privileged in my time. At fourteen I composed verses in Latin and Italian, corresponded with Metastasio, and wrote a play called *The Triumph of Virtue*, which I dedicated to the Marquis de Pombal. My verses circulated in manuscript and were praised. I wrote an epithalamium for the marriage of the King and Queen in 1768; I was sixteen, the same age as the Queen. I wrote several economic treatises, including one on a project for establishing a national bank. I married late: I was already twenty-five, and my unsuitable husband was forty-four. I continued my studies of mathematics, physics, and botany. My husband and his friends thought me an odd, an unsuitable wife. I was brave, as a woman, for my time. I did not simply leave my husband seven years later or, what was more common, have my father and brothers speak to him sternly and secure his agreement to our living apart. I sued him for a legal separation. There was a trial, in which I testified about some of his many infidelities, and he countercharged me with spending most of my time reading, being an atheist, and having an affair with my mathematics tutor, as well as other, more diffused debaucheries. Despite the scandal I had unleashed, I won my decree of separation. Then I stood alone.

I went on reading, writing, translating, studying. I had a stipend from the court for my literary activities. My translation from Latin into Italian of a history of papal influence in the Kingdom of the Two Sicilies was dedicated to the King when it was published in 1790. I became a republican and broke with my royal patrons. Shall I recite my Ode to Liberty—the one for which I was jailed? No. I was no more than a conventionally gifted poet. My strongest poems were written years earlier—sonnets on the death of my child, Francesco, only eight months old.

The revolution exploded and I exploded with it. I created the principal newspaper of our five-month-long republic. I wrote many articles. Though hardly unaware of practical economic and political problems, I do not think I was wrong to consider education the most imperative task. What is a revolution if it does not change hearts and minds? I know I talk like a woman, though not like every woman. I know I talk like a woman of my class. I had read and admired Mary Wollstonecraft's book when it was published in Naples in 1794, but I did not, in my newspaper, ever raise the issue of the rights of women. I was independent. I had not sacrificed my mind to some trivial idea of my sex. Indeed I did not think of myself as a woman first of all. I thought of our just cause. I was glad to forget I was only a woman. It was easy to forget that I was, at many of our meetings, the only woman. I wanted to be pure flame.

You cannot imagine the wickedness of life in that kingdom. The depravity of the court, the distress of the people, the falsity of manners. Oh, do not say it was splendid then. It was splendid only for the rich, it was gratifying only if one did not reflect on the lives of the poor.

I was born into that world, I belonged to that class, I experienced the charms of that very agreeable life, I rejoiced in its unlimited vistas of knowledge and skill. How naturally human beings adapt to abjection, to lies, and to unearned prerogatives. Those whom birth or appropriate forms of ambition have placed inside the circle of privilege would have to be dedicated misfits —disablingly sanctimonious or bent on self-deprivation—*not* to enjoy themselves. But those whom birth or revolt have cast outside, where most beings on this earth live, would have to be obtuse or slavish in temperament not to see how disgraceful it is that so few monopolize both wealth and refinement, and inflict such suffering on others.

I was earnest, I was ecstatic, I did not understand cynicism, I wanted things to be better for more than a few. I was willing to give up my privileges. I was not nostalgic about the past. I believed in the future. I sang my song and my throat was cut. I saw beauty and my eyes were put out. Perhaps I was naïve. But I did not give myself to infatuation. I did not drown in the love of a single person.

I will not deign to speak of my hatred and contempt for the warrior, champion of British imperial power and savior of the Bourbon monarchy, who killed my friends. But I will speak of his friends, who were also so pleased with themselves.

Who was the esteemed Sir William Hamilton but an upper-class dilettante enjoying the many opportunities afforded in a poor and corrupt and interesting country to pilfer the art and make a living out of it and to get himself known as a connoisseur. Did he ever have an original thought, or subject himself to the discipline of writing a poem, or discover or invent something useful to humanity, or burn with zeal for anything except his own pleasures and the privileges annexed to his station? He knew enough to appreciate what the picturesque natives had left, in the way of art and ruins, lying about the ground. He condescended to admire our volcano. His friends at home must have been struck by his fearlessness.

Who was his wife but another talented, overwrought woman who thought herself valuable because men she could admire loved her. Unlike her husband and her lover, she had no genuine convictions. She was an enthusiast, and would have enlisted herself with the same ardor in the cause of whomever she loved. I can easily imagine Emma Hamilton, had her nationality been different, as a republican heroine, who might have ended most courageously at the foot of some gallows. That is the nullity of women like her.

I will not allow that I was moved by justice rather than love, for justice is also a form of love. I did know about power, I did see how this world was ruled, but I did not accept it. I wanted to set an example. I wanted not to disappoint myself. But I was afraid as well as angry, in ways I felt too powerless to admit. So I did not speak of my fears but rather of my hopes. I was afraid my anger would offend others, and they would destroy me. For all my certitude, I feared I would never be strong enough to understand what would allow me to protect myself. Sometimes I had to forget that I was a woman to accomplish the best of which I was capable. Or I would lie to myself about how complicated it is to be a woman. Thus do all women, including the author of this book. But I cannot forgive those who did not care about more than their own glory or well-being. They thought they were civilized. They were despicable. Damn them all.